התקוממות

Insurrection

Ξεσήκωμα

*An epic novel about
the Maccabean Revolt*

BY BRANDON TESKEY

For all those who have ever taken up arms
in the defense of liberty

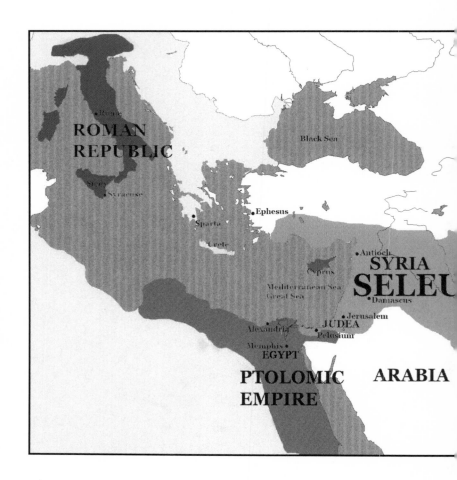

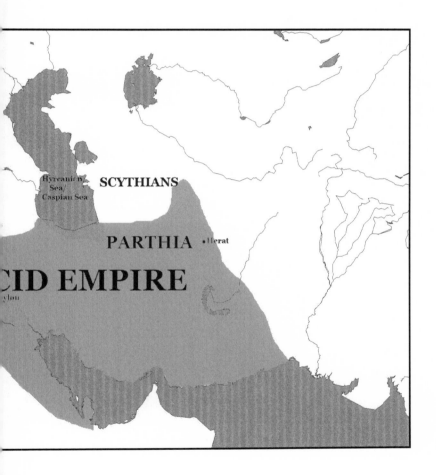

A Note to the Reader

THIS NOVEL, THOUGH based on true events, is a work of fiction. The author has invented scenes and characters. Much of the dialogue and characters' thoughts are a product of the author's imagination. Creative license has been taken sparingly with chronology as well as with some historical events. Speculations have been made, especially in resolving conflicting historical sources.

Interchangeable terms have been used to represent two major national identities: Jews and Syrians. Jews may be referred to in the text as Israelites or Hebrews, while Syrians may be called Seleucids or Greeks. The author has used some anachronistic terms for earlier concepts, and employs language he feels most accurately reflects the Hebrew and Greek thought of the time.

Nevertheless, this novel does remain true to the spirit and the occurrences surrounding the Maccabean Revolt, and most of the unbelievable parts of what follows actually happened.

By 331 BC, Alexander of Macedon (Alexander the Great) has conquered virtually the entire known world, uniting every conquered region under the banner of his Greek Empire.

On his deathbed, fighting bouts of delirium and having proclaimed no heir, Alexander issues an order to leave his empire to "the strongest."

His kingdom is subsequently divided among his four generals.

Ptolemy and Seleucus are the two most powerful. Ptolemy takes control of the west, establishing his kingdom in Egypt, and Seleucus takes the east, placing his capital in the region of Syria.

In 274 B.C. a perpetual war breaks out between these two world powers that will last for more than one hundred years.

Between the two dynasties lies the land that divides their empires, the land over which they war, the land both claim dominion over.

This is the region known as Judea.

Prologue

Hear, O Israel: the Lord your God is one.

FLAMES DANCED ATOP golden candlesticks, flickering in the warm breeze that traveled across the floor of the dimly lit synagogue. The words, uttered in Hebrew, echoed in the boy's mind. Finely woven, dark-red curtains lay draped across walls of large gray stone.

The boy looked up at the imposing figure of his father, whose thick black beard was bordered by a streak of gray on either side that ran downward from his mouth, making him look still more solemn and regal. The boy looked back at the *bimah*, the altar upon which the thick scroll was placed, still partially unrolled. He could smell the burning oils mingling with the rich smoked scent of lamb meat that lingered outside in the dry air.

"Remember," the priest said in Hebrew, looking down at his son, "The Lord your God is one. Never forget who you are and where you come from." He switched to Greek. "You come from a people set aside by God. Did God not proclaim to Abraham that, in him, the nations of the world would be blessed? We are the chosen people, my son—a strong people!"

"Yes, Papa," the boy whispered.

"A strong people," the priest repeated to himself. He turned, as a faint pulsation rose in the distance. The sound grew in strength, like the onset of a storm. Two large columns of Chrysaspides infantry soldiers marched along the dirt roads of Modein, proudly bearing the golden shields that marked their Greek corps. The boy could feel the vibration of their steps through the synagogue floor, and quivered with fear as it rose. The priest bowed his head, closed his eyes as the sound of advancing men grew closer and closer.

When the sound eventually faded and silence returned to the synagogue, the priest looked down at his son. "One day soon we will be strong again," he whispered. "We will not always be trodden down by the pagans. There will come a day when God remembers His people and anoints for us a leader who will throw off the yoke of the idolater, and Israel will once again be free."

"Will kings ever reign in Jerusalem again, Papa?"

Suddenly a heavy fist banged on the synagogue doors. There were men outside.

"Open up!" demanded an angry voice in Greek. "In accordance with the law, we're conducting a search of this building!"

The soldiers outside struck the doors once more. The boy trembled, but the priest stared into the distance and answered his son.

"Yes. One day, I promise you—one day, they will."

סֵפֶר אחד

Book I
The Line in the Sand

168 BC

"*And by him the daily sacrifice was taken away, and the place of the sanctuary was cast down. And a host was given him against the daily sacrifice by reason of transgression, and it cast down the truth to the ground; and it practiced, and prospered. Then I heard one saint speaking, and another saint said unto that certain saint which spake, How long shall be the vision concerning the daily sacrifice, and the transgression of desolation, to give both the sanctuary and the host to be trodden under foot? And he said unto me, unto two thousand and three hundred days; then shall the sanctuary be cleansed.*"

~ Daniel

Βιβλίο ένα

Chapter 1

A CLOUD OF DUST drifted aloft as the old man raked the staff across the sand, leaving a deep line in the fine, powdered earth. Tall palm trees swayed in the strong, southwest wind.

"The line is drawn!" he shouted, driving his staff into the ground behind the line. The shoes he wore were those of a soldier. Over his steel-plated armor, draped across one shoulder, a crimson cloak snapped in the wind, flapping violently around his shins. His hair was streaked with silver, his features chiseled like stone, and his face shone red from the relentless sun. His cold gaze rested on the advancing horsemen. At his back, three ranks of cavalry soldiers, ten men across, sat as rigid as statues on their tall horses. The wind continued to kick up dust from the sand dunes behind them, carrying it across the uneven desert terrain.

"The line is drawn!" the man shouted again, as King Antiochus IV and ten of his bodyguards approached. Behind them: four-hundred cavalry guards, the Amega. Behind the guards, a column stretched for miles, punctuated with pack mules, chariots, cavalry, and carts laden with artillery and siege equipment. Behind this, engineers, archers, infantry, scouts, war elephants, and a supply line of tents, food, and water spanned halfway to the coast, where the king's navy had landed nine days earlier.

Two days later, they had begun their advance toward Alexandria. So far, they had marched eighteen miles along the coast with the wind at their backs, after having sailed up the

Nile River in their boats. They had successfully taken every strategic village and town along the way, and now the city of the late great king, Alexander of Macedon, was in sight.

Four hours before the king's arrival, his Hetairoi scouts, led by Apelles, had spotted the small cavalry contingent blocking the road. Apelles had ordered a full-speed advance, but the cavalry had refused to scatter, stoically blocking the highway. The Hetairoi slowed as they approached the unmoving barricade of horses and men, their disbelief evident.

"Clear the road!" Apelles had demanded with a shout, bringing his fifty men to a halt. They waited, ready to attack, their V-formation flanking either side of the road. It was clear by the cavalry's armor, helmets, shields, and standard who the men blocking the road were. The old man with the staff stood in front of his troops, his other hand clutching the hilt of a gladius sheathed on his belt.

"In the name of King Antiochus, I command you to clear the road at once," Apelles bellowed. Unflinching, the old man stood his ground.

"We don't recognize your king's authority in this part of the world," the elderly man calmly replied. "As emissary, I will wait here to speak with your king."

Apelles jerked his horse angrily to the left. He quickly weighed his options, wanting only to run the man through with his javelin to teach him the price of insolence. He had the advantage in troop size and strength, and could swiftly destroy this paltry band of men. Yet King Antiochus was known for his choleric disposition and insane fits of temper. If the king were displeased with his actions for any reason, he would have Apelles crucified without hesitation. He looked down at the emissary in contempt. They were cursed by the gods, all of them. Soon they would be dead, and the stench of their foul leavings would fill the air. The king, he decided, would best determine the fate of these wretches.

Apelles turned his horse and signaled to his men, who fell in behind him. In two tight columns, they traveled back at a gallop.

Now King Antiochus and his entourage of four-hundred guards rode hard toward the small band of men. The front rows of the formation fanned out, creating a skirmish line. For a moment, the silence was profound as the king dismounted and strode forward, flanked by his bodyguards. Scattered among the sand dunes north of them, Antiochus had placed archers, well-positioned to reach the small troop of cavalry blocking the road. He had but to lift his hand, and these men would be cut down by volleys of arrows.

King Antiochus was a man of average height and gaunt build. His hair, mid-length and wavy, was brushed forward in the Greek style. His cleanly shaven face looked young for a man of his age. His eyes glittered with hate as they came to rest upon the standard of a golden eagle held by one horseman planted in the road ahead. Beneath the eagle, emblazoned in gold, were the initials SPQR, the Latin insignia representing *The Senate and People of Rome.*

As the king strode toward the cavalry, the old man brandishing the staff shouted again.

"The line is drawn!"

As the king drew near, the man lowered the staff, bearing himself proudly.

"I am Gaius Popillius Laenas, former Consul of Rome, and ambassador here on behalf of the senate for the people of Rome." After a pause, he continued in his resolute tone. "Be forewarned that, should you cross this line, Rome will regard it as an act of war. The safety of the Ptolemaic Dynasty is of vital importance to the interests of Rome."

"Who do your senators think they are, demanding I do anything?" Antiochus answered, his hands trembling at the man's impudence. "Egypt has made war on me! They harass our borders—"

"I don't care who started what with whom," Laenas interrupted, his tone dismissive, "nor do I care about your pathetic ambitions to rekindle the empire of Alexander under your banner."

Antiochus went rigid as Laenas casually strode past him, turning so he was standing directly behind the king. The hands of the bodyguards went immediately to their swords, waiting for the order to strike the old fool down. Antiochus felt no fear, only anger, as Laenas breathed hotly down the back of his neck.

"Especially the banner of a spoiled Syrian whelp who couldn't keep from shitting himself the last time he was confronted by Roman might," Laenas taunted. Glancing down, Antiochus saw that he had drawn a circle around him with the staff. His face flushed in anger.

"Before you move from within this circle," Laenas continued, his voice soft with menace, "I want your answer. If I do not get it, consider yourself in a state of war with Rome." He circled Antiochus until they were face-to-face again. His voice grew louder. "You will remove your armies from Egypt and Cyprus now and retain your troops, or you will be forced to leave later without them."

"I can assure you that the grain flow into Rome will not stop—"

"Of course it won't. You are mistaken, though, if you think you will control that."

The silence lingered a moment before Antiochus answered, "I need to consult with my chief generals."

"If you move one inch outside that circle without giving me your answer, I will bring down the full might of the Roman Republic upon you."

Antiochus stared at Laenas.

With even just a small amount of Roman reinforcement, he knew his advance toward Alexandria would lose traction; if Rome committed a few legions to the fight, it would be over. They would likely send their legions toward his own shores, while pinning him there, helpless to stop them. They would surround him, cutting him off from his supply line, and set his country ablaze, just as they had done to Hannibal. Years of preparation and war—all for nothing. Antiochus cursed inwardly.

There had to be a way to win, he thought. *I just need an army large enough to hold off Rome and keep them distracted while I go for my prize, and take control of the Ptolemaic Kingdom from these low-bred Roman vassals. Ptolemy Euergetesis was weak as a eunuch. Cleopatra, the slut, has always been the real power behind the throne.* He needed time. He could win, and take this kingdom. Not now, but five years should be enough to build an army large enough to halt Rome and take Egypt. He knew their methods. He knew their tactics. Although they were disciplined, well-trained, and methodical, they could be beaten. And he would be the one to do it.

Antiochus was well aware how the oracle of Zeus had foretold he would be a great conqueror, successful in all his endeavors. And indeed, as predicted, he had successfully seized the throne and maintained control, holding off the Parthians to the east.

Patience, he counseled himself. *This is not the day. You are a god of men, and soon enough Rome will realize it. The world will realize it.* He took a deep breath.

"If you can keep Egypt at bay, I will take my men and retire at once from this place." Antiochus glanced down at the circle in the sand.

"Turn the men around," he said to the general beside him.

"At once, Your Majesty."

Chapter 2

BY DUSK THEY had made it four miles along the coast. A storm was on the horizon, and dark gray clouds veiled the sky. Antiochus's mood was equally dark, as he sat on his horse, waiting impatiently while slaves hurriedly prepared his tent. His officers waited with him, the horses fidgeting. Rain began to fall lightly, the droplets hardening the powdered sand.

"After the camp is set up and secure, assemble the men in formation," Antiochus ordered, "and send a dispatch to Cyprus informing Seron to prepare for evacuation."

"Yes, my lord," replied Lysias his cousin, one of his lead generals.

Within the hour, the troops were mustered. The Argyraspides, that elite unit of infantry warriors bearing their trademark silver shields, assembled at the head. To the right, in the place of honor, stood five-thousand cavalrymen. The remaining three main cavalry divisions—three-thousand Amega, Hetairoi, and Nisaioi—lined up facing them. The Chrysaspides, the main body of infantry, stood opposite, with the Politikoi at the rear, assembled beside the Greek hoplite militia and twelve-thousand Persian mercenaries.

Antiochus rode stiffly upright between the lines on his white horse, a proud look on his face. Any indication of his lingering temper from the day's earlier events had been suppressed, if only temporarily.

"We have marched across a continent with the greatest army since Alexander of Macedon!" There were murmurs of assent among the troops.

"We have destroyed the Egyptians, and pushed them back into their shithole ramparts! As we speak, Ptolemy has barricaded himself, hiding among his slaves!"

The murmurs grew louder at the king's words, and several voices cheered. Antiochus eyed his men. How easy it was to manipulate the sheep of the world, he thought, and who was more of a sheep than a common soldier? And who better to manipulate them than their king—rightfully their god—whose destiny it was to subject nations beneath him?

"I come before you as both your king and fellow countryman to tell you the war is over, and a new era of peace and prosperity is upon us!" He paused as a roar of elated voices broke out.

"The cowardly Egyptians, too broken and ashamed to show themselves, have surrendered behind the skirts of their masters, the Romans, and today I tell you that I have successfully negotiated a peace agreement to end all hostilities! You men have fought hard, and I am proud of you. There are barrels of cool wine and ale and hot food waiting for us at the ships before we depart for home.

"Victory is ours!" Antiochus cried, over the shouts of delight. He wheeled his horse around and headed for his tent, his officers in his wake.

§

Inside the king's tent, his military advisors and generals milled about, talking among themselves. Antiochus stood before a chart, a map of the world—his face dark with malice. This was his by right, but inexplicably it now seemed far out of his grasp. Outside, the rain fell heavily in the night, the drops beating a staccato rhythm on the tent overhead. Candles within dispelled the gloom. Urion, the king's trusted advisor, who had served the king's father and brother, observed the mood of his liege and was the first to speak.

"Yours was a wise decision, Your Majesty. With Rome in the fight, the fates would not have favored us. Not yet."

"Rome does not have our tactics," contradicted General Nicantor, an officer with an immaculate reputation as a tactician. He did not care for this Urion—a mere upstart, who in his opinion had risen far beyond his intended station. "They rely too heavily on their infantry, while we have the strongest cavalry in the world. We would have attacked their cohorts from all sides, and outmaneuvered them on the battlefield. It might have been risky, but certainly not impossible."

"I disagree," said General Lysias, shaking his head. "Their sheer numbers would have destroyed us. A war with Rome is not possible now. It would mean the end of the empire! For all we know, they might already have a legion in Egypt."

"Indeed, you made the right decision, my lord," Urion murmured. "I commend you on your wisdom and prudence, your patience and farsightedness. You will strike when the time is ready."

Their words flowed over the head of Antiochus, who was lost in his own internal debate. *I am probably the laughingstock of Rome now*, he thought, furiously. *They'll all be talking of how Gaius Popillius Laenas bullied the king of the Seleucid Empire into submission with mere words and a line drawn in the sand—those bastard peasants who elect dogs to keep order and conquer lands. Fools! I should have taken his head, paraded it through the camp, and then sent it back to the Roman Senate.*

He turned and looked at his officers.

"I have seen the ingenuity of the Roman army, and I will use *their* ways to conquer them. We will wait, as they do, until they are weak and involved in other conflicts. Then we will strike with the ferocity and strength of our entire army, taking advantage of our cavalry to force them into submission."

"We need not even destroy or conquer them," Lysias added. "We only must make it too costly for them to continue, so they lose their will to fight for Egypt."

"Then it is ours for the taking," General Gorgias crowed.

"Tomorrow we head for home," Antiochus declared. "Five years from now I want to be dining in Alexandria." His leaders grinned. "Go prepare the men for the morning's march and the journey home."

Urion waited until the others had filed out of the tent. Persian by birth, he had been sold as a child to a wealthy Greek, and his name, Naseem, had been changed to Urion. He kept his face cleanly shaven, and his dark hair short, in the Greek style that mimicked the king's. Antiochus's father, having recognized the slave's shrewd mind and strategic skills, had elevated him to his personal advisor, to the dismay of the generals.

"Be patient, my lord. Someday Rome will pay. Not just for this, but for what they did to your father."

He referred to the incident which had happened twenty years earlier. Antiochus had been captured and taken hostage by Rome while his father, Antiochus III, had been king. After the treaty of Apamea, when Rome hamstrung the Seleucid army, Antiochus III negotiated his son's release, reluctantly trading his grandson, Demetrius—a son by Seleucus, Antiochus IV's elder brother.

Comfortable in his ability to speak openly and honestly with the king, Urion did not flinch when Antiochus exploded. "I have yet to avenge myself or my father of anything that Rome has done to us!" Antiochus spat, no longer making any attempt to curtail the rage that had simmered below the surface. He slammed down his fist. "And *this* is how I act, when I have the chance? Cowering, like a whipped dog in disgrace, just as I was forced to do when captured in my youth?"

"They are trying to incite insurrection," he roared. "They bribe the Scythians and Parthians to the east to cause trouble in our border towns and villages." The king began pacing, his eyes transforming to that dangerous vacuity that Urion knew so well.

"I want Rome burned to the ground! I want their whole

system of peasant rule eradicated. I want them wiped clean from the pages of history!"

"They *will* pay, my lord."

Antiochus knew he had enemies everywhere. His troubles did not end with Rome. Word had come from his spies that his brother's widow, Laodice, whom he had married after his brother's death, was scheming to put her son, Antiochus's child-nephew, on the throne in his place. There were those who had argued that the boy was the rightful heir and that Antiochus should never have been permitted to wear the crown.

As much as he despised the woman, he knew it was imperative to return home and sire a child with her and thus end any claim his nephew may have to the throne. To cement his position, he had long considered having the wretched child poisoned. Best to take him out of the picture altogether, he decided, as long as the act could not be traced back to him.

Things would be so different if he had taken Alexandria. He had been so close. Within days the Ptolemaic empire would have been his, and he would have annexed new lands, wealth, and thousands more soldiers. Back home, they had begun calling his father Antiochus the Great, and he wondered how the world would remember his own legend. What would they call *him*? Would they remember his great achievements? Would there be greatness to recall? At that thought, he seethed within.

Urion watched the king, knowing he needed some kind of physical distraction or the fixation of his thoughts would consume him and split his mind asunder.

"Shall I send for one of your concubines, my lord? Or perhaps one of the slave boys?"

"Send a boy," Antiochus said, indifferently.

Despite his earlier life as a slave, Urion felt only a detached pity for those helpless innocents who were summoned to the king's chamber. Antiochus was the king as decreed by the gods, and it was no man's place to question the king's doings. He had killed six in the past year, and Urion wondered how long it would be before the king *needed* to kill to achieve sexual arousal. Rumor had it he was all but impotent unless whoever shared his bed was writhing in agony. Urion bowed slightly and left, his soft steps making no sound on the carpet of sand.

Alone, Antiochus walked back to the map of the world lying on the table. His eyes went to Egypt. Enraged, he slammed his fists into the table, overturning it. He kicked over every single chair. Picking up one, he lifted it over his head and brought it down hard. He grabbed a golden jug of wine and hurled it against the tent wall. Wine spattered the tan canvas like a spray of blood. He stood there, red-faced and breathing hard, when a subtle noise made him turn. A slave boy stood in the entrance, shaking with fear.

Antiochus closed the distance between them in three long strides and grabbed the youth by the hair, jerking his head down and knocking him to the floor.

After minutes, the callous and preoccupied slaves passing hurriedly outside the tent heard the screams of struggle transform to sounds of choking. After a time, there was only silence. Within the hour, the slaves removed the boy's body.

Chapter 3

THE SKY WAS clear overhead, but the sultry wind blew hard in their direction, dark clouds lining the horizon. The shoreline was littered with beached galleys. Kalisto, one of Antiochus's naval admirals, stood beside Urion, staring at the waves crashing violently against the shore, as men worked furiously to ensure the king's camp would survive the storm's onslaught. Of medium height and a stocky build, Kalisto bore burn scars on his arms, a souvenir of the day his galley had been torched during the battle of Eurymedon, in the days of Hannibal's retreat.

"There's no way to get out," he said. "The squalls have us locked in. I know it looks clear enough now, but once we're out at sea, it will be a nightmare. Boreas is blowing the storm right in our direction." He suddenly wondered about the ship he had spotted earlier, which had fought its way past the storm's relentless tide, forced to head west into enemy waters to avoid being dashed against the shore. It was considerably lighter and swifter than the vessels he commanded—carrying dispatches, no doubt. He wondered if the ship bore runners to deliver the dispatches and whether they would be able to make their way through enemy territory. He hoped the ship had made it safely past the treacherous reef. Well, they would know soon enough.

"I would advise the king against ordering us to set sail until the storms clear."

"And when will that be?" Urion demanded. Kalisto bit back the retort that rose to his lips. What did this slave know about commanding a fleet? However, he understood the frustration. No one wanted to give the king information he did not want to hear, although Urion seemed to have some strange immunity to the king's notorious wrath.

"Three days, perhaps even a week. It's hard to say at this point."

Urion's face hardened.

"The king is already displeased, I need not remind you. You'd best find a way to make progress. You wouldn't be the first naval commander the king has put to death, and by Zeus, we will find someone competent who can get us off this cat-worshiping, godforsaken sandpit!" Kalisto watched Urion storm off. *Yes, Urion, my little royal stooge*, he thought to himself. *How unfortunate if you were to meet with an accident at sea, and get bumped off the ship. Eunuch! Castrated dog! Now go wipe the king's ass for him, and see to his boys and mistresses, you stubby little woman.* Did the king think he was Poseidon, that he could control the seas? Let the king order him put him to death, if he so wished. Setting forth in this weather would likely be a death sentence anyway.

The wind pushed inland, and the ominous clouds drew nearer, darkening the seas and land beneath. Over the hill, far out to the west, Kalisto spied a single runner making his way in the direction of the camp. It looked like that ship he had spotted in the distance hours before, had made it through after all.

§

Persias, a young man of twenty-two, raced toward the camp. The tall, blond-haired runner, son of a Macedonian colonist, had been conscripted into service. Persias had been charged to deliver a written scroll directly into the hands of the king and no one else. He burned with pride over this honor and respectfully refused the demand of several of the king's officers to deliver the message to them instead.

Finally he was ushered into the king's tent. The king was

studying a scroll upon which were writings of the philosopher, Epicurus. Persias felt a sudden shiver of apprehension, conscious that he was towering over the king, unsure whether he should shrink down and bow or stand at attention. He remained inert.

"What message do you bring?" Antiochus asked, with a pompous tone, without looking up from what he was reading.

"My lord, I was instructed by Governor Apollonius to deliver this scroll directly into your hands."

Taking the scroll, Antiochus broke the seal and unrolled it on its heavy wooden rollers.

"Do you know what it says?" the king demanded, again without looking up.

"Yes, my lord. I was instructed to destroy it if we fell into enemy hands."

The king began to read.

My Lord, the Descendent of Zeus:

Regrettably, I must inform you that riots have erupted in Jerusalem, led by Jason, the Jews' former high priest, whom you have replaced with Menelaus, a more suitable choice. Unfortunately, members of the traditional Jewish sect are irate over the appointment of one to the office of high priest who is not a Levite, lineal descendent of Aaron. Menelaus had Onias, Jason's brother, poisoned to protect his position. Once word of this spread, Jason rebelled, leading his band of men to rid Jerusalem of its Greek influence. Not adhering to the strict interpretation of their ancient texts, Jason does not have the support of the Hasideans or other Jews who follow the precepts of Moses, so resistance is divided. Nevertheless, much of the city remains in the hands of the rioters, and our situation is dire. The rebels are openly hostile to our colonists, and my men are overextended. Many have been injured in the fighting, and some have died. I formally request every soldier you can spare to quell this uprising and reestablish order in the region.

Your true servant,

Apollonius of Tarsus, Governor of Judea, Coele-Syria and Phoenicia

Antiochus's livid glance shifted into a blank expression. Gripping the scroll's heavy rollers in both hands, he swung hard and struck the side of Persias's head, grimacing at the impact that sent a shockwave up his arms. Persias let out a groan of terror as he folded to his knees, swaying. The king brought down the roller again, harder this time, over Persias's eyebrow.

"Stop! Please stop," the young man cried, as blows continued to rain down on him. He lifted his arms in a piteous attempt to protect himself as he curled into the fetal position. His voice grew shrill. After the seventh blow, his cries were silenced, but Antiochus didn't stop until he was too exhausted to lift the scroll, now so heavily stained with blood as to be unreadable. Persias's chest heaved once more before he stopped moving. His beaten face was an unrecognizable pulp.

§

The mood was somber as Antiochus stood with his chief generals and top advisors around the large table inside his tent. Despite the falling rain outside, the sound of tents being broken down and cargo being loaded onto galleys rang out in the night as the spent storm finally retreated west. A map of the Mediterranean was on the table, with all eyes fixed on a little place called Judea.

"We will rendezvous with our ships from Cyprus and land here," General Lysias said, pointing to just outside Gaza on the map. "From there, we will march inland toward Jerusalem."

"These are people of deep tradition, with strong cultural and religious ties to the land," General Nicantor put in. "With that comes a deep spirit of independence and the desire to govern themselves. We must ensure the insurrection is broken at its roots. Until—"

General Gorgias interrupted, his tone dismissive. "My lord, we have spent millions of talents of gold trying to Hellenize a desolate part of the world where the most valuable commodity is the camel shit. We should simply bribe the Samaritans to burn the city down."

"They believe their god gave them that land," Lysias pointed out. "The Babylonians uprooted them under Nebuchadnezzar, and still they managed to find their way back after Babylon fell to the Persians."

"They're like god-cursed ticks," sneered Gorgias.

"I don't need a history lesson!" Antiochus shouted, slamming his hand down on the table. "When I'm done with them, they will never again defy me. I will deliver such a reproach that they will never dare raise their voices again in dissent. I will denigrate and desecrate their god. The whole earth will quake at my very name and the superiority of my gods."

Antiochus looked around, meeting the eyes of each man in turn, as he spoke slowly and distinctly. "Gentlemen, give me a massacre."

Chapter 4

KALISTO WAS GRATEFUL he had escaped with his head. The temperamental king, instead of raging against his insistence that they wait out the storm, had placidly agreed. Now a cool breeze brushed Kalisto's face, as his galley led the course of the fleet. Behind him, in the center, sailed the ship of Antiochus, its golden sail flying the embroidered royal crest.

The ocean was filled with ships and war vessels of all shapes and sizes. The septrireme and the hexareme—designed for strength—sailed among the heavier war ships, while lighter, more nimble triremes—such as the trihemolia—were present in fewer numbers. Large cargo ships transported the chariots and heavy equipment, while a division of cavalry, war elephants, and infantry marched separately up the coast. Kalisto's trireme was a trihemolia, one of the king's swiftest ships when under Kalisto's command. Excluding the company of soldiers aboard, it boasted a crew of one-hundred-and-forty-four men, one hundred and twenty of which manned its oars.

The rhythmic drumbeat from below, where rowers propelled the ship, was audible on deck. The coast was still visible from the starboard side. Kalisto pursed his lips. Best to hug the shore, he decided. If they ventured too far from the coast at this time of year, they risked being hit by a storm and losing their entire army. Rumors had already begun to spread as to where they were headed. Even the ship commanders had only been issued a bearing.

We are headed to the Sinai, to Gaza, mused Kalisto, *where we will undoubtedly converge with Antiochus's second army division, traveling up from Cyprus.* And from there? The riots in Jerusalem were no secret. Even the king's servants were talking of his growing rage toward the Jews. They said when the madness took him, Antiochus would yell for hours, vowing to exterminate the whole Hebrew race for being a threat to his empire.

Kalisto rubbed his tired eyes. The Jews had always been contentious, ever since being annexed to the kingdom some forty years before. He had heard strange, even macabre stories . . . how they cut off part of their phalluses as a covenant with their god. He shuddered. The stories of their god were even stranger . . . tales of terrible things he had done to the Egyptians, afflicting them with plague and famine. Most were likely nothing more than legends. Still, if even half the stories were true . . . In Babylon, they talked of the Jews and their god, speaking of the horrors he rained down upon them. Even the great King Alexander, after laying siege to Tyre, had refrained from attacking the Hebrews, in spite of their aiding the Persian dogs. Men whispered that he was afraid of the Jewish god. And if that were not strange enough, the Jews believed theirs was the *only* god. Kalisto shook his head at the oddity of such a people. No wonder they were scorned.

"We've the wind at our back, sir." The words of Jorrin, the lead navigator, cut into his thoughts.

"For now."

"If the winds change, those clouds will be heading straight for us," Jorrin said, pointing northwest. Kalisto looked back at the king's ship in the distance.

"Hopefully, after this we can sail to Antioch, up the Orontes," Jorrin added. "By Zeus, I will spend my entire year's wage!" His toothless mouth spread wide in a grin. "I will drink dry the wine presses and fuck every whore in the city, feast on fattened pig, play dice, and buy a new set of clothes fit for a nobleman." Kalisto's attention was on the direction of the tide as he scratched his thick, lice-infested beard.

"After this war, I'll head to Tempe," Jorrin continued. "There is a village out there where my father lives. My wife is there with our children. Do you have family, sir?"

"I did once."

"I'm sorry, sir. Your pardon for my asking."

Kalisto was silent a while, looking out to sea. "Four years ago, a courier brought me news that our village was destroyed by plague. I was in Thessaly, bringing in troops and supplies to help the Macedonians fight Rome."

"Did you ever go back?" Jorrin asked after a moment.

"I'll never go back."

"They could still be alive."

Kalisto ignored him.

Chapter 5

THE SELEUCID GOVERNOR of Judea, Apollonius, sat at his desk, writing a letter. He wore a white-and-maroon, Greek-style tunic that came nearly to his knees. He shifted in his chair, feeling unaccountably stifled. Although the room was large, Apollonius hated it, feeling confined in the old Jewish-style building. Having the balcony open helped, but he vastly preferred his office in Syria. He looked up as a knock sounded at the door.

"Enter."

A young man came in, dressed in a similar red-and-white tunic.

"A dispatch, sir."

Apollonius set aside his papyrus and signaled the man to hand over the scroll. He noted that it bore the royal seal.

To my trusted servant Apollonius:

My army and I are currently positioned thirty-two miles south of Jerusalem and will reach the city in three days. Upon my arrival, I want all the gates sealed and sentries posted, except for the southern entrance. Keep that open, awaiting our arrival. It is time to collect the fee for treason against the king and to break the will of this obstinate people. I will make an example of those who dared to betray me. In three days, we will break their spirit and put an end to their illegal religion as well. I have heard reports that the Jewish population is exploding to the point where they can hardly be enumerated in a census. In three days, this burden will be lifted.

Antiochus Epiphanies, Son of Zeus

By the gods, thought Apollonius, *does he not know the riots ended months ago, that the conspirators fled or were killed?* Even that rotting worm Jason had fled. Did the king know but no longer care? Rumor had it that the children of Syria were already mocking his chosen name, Antiochus Epiphanies (Antiochus the Deified). They laughingly changed it to *Epimanes*, "the mad one."

"Assemble the guards and the troops," Apollonius ordered. "No one is to leave the city without permission from this office. Do you understand?"

"Yes, General," the young man replied, backing out of the room and closing the door behind him.

Apollonius rose from his chair and strode out onto the balcony. His hazel eyes stared down at the streets below, his expression thoughtful. His face belied his thirty-odd years, as did his narrow waist, broad shoulders, and thick, sandy-blond hair.

These streets will be flowing with blood in a few days, he thought, feeling a twinge of regret at the inevitable loss of life. "The earth is a tomb for the living," he whispered to himself, recalling the popular expression. If these people of Jerusalem refused to be ruled, then they would die—it was as simple as that. They would have to submit to the king in all things, including religion, or cease to be. The king had taken drastic measures to instill in them the Hellenistic customs. He had built a gymnasium, repaired roads and buildings, and still they refused to change. The whole world was to become Greek. That was the will of the gods.

Apollonius stepped back inside his office. His eyes locked

upon his sword, mounted above the mantle. There was none like it in the entire kingdom. It had been a gift from his father, when the old man was on his deathbed. The hilt of his xiphos was gold, the handle bound tightly with leather. The blade was slightly longer than most, comprised of an unusual compound of metals. The blacksmith had been a man from the far eastern end of the known world who was indebted to his father for saving his life. As payment, he had imparted to him the most valuable sword he had ever made and, in turn, his father had passed it to Apollonius.

§

Riding out with a column of bodyguards to meet the king, two days after receiving his message, Apollonius wondered if the riots would cost him his own life as well. There was no doubt in his mind that massive bloodshed would ensue. The king was coming to make it abundantly clear that the Jews' disloyalty and insurrection would not be tolerated. Their women, their children, their god—they would all pay for their defiance, and incidents like these would cease to happen. *Fear is a powerful ally*, Apollonius reminded himself.

He reflected how the king had recently had General Andocides nailed to a post and used for target practice by his archers' children. Andocides' only crime had been suggesting they delay the march until preparations could be made regarding the food supply. It was rumored that the king had taken a dislike to Andocides because of his tall stature. Though the king was cordial in his last correspondence, Apollonius wondered if he was riding to his death.

Antiochus's massive army was no more than a mile from the city. It was a vastly intimidating ocean of men. The Hetairoi rode out front. The Argyraspides infantry stretched out behind them, along the road toward the rising sand dunes and rock formations. Their silver hoplite shields glistened in the piercing rays of the morning sun. Apollonius and his ten men were quickly surrounded by Amega cavalry lances, which lowered in warning. He halted.

"I'm Governor Apollonius," he shouted over the thunderous marching, choking slightly on the dust cloud that filled the air. "The king notified me of his coming. I must speak with him at once," he said, holding up the insignia on his ring for the soldiers to see.

"Go inform General Nicantor that the Governor Apollonius is here to see the king and requests an audience," the commander ordered one of his men. The man rode off against the tide of soldiers. Apollonius and his company were escorted to one side as the massive body of soldiers marched past.

§

One soldier marching past that day shifted the weight of his round silver shield strapped to the back of his wicker rucksack. He carried the two sections of his weighty sarissa—a twenty-foot spear that fastened together before battle—in a lanyard slung around his neck, holding it upright against his shoulder. He was blond, tall, and twenty-four years old. His family had been military colonists under the Seleucid regime, originating in a Spartan town called Argos. His father named him Nabis, after the ruler of Sparta, under whom he had served in the Spartan war with Rome. His father had lost his right hand fighting at the port of Gytheum.

After the battle was lost, Argos had been annexed by Roman interests, and the family was forced to relocate east. Nabis, eager to live up to his father's reputation for valor, had volunteered for enlistment and fought through the Egyptian campaign. He experienced his first combat at the battle of Pelusium when his company had been called to the lines against the Egyptian infantry.

He had been terrified. The first four ranks, their towering

sarissas braced, had thrust them into the enemy lines upon command. Nabis had been in the third rank. The long pikes stabbed, slashed, and punctured the Egyptian soldiers. The fifth rank held their pikes angled above the heads of the first four, readying for their turn. After the initial crash, the soldiers who were wounded or whose pikes were broken or impaled in the enemy, shifted their bodies sideways and moved back between the columns toward the rear of the phalanx, while the squires rearmed them. The commander would call out for a shift of ranks after every four thrusts of the spears.

Nabis, in the third rank, could see the enemy clearly. The fury with which they fought was terrifying. He heard the screams as they struck and saw the bodies drop. He kept his focus on the enemy before him, his peripheral vision hindered by his Chalcidian-style helmet. As the ranks about him shifted, a spear flashed, slicing the neck of the soldier directly in front of him. The man dropped instantly, the artery fatally severed.

Nabis held his silver-plated shield beside his left shoulder and face, his sarissa at the correct forty-five-degree angle. Adrenaline flowed through his veins, and despite his nearly paralyzing fear, he continued to move forward as he had been trained, past his fallen comrade whose chocking sounds grew quiet as his hand dropped away from the pulsating wound.

"Doratismos," the commander bellowed, and obediently he thrust his spear forward. His first strike was a miss. The tip of his spear strayed, flying high and right of an enemy soldier. As the counterattack came, he instinctively raised his shield and braced for impact. Nabis felt his shield jerk sharply up and to the left as the enemy spear crashed into him. The second order was shouted, and he thrust his spear forward again. This time he held steady, but his blow was deflected by the bronze shield of his enemy. The soldier to his left dropped his target. Nabis ducked behind his shield as his opponent struck.

The command sounded once more. This time his spear thrust was low and grazed the lower rim of his target's shield before sinking into his opponent's waist. Even with the twenty -foot spear's length between them, he saw clearly the look of confusion and pain in the Egyptian man's face. Nabis pushed the spear forward as he was trained to, impaling the man, and felt his deadweight dragging his spear downward. Two other pikes struck the soldier before he sagged to the ground.

At the command, Nabis moved back behind the ranks. The smell of blood filled the air, the stench of loosened bowels wafting over the dust. The dying man's visage blanketed his gaze, and Nabis dropped to one knee, vomiting. A hand jerked him to his feet.

"Get to your feet, shield humper! Get back into the fight!" Falling in at the rear rank as the phalanx moved forward, he stepped over the man he had skewered. His eyes were lifeless, but his body was still twitching. Nabis looked in time to see the cavalry reserve charge forward three hundred feet to his left through the enemy line, as Egyptian soldiers began to break for the walls behind them.

That had been the only man Nabis had ever slain, and he relived the memory every day. Now he was in Judea, marching toward the gates of Jerusalem, and he didn't understand why. The uprising had ended months ago. Perhaps the army was designed merely to be a quick show of force, a flexing of the king's muscles, before heading home.

On they marched, toward the city, which loomed in the distance. Nabis cursed his armor and shield, which felt increasingly heavy around his shoulders with every mile they advanced. His feet and legs ached in a constant dull pain. His back felt like he had been struck by a battle-ax, and his arms throbbed from carrying his sarissa. A part of him wished only to drop his weapons and uniform and seek passage on the next ship headed for home.

His father hadn't been well when he left, and Nabis hoped he was still alive. The old man hadn't wanted his son to become a soldier, especially not in the infantry, and especially not in the

Argyraspides. This had perplexed and angered Nabis. Surely he was doing just as his father had done. His father was a Spartan, duty-bound to glory. But after Nabis killed that Egyptian, seeing the look in the man's eyes as he died, he felt he understood his father's reservations.

Chapter 6

THE BLINDING SUN beat down on the massive Syrian army. Impervious to the heat, Antiochus sat on his horse at the side of the dirt road that led into Jerusalem. The ranks of his soldiers spread out like a sea before him. The infantry formations were in front, led by the Argyraspides, their silver shields glinting and their immense sarissas held high. The cavalry followed, with a restless detachment of elephants behind them.

"What's coming serves them right," Antiochus grumbled to Apollonius. "It's good to remind the rabble that treason will be punished—swiftly and with vengeance. Now and forever, this place will stand as a monument to the rights that kings have over their subjects."

"General Hermon," Antiochus ordered, his eyes bright with anticipation and bloodlust, "open the gates of Hades."

Hermon hesitated before nodding to a herald, who lifted his long horn to his lips and let out a deep and long-sustained note, as other horns quickly joined in. At once, the flags were raised, and the infantry formations marched forward again. Their feet kicked up dust as they moved to the call of the horns.

"I hope the boatman's been paid in advance," Antiochus said, referring to the toll that must be paid to ensure the dead's passage to the underworld. His eyes narrowed. "Those who remain will surely remember."

Shouts and women's cries of panic rose in the air as the soldiers turned a corner, moving forward in their modified phalanx formation toward the marketplace. When the sarissas in the front ranks dropped ninety degrees, the shrieks grew louder.

§

Marching toward the center of the city, Nabis's eyes moved past the overturned shop tables over the scores of dead bodies strewn in the marketplace and streets. The soldiers had created a parameter within the city gates, blocking all the alleyways. Nabis's thoughts screamed. *These people weren't even armed. They never even had a chance.*

After a short security halt, his modified phalanx patrolled deeper into the city until they trapped a group of Hebrews in a dead-end alleyway. The front rank lowered their pikes and impaled the cornered group. One young woman tried to duck beneath the sarissas, but she was quickly speared by multiple pikes. One spearhead broke off between her ribs, and she began convulsing.

They continued their march. The streets were in a state of bedlam. Cavalrymen galloped down alleyways. Families were dragged from their homes. The men who resisted were hacked to death by short swords. The male children were publicly inspected for illegal circumcisions and the circumcised children, butchered before their parents. Nabis saw women atop the walls holding their newborns, begging for their lives as they were forced off at spear point, falling to their deaths below. Nabis thought of his Spartan father and what he would have thought of this massacre.

"This isn't honor!" he whispered, as they marched. Owning weapons had been illegal for the Israelites years ago, so the poor fools didn't even have means to defend themselves. *May the gods forgive us!*

Nabis's mouth was parched. Sweat dripped down his face as they approached the central market square. Up ahead, on a stony hill, sat the temple. Unique among the buildings in Jerusalem, it was surrounded by an outer wall accessed by stairs. Nabis saw an elderly man dressed in white walking toward them, at the head of nearly fifty people, mostly women clutching small children. The man held up his hands.

"Stop, please!" he implored the soldiers in accented Greek. "In the name of God, stop!" His beard was as white as his garments, as was the hair on his balding head. He was likely a priest or a holy man, Nabis thought.

"These people are unarmed! We don't want to hurt anyone," the old man pleaded.

The officer shouted an order in response, and the first four ranks of the phalanx lowered their spears. Nabis, from the fifth rank, could see the faces of the crowd as they began to panic. Opposite the courtyard square, unnoticed by the priest and the cowering townspeople, archers and cavalry fanned in from several adjacent streets. The archers lined up in two columns on the left, while the cavalry blocked any possible escape to the rear. Nabis heard his officer give the order to advance, and he obediently moved forward with the phalanx, bracing himself for the coming slaughter.

The old priest lifted up his eyes to the heavens and slowly raised his hands, palms open. He spoke in a language Nabis did not recognize, in a rhythmic pattern that was almost musical. Nabis realized he was speaking to his god.

As the formation moved forward, the crowd scattered, and arrows were loosed. Most hit their marks. The survivors, with nowhere else to go, ran straight toward the cavalry, which hacked them to pieces with their javelins and the curved, convex blades of their kopides. The archers shifted their direction of fire into the scattering crowd. Nabis flinched as three spears drove deep into the old man's chest, pushing him off-balance. One of the soldier's spear tips broke off as he pulled his sarissa free. The other two soldiers dragged the man forward and tore their pikes from his chest, leaving gaping wounds. The old man staggered, then sank to his knees. He stared vacantly, blood pulsing from the wounds with his every heartbeat. Rapidly the dark red stain spread across his white garments. His senses quickly faded, and his face went ashen as he fell forward, his whole body seizing in spasmodic tremors of shock.

Nabis saw the cavalry formation that had charged the scattering crowd. He watched as a javelin dropped a young girl, and a soldier on horseback cleaved an elderly man's skull with his sword. The phalanx shifted, and Nabis found himself with his sarissa poised, at people who had nowhere to flee. He prayed his sarissa would not find a target.

In moments, it was over. The bodies were strewn across the square, the wounded groaning in pain. The scent of blood and urine filled his nostrils, reminding him of his first battle in Egypt. Those were armed soldiers, not innocent, unarmed civilians. That was war. This was an atrocity. He wondered at how the Seleucid kings had been so tainted by eastern influence as to completely disregard human life.

He smelled smoke. A nearby synagogue had been set on fire. The smell of burning wood and roasting flesh filled the air, overpowering the other scents surrounding him.

"Recover!" his phalanx commander shouted. As the men hastily realigned their formation, he pointed to half a dozen soldiers, including Nabis. "You, you, and you," he barked. "I need finishers to put these Hebrew bastards out of their misery. Pick your lanes."

Nabis and the five other men stepped out of formation, their sarissas pointed upward. They lined up fifteen feet apart, preparing to use the metal rear tip of the sarissa to drop in a downward motion, over the dying people. The first victim in Nabis's path was choking up blood and barely conscious. Nabis averted his gaze as he brought the sarissa tip down through the man's forehead. He heard a loud crack as the man's skull shattered, and he lifted his sarissa.

"Hurry up, Nabis, you're falling behind!" his commander yelled amidst the surrounding cries of pain and pleas for mercy.

The next person in his path was a young woman, barely

wounded with an arrow shaft through her calf. Nabis swallowed hard, noticing she was pregnant and heavy with child. He felt paralyzed and lowered his pike slowly back down to the earth—staring at her, taking in the fear in her face and the tears running down her cheeks.

"What in the name of Athena's cunt is the matter with you?" the commander barked. "Are you wounded?"

"I'm not an executioner. I'm a soldier," Nabis muttered.

"You're an Argyraspides infantryman! When your king orders you to kill, you kill!" Nabis felt the eyes of his phalanx on him, in a mix of empathy and disgust.

"There is no honor in this," he insisted.

"Who do you think you are, disobeying the orders of your king?"

"I can't do this!" Nabis groaned, standing motionless.

"Coward!" The commander grabbed his sarissa, tearing it from Nabis's grip. He aimed it at the woman, who raised her arm instinctively to protect her face. Instead, the commander brought the pike down into her curved stomach. She shrieked. The next blow tore through her cheek, breaking her jaw. The shrieks of pain became a gurgling squeal. The final blow through her forehead silenced her.

"Some Argyraspides," the commander sneered. "You would be pathetic in a regular infantry unit. Stand over there," he ordered, pointing to the far wall of the square. Nabis felt the eyes of all the soldiers staring at him. Everything felt cloudy and distant.

His commander selected six more men of the lowest rank and ordered them to stand next to Nabis. "You seven women are on execution orders, to guard the crucifixes on the south side of the city." He turned to his second in command, whom Nabis outranked. "Make sure Nabis doesn't start wailing like a woman in childbirth, and hopefully you can all accomplish this without shitting your loincloths."

Moving toward the Southern Quarter, Nabis saw Jews,

their faces streaked with blood and soot, weeping outside smoldering synagogues. A dazed shopkeeper with blood running down one side of his head walked aimlessly, barely able to see through his tears. Nabis saw soldiers beating and taunting a man clearly of different dress and look than the Jewish population, whose protests that he was a Samaritan and no friend of the Jews went ignored. All around lay decapitated bodies, whole families stacked on the side of the road in heaps. Flies swarmed gleefully over the corpses. The images accosted the young man's consciousness. They felt like scars on his soul, being etched forever into his innermost being. He felt removed, detached. His youthful innocence was a thing of the past. He had witnessed humanity in its most ruthless manifestation and would never again be the same.

When they marched into the square near the southern entrance of the city, short crosses lay randomly about the quarter. Engineers finished chiseling away at the stone streets to create short, square holes in which to securely fit the crosses. They reported to the commanding officer, who ordered them to stand by.

Prisoners were led or dragged into the spacious square by Persian mercenaries. The men were barely conscious, the women led by ropes around their necks and holding naked babies, all male and all circumcised. Nabis noticed that the women looked like they had been beaten into submission. One had blood running down the inside of her thigh. Babies were crying. When the prisoners spotted the crucifixes, some panicked, fighting desperately as they were hauled toward the crosses. One woman took a step back in disbelief, until she was met by a shove from her captor. Others just started to cry in helpless desperation.

Nabis stood guard as the first of the prisoners, a woman, was hammered to a cross. The Persian mercenaries laughed as they tied the circumcised babies by the neck with thin strands of rope, and fastened the other end loosely around the necks of the infants' naked mothers. The screams of the babies went silent, one by one, as the mercenaries hoisted the crosses up along one side of the road. In place of the babies' screams were the horrific cries and hyperventilating sobs from their mothers.

The hours passed slowly. Nabis glanced down at the dark puddle of blood that had accumulated near his feet and felt sick. To the west, the roads were lined with crosses, each adorned with a naked, swaying body that arched forward under dislocated shoulders. The graystone streets were stained red. At the king's order, scores of women across Jerusalem had been crucified, slaughtered with their babies. It was the king's punishment for ignoring his decree outlawing the non-Greek custom of circumcision as a barbaric form of Jewish nationalism.

At least the dead weight of the infants quickened their death and ended their suffering, Nabis thought, fighting the tears from his eyes.

It was eight more hours before he and his men were relieved. Some of those crucified, mostly men, still clung to life. The eerie silence of the night was broken by the crackling flames that still burned in places throughout the city.

Anxiously, Nabis watched the glowing red sky, wondering what atrocities tomorrow would bring, and what awaited him for disobeying an order.

Chapter 7

THIN FINGERS OF light stretched up from the eastern skyline, staining the pre-morning gray. A large cart pulled by two mules rolled up to the temple mount by the court of the Gentiles in the northeastern section of the city. On the cart, covered by sackcloth, was a large, weighty object.

At the foot of the stairs to the temple, King Antiochus stepped down from his horse and surveyed the scene in front of him. He grunted with amusement and strode up the white steps, now lined with hundreds of soldiers. Behind him, slaves carried a wooden cage lashed to two poles. A group of priests in the outer courtyard, surrounded by armed guards, watched their approach.

When Antiochus and his entourage reached the temple, they set the cage down, opened the door, and stepped back. The squeals of a young swine could be heard as they raced into the temple. The priests, outraged, rushed to intervene, but the guards easily held them at bay. The king wore a smug smile, his hands clasped behind his back.

It took eleven slaves to move the ten-foot statue from the cart up the stairs. It was an image of Zeus, his body naked, brandishing a chiseled lightning bolt that had broken. The visage was in likeness of the king. The priests cried out in anger, and one of them tried to break free of the guards. One swung his javelin sideways, smacking the wooden haft against the side of the priest's face, knocking him unconscious and loosening several of his teeth.

The king led the slaves into the temple, passing through the inner court toward the rear, behind the veil, to the Holy of Holies, the sacred room that once housed the Ark of the Covenant. There the statue was set, and Antiochus fell to his knees before it, looking up into his own angry eyes. A slave nearby struggled to hold onto a squirming sow that was squealing in fear. The king reached out and gripped the animal by the neck. He pinned it to the cold stone floor as another slave scurried forward, nervously bowing, bearing a red pillow with a golden, sacrificial knife. The king took the blade and raised his eyes to the statue towering over him.

"Zeus, I make this offering in your name to show the world your supremacy over these barbarians and their false god!" With that, he plunged the blade into the pig's neck. Its snorts turned to loud squeals as it struggled hopelessly. The king stabbed it again and again, drunk with the godlike power he wielded over life and death. All would be subject to him. The pig's screams faded to shallow grunts until only its hooves moved back and forth. Then it grew still.

The king got to his feet and looked about at the myriad priceless gold and silver objects: the shields, lamp stands, plates, and wash bowl.

"Urion," he said, as his advisor scurried forward, "have everything of value removed to the treasury. Leave the statue …"—he paused and gave Urion a vicious grin—"… and burn the pig on the altar."

Antiochus walked toward the temple entrance as the puddle of blood from the swine spread across the stone floor. The king's smile only grew as he saw the weeping priests before him, humbled and broken.

§

Within hours of the king's desecration of the temple, the news had spread, the proclamation read in every quarter of the city and public forum for the gathering crowds to hear.

The worship of the deity known as YHWH is hereby outlawed. Any practices associated with such worship are punishable by death. Anyone with a copy of sacred writings, the Torah, or books of so-called prophets will be executed. All copies of these must be turned over to authorities by sundown and destroyed. Any circumcised infants will be executed, along with their parents. Any attempts to organize meetings or religious gatherings will be punishable by death. Anyone caught speaking or writing of the deity YHWH will be put to death immediately.

Chapter 8

ANTIOCHUS SNEERED AS he eyed a group of the newly captured slaves in the wood-barred confines west of Jerusalem. He was bored.

"We've been in this shithole for over two weeks," he grumbled to Urion. "How long until the army is ready to leave for Antioch?"

"They are ready now, my lord. It is the slave carts being assembled that delays us. There are over ten thousand, and it would be best to wait rather than leave them behind. They should bring a good price at market, and the treasury is in great need of supplementation."

"I want them fed only pork."

Urion's eyes widened.

"We'll see how long it will take to break their spirit," Antiochus added with a grin.

"My lord—"

"And appoint Apollonius as my general of the western army. Give him all the troops he needs and oversight of the building of the new citadel."

"Yes, my lord. If I could just—"

"And I want that citadel built quickly. Our troops need a permanent base of operations here. I'll appoint Seron as governor. That worm's ambition might even subdue these people."

"My lord, if you please—"

Antiochus wheeled around and glared at Urion.

"What!"

"My lord, I fully agree with you in wanting to break the spirit of these barbarians, but my fear is that, if we feed them only pork, one of the foods their god forbids, they will choose starvation. If they become sickly or die, that is money we will lose, money we need to pay our soldiers, who have just undergone a lengthy campaign for you. And may I remind you, that unpaid armies in times of peace after prolonged times of war have often proven disastrous to kings throughout history."

Antiochus shot him a deadly look of both anger and amusement.

"Are you questioning the loyalty of my troops? Or have you secretly become Jew?"

Urion felt a frisson of fear.

"No, my lord. I merely have your best interests in mind, to preserve the health of these dogs solely for your profit."

"I want them fed pork. We'll see how strong their beliefs are when the only other option is death." He cast Urion a cruel smile. "I'll wager you half your year's pay. You can return to being a slave, if I am right."

Urion's heart sank.

§

Nabis stood at attention before the Argyraspides commander. "I was told to report to you, sir."

"Ah, yes. Nabis, right?"

"Yes, sir."

"By recommendation of your superior commander, your enlistment has been extended. You are reassigned as a sentry here in Jerusalem, part of the show of force the king wishes to remain behind to maintain order. If you prove yourself, there'll be opportunity to advance."

"I'm no longer in the Argyraspides?"

"Is that not what I just said?" The commander chuckled pompously.

"For ... for how long?" Nabis stammered, hiding his blinding disappointment. "When will I be allowed to return home?"

"Five or more years." At Nabis's dismayed expression, the commander softened. "It would be best to think of this place as home, at least for now. You will be serving under Apollonius. Your commanding officer will inform you where to report tomorrow. That will be all."

Nabis turned, maintaining his military bearing, and walked away. He looked down at his silver shield, the symbol of pride to the Argyraspides, which he would now have to relinquish. In finding no honor in the battle they had waged, he had been stripped of what little honor remained of his service.

§

The guards pushed the Hebrew woman, unbound, before the king. Within his open tent, she fell to her knees and bowed her head low on the white-and-red carpet.

"Rise, my dear," Antiochus said, giving her a kind smile that belied the glint in his eyes.

Immediately after, her seven sons, their feet shackled and hands bound behind their backs, were lined up by age behind her—the oldest in his mid-twenties to the youngest, only four. None of them had eaten in days and were faint with hunger.

The king waved his hand, and one servant brought in a short square table, upon which another placed a metal tray bearing a sizzling rack of pork ribs. Seasoned with salt and garlic, the tantalizing aroma filled the air. Several of the boys closed their eyes, swaying slightly.

"Woman, what is your name?"

"Hanna."

"Hanna, I would be pleased if you would dine with me here."

She glanced at the platter of ribs, and her face went ashen.

"As your humble servant, I do not deserve such an honor."

"Indulge the wish of your king," Antiochus said, his tone slightly mocking.

"My lord," she stammered, "our God has forbidden us to partake of pork. It would be a reproach against God to do so. I would be happy to accept the king's most generous hospitality and eat anything else . . ."

Antiochus's eyes narrowed.

"Your god isn't real, and mentioning him is illegal, as well you know, and punishable by death." He relaxed slightly and gave her another smile, his eyes cold. "I will grant you and your children your freedom if you but eat what has been placed before us."

"Please, my lord, I cannot. My lips have never tasted of anything unclean," she whispered.

"You call *my* food unclean?" Antiochus bellowed, towering over her. "Your king orders you to eat!" Trembling, the woman sank to her knees.

"God, my lord, is my king." At her words, Antiochus went apoplectic.

"I am the one true king," he roared. "Your god is a myth! If you do not eat this now, as I command you, your children will die! One by one. In front of you! Do you hear me? They will all die, and you will be responsible for their deaths!" Antiochus drew his xiphos slowly from his scabbard, and walked to her eldest son. Lifting the young man's face, the king set the tip of the blade beneath the chin, enjoying the look of hatred in the proud lad's eyes.

"I offer you the chance to save your family's lives. If you eat as your mother would not, you can still save them."

The young man drew himself up as straight as he could and looked defiantly at the king. "We prefer death to disobeying God, to transgressing the laws of our ancestors! You may dismiss us from this life, but know that the true King, of this world and the next, will raise us up to an everlasting life, because it is He that we die for."

The king grabbed the youth's lower jaw, slipping his sword into his mouth, slicing open his cheeks. Signaling a guard to hold back the head, he pried apart the jaws and cut out the tongue. The young man fell on his knees, groaning in agony. Antiochus stepped between him and his mother, who had lunged for her son.

"Eat the food!" Antiochus growled at her. He held up her son's tongue before her. She closed her eyes, her breath coming in deep sobs. Antiochus turned and drove his sword into the young man's stomach, watching with fascination as his victim's eyes altered. He leaned hard on the hilt of the blade, sawing it back and forth, cutting the flesh down to his waist before jerking the blade out. The young man collapsed on the ground, his intestines bulging from the wound. He looked down in horror, then looked up at his mother before he shut his eyes.

Antiochus looked at Hanna. "Are you going to eat?" He stepped behind her second son, in his late teens. Glancing at Hanna, he drew his blade back and forth across the boy's neck. Hanna cried out, as her second son gasped in violent chokes. "Please, please stop!" she pleaded.

"Are you hungry yet?" the king shouted, shaking in rage at his inability to force her to obey him. He stabbed the third boy through the base of his skull, holding him upright by his hair. One by one, the king slaughtered the first six of the woman's seven sons. By this time, the four-year-old boy was nearly hysterical with fear. With five brutal strokes, Antiochus hacked the child's head off. He picked up the head by the hair, and dropped it in front of Hanna.

His hands dripping with blood, the king tore a fatty piece of the cooling meat from the plate, grabbed Hanna by her long black hair, and shoved the meat into her mouth. She struggled to break free, but the king persisted. "You heartless bitch!" he shouted. "You wouldn't eat to save your own family!"

Cursing, the king let her go. Gasping, Hanna spat out the pork. "It's the last thing you'll ever taste!" Antiochus roared.

Bringing herself back up to her knees, Hanna cried out in Hebrew, "I have nothing to fear from a butcher and cruel tyrant! You are the most defiled of all men. God in heaven will protect me and my sons."

"What is she saying?" the king demanded, trying to catch his breath. His guards shrugged uneasily. None knew Hebrew. "No matter. Take her out front, nail her to a stake, and burn her alive."

Soon Urion could smell the stench of burning human flesh and hair, from where they stood inside the tent.

"I guess you won the wager," the king said, his eyes glittering in fury as he wiped the blood from his hands. "The slaves can feast on animal feed to keep them alive. I want armed convoys sent to every neighboring village and town in Judea. I want a forced worship service to the gods, and everyone to bow before a likeness of Zeus in submission to Greek culture and religion. Any who refuse to bow are to be burned alive, just like this whore of a woman."

Book II
The Defiant

167 BC

*"As between lions and men there are no oaths of faith, nor do wolves
and lambs have hearts of concord but are evil-minded continually one
against the other, even so is it not possible for thee and me to be friends,
neither shall there be oaths between us till one or the other shall have
fallen, and glutted with his blood . . ."*

~ Homer

βιβλίο Δύο

Chapter 9

THE DARK GREEN hills glistened with dew as the sun crept above the horizon. Pockets of light provided visibility on the grassy plains for the shepherds walking south through the meadow below. On the ridgeline above, fifteen men crouched and began a cautious descent toward the valley, concealing themselves as best they could behind the brush and foliage, their light brown garments assisting in the camouflage.

Judah was twenty-three, and the brown beard did little to exaggerate his age. For a year now, he had tracked down numerous brigands across the land. The owners of large herds of cattle, horses, mules, and sheep paid the most for his services. Their drovers had the most to lose, often suffering considerable losses as the herds were driven from the northern open plains toward Jerusalem and its surrounding villages. Despite his youth, Judah commanded men as much as fifteen years his senior. Apprehending thieves had become a lucrative source of income, and herd owners were paying ten to fifteen percent of the value of what he recovered.

A resident of a neighboring village had approached him three days earlier and asked him to bring back his oxen that had been stolen on the way to Jerusalem. The thieves had wounded three of his drovers in the robbery, but were notably slow in making their escape. Judah knew the land well, and knew that the Samaritans who had raided this particular herd would be moving east. No herd would move easily over the steep, mountainous terrain and so, by taking the mountain ridge, he and his men would easily intercept them despite their four-day head start. The Samaritans, he guessed, would head for the nomadic Bedouin villages in an attempt to unload some of the herd. Judah was very familiar with the mountain pass the Samaritans would have to move through, Wadi Haramia, and surmised which caves they would likely use to break their journey.

He had guessed correctly. At the base of the ridge, the fifteen men crept down off the rocks, dropping onto the solid earth and concealing themselves among the stolen oxen. They drew their antiquated short swords, daggers, and slings, moving slowly so as not to alarm the animals and alert the Samaritans. The sling, though somewhat obsolete, was still a favorite weapon of the Benjamites, an Israelite tribe known for accuracy of up to three-hundred-and-eighty yards. The three-foot-long leather-twined straps were sown to a pocket in which they would place a smooth stone. Several men wielded staffs, which they preferred using for the close-range fight they expected.

Glancing into a cave entrance, Judah counted the sleeping forms, their cloaks covering their heads. He glanced to his right, and signaled to his younger brother, Eleazar, and the other men, to move in.

The cave was dry. They could smell the remains of the thieves' fire from the night before. The fifteen crept forward, closing in on the sleeping men.

The crunch of a loose rock sliding beneath Eleazar's foot caused one of the thieves to stir. The man lifted his head and peered out from beneath his cloak, groggily regarding the intruders. Before he could react, two flat stones were loosed from spinning slings. Each thudded into the man's skull, and he dropped without so much as a sound. Judah's company sprang upon the rest, who struggled unsuccessfully to get to their feet as their attackers clubbed them with staffs and the hilts of short swords. One of Judah's band used his loaded sling as a club, swinging it into the cheek of one Samaritan, who was scrabbling around, trying to find his blade. The blow knocked him unconscious, and he pitched forward, bleeding from the mouth.

Quickly the shouts fell silent as the melee ended. Judah's face broke into a smile as relief washed over him. He and his men stood over the unconscious and groaning Samaritans, who were quickly bound.

Within moments, three of Judah's band began piling large stones in front of the thieves. Eleazar looked over, incredulous at the sudden realization that they were preparing to stone these men. This pursuit had been Eleazar's first in accompanying his brother.

"You can forget this one. He's as good as dead," Ahab, one of the company said, standing over the Samaritan who had been struck by two loosed stones at the onset of the struggle. He was lying facedown in a dark pool of blood, and a clear fluid dripped from his left ear.

"Well, there's plenty more we still have to take care of," another man said.

"We can't do this," whispered Eleazar to his brother in moral protest. "We can't let this happen." He raised his voice louder this time. "These men didn't kill anyone. They stole oxen. They're thieves, not murderers."

"They're not murderers only because their victims were fortunate not to die of their wounds, after the robbery," said Ahab, overhearing the young man.

"Judah, is this godly?"

"Father is the priest, not I," Judah said, replying with indifference.

"He that sheds man's blood, instead of that blood shall his own be shed, for in the image of God I made man," Eleazar quoted from the Torah. "Would you make us worse than these thieves?"

Judah stood silent a moment as his crew argued. He considered both his brother's youthful naïveté and also the hard truth that he was right. Eleazar did have the innocence that only the son of a priest could possess, but it was true: these men hadn't killed anyone, at least not that he knew of.

"We're letting them live," Judah said decisively.

Murmurs quickly arose among the others. "Why, to be prey for these criminals later on?" asked Ahab. "So they can steal again, and next time, actually kill someone? These heaps of swine dung aren't worth the ground they lie on." Judah searched the faces of the Samaritans. They were terrified, pleading with his eyes for mercy. Finally, Judah spoke in a stern but quiet voice, "My decision is final."

"Who are you to give such an order?" Ahab growled with menace.

"If you want to butcher men, there are employers for such professions. We are charged to bring back the oxen, and that is all." Ahab, kept silent, his face contorted in a scowl. Finally, he turned and walked out of the cave in anger.

§

Judah and Eleazar led their mule by the reins, with only the light of the narrow moon and stars to guide them down the fiercely black road of Modein, their small village. It had taken one full day to reach home, and they were relieved to see the familiar outline of their father's house ahead.

Judah had considered the incident in the cave for most of the journey, pondering whether he had made the right choice. Ahab did have a point. Killing the Samaritans would have been a safeguard against retaliation. Judah and his men had killed people in the past while recovering stolen herds, but almost always it was done in self-defense, or they had stoned people guilty of murder. Judah thought about how fractured their group had become, after his decision, and the unspoken tension right until they were paid and all went their separate ways. *Eleazar is young*, Judah thought, *young and naive, sheltered by the pieties of our father. It must have been a shock to him seeing our companions, hearing how they talked.* Judah didn't know why he had turned out so different from Eleazar and his other brothers. He didn't have the sensitivity they did. Nevertheless, it would have been wrong to stone those men.

Wearily, Judah and Eleazar stopped outside their father's house. Eleazar crept inside quietly, once the mule had been stabled. The L-shaped house was spacious compared to other homes in the village, and Judah's father, Mattathias, kept the place fastidiously clean. The house had a flat roof with a balcony, and Judah had his own separate quarters within the outer wall, which had been added to the structure when he married. The extension had its own entrance across a causeway, and was secluded from the rest of the house.

The door to Judah's living space was heavy cedar, and the walls, made of basalt bricks, were held together by mortar. He walked through the door, taking great care not to make any sound that would disturb his sleeping wife.

She lay on her side on their small bed of wool-stuffed animal hides. It stood a foot off the ground, on top of a brick-slab frame. A blanket was pulled up around her shoulders. Her face was without blemish and her skin fairer than most daughters of Israel.

Although Eleazar had gone straight to his room still stinking, Judah had taken time to bathe in the stream just down the slope from the house, adhering to mikveh, the Hebrew ritual bathing. Donning fresh garments and tightening his sandals, he had walked back up the slope toward his sleeping wife.

Adi and Judah had been married for three years. His wedding to the seventeen-year-old daughter of an architect had been arranged by Judah's father when the boy was twelve years old. Since his early childhood, Judah had been infatuated with the girl. His father took notice and, when he was assured that she came from a good family, he made the arrangements, paid the *mohar,* her dowry, and the Erusin—the betrothal ceremony—was performed.

Although a poor housekeeper, Adi was adored by Judah. Now nearly twenty, she had been devastated when they lost their first child six months into the pregnancy only the year before. She was ashamed that, after three years of marriage, she had not only failed to bear a son but any children at all, their one conception dying within her. She prayed constantly that God would bless them with offspring, but so far her prayers had gone unanswered.

Her eyes were closed as Judah climbed under the heavy sheep's wool blanket. She stirred ever so slightly, and a smile touched her lips. She rolled over, her warm nakedness pressing against his cold body. He put his arms around her.

"You're so warm," he said, burying his face in her neck.

"You're still wet," she murmured, caressing his still-damp beard. He pulled her body against his and felt her heat seep into him.

"I missed you," she said softly, her lips brushing his ear.

"I'm here now," he said, smiling, with a tenderness only she would ever see. He moved back a strand of her hair that fell across his cheek and ran his hands down the length of her. She leaned into him, excited by his touch. She stared into his eyes and kissed him, moving her legs around him. Judah forgot his weariness, kissing her ceaselessly as he lost himself within her.

Chapter 10

ADI'S SIDE OF the bed was empty. Judah arose, ignoring the chill on his feet as he stood up on the cold stone floor. Donning his house garment, he walked down the connecting causeway and entered his father's house. The sun was bright and the morning brisk.

Eleazar was sitting on the floor at the table, eating. The house smelled of wheat porridge.

"Where's Adi?" Judah asked, yawning and rubbing his eyes.

"At the market," Eleazar said, between mouthfuls of porridge. "She left not long ago."

"Where's Father?"

"I don't know. I heard him moving around early, but then I went back to sleep."

Judah eyed his brother's bowl hungrily.

"There's more in the pot, if you want it," Eleazar offered. Judah scooped some porridge into a small clay bowl with a wooden spoon and dropped down onto a cushion on the floor opposite Eleazar. It was good to be home.

"Adi said Gaddi and Simon are coming tonight to dinner," the younger man said.

Gaddi and Simon were their older brothers, who had both moved out of their father's home once their wives had borne them children. Gaddi was heavily involved in the town council, making frequent official trips to Jerusalem to petition the Syrian tax officials to allocate more funding to help masons reconstruct the old wells. Simon was being groomed to become a priest, just like their father. He spent much of his time studying the

Torah in Hebrew, rather than the Greek Septuagint translation, which had become so popular. One day he would minister to the people of Modein alongside his father. He wasn't as fiery an orator as Mattathias, lacking his father's zeal, but his knowledge and love of God and the scriptures were unsurpassed.

Their father had moved them from Jerusalem to Modein when the oldest of his five sons was still a mere boy. He wanted to raise his family away from corruption and Hellenistic influences. Even the office of high priest had been perverted by Greek culture, and a new sect of Sadducees had developed, grown from the Greek philosophical influence. Long ago, when the new edicts had been issued, it had become not only politically problematic but virtually impossible to worship God in the traditional Mosaic fashion. Disgusted, Mattathias had moved his family west where he could worship the way he pleased, the way Judaism, he said, was meant to be practiced.

Jonathan, the youngest at seventeen, walked into the kitchen.

"Shalom," he greeted his brothers in a sleepy voice. "When did you get back?"

"Last night. Well, early this morning," Eleazar said.

"Why are you even awake?" Jonathan asked, shaking his head. He threw Eleazar a sly, taunting glance. "Were you at least successful this time?"

From the satchel next to him, Eleazar pulled out a leather bag filled with silver shekels and casually dropped it on the table, where it made a satisfying thud. Jonathan looked impressed.

§

Long after Adi had returned from market, Mattathias stepped into the house from outside, his tall form filling the doorway. His eyes were red, dust covered his hair, and his clothes were torn.

Glancing up from where he was reading, Judah knew at once that something was terribly wrong.

"Father?" he said, standing.

"My son," Mattathias muttered, in a shaken voice, "God has abandoned Israel." He leaned against the doorframe, buried his head in his hands, and began to weep bitterly. Judah was in shock. He had only seen his father cry once, and that was four years before, when his mother had collapsed without warning and died.

"Father!" Eleazar shouted, appearing from the adjacent room. His eyes moved questioningly to Judah's, but all he saw there was uncertainty and fear.

Judah grabbed a cup and poured his father some wine, then led him to the table, where Mattathias sank onto one of the pillows. "Father, what is it?"

"Jerusalem has been massacred! Rape, torture, murder, enslavement and horror upon horror: the temple has been desecrated!" Mattathias spilled out the story that Gaddi had come bearing, the story now spreading rapidly through the village.

Judah sat, his mouth open, as his father described the new proclamation by the Greek king outlawing all practice of Judaism, including private worship of God, and reinstituting the ban on ownership of weapons or symbols of national identity. Judah was struck with a flood of emotion. He felt his throat swell and tried desperately to remain stoic, realizing this moment would forever divide his life between a distant past and a changed world. Their national identity was being eradicated before them.

"Why be born?" Mattathias murmured, a heavy tear streaming down his cheek. "To see this? The ruin of my people? The ruin of the holy city? Everything given over to the enemy? They've taken everything from us. The sanctuary is in the hands of aliens. Our people, no longer free. We have become slaves, and our glory is laid waste while the Gentiles profane us! Why should we even live?" he choked.

Judah was too stunned to speak. Eleazar sat, his eyes brimming, staring at his father. The world had become a dark place. And it would never be the same again.

§

After their meal together that afternoon, all five of his sons sat quietly as Mattathias uttered a short prayer for the souls who had died in Jerusalem. The table had been cleared but for small clay cups of wine. The women had departed into another room, and a heavy silence descended on the men as they sat.

"Antiochus is sending patrols to every town and village in the region," Gaddi said at last. "They'll hold a public worship service to their pagan gods and force everyone to sacrifice to an idol. Those who refuse . . ." He shook his head in disbelief. "Those who refuse," he continued, his voice a whisper, "will be crucified and burned alive." He looked at his father, whose eyes appeared distant. "If the detachment of cavalry leaves as scheduled, they will be here within two, maybe three days at the most."

"I'm not going to bow down to some God-cursed statue!" Simon cried, slamming his cup down angrily on the wooden table. "I'd rather die!"

The table remained still after this outburst. "I was thinking perhaps we should head south, beyond Jerusalem, where the damage has already been done," Gaddi murmured. "Avoid major cities and the larger villages for a time. But we don't want to be caught traveling on the open road. The patrols of soldiers would be as likely to kill us for sport as to let us pass. So, in truth, it may be safer to remain here."

"Father, I think we should leave Modein," Simon said over his brother, growing even more aggravated. "Head east for the caves and avoid the Syrians entirely."

"I agree," interjected Eleazar. "We can't just stay here."

Gaddi rolled his eyes.

"You think we're like David and his mighty men, hiding out in the caves?" he scoffed. "You've been spending too much time wrapped up in the scriptures. This is a different time!"

Judah looked back and forth between his two elder brothers. Gaddi was in his mid-thirties, his skin darker than Simon's, and his eyes dark brown. He kept his hair shorter in the popular Greek fashion, and he sported a neatly trimmed beard, while Simon, five years the younger, wore his curly hair unfashionably long and his beard untrimmed in keeping with a strict interpretation of the Torah. Although a man at twenty-three himself, Judah felt the seven years that separated him from Simon were more like a lifetime, making both brothers seem a generation older.

"What do you suggest?" Simon shot back, annoyed. "Stay here and count ourselves among the idolaters?"

"No, but that doesn't mean we throw our lives away, or act like children at play and—"

"We can't wait for them to show up," interrupted Eleazar.

The eyes of Jonathan, the youngest, darted back and forth toward whoever was speaking, but he remained silent.

"Do you actually wish to prostrate yourself before the graven image of some animal-fornicating false deity?" Simon almost yelled at Gaddi.

"Enough," said Mattathias, raising his hand, silencing them both. Drawn forth from his reverie, he moved his eyes slowly from son to son. "We will not be fleeing the town for some distant village, nor will we be heading for the caves to the east. At least not yet."

"Then what," pleaded Simon. "Become martyrs?"

"We kill them," said Mattathias, evenly.

No one said anything for a moment. Spoken by their peace-loving father, the words came as a shock.

Mattathias slowly stood and walked over to a cupboard. He

pulled away some of the boards that made up a false back, and drew forth a cloth-covered bundle. He rested it on the table and took his seat again.

"I have been saving these for a long time," he said, as he began to unroll the cloth, revealing well-worn Greek short swords. "These date from when the Ptolemaic Empire ruled this part of the world, when it was legal for our people to own weapons. Years ago when the soldiers searched our synagogue and the people's homes for weapons, they never found these."

"Father," exclaimed Gaddi in a distressed voice. "Do you realize what could happen to me and my appointment as the magistrate here, not to mention your life, if someone informed the Syrian authorities that you have these?"

"Shut your mouth!" Eleazar barked at his older brother, disgusted. "I think we are past that."

"Keep your thoughts to yourself, you feeble-minded, pubescent whelp!" Gaddi snapped back.

"Gaddi! Eleazar!" their father roared, bringing silence back to the room.

Judah stared at the dull and jagged blades. One was missing a part of its wooden hilt.

"This could turn disastrous quickly," he said under his breath, steepling his hands. "We have no idea how many Syrians are actually coming, how far away their reinforcements are, and if we do try and fight them, we don't know how our fellow citizens will react. Even if we convince people to fight and not betray us, they may join the Syrians once the fighting starts, or they may stand by idly and watch us just get slaughtered."

"There's something else," Gaddi said. "Onias, the horse breeder's son—he's been an agent spying for the Syrians for months now. He's informed the head of Antiochus's scouts about this town and all the surrounding villages he trades with. He specifically told him about you, Father, about your synagogue and the tone of your sermons."

"How do you know this?" Simon demanded.

"He told me. I saw the son of a whore when I arrived in Jerusalem just after the massacre occurred. He said they were expecting trouble from us, and that if I could convince you, Father, to lead the pagan worship, the people would then follow, and it would save countless lives. He said the empire would be eternally grateful, and we would be showered in wealth."

"The only wealth I wish to gain is the glory my God will shine upon me, when I drive mine enemies from this land forever," Mattathias said, his eyes flashing.

"Judah?" Gaddi asked. "In fairness, you're the only one here with experience in—in such matters." All eyes turned toward Judah.

"If we attack the Syrians, and don't get killed right away, there is no turning back," Judah said. "Our very act of resistance will be a declaration of war against what's probably the largest military might on earth. Even if we survive, and the village supports us, things will get much worse before anything gets better, if we can even make a difference at all. Strategically, there's no way we could ever meet the Syrians in pitched battle in the open and survive. We'd have to organize decisive forays, against weak and exposed targets, and withdraw into hiding while bleeding their resources dry. We'd have to fight like Gideon and his three-hundred men when they made war on the Midianites. For us to win—to throw off the yoke of the Seleucid king, if that's what we're talking about—we would have to win every single engagement. They would only have to win once. One victory for them would mean our annihilation."

"This folly means throwing our lives away," said Gaddi. "We can't fight armored and mounted professional soldiers."

"We can," Mattathias argued, "and we won't be throwing our lives away even if we are slain. Almost every animal under the sun has its limits to the abuse it's willing to endure before lashing out in defense, or anger, and we've far passed the limits of tribulation. If this indignation against Israel doesn't rouse the spirit of our people to fight back, then slaves is what we've become, and slaves is what we'll always be, and our ancestors should never have left Egypt. There would be no worse death to suffer, no worse torture to endure, than to live like *this*, a life in submission, with forced smiles while they desecrate our God, our people, and our very existence! No, we must fight, and even if we die, we must fight for our God, and for our nation."

§

The news was devastating. There was hardly a family in the town that hadn't been affected by what was now being called the Abomination of Desolations. Brothers, sisters, cousins, parents, and friends—it seemed everyone had suffered the loss of a loved one. The word was that more than eighty-thousand people had died and another ten thousand taken captive since the massacre. Conflicting rumors saturated the town. Some claimed that pagan worship was being enforced in every city. Others said Antiochus had pulled his army out and moved on, leaving only enough soldiers to keep order, but not enough to undertake police actions throughout the entire region.

"Of course it's not true," Mattathias heard an old Jewish woman say, inside a shop. "To outlaw a religious practice is one thing, but to force a whole country to worship idols? They can't be everywhere at once."

Mattathias shook his head at such childish naïveté. How many more would blindly put their heads in the nooses their enemies held out before them? When, he wondered, would they learn that the only thing that could be done when one faces pure evil is to stamp it out, at whatever cost necessary to ensure one's survival?

Gaddi and Simon arranged for their wives to stay with family in Lydda, a village five miles away. Judah's wife, however, refused to leave his side, no matter how much he pleaded.

"It will be safer not only for you but for me, don't you see?" Judah argued. "I won't have to worry about protecting you from danger if the Syrians pass this way. They won't bother with Lydda. It isn't heavily populated. It's too secluded, and it's too far west. It would take them out of their way. If they're coming, it will be to Rathmin after Modein." His pleas and countless arguments fell on deaf ears. Adi refused to leave his side.

The night before, Adi had cried herself to sleep, while Judah, his father, and brothers made plans. Adi had three married sisters who had moved to Jerusalem with their new families. Their unknown fate filled her with dread. *None of this would have come to pass if the Greeks had let us live in peace*, she thought to herself. *They've manipulated our people for over a hundred years. The Macedonians brought their apostasy, their idol worship, their open debauchery. They despise anything that isn't Greek. They think they're so superior. They think our God won't punish them.*

Adi wondered if God would hear their prayers, or was this His punishment for the Jews allowing themselves to become Greek at heart? Maybe it was she who bore the most blame, at least in this family. Why would God not bless them with a child, if He was not angry with her? *I am a barren, worthless woman*, she thought, sobbing into the pillow so the men could not hear. She was terrified Judah might replace her with another woman because she could not give him a family. How long until he tired of her? But these fears were not the thoughts that most tormented her this evening. Her mind was possessed of worry for her sisters, for Judah, and for them all.

Hours later, when Judah had finally come to bed, she pretended to be asleep. But she had already decided, lying there in the dark, that no matter what the peril, she would never leave his side.

Chapter 11

HOW IN THE *name of Dionysus's fornicating cock did I end up with this assignment?* Apelles swore under his breath, his horse leading his two columns of the Hetairoi cavalry at a sedate pace. While the king and his generals enviably marched north to conquer new lands or sailed home to Antioch, Apelles had spent the last three weeks on this cursed mission, attempting to build "diplomatic relations" with the wretched indigenous locals by indoctrinating them with Greek customs and religion. The idea had been to ensure they submit to the king, that Apelles root out any and all dissidents and make an example of them. *As if Jerusalem weren't enough,* he thought.

The Jews in Adasa hadn't put up a fight, everyone swiftly dropping to their knees to bow down before Zeus. In Berea, Apelles had only to crucify the priest and his family to gain acquiescence. Emmaus had been the same, with only half a dozen people killed, their heads placed on pikes. Caphor, their most recent stop, had been the easiest one yet. *It would have been sad if it weren't so funny,* he'd thought, flippantly. *The Jews have no spine. Just look at the fool next to you.*

Apelles glanced over at Onias, masking the disgust he felt for this Jew riding next to him, who gave Apelles an eager grin. *The scum jumps at the chance to betray his kinsmen for money so he can suckle at the breasts of his cheap whores,* Apelles thought. *How very Greek of him.*

Apelles didn't understand the Jews who did offer resistance. To be willing to die for a belief? How irrational could you be? He wanted to grab these idiots by the neck and scream at them, *"There are no gods! Yours, mine—they're all nothing but myths! They don't exist!"* However, Apelles wisely kept such thoughts to himself. King Antiochus IV was as ardent a believer in the gods as one could be—particularly in Zeus, whom he credited with his success in ascending the throne. Apelles spat. *If there were such a thing as a perfect being*, he thought, *creatures like us wouldn't exist.*

He cursed inwardly at the absurdly slow pace they were forced to maintain. It was all thanks to that wretched cart filled with that wretched rock, purportedly carved in the likeness of Zeus but in fact carved in the likeness of their king. They'd been forced to drag it to every town they conquered—that and the crucifixion equipment—although the latter had proven not just a necessity but a blessing for the sake of expedience.

"Let's hope there are no problems with this next town," Apelles muttered. He just wanted to get this assignment over with. He hadn't realized he'd spoken aloud until he heard Onias reply in Greek, in his tortured accent.

"I hope not. This is the town I hail from." He tossed Apelles a worried look. "There is a priest here, very staunch in his beliefs and his interpretation of the scriptures. He's a skilled orator. He easily moves people, and they listen to him."

Apelles barely heard the words. *What a disgusting accent these Hebrews have*, he thought. *They have been speaking Greek for hundreds of years now. You'd think they'd learn to speak it properly.*

"We've dealt with such priests before," Apelles finally answered, dismissively. "There is a solution for that as well."

"His oldest son is a bureaucrat here. I told him to tell his father we'd pay a handsome sum if he cooperates and gets the townspeople to peacefully submit," Onias said.

Apelles chuckled.

"If there's one truth I have learned, it's that money changes people's ideology, loyalties, and even their religion, more persuasively than anything else on earth—even the sword."

Onias hoped things would go as he planned. He hoped the priest, Mattathias, would listen to his son, and not bring destruction upon the townspeople. He knew the power the priest commanded. He also knew that he himself—Onias—would be facing the family, friends, and neighbors he had grown up around, and would have to look into their eyes this day. He knew if things didn't go according to plan, it could be his own life that might be forfeit.

§

The people of Modein trudged toward the marketplace at the center of town, as ordered. Preventing anyone from leaving, the Hetairoi cavalry guarded the street that split from the main road and ran through the village, dead-ending on the town's far side.

Forty Hetairoi had ridden into town just hours before dusk, followed by Apelles, as commanding officer, suffering the presence of Onias on his right to demonstrate to the populace the king's tolerance of Jews who embraced Hellenism.

Arriving at the town's center, Apelles spied the platform set in the market square—a stage often used for entertainment or announcements—and ordered ten soldiers to erect a heavy altar on top of it. Three square blocks served as a base for the rectangular slab that required at least four men to lift. The remaining Hetairoi were ordered to comb the town and summon every inhabitant to assemble in the square.

"It's happening," Gaddi said, peering out the door of his father's house. "They're forcing an assembly."

Mattathias and his sons strode toward the marketplace in a tight group, Mattathias and Simon conspicuously dressed in the traditional white vestments of Jewish priests.

Judah had ordered Adi to stay behind until they returned and to hide behind the bed in case the soldiers searched the homes.

"*Shalom*, Mattathias!" Onias cried, dismounting from his horse when he spotted the priest. Mattathias ignored the man, shooting him a look of resentment. He was repelled at the sight of Onias, clad in a red and white Greek tunic, its hem fashionably high around his thighs. His beard had been shaven, and his sandals also were Greek. *He looks like a damn harlot*, Mattathias thought. Onias hurried forward and fell into step alongside.

"Mattathias, you can save countless numbers of our people's lives today," Onias said, his voice wheedling, like a merchant trying to sell cheap goods.

"*Our* people?" Mattathias shot back.

"Of course, our people. These are my people as well as yours," he replied, as if his feelings were hurt.

Mattathias failed to respond. "Your king asks for your support, and your people need their king, whether they know it or not."

Mattathias quickened his pace. "You'll have one chance to save your life today, and your family's. All you have to do is bow."

They neared the crowd of six hundred. "You don't have to be sincere, you know. God understands. You are surely no good to Him dead. Your disciples will follow your example, and the town will be spared without losing a single citizen. Think of that. Undoubtedly God is best served in this way. Be reasonable. Think of your children.

You will be the first to be summoned."

Mattathias glared at Onias as the man turned and walked toward the altar with the sculpted bust of Zeus propped above it. On the altar, embers smoldered, awaiting the coming sacrifice.

"People of Modein!" Voices hushed as Apelles addressed the crowd. "Our king has decreed that each of his subjects demonstrate their faith and loyalty by kneeling before this image of the Lord God Zeus, where, collectively, we will offer sacrifice. I am familiar with your traditions and the mythology that has permeated your culture prior to the enlightened Greek rule, and I ask you to prudently put these aside and, in accord with the law, submit to the nation that now rules the world and the gods that made it so." There was a brief pause while Onias whispered something in Apelles's ear.

"Your priest, your religious leader Mattathias, has been honored by the gods to lead your town in our worship and sacrifice."

There were audible gasps as eyes sought out Mattathias, and a gap formed around him. Mattathias drew himself up, his voice booming as he spoke with measured words.

"Regardless of whether every nation this king governs chooses to obey him, my sons and I will continue to adhere to the commandments of the one true God and to live by the covenant our ancestors made with Him." A shock of emotion seemed to pass through the crowd, and Apelles, amused, shook his head from side to side in disbelief. Apelles then signaled two of his soldiers, who closed in on Mattathias.

"Far be it from us to desert our law and ordinances! We will not obey the king's words by turning aside from our religion," Matthias cried, as the soldiers grabbed his arms. Both soldiers placed their free hands on the hilt of their short swords, ready to draw them.

"People!" Onias cried. "I will lead the worship and provide salvation for our town. Do not be foolishly led astray by traitors like Mattathias. Save your lives and your families. It isn't God's will that you die here."

The two soldiers dragged Mattathias from the crowd. Without warning, Eleazar stepped in behind them, drew a rusty blade from his waistband, and nervously but speedily hacked down upon the neck of one of the two men. The soldier reflexively drew his sword, slashing horizontally at Eleazar, slicing through his garment and into his abdomen. Suddenly seeing the extent of his own wound, and the blood flowing down his shoulder, the soldier staggered forward, his face growing ashen. He tried to swing once more at Eleazar but fell to his knees, then dropped into the dirt.

The crowd had not yet realized what had happened when the second soldier rushed at Eleazar with his sword arm diagonal across his body, ready to strike. Judah stepped forward and jammed his ancient sword into the soldier, penetrating his waist below the armor, making short sawing motions until the man went limp and slumped to the ground, screaming. Mattathias, now free, drew his own sword from under his garment and cleaved the dying Syrian's head, sending his helmet toppling.

Mattathias looked up at the stage, the crowd as well as the soldiers now privy to what was happening, and saw Onias's jaw drop in amazement. Apelles barked orders for his men to close in on the Jews. Mattathias darted onto the stage and stabbed his blade deep into Onias's chest, beneath his third rib. Then the crowd erupted, violently attacking the Syrians, dragging cavalry soldiers from their panicking horses and crushing them, as Apelles shouted more orders amidst the chaos.

Judah picked up the dead Syrian's sword and engaged a soldier next to Apelles, who drew his kopis. The soldier rushed Judah, his seven-foot spear held overhand, ready to lunge. Judah blocked the strike, knocking the spear tip aside, which narrowly missed his chest. He spun around, swinging the blade of the dead Syrian across the neck of the attacking soldier, slicing his throat. The man's body dropped suddenly as escaping air hissed thorough his windpipe. Blood sprayed and bubbled from the laceration as the soldier dropped his spear and clutched his wound, his life ebbing.

Another Syrian was nearly on top of Judah, wrestling to remove his sword from its scabbard. Judah brought his right hand around, swinging the ancient sword Mattathias had given him into the man's helmet. The blade shattered on impact, but pieces of the sword broke through, rending the man's skull.

With his kopis, Apelles swung at Mattathias, who was struggling to free his sword from Onias's chest. Mattathias pivoted, turning Onias's body into the path of the blow. The body fell to the platform. Unarmed, Mattathias braced for

Apelles's second blow, when Gaddi lunged from the crowd and threw himself at Apelles, slicing the cavalry commander's left triceps through to the bone. Apelles dropped his blade. Gaddi, off-balance, lunged again and stabbed Apelles in the thigh. He sank to the ground, gripping Gaddi's garment with blood-soaked hands.

Groaning, Mattathias labored to lift the three-foot marble bust of Zeus. He brought it down on Apelles, the idol cracking in two as it crushed the commander's head against the stones.

The remaining cavalry soldiers, who had been holding their posts along the perimeter, charged at full gallop toward the foray. Jews armed with the weapons of fallen Syrians attacked the mounted soldiers with unexpected ferocity as the women and children fled. A spear thrown from the crowd struck the lead Syrian horse in the neck and its rider was flung forward, crushed by the angry mob. Nine Israelites were wounded as they attempted to bring down another rider. One by one, the cavalrymen were pulled from their steeds and slain.

Mattathias gripped the altar by its base, his legs and arms straining as he heaved with all his might. The orange embers glowed as he hoisted the stone slab at an angle, his body shaking with the exertion. His young son, Jonathan, wedged a shoulder against the slab and pushed upward, gripping the edge with his hand. The altar gave, toppling over and spilling the sparking flames. The wooden stage ignited, flames crackling and smoke billowing black and thick.

Looking around, Judah spied a dismounted cavalry horse whinnying. Anchoring the Greek kopis in his belt, he picked up a spear lying next to its former owner and swung himself onto the steed. He turned it onto the main road and charged toward the edge of Modein, where the remaining ten Syrians were waiting.

A crowd of men followed Judah on foot, armed with rocks and enemy weapons. The Hetairoi troops charged, javelins gripped overhead, ready to throw. Judah hurled his spear forward just as the spears of the Hetairoi on the left flank threw theirs, the distance between them closing at breathtaking speed. Judah's spear spiraled from his fingers and punctured one soldier's armor, lodging beneath the collarbone. Judah felt his horse buckle and saw a spear protruding from the animal's chest. He held his breath as the animal's front legs folded. Judah struck the ground hard and grunted in pain. He tasted blood, the dust nearly blinding him.

He fought as he felt himself being dragged along the ground by his wounded horse. He kicked himself free in time to see that most of the remaining Hetairoi had been pulled off of their steeds. The three still mounted chopped through the crowd with their kopides before breaking free and galloping out of town.

Judah watched helplessly, the crushing pain in his ribs preventing him from being heard.

"Stop them," he groaned, trying to bring himself to his feet, unable to get air into his lungs. "Don't let them get away!"

But his words were lost in the triumphant roar of the crowd, too busy celebrating routing the king's men. The three soldiers made their escape, all but unnoticed.

The sun was setting fast as Judah limped back to the marketplace. Mattathias addressed the crowd in front of the burning platform.

"People of God! It is written: 'Who knows whether it was not for such a time as this that you were made?' Each of us has been put on this earth for a purpose! And now, in our own time, an atrocity has come to pass, one so grievous that the only recourse left to us is to rise up in insurrection!"

The crowd roared its approval.

"People of Israel," he cautioned, "what was done here today will ultimately prove a victory for the king unless we unite! Our darkest time indeed still lies before us. Within days more Greeks will arrive, and they will tear this town from its foundation and kill everyone in it. But it will be far better for every one of us to die than to live so ingloriously under the subjugation of tyranny and evil, forced to turn our backs on our God." The crowd fell silent.

"Each of you is free to do as he pleases. My sons and I will be leaving for the wilderness, and I invite anyone who is zealous for God's law, for his country, and for freedom, to follow me!"

A man from the crowd cried out. "Are we to conceal ourselves in the forest like wild animals, living as cowards and bringing shame upon our heads for the remainder of our days?" Another voice in the crowd called: "You're saying we should surrender our town into the enemy's hands, and accept defeat while we hide like dogs?"

"No, not defeat!" Mattathias shouted. "We will give them a war unlike any they've ever fought. We'll show them the price of their idolatry, and prove to them that our God is sovereign over all, even their king. In their pride, they will be humbled before God!"

Chapter 12

THE SUN WAS long past setting when Judah half-carried Eleazar, groaning, into the house. Pressing a blood-soaked cloth against his abdomen, the youth sank onto the table.

Adi rushed to Judah and touched his forehead with delicate fingers. Scrapes and cuts lined his face, which was caked in dried blood and dust.

"Adi, a needle and thread. Now!" Mattathias ordered, entering the house behind Judah. Exhausted, he dropped onto a cushion. "We are going to have to leave this place by morning."

"Eleazar won't be able to move," Adi said, hurrying to examine the wounds of her brother-in-law.

"He'll have to," Mattathias answered.

Adi ran out of the room, returning with a bucket of water. A wet rag draped over it and her sewing kit.

Mattathias pushed Eleazar onto his back. He and Judah held him down as Adi stitched the four-inch laceration with trembling hands.

Jonathan applied a wet cloth to his own hand, where the pagan altar had scorched it.

"We can carry him," Jonathan said. "We'll easily have a third of the town coming with us into the wilderness."

Judah nodded, as Adi tenderly washed the blood from Eleazar's face.

"We'll have to move further north than we told them, though." Judah's voice was thick with fatigue. "Many will head to neighboring villages and take refuge with relatives, but those who remain here will tell the soldiers information, even if unwillingly."

The door opened, and Judah and Simon leaped to their feet, reaching clumsily for the weapons they had discarded. They relaxed when they saw it was Gaddi. He was alone.

"Father! I need you to come with me. There's something you should see."

Mattathias rose wearily. "Pack the mules," he said to Jonathan, "We leave before dawn."

§

"He's in a lot of pain, but he can still talk," Gaddi said, as he led his father into the nearby house of Joseph, a neighbor. "So far he's refused to tell us anything."

In the center of the room, dimly lit by a flickering candle, sat a Syrian, with his hands bound behind his back and his feet lashed to a table. Joseph stood over him, alongside his two sons. One held a broken Greek javelin in his hand like a club, and the other held a sword.

The man's face was pulped, his nose broken, and a makeshift dressing seeped blood from his calf where a sword had left a deep gash in his leg.

"What's your name, Syrian?" Mattathias demanded. The fear in the Syrian's eyes was unmistakable, but he remained silent. Joseph's son jabbed him in the side with the broken spear, enough to increase his fear but not enough to draw blood.

"Theon," he blurted, his voice raw.

"Are you Greek?"

"My father was Greek. My . . . my mother is a Persian." He said the words with effort, through bleeding lips.

"And how long have you been in the Syrian cavalry?"

"Six years. Six, I think."

Mattathias turned to one of Joseph's sons.

"Get me something to drink."

The youth poured wine into a cup and handed it to Mattathias, who held it up to the Syrian's lips. He drank greedily, wincing as the wine sluiced across his beaten mouth.

"Theon, tell us where the closest Syrian force is, and how many there are."

Theon hesitated.

"I can't," he whispered.

"I'm only going to ask you once," Mattathias advised, his voice steady and even, his manner convincing. "If you don't tell us the truth and quickly, Joseph will make what your people did in Jerusalem look like an act of charity. And I assure you none of us will see fit to intervene."

"We have his cart filled with crucifixion equipment," Joseph growled, and the Syrian began to cry.

"There's a handful of infantry soldiers at Emmaus," he choked, "and a cavalry detachment about twice the size as ours headed for Michmash. We were to rendezvous with them at Mizpeh two days from now."

Theon haltingly explained what supplies and equipment they had, who was leading them, and what their plans were.

"Three soldiers fled the town. Where would they head? Michmash or Emmaus?" If Emmaus, it would be to a smaller band of men at a closer distance, giving the Jews less time to escape should the Syrians give chase. If the soldiers went to Michmash, the villagers would have two, maybe three days, but then would surely face a formidable force.

"I don't know," Theon answered miserably.

They would have to prepare for the worst. Mattathias would have chosen Emmaus.

"We must leave." He looked at Joseph.

"What should I do with the heathen here?"

"Let him go."

"Let him go?" Joseph repeated in astonishment.

"There is nothing to gain by killing him. Let us not be

animals such as they are. Maybe God will show us favor if we are merciful."

Gaddi and Mattathias left for home. "I want you and Simon to take a couple of torches and scout out the road east of Modein," said the elder man. "See which direction you think those riders were headed."

"Father," Gaddi said hesitantly. "Simon will no doubt remind us that it's now the Sabbath. I do not believe I can enlist his help for anything before tomorrow night."

Mattathias stared, incredulous. "Surely he would not be *so* foolish. The Sabbath is there to honor God, not to get us slaughtered. No glory will come to Him in our death. You tell him—no, never mind. I will tell him myself."

Chapter 13

THE PALACE WALLS glistened in the dawn's first light, as Queen Laodice strode through the kitchen, passing a knowing glance to Theophilus, the head of the cookery.

"I can have it brought to your room, your majesty," said a servant girl, holding a plate of fresh fruit.

"No, I'll take it," Laodice said pleasantly. The servant handed the queen the plate as the cooks began preparing her meal, which she would take within the hour.

She passed down the corridor up the steps toward the second floor and glided down the hall past her son's room to her own bedchamber. She plucked a grape from the cluster and ate it. Then she set down the plate on a small table and stretched out across the bed. Naia's scent was still on her sheets. She breathed a satisfied sigh. A dog's barking outside broke the silence.

Though she was sure Naia was all right, Laodice hoped no one in her priestly order suspected their little dalliance. If she were ever discovered by the priests, Naia would be flogged. In truth, the danger excited both of them, made it more real for both of them.

Boredom—that's the one thing she couldn't abide. And thanks to her three lovers, boredom was rarely a problem. First, there was Aetos . . . first not for pleasing her but because he served a strategic purpose. Aetos was one of the king's bodyguards and captain of the sentry, tasked to guard the royal family. An older man with broad shoulders and leathery skin, he was Laodice's potential weapon against the king. If she wanted someone to kill Antiochus, Aetos was both in the right place and capable of the assignment. If the king ordered *her* to be executed, Aetos would likely be given the order, and she could possibly convince him to let her escape.

It had not been difficult to persuade him to betray his king by bedding her. She slowly seduced him, toying with him and inviting him into her bedroom on lonely nights, implanting the idea in his mind. During those evenings, she devoted herself to his pleasure, until he had no resistance left. She led him to believe that it was he who had taken advantage of her, and not the other way around.

Theophilus, who ran the royal kitchen, was her second lover. In charge of the cooks, he personally took her orders every day, whenever she was hungry. He was short and precise in his actions and not particularly attractive, but she saw the way he looked at her. She reveled in being the object of his worship. How easily she had possessed him, pretending to be overcome with passion and offering no resistance. Like a beast taunting its prey, she played with Theophilus, only coupling with him a few times, enough to keep him tormented and obsessed.

Never had she experienced the kind of love the poets celebrate. She had been sheltered, and her father had married her as a young girl as soon as she could conceive—first to her eldest brother, the crown prince, who died soon afterward, and then to her brother Seleucus, when he became heir. Seleucus had given her two sons, Demetrius and Antiochus. When Seleucus died, Demetrius was in the hands of Rome and soon after was reported dead. This made her son Antiochus rightful ruler at the tender age of nine. Laodice had reluctantly married her younger brother then, who adopted the young Antiochus and set himself up as co-regent, taking the name of Antiochus IV Epiphanes for himself. This man, her current husband, now called himself king.

No, it was never love that Laodice found in any of these marriages, nor was it love she sought. Instead, it was the power to manipulate—a power she carefully cultivated to ensure her own survival. A smile, a tantalizing look, the clothes she wore, the parts of her body she left exposed—she bent the will of others to hers, using their own desires, insecurities, and fears against them, with her innocent smile.

Naia, however, had been different. Naia was purely for pleasure. And it was Naia whom she had arranged to meet the previous evening.

Naia was a priestess in the temple of Apollo. She was summoned to the palace once a week—ostensibly to bless the queen and her family, performing ritual acts and divination—but the queen's servants knew that Naia had violated her priestly vows of celibacy long ago, causing her sacred internal fire to die out. She desired the intimate touch she had sworn to forsake, and found it in the arms of the queen. It was for Naia that Laodice felt lust, a lust that readily usurped her thoughts and influenced her actions.

From her window, Loadice watched the eastern sky turn gold with the rising sun, and she sighed. It was time to wake her son and check on him. What she felt for him was the only love she'd really ever known. She hoped he was not still sick this morning. Last night when she put him to bed, he'd complained of a stomachache. She exited her bed chamber and glided down the hall to the boy's room.

A woman's shrieks broke the tranquility of the morning, echoing down the palace corridors. Laodice didn't realize the cries were coming from her. On the floor at her feet lay her child—twelve years old, the life gone from his body.

His corpse was as pale and cold as snow, stiffly unyielding as she tried to fold him into her arms. Her keening as she rocked back and forth was unearthly. Servants rushed to help, which only agitated her further.

"Get out!" she screamed, and they did not argue.

The boy had complained the night before of feeling poorly, but she had done nothing more than put him to bed early, assuring him he would feel better in the morning. Instead, he was dead. His lips were blue. Blood and bile had dripped down the white silk sheets of his bed where he had vomited, pooling on the floor.

She rocked his still form back and forth, repeatedly crying out his name.

It was her fault, she thought, filled with hate for herself. She had not wanted a sick child to distract her from the evening's pleasures. She was sure she was being punished for her part in Naia violating her vow of celibacy, cursed by the gods for indulging in such wanton pleasure with a priestess. Naia was more than a priestess; she was a sibyl, a diviner of visions. In recent weeks, she feared the visions were being withheld from her by the gods. Even when she inhaled the divine vapors, she saw nothing. Was that Naia's punishment? She had confessed to Laodice that she saw nothing even when she tried inhaling more vapors than usual. Fearing gossip and discovery, Naia had lied to her order and invented prophecies—yet another grievous sin worthy of punishment.

Laodice rocked back and forth, her keening now reduced to whimpers. Her son was dead—her son, the rightful heir to the throne of his father, now occupied by his mad uncle. All her plans to unseat Antiochus and ensure her own survival had turned to dust, just as her son now would. She dreaded the king's eventual return. When they were children, she had been tortured by him. It was Seleucus who had intervened, protecting her. She buried her head in her son's neck and collapsed across his body.

§

"I am a god, and I cannot die," Antiochus crowed, his eyes glazed. He stared in wonderment across the dock of the harbor, the dripping, razor-sharp tip of the sacrificial dagger in his hand. He had drawn it across his thin chest from shoulder to waist on each side of his body. He looked up at the full moon and laughed in delight.

"I am divinity, made manifest!" A string of spittle dripped from his lower lip.

"My lord, please, you are unwell," cajoled Urion, as he cautiously approached the king. "Let me have the knife, and I shall have someone tend to your wounds."

Eyes glittering, Antiochus turned and slashed at Urion's neck with the knife, narrowly missing him, as Urion jerked back.

"You're trying to poison me! You want my throne!"

The king had lost weight over the past few weeks and looked pale. Urion had spoken with the king's physician about his episodes of mania. The physician explained that, if not brought about by the gods, then it could likely be controlled by a balance of the four humors. In the king's case, judging by his symptoms, the imbalance was most likely located in the gallbladder or spleen. The king needed an increase of yellow and black bile, and cooler temperatures would balance the humors, returning them to their natural equilibrium.

They had sailed north and docked at Sidon, Urion hoping that the milder northern temperatures would cool the king's agitation. Instead, he had become withdrawn, retreating into himself and refusing to speak to anyone.

"They're all after my kingdom," Antiochus muttered, pacing back and forth, apparently now oblivious to Urion's presence. "I have no choice. I must protect what is mine. I must kill them all." He stopped in his tracks. What if this was the work of his brother, the brother he thought was dead? What if, instead, he was still alive? Antiochus shook his head, trying to clear his confusion.

"No, no. I saw him burn on the pyre," he argued with the voice in his head. "But what if Hera has raised him up in revenge for Zeus begetting me, and putting *me* on the throne?" Yes, yes, he must kill them all. All those around him were a threat, doing Hera's bidding. She had lashed out before!

Without warning, Antiochus swung the dagger, but Urion was several feet away and safely out of range. Frustrated, Antiochus lost his balance, falling forward onto his knees. The dagger fell from his hand, unnoticed.

"Eat the food! *Eat the food!*" he cried, sitting on his haunches, swaying slightly. "*Eat the food!*" he shrieked. "Eat the pork!" His cries turned to groans. He wrapped his arms around his body, rocking back and forth. "Eat the food," he whimpered. "Eat the food."

Urion motioned to the captain of his guards.

"Get him on board the galley. Quickly! Don't let anyone see him like this."

Chapter 14

IN THE PRE-DAWN hours, Mattathias and his family trudged northeast. Two-hundred-and-twenty-six people followed in their wake, mostly on foot, their mules laden with food and goods. They had been traveling most of the night.

"Seventy-six," Judah told his father. "Seventy-six men that are of fighting age and can hold a spear."

Judah and Adi were walking on either side of Eleazar's mule. Seated on the animal, Eleazar was barely conscious, in considerable pain, and even in the dark Judah could see he was frighteningly pale. Judah put a hand on his brother's leg and was rewarded by his eyes opening. Eleazar looked at him blearily.

"How are you doing?"

"How long until we stop?" Eleazar croaked.

"Not long—just a few more miles."

Eleazar shot Judah a subtle look of distress, but not for his wound.

"Once all this blows over, we will come back, and you can find Elizabeth," Judah said, reassuringly.

"They've gone to Ekron."

Elizabeth was the daughter of a mason in Modein. Eleazar was deeply infatuated, and had been for over a year. He had begged his father to secure a dowry for him to take the girl as his wife. Her father, however, bore a grudge against Mattathias after another mason had been chosen to rebuild the town's synagogue. Mattathias tried to discourage Eleazar, but Eleazar pleaded. The girl's father had refused the match. Eleazar now feared he might lose Elizabeth to another man in his absence.

"Israel is a small country," said Judah. "I'm sure you will see her again." As the words left his lips, Judah found himself wondering if Israel itself would survive the tyranny of this insane king.

Mattathias was wrestling with a different problem. They were headed north as agreed, but it did not sit well with him that they were ignoring the plight of the people at Mizpeh. He wondered if it was his group's responsibility to veer south and warn them of the coming soldiers. If that Syrian had told the truth, there was still one more day before the eighty-man force arrived at Mizpeh from Michmash for the intended rendezvous.

By the tracks Gaddi had found, it appeared the three soldiers who had escaped had headed for Emmaus. Mattathias's instinct for survival said to march hard for the north and leave Mizpeh to the will of God.

"*Ratzon ha'El,*" the priest said, under his breath. *God's timing, His will. I could send a runner to warn them, but then the enemy might discover where we are and what happened at Modein. They might take their anger out on Mizpeh on a far greater scale than what would occur should we leave them to their fate.*

Their fate. Matthatias had often contemplated that word. The Greek word, *fate*, was not quite the same as the Hebrew *ratzon ha'El*. Fate was a set path one could not alter—predetermined and solidified, regardless of choice. *Ratzon ha'El,* on the other hand, was a fulfillment of the purpose of God manifested through the free actions and choices of men. Mattathias had meditated on the concept for hours on end while studying the Torah. Other priests in Jerusalem would use faith as the intelligent dismissal of any concept they couldn't comprehend, but Mattathias was drawn to the belief that actions performed were part of what God always intended or had always known, one's *ratzon ha'El,* and that God gave his creatures the freedom to act as they wished and to live with the consequences of their actions.

Freedom. That was another word Mattathias spent significant time meditating upon. Autonomy was granted to Adam in the garden east of Eden, and to his descendants: the freedom to choose between good and evil, right and wrong. If God Himself would not interfere in the autonomy of man, who were these foreign kings to tell a country, or a people, what to believe or how to live their lives?

He wondered again what to do about Mizpeh. A thought struck him. What about Nathan Ben Isaac? Nathan was a priest at Mizpeh and his friend—they had studied in Jerusalem as young men together.

Nathan was rigidly devout. There was no possibility that Nathan would bow down to an idol, to a false god. *Oh, God, please tell me what to do.*

It would be wrong of him, he knew, to let their brethren go to their graves without a warning. But even if he did warn them, would they not still choose to stand fast as martyrs? Would going there be a vain exercise should the Syrians arrive early and destroy the city before they arrived? He would be subjecting nearly three hundred of God's faithful servants to their deaths needlessly, after they had already fought so hard to survive. Could he justify such a sacrifice? On the other hand, there were many strong men—believers—in Mizpeh who might choose to join them in their fight.

"Mizpeh is only five miles south of here," Judah commented, as if reading his father's thoughts. "Many faithful live there, Father. We could make it there in less than two hours."

At this, Mattathias's mind was decided. He gave his son a resolute glance.

§

Mattathais had pushed the entire group south as swiftly as they could go. When they climbed to the northern gates of Mizpeh, Nathan and the other city elders greeted them, having seen them approach in the distance. Mattathias wasted no time telling the growing crowd what had happened at Modein, why they were on the run, and why he felt compelled to detour and warn Mizpeh's citizens. As more and more residents approached, he spoke of the attempted religious subjugation, how his people had defeated their attackers, how several soldiers had escaped on horseback, and how the soldiers were headed this way to exact the same sort of subjugation and punishment on Mizpeh.

"Anyone faithful to God is welcome to accompany us north into the wilderness," Mattathais said.

"Escape? North? Do you suggest we simply abandon our city to the Gentiles?" Nathan demanded. "We must stay and face them here—seal up the city and defend our homes!"

"Mizpeh has withstood sieges before," came a voice from the crowd.

"These are soldiers, and we are forbidden by law to bear arms. We have few weapons," another voice cried.

"We must go now! We can do more alive than dead," shouted someone else.

"We cannot run like cowards!"

"We cannot bow down to them and forsake all that we believe in—"

A cacophony of voices rose in argument until finally Judah shouted for silence. To his surprise, the voices subsided, as all eyes turned to him—some suspicious, some desperate.

"You cannot stay here! We know—we saw—what is awaiting you, what is awaiting all of us if we tarry. The Syrians are sending an army to tear this place to the ground if you do not embrace their idolatrous ways." As voices rose in argument again, Judah held up his arms in supplication.

"But you are right. We can't simply abandon the city and hasten to the wilderness, as they will surely ride us down and slaughter us on open ground."

"What do you suggest?" asked Nathan.

A hush came over the crowd, as Judah continued.

"We permit them to enter and pretend they have caught us unawares. They will likely approach from the south, but we must be prepared at all sides. Once they are inside, we ambush them from the city walls and rooftops, trapping them." He looked around the crowd at the intent faces. "And then we kill them all."

After a moment of silence, Nathan swallowed hard and then shouted in Hebrew the ancient Israelite war cry, "For God and for Israel!" The shouting erupted again, but this time it was different. It was synchronized and united.

§

"There isn't enough blood on earth to satisfy Ares—or our king," Amillius said to Jason, not bothering to lower his voice as the two mounted columns ascended up the shallow incline of the hill. "And this will never end, not with these half measures. You can't reason with Hebrews. They are truly impervious to reason. They actually believe in their stupid religion! They believe wholeheartedly, which is why we should do ourselves a favor and just kill every one of them."

His companion grunted in reply.

"I've been a Hetairoi for four years now," said Amillius, continuing his rant. Before that, I was an Amega. Don't believe what they say. The hostility isn't going to end any time soon, just because we make them kneel and they pretend to give homage to Zeus. What's more, the king knows it. Why else would he be having his citadel in Jerusalem erected right now? Mark my words. This fighting is sure to last a *long* time—"

"Amillius, shut up!" barked their commander who was five horses ahead of them, leading the columns. "We're almost there," he called to the men.

"Yes, sir! Right away, sir!" Amillius muttered—sarcasm in

his voice. He tossed Jason an eye-rolling glance. The commander ignored him.

"I want strict silence from here on out," the commander said, his quiet, steady voice carrying through the air. "We're early, and reinforcements are yet half a day's ride from here, coming from Modein, so stay alert. Stick to standard procedure unless otherwise told, and remember your places. Understood?'

"*Eleleu!*" grunted the cavalry soldiers in unison.

"Rah, rah," Amillius mocked, under his breath.

It was not long before the white stone wall of Mizpeh came into view, pocked with square houses of uneven, compacted cut stone. Over the city's south entrance stood an overpass. The narrow passage below cut through the sixteen-foot-thick wall and led inside. Identical gates guarded the city's entrances on the north, east, and west.

Mizpeh meant *watchtower*. Because of its close proximity to Zion, just seven-and-a-half miles away, the city—with its strong stone walls and hilltop position—made an ideal watchtower for, and stronghold against, enemies marching on Jerusalem. When Israel was young and still ruled by the Judges, a Levite woman had been raped by the men of Gibeah. The sons of Israel had gathered at Mizpeh to coordinate a retaliatory attack. In later years, after the Ark of the Covenant was lost to the Philistines at the battle of Aphek, Mizpeh was the rallying point where Samuel the prophet gathered the people in prayer and preparation for the coming war, and later to anoint Saul as the first king of Israel. The city was large and densely populated.

Traveling through the narrow opening in the wall that permitted no more than two riders abreast, Amillius could see a dense array of square houses of all sizes beyond the southern quarter. Their flat roofs rose along the north of the city, which was higher up the slope. The houses spread maze-like toward the western wall. The city was oddly quiet. It almost seemed abandoned.

Amillius stiffened. Clearly their arrival had been noticed, but it was unusual in a city this size for the streets to be so empty. As the columns filed forward into the open square, Amillius spotted a man on a rooftop watching them, who then ducked behind a parapet, out of sight.

Suddenly, a high-pitched scream came from behind. Turning, Amillius saw a man standing near the rear of the column, plunging a long spear into the side of one of the Hetairoi.

In disbelief, the soldier next to the Hetairoi drew his sword, as the attacker wrested the spear from his victim. As the soldier lifted his sword to strike the man, an immense rock came crashing down from the top of the wall and knocked the soldier from his horse, shattering his collarbone and crushing his sword arm.

Confused, the Hetairoi wheeled their horses as figures emerged along the top of the city wall and the flat rooftops—wielding slings, rocks, staffs, and clubs. Stones were hurled, bombarding the riders, knocking them from their mounts. More rocks rained down from the wall's overpass, killing the soldiers emerging from the entrance. Jason was struck in the face by a sling-fired stone, fracturing the bone beneath his eye. His eyes rolled back; he lost consciousness and slid from his horse.

Amillius, seeing no escape from the entrance littered with bodies, turned and charged toward the housing district. The screams and deafening tumult added to his confusion. He jerked as a stone struck his thigh with fearsome force, and he roared in pain. He continued forward, anxiety gripping him. Suddenly, his horse reared as a crowd of men rushed them. He struggled to keep his seat despite the pain in his leg.

Hundreds of people poured out of the buildings and into the streets. Behind, he heard a scream and turned to see the crowd rip the commander from his horse and club him to death. Amillius's horse whinnied in agony as a spear struck its neck and its legs collapsed. Amillius collided hard with the ground—his injured leg pinned to the ground by the dead weight of the animal.

He raised his head, trying to get free. As his vision came into focus, a foot slammed into his chest. Amillius was screaming, although he did not know it. He looked up in time to see a sword drive down toward his face before everything went black. His body jerked sharply as Judah yanked the blade free.

§

"Simple drunkards!" Mattathias mumbled, looking past Nathan and walking to the table outside the tavern where Judah and Jonathan were seated. The echoes of drunken revelry sounded through the city's dark streets.

Mattathias shook his head.

"We should be preparing to leave, not celebrating. We may have won a small skirmish, and only because the Syrians weren't expecting it. We should make haste. Jerusalem is only seven miles from here."

"Closer to eight," Nathan said, taking a seat across from him at the wooden table. He took a sip from the clay cup in his hand. "Be patient, my friend. We have not triumphed over tyranny since the days of Hezikiah. The people are jubilant." He leaned forward and looked at his friend intently. "Do you know what this means? It means we will survive as a nation. It means God will punish those who have slandered His name. It means Israel has the spirit and the faith to fight!"

"It also means that, by morning, the Greeks may be at the city gates and descend on us with an army large enough to murder us all," Mattathias retorted.

"We will accompany you," Nathan said. "Of that you can be sure. Many of the elderly, the Syrian sympathizers, and those who are simply stubborn will remain, but the dedicated will follow you if your aim is to fight."

"Of course we plan to fight," murmured Mattathias.

"How is Eleazar?"

"No worse, but no better either. He's with the physician now." Mattathias sighed. "It will be hard on him to keep moving."

"All the more reason for you to be a little patient, my friend."

Nathan turned to Judah.

"They've been talking about you, the men of Modein. They're saying your bravery was unparalleled. They said at Modein you charged on horseback, singlehandedly, against ten mounted men, with nothing more than a spear."

Judah responded with a look of surprise.

"People exaggerate."

"Maybe." Nathan grinned. "Have you heard what they're calling you? *Maccabee*, The Hammer." He repeated the word in Greek. "Your tactics for the surprise attack here were certainly effective. How did you know it would work?"

"It's not my first time being in Mizpeh. I was fairly certain which direction they'd come from. I know your city's layout. And naturally, if we forced them into confusion and desperation, blocking the exits, they would have no escape."

"A natural strategist, then," Nathan said, giving Judah an appraising look. The young man displayed a confidence—an authority and wisdom—decidedly beyond his twenty-three years.

Judah leaned toward his father. "I'm going to the physician's house to check on Eleazar."

§

Adi looked up at Judah standing in the doorway and gave him a heartfelt smile.

"He will be all right. He's strong, and the doctor says he should recover quickly, as long as infection or leprosy doesn't set in. He has given him something to help him rest."

Judah looked down at Eleazar, sleeping peacefully.

His eyes shifted from his brother to his wife, taking in her soft, dark features and tired eyes. He leaned forward and kissed her forehead. Adi took hold of Judah's arm and rested her cheek on it, closing her eyes. Her cheek felt warm and soft. She eased the panic he felt over his brother.

Chapter 15

L AODICE LAY IN bed, pressed against Theophilus's chest, listening to him breathe. Her eyes filled with tears as her thoughts invariably returned to her son. Desperate for some kind of distraction from her sorrow, she had turned to the kitchen master. She had been tempted to turn to Naia, but Naia made her feel happy. She didn't want to feel happy. She didn't deserve to be happy. The cook, on the other hand, a man of diminished status, meant nothing to her. That was what she wanted to feel. Nothing. Empty.

"Do you think someone might say something?" Theophilus asked. "They say the king will return soon."

She did not reply.

"Will he find out? About us, I mean."

"The Parthians are already attacking the eastern fortresses. His mind will be elsewhere. He and his army will leave, and things will return to normal."

Normal . . . her voice trailed off at the word. She realized she had never known a life resembling normality. She was barely a girl when her father gave her to her brother Seleucus for wife, but not before Antiochus had violated her. Father never cared; Mother just pretended not to know.

"Laodice . . ."

She sighed. "What?"

"There's something I must tell you. About the night your son became ill."

The queen went rigid. She sat up in bed.

"Tell me," she demanded.

"I didn't question it at the time—it's not my place to question orders—but the day before the boy fell sick, two of the king's servants returned to work in the kitchens. They insisted on handling the food for your son and yourself—the way they usually do for your husband. After that, they just disappeared. No one's seen them since."

Laodice stared at her lover. Her eyes seethed pain and shock. The king had murdered her son! She began to tremble—eyes brimming over, face contorted in torment. *It must be true*, she thought. *The bastard discovered my efforts to gain support to make the boy king. He killed him, even after adopting him as his own.*

"I see I have upset you. I just thought you should know. Please forgive me." The cook was confounded: he had upset the queen! But Laodice barely noticed him.

She composed herself, brushing the tears from her cheek.

"Thank you for telling me," she murmured. He took her hand and kissed it, while she stared absently across the room.

"I would do anything to bring you peace." He wanted to touch her, but did not—still confused, not knowing his place.

The queen did not hear him.

"It's probably nothing, just my own foolishness, you know. My imagination," Theophilus said, awkwardly trying to smile. "Even if it were true—really, what could we do?"

"Kill him," Laodice whispered.

"*What?*"

"We will kill the king."

§

Nabis emerged from the tent set up outside the station where he and three other soldiers were quartered. The sky was pale with the dawn, the air cold, and the camp seemed to be in a frenzy.

"Something's wrong," he said to himself out loud. In the

background he could hear the masons' hammers pounding ceaselessly on the citadel a few hundred yards away.

"What's happened?" Nabis called out to a soldier walking past him, noticing the man was of a lower rank.

"Another uprising. This time at Mizpeh. Two Hetairoi units were completely slaughtered. All the infantry units are mobilizing patrols to chase them down."

"Is the cavalry mobilizing?"

"Don't know," the man said, hurrying by.

Nabis's unit was an infantry attachment assigned to travel as support with a cavalry unit. When his commander discovered he was a former Argyraspide throughout the Egyptian campaign, they had made him a column leader. His unit was much more relaxed than any he had been in with the Argyraspide, and most of the men—even those who outranked him—looked up to him for being a prior member of the elite group. Although it had been only seven weeks since he failed to obey orders during the Jerusalem massacre, his role had changed, and his men admired him.

§

"It is imperative we contain this rebellion immediately," Apollonius snapped at Seron. "If the king hears of this, he'll return here himself, and we'll be hanging on crosses by year's end."

The general tapped his fingers on the map. "The latest intelligence reports show the rebels moving north from Mizpeh," he continued. "I'm sending patrols along the main paths and cavalry to cut off possible escape routes. That should box them in. The rebel band is reportedly nine hundred in size, but growing with every town they enter."

Seron pretended to study the map. Apollonius threw him a contemptuous look. The only reason this incompetent fool had replaced him as governor was because of the provincial policies of the king. Apollonius could have predicted how poorly the king's insistence on eradicating Judaism would unfold, and yet he himself was paying the price. To add insult to injury, he was expected to advise this stooge.

"They are moving mostly on foot—men, women, and children. We should apprehend them within the week."

"See to it, then," Seron replied.

"I'll initiate the infantry's forced march by nightfall. They will average twenty miles per day. It's only a matter of time before we find them."

"The king wishes to make an example of them," said Seron. "Make it so."

§

Antiochus walked to the bow of the galley, his frail hands gripping the railing. He stared down at the glassy, dark water. Alongside the ship, rows of oars kept a steady pace with the drumbeat.

When word had come of the Parthian attacks on the eastern buffer zone, the king had flown into an insane rage, followed by delirium. The hysteria had lasted several days, and in the week that followed, Urion had remained at his side to ensure the king's recovery. It had been an enormous relief when Antiochus opened his eyes and was himself again.

Now, Urion had to focus on the king regaining his strength after days of refusing to eat, babbling about someone trying to poison him. Urion had a different member of the crew taste each of the king's meals before he personally served them, to make sure there was not a grain of truth in his master's suspicions.

They had left Sidon three days before, headed for Antioch, Urion confident the king had recovered.

By now, my brother's son is dead, Antiochus thought, *and that threat is contained.* But the dispatches had informed him that their eastern fortresses had been attacked by the Parthians. He felt beset by enemies. From the Egyptians and the unruly Jews, to the Parthians and the Scythians, to the Persians' failure to pay their taxes, to his wife's feeble attempts to rally support to put her brat on his throne, he felt the world was crumbling about him.

They don't understand that I am a god manifested in human flesh, he seethed. *They don't comprehend that I can right the wrongs of the world if they will simply bow to me. Even my own officers are too obtuse to recognize my divinity. They abandon their posts.* He thought of his admiral, Kalisito, who had stolen a ship the day before they left Sidon. He had sent two of his fastest ships to chase the coward down and kill him.

Antiochus turned to find Urion watching him closely. He felt a flash of irritation.

"Within three months of arriving home, we will depart Antioch for Persia, and I will personally find out why those heaps of dung have not sent me the required tax revenue necessary to run this kingdom. I'll put to death whoever is responsible. I've changed my mind about taking General Lysias on the eastern campaign. I'll appoint him in charge of the capitol in my absence. He is the only one of my generals these days that I can trust."

Urion bowed. "Yes, my lord."

Lysias was an excellent general and a loyal supporter of Antiochus. Long suspicious of the queen, he had privately voiced his concerns when the king had announced his intentions to take his deceased brother's wife as his own. *I should have listened to him then*, Antiochus thought. It was Lysias who later suggested that the king have his head guard, Aetos, attempt to seduce her to test her fidelity. When she failed the test, Antiochus, in a rage, wanted to kill them both. It was Lysias's cool head that prevailed. He had suggested that, instead of destroying them, the king might use Aetos to keep an eye on Laodice and report her every action, thereby ensuring the guard's continued loyalty while keeping the king a step ahead of his treacherous wife. Even Urion did not know about the queen's escapades, although he did not approve of Laodice. The artifice appealed to Antiochus, and he contented himself with daydreams of the intricate revenge he would devise to ultimately punish the whore. And now his spies were telling him she was defiling a priestess. He just wished he could have been present to see it, to witness the queen's distress when she received the news of her son. *Soon*, he thought.

§

Thank you, God, Adi prayed fervently. *Please let it be true.* She looked down from the mule she was riding, to her husband, Judah, walking beside her.

It had happened while she was tending Eleazar. Mary, the physician's wife, had kindly asked how she was feeling. Adi looked a bit pale, Mary thought. Adi said the traveling had been unusually wearisome and that she was feeling achy, but she assumed all the stress of the last few days had caused that. She was, Adi admitted, concerned that she had suffered nausea for several mornings, since that might hinder them when they set out again. When Mary asked when her last period was, Adi blushed in shame, admitting that, in fact, her flow had ceased a couple of months earlier, and she feared she was barren.

Mary asked if she could examine her, and afterwards gave Adi a reassuring smile. "I think you are with child, my dear. It will be a little more time before you'll know for certain."

Adi buried her face in her hands and wept. "I pray you are right," she said through her tears.

Now, as she looked fondly down on her husband, she reflected on how, despite the circumstances, God had still chosen to be generous to her, to them—to give them hope for the future. *God, give me a son to give Judah*, she prayed. *But I can't tell him yet, not until I know for sure. If it's true, it means God has*

heard me in my tears, just like Hanna who bore the prophet Samuel.
Adi's heart filled with elation, thinking of how thrilled Judah
would be.

She glanced back at Eleazar, riding a little behind them.
Much of his color had returned, and he was able to ride and
walk without assistance.

"It is amazing, is it not, how, with just one small event, the
tides of the world can be altered by the hands of God."

Startled, Adi looked down at Nathan, but he was addressing
her husband.

"R*atzon ha*'E*l*," Nathan continued. "The armies of God
have assembled. Soon we will be able to make a stand on open
ground and drive them from our lands forever."

Judah gave him a sidelong glance.

"With our numbers versus theirs, I think we would be
advised *not* to make an open stand against the Syrians."

"But we have God guiding our every move. How *would*
you have us fight?" Nathan asked.

Judah rubbed his eyes wearily.

"The Syrians have one of the best-trained armies ever
assembled since that of Alexander the Great. To fight them
in phalanxes on open ground would be willingly placing our
heads into nooses and letting them kick out the stools. They
do have one weakness, though," he added before Nathan could
argue. "Their treasury."

"Oh, come now! They are easily one of the richest
kingdoms on earth!"

"But they have been at war for almost one hundred years
now, and that has surely taken a toll. They have hostile forces on
both fronts, and have been exhausting every resource they have
to quell them. Their coffers must nearly be empty, and their
armies are spread too thinly across an empire too vast for them
to control. Then there are the rumors that the Persian governor
withholds revenues and may attempt secession."

"So how do you think we should fight them?"

"We attack in small groups and strike where they are weak. We select targets costliest to their kingdom, in both their personnel and purse."

Nathan hesitated.

"I understand your thinking, but I still think we would be victorious on open ground." Nathan held up a hand as Judah began to interrupt. "Let me tell you why. Pride. We can use their pride against them. As it is written, *"When pride comes, then comes disgrace, but with humility comes wisdom."*

"Yes," Judah replied, "but I'm not sure I'd be willing to stake so many lives and such an important victory on whether their pride alone will prove to be their undoing."

Nathan shrugged and smiled.

"The sun is going down," he said. "Let us proceed another mile or so to those caves up ahead, which we should reach before sundown. Then we will stop and rest for the Sabbath."

Judah felt his heart sink.

Chapter 16

"THEY'RE DEAD!" ANNOUNCED Hippolyte, the commanding infantry officer, moments after entering Apollonius's office. "They're all dead."

"What? Who are you talking about?"

"The rebels! We killed every one of them. They're *all* dead."

Apollonius looked at him with disbelief. "Thank the gods!" he said jubilantly. "Tell me exactly what happened."

"We marched for twelve days, then encountered a family of Iudomains who had spotted them moving north. We tracked them to a large cave where they were sheltering with their families."

"How many men did you lose?" Apollonius demanded.

"None," answered Hippolyte, dispassionately.

"*What?*"

"We didn't lose a single man. We expected a fight to erupt immediately, but they didn't even come out to fight us, they just stayed inside the cave. We barricaded the entrance with wood and dead grass and set it on fire. We were prepared for them to charge the barricade, but they stayed inside. They began singing. Once it was silent and the fire burned out, we charged the cave. Everyone had suffocated. We counted nearly a thousand of them."

"And was their leader, this priest with them?"

"He perished as well."

"How do you know?"

"One of them was dressed in priestly garb. We assume he was the leader.

"Singing? Why didn't they fight?" Apollonius was perplexed. Why, after starting such a rebellion, did these Jews do nothing when attacked?"

Hippolyte suddenly looked ashamed. "I couldn't be sure, but I believe it was because we attacked them on their Sabbath day."

Apollonius's eyes grew wide. He exploded into guffaws. He threw his arms around Hippolyte and embraced him, tears of laughter spilling down his cheeks. Hippolyte however, remained solemn, remembering the sounds of the hymns to their god amidst the crackle of the flames. Then the singing took on a different dimension—laced with suffering and desperation. Then the singing had ceased, and only screams and the sound of babies crying could be heard. Then, nothing.

"You'll be promoted for this," Apollonius said, still trying to control his laughter.

§

Laodice gazed into her mirror, beholding her own image and the anguish in her eyes. *Who are you?* she asked herself.

In the days following her son's death, Laodice disguised herself and spoke to various alchemists about his poisoning. They suspected belladonna, a green-leafed plant with berries that are fatal when ingested. Now, she worked on her plot to kill Antiochus. It was a possibility she had always considered, but now she could think of little else. Killing him had become an obsession.

She could lure Aetos into drowning the king in his bath. On the other hand, she could have him poisoned by Theophilus, the only person who knew the king was responsible for murdering her son. There would be no freedom for her in this life, as long as her husband breathed. She knew now the king was coming home. The advanced parties had all arrived, and the king would be only days behind them. Soon he would be in his beloved palace, where she could get close to him, where she could kill him.

§

Water dripped slowly, rhythmically, from the roof of the cave near the Gophna hills. The humidity of the sleeping multitude mingled with the smoke of small fires scattered about the group taking shelter there.

Mattathias had assigned shifts for ten armed lookouts at or near the entrance. One of those men was approaching him now, accompanied by three strangers.

"These three men escaped from Nathan's camp."

"*Escaped?* What do you mean 'escaped'?"

"Nathan is dead," one said, his voice trembling, tears building in his eyes. "They attacked us on *Shabbat*."

§

Mattathias had stared at Nathan when he made the announcement once they had reached the caves.

"Nathan, I appreciate and understand wanting to observe the law, but we *must* keep moving."

Nathan shook his head. He was implacable.

"It is the Sabbath day. We do not work or travel, according to God's law. Did not God command that, 'Six days ye shall gather it; but on the seventh day, which is the Sabbath, in it there shall be none?' Did not God command Moses to put a man to death for merely gathering sticks on the Sabbath during their wandering in the wilderness? How are we different? Why would God bless us in battle if we don't honor His commandments?"

"Nathan," Mattathias said, his voice gentle but steady, "did God reprimand David when he took sacred bread from the priest Ahimelech? No. David acted to save the lives of his men and his own and broke God's law so they would not fall into the hands of Saul." Mattathais gave his friend a beseeching look. "Like David, we are fleeing for our lives from a wicked king, and it is imperative that we travel on the Sabbath to save the lives of God's people. The law is not a snare to trap us, nor a stumbling block to make us fall into the depths of *Sheol.*"

"If we don't keep moving quickly," Judah put in, "the Syrians will catch up with us, and run us all down! All we have done will be meaningless."

The argument spread through the crowd until it had firmly divided them into two camps. Two-thirds of the group, all from Mizpeh, allied with Nathan.

"Stone them! Stone them!" one woman had cried, as the five-hundred-some who chose to follow Mattathias gathered their things and prepared to move on.

Simon had chosen to follow his father, although conflicted about his decision. In truth, a part of him had been swayed by what Nathan had to say, but he knew his father and Judah were right, that to stop there would be the death of them. In the end, it was only because they were his family that he chose to keep his mouth shut and follow Mattathias.

"The law is not an anchor to be wrapped around our necks in order to drown us," Mattathias had grumbled, as his group— dividing itself from Nathan's—prepared to continue north.

§

Simon heard the stranger's words—that Nathan and his followers had all been slaughtered—and sagged against the cave wall. Sightlessly, he stared at the flames of the fire that burned before them.

"They attacked us on Shabbat," the man continued reporting to Mattathias, "as you predicted. We heard their approach from inside the cave, and people began to plead with Nathan that we at least should try to escape. Others pleaded that we should fight. But Nathan was stalwart, and panic began to surge. He called out to the people: 'How can we call ourselves Jews if we disobey the word of God? If we are to die, then it is His will, and God will avenge us when our blood cries out from the land.'

"Nathan rebuked those who wanted to fight. 'We would die in our blasphemy, as heathens. How can we expect God's deliverance for our country if we don't hold to His precepts and statutes?' he said.

"Smoke began pouring into our cave from a pyre the Syrians built, blocking the exit. The wind blew hard. Smoke filled the cave, and we were terrified. Nathan began singing a psalm of David, and soon most everyone joined him, not knowing what else to do.

"My friends and I were in the innermost recesses of the cave, furthest from the smoke. One of us spotted a crevice further toward the back and shouted for others to follow. Ten of us squeezed our way through." The young man looked sick. "I saw Nathan just before I ducked into the crevice. He looked right at me, disappointed. The singing had mostly ceased, and everyone else was coughing badly. The only thing he said was, 'Tell my friend Mattathias goodbye for me.' We made our escape, but everyone else perished."

Though his voice did not break, tears began to fall down the young man's cheeks. Mattathias put his hand on the youth's shaking shoulders. He could see the haunting guilt in the young man's eyes. "You did nothing wrong, son," the priest said gently.

§

Laodice stared at her shivering reflection. It was the vestige of a stranger—unfamiliar and hideous. Her eyes were blackened and bruised, and her nose horribly disfigured with a deep, livid slash from her husband's ring where he had backhanded her across the face. She could barely breathe with the swelling the break had caused.

She touched her throat delicately, brushing the spots where Antiochus's fingerprints were still clearly visible. She pressed one hand on her belly, wondering whether the child would be a monster, as his father was.

When Antiochus had stepped off his ship in Antioch harbor, every politician and important figure in the city had been there, amidst huge crowds, to honor him. Laodice had gone to great pains to look alluring, gracing him with a warm smile that completely masked her contempt. She kept her eyes on him, waiting for the king to look at her, to acknowledge her, so she could gauge his mood. He never did. She carried herself proudly behind him, as if in reverence of his power and strength. Only when they approached the bejeweled chariot did Urion touch his elbow, signaling that he should let his wife enter first. The king's eyes flashed, but he stepped back ever so slightly to let the queen pass. Laodice attempted a smile and graciously nodded at Antiochus, but he kept his gaze on the crowd.

Once at the palace, he strode to his private quarters.

"My lord," Laodice began once they were alone save for Urion and a few servants.

Without warning, the king had whirled around and whipped the back of his hand across her face. She fell onto the floor, startled that the beating had begun so soon. He grabbed her by the hair and dragged her into a bedroom, slamming the door shut, leaving Urion and the uneasy servants in the corridor.

The servants disappeared with great haste. Urion stood for several moments, listening to the crashes and cries that emanated from the adjacent room.

She had tried to dull the pain with shouts, accusing him of murdering her son. Those shouts he silenced with a more fervent beating before tearing her extravagant dress from her body.

After he had ravished her, Laodice lay curled up, naked, on the floor—her body aching, her wounds stinging, blood trickling from between her legs. Antiochus cursed at the blood stain on the sleeve of his tunic and tore it off.

He glanced at her on the floor and felt the stirrings again within him. She would bear him a child, of that he would make certain.

"Stop sniveling about that whelp of yours. I'll give you a son, and rightful heir to my throne, but this one will have a god's lineage, and my blood flowing through his veins."

She groaned something unintelligible. He smiled with malice.

"Oh, your whore is dead. That befouled priestess. Her infidelities were not looked upon mercifully when my agents informed her order of her licentiousness. Upon my request they may have taken her chastisement a bit far. Do you smell the air? That's her—burning on the pyre out there beyond the river." He laughed, not knowing if his words were true, and not caring.

He knelt down and flipped the queen's body over. She lay there, limp, as he forced himself into her once more. She bit her lip hard to keep from screaming. She would not add to his pleasure. She smelled the smoke and wanted to weep for Naia.

The king finally finished, and stood up. "Now that I'm done, I can have Aetos come in and see to your servicing, since you two have gotten so close," he said with a smirk.

Laodice pressed her eyes tightly shut, willing back the tears.

For two weeks, the violation had continued. The beatings eventually stopped, as Antiochus did not want to endanger the chance of the queen bearing him a son, but he still inflicted pain in any way that he could. When his physicians confirmed she was with child, he soon tired of her unresponsiveness and abandoned her in favor of his male servants.

When the queen crossed paths with the king's guard, Aetos avoided her gaze. He looked guilt-ridden. So the king knew—had perhaps known all along. That Aetos was still head of the king's guard, that he was alive at all, told her that she—not the king—had been the unwitting fool. *Antiochus must enjoy that,* she thought.

What of Theophilus? she wondered. Could she trust him? Or was he, too, a puppet of the king? She thought back to the last time they were together, when he confessed his worry that her son had been poisoned. No, she decided. Although the cook was fearful of the king, had he been part of the scheme, he never would have alerted her to it. Theophilus was not her enemy, but was he her ally? Would he have the fortitude to defend her, now that Antiochus had returned? Would he help her to murder the king?

סֵפֶר שְׁלִישִׁי

Book III
Uprising

166 BC

"Arise, O Lord, in your anger; lift yourself up against the fury of my enemies; awake for me; you have appointed a judgment."

~ King David

βιβλίο τρία

Chapter 17

FOUR FIGURES WADED through waist-high grasses that filled the dried wash on one side of the Tephon garrison. Emerging into the pre-dawn shadows, they crept between two watchtowers toward the palisades made of lashed cedar trunks that loomed sixteen feet above them.

Reaching the wall of the fortification, one of the men hoisted up the others, who grabbed hold of the ropes that bound the logs. Swiftly and silently, they scaled the wall, which creaked slightly with their weight as they dropped down onto the other side, unnoticed by the watchtower sentries. Judah reached the ground first. Eleazar, who had remained outside, faded back into the grassy wash.

Concealed by the shadows of storage buildings, armories, and troop housing, the three men paused in trepidation as a sentry approached, his heavy steps thudding on the ground. All three silently drew their short swords and watched with foreboding, as the long moon shadow edged toward them.

Judah signaled Joel, who waited motionless until the man came into view, then leapt upon him, forcing him to the ground between two of the buildings. Driving his blade between the upper ribs, Joel clamped his hand over the sentry's mouth, muffling his cries. Blood spewed from the sentry's nostrils, between Joel's fingers as the sentry struggled under Joel's weight until finally going limp. Joel removed his blade, and blood pooled heavily beneath him.

They waited—hearts pounding, straining to hear any signs of disturbance. Nothing. Judah signaled again, and the three crept forward toward the watchtowers that flanked the front gate. The gate consisted of two large wooden doors bolted shut by a heavy wooden beam from the inside. Two sentries stood there, leaning against the gate, idly chatting. Judah and his men inched along the wall shadows. Drawing near, they could hear the conversation.

"Jewish women wouldn't copulate to save their father's life," one man muttered. "Not willingly, anyway." He laughed. "The Samaritans up north—those sluts are warmer to a man. I tell you, the deployments here are endlessly boring. You'd be wise to take a second wife."

"Did you?"

"What do you think? I've been in this cursed region five years. I don't even know if my wife back home is still alive. Neither of us reads or writes. I found a round Idumaean woman whose cunt is as wet as—"

Only the terrified look on his companion's face gave any warning as Judah clamped his hand over the speaking man's mouth and dug his blade into the base of his skull, wrenching the hilt, severing the man's top vertebrae. Before the other guard could react, Joel plunged his sword downward between the man's collarbone and shoulder blade, into his chest. Simultaneously, their third companion loosed a flat stone from his sling, striking the guard manning the nearest watchtower squarely on his forehead as he glanced down to identify the disturbance. The other tower showed no movement, suggesting it was unmanned. Hurriedly, Judah and the others labored to lift the heavy plank that secured the wooden doors. The gates swung open slowly, the hinges creaking loud enough to make Judah wince.

He stared out into the empty darkness.

Suddenly, the darkness came to life. Five hundred men, led by Mattathias, poured up from the embankment and moved voicelessly into the outpost. Half the Syrian soldiers were dead before the first screams were heard. Within ten minutes, it was all over, the crackling flames of the fortress reddening the dark sky.

In the past six months, Mattathias's army had ambushed no fewer than twelve patrols, hijacked a large shipment of grain and Syrian horses en route to the citadel inside Jerusalem, and raided three small fortresses. Every one of the attacks had been meticulously planned by Judah. He had a gift. He could envision the way an attack would unfold before it happened. He almost knew how the enemy would react before the enemy did, but every attack he planned was unpredictable and equally devastating. Judah had organized the men as Moses had organized his army, appointing officers to groups of tens, fifties, and hundreds. He targeted weak, undefended objectives rather than fight in the open as the Greeks did. The sheer number of the Greeks would have ensured their defeat, in a pitched battle.

We owe so much to his prowess, Mattathias thought as he stood next to his sons, watching the flames consume the garrison. Though new recruits flocked to them from every town and village they passed through, Mattathias wondered what they would do when the Syrians mustered their entire southern army. Then what? *Our people need a place. They need to survive*, he thought, smelling the smoke that filled the air, warming him.

Then he felt his gut abruptly clench, and the thought of his recurring illness shot fear through his mind. He had prayed it would not return—the relentless vomiting and stomach pain. *At least you are alive today*, he thought to himself. *You are alive today.*

§

Adi stared across the barren plain as the sun began to rise, her hands wrapped protectively about her belly. The plateau was dense with vegetation, long dead in the intense sun, but Adi could make out a thin outline of life—a slender green strip that flanked the river a quarter-mile away. Built across the plateau was their camp, dotted with scores of Syrian tents they had acquired when Judah and his men attacked a Seleucid supply convoy headed north. Several small fires from the night before still smoldered.

Judah had been gone for two days and, although she always worried when he was away, this time she had been gripped by fear. Perhaps she was just more afraid for the baby's sake, now that her time was nearing. Eight or nine weeks, she guessed.

She had been relieved to learn they were moving south, away from the wilderness and toward the cities and villages. That would give them increased levels of support and draw the Syrians out of Jerusalem into the open, where they were more vulnerable to Judah's unconventional tactics. Every waking moment, Judah seemed focused on strategy. He had been elated, following one attack, when they found maps detailing the location of all Syrian fortifications and outposts.

Gaddi, she knew, had suggested they solicit support from Rome—an empire that hated the Syrians as much as the Israelites did, for the support Syria gave the Carthaginians. Mattathias, however, disagreed, saying they would merely be trading one brutal sovereign for another. Simon insisted Rome would never help them anyway, and Judah listened to all opinions objectively. *If Rome sends legions, we may actually have a chance to survive this madness,* Adi thought.

She just wanted to rid herself of the fear that possessed her. It consumed her. Adi looked down at her belly and prayed Judah would be there to see this infant come into the world. *God, let it be a boy, and let this one live*, she prayed. She remembered the look on her husband's face when she told him she was with child —the way he lit up, the joy in his eyes.

I just want it all to end. I want our children to grow up in Modein in peace, the way things were before. Then she felt a sharp pain in her stomach.

§

Mattathias gripped his abdomen and retched behind a pomegranate tree—out of earshot, he hoped, of Judah and his men. The cool dawn air brought no relief to his stomach, which twisted inside of him. It was getting worse, he realized, wiping his mouth, and it would not be long before his condition was discovered. Another spasm shook him. He leaned forward and vomited again. His face was pale, beaded with sweat. He trudged back toward the camp.

A month earlier, he had thought it was simply the flu and believed the vomiting and dysentery would pass in a few days. It had taken him nearly two weeks to recover, and now, to his dismay, the symptoms had returned. Shaken, he thought of Modein and their home on the edge of the brook. He thought of his wife when she fell ill and died.

Judah saw his father coming back into camp and fell into step with him. One glance at the priest's face revealed he was unwell.

"It's back, isn't it."

"Yes," Mattathias whispered. "I'm going to need to see the physician."

A distant movement caught Mattathias's eye, and he stiffened. "A rider."

"Someone from camp?" Judah murmured, turning to look.

"Hard to say."

"I'm going to wake them."

Judah's men leaped from their blankets and, moving with practiced speed, armed themselves with Syrian javelins, short swords, and bows that were more accurate at greater distances. A few also carried slings and stones. They hurriedly stowed their blankets and cloaks in their satchels as they readied their arms.

Judah stared intently into the distance at the rider, who was approaching at a swift gallop.

"It's Simon!"

Judah raced out to meet him, his heart filling with sudden anxiety. Had the Syrians attacked their main camp when most of their force was not there to protect them?

Simon dismounted, and Mattathias watched as his sons exchanged a few words. Judah then mounted Simon's horse and sped away. Simon joined Mattathias, collapsing wearily beside him.

"What is it?" Mattathias asked, when Simon didn't speak.

Sighing, he looked into his father's eyes.

"It's Adi. She gave birth yesterday, and she's very ill. That's all I told Judah." He shook his head. "The child didn't survive. It was a girl."

Simon's shoulders sagged. "Adi was grief-stricken. There was a problem with the delivery." He remembered what the old physician had said about the spreading infection, how she wasn't likely to live through this. At least it wasn't a son that was lost, he thought, remembering how much they wanted a child. *Ratzon ha'El,* he thought.

§

It took two days for Mattathias and the men to return to the main camp.

As he and Simon moved through the rows of tents, Gaddi's wife, Rebecca, came running toward them.

"They're gone!" she shrieked. "Judah took her."

The two men looked at Rebecca in confusion.

"She got weaker and weaker," the young woman gasped, "and then she didn't wake up. Judah took one of the horses and rode with her to Emmaus."

"That's more than seventeen miles away!" Mattathias exclaimed.

"She wouldn't wake up!" Rebecca repeated, choking on the words.

§

O N GETTING SIMON'S horrible news, Judah had spurred the horse toward Adi, galloping fervently south. He had ridden the beast relentlessly—almost to death—trying to make it back to the main camp. He had run toward the tent where Adi was wrapped in blankets—pale and clammy, barely responsive. Rebecca stood beside the mat that served as a bed. The physician quietly informed Judah that the infant had not survived.

Judah had commanded everyone out of the tent. He held his wife for what seemed like a lifetime. "I'm sorry," she whispered over and over. "I would have loved to have given you a child."

"Hush," he whispered, trying to reassure her, to calm her. Finally, the convulsions and shaking lessened, and she fell asleep in his arms. He stayed with her all day and through the next night— praying and fasting, pleading with God not to take her away from him. The second day she seemed a little better, but still had no color and could barely move. That evening she worsened rapidly.

"There's nothing more I can do for her out here," the doctor had said. "She needs a physician with medicines and healing herbs. She's in the hands of God now."

Emmaus, the closest large city, was twenty miles away. It would be risky, carrying her on a horse all that distance. And there could be Seleucid convoys tracking them. Judah agonized over what to do.

"I'm *so* very cold," Adi had whispered, as he held her close. She was burning up, and the night air was warm and humid. He made up his mind. If they stayed here, she would probably die.

He saddled a fresh horse, and readied supplies for the trip. When he returned to his wife's bedside, he could not awaken her. He lifted her onto the horse, cradling her against him, and rode south as fast as they could manage.

Adi had a blood sickness. The doctor said some of the larger cities had Greek remedies made from mold that might cure such a condition. Judah felt a rush of trepidation pass through him again, and he spurred the horse once more, even though it was lathered in sweat. Every time the beast slowed, he gave it another kick, unsure of how much more it could take. He saw a stream in the distance, and knew he had to stop or the animal would die.

Adi's eyes opened briefly. She looked and saw the worry on Judah's face. *I love him*, she thought. She felt so tired. She wanted to speak, but felt herself drift away again, now feeling no pain, just the warmth of Judah.

When they reached the stream, Judah slid from the saddle with Adi in his arms. The horse continued forward and began drinking greedily. Suddenly Judah panicked as he noticed the utter limpness of the body he held. Overcome, he laid his wife gently on the grass. He touched her skin. It was neither warm nor cold, but matched the outdoor temperature. Judah was terrified to investigate further, terrified of the truth. He shook Adi, tears streaming down his face into his beard.

As he lifted her head, the realization came: she wasn't breathing. He shook her again, crying her name, but her head lolled back. Her body was lifeless. He pressed his cheek to her mouth. Nothing.

He lifted her body to his. The grief-stricken screams that came from him sounded anything but human.

Falling on his face, he tried to fill his lungs with air but couldn't seem to take enough in. He shouted in his thoughts, asking himself, *What more could I have done to save her? Why did I ride away? At camp she could at least rest, and be in peace. I should have told her I loved her. Why didn't I say it one more time?*

Chapter 18

A POLLONIUS STARED UP at his father's sword, his
treasured xiphos, a symbol of Greek triumph over the
known world. The sword was unparalleled. But now, the
empire was in derision. The general had just been informed of
the latest attack, this one on the supply train of carts headed
for Jerusalem. It had contained gold from the north, the payroll
for his soldiers. The carts were heavily armed, yet not one of
his men had survived. The gold was gone.

Apollonius suspected the Hebrews militants he thought he
had vanquished months ago, were responsible for the continuing
slate of attacks. The few survivors of several onslaughts had
claimed their attackers were Jews, led by a priest.

His hopes of quickly ending the revolt had been shattered.
They were traveling north, that much he knew. He pinned his
hopes on the envoy he'd sent arriving in time at the garrison
south of Tephon, where they could track them down and wipe
them out once and for all, hopefully by month's end. For all
their lack of sophistication, skill, and experience, the Jews had
revealed themselves to be master strategists and fearless soldiers.

Apollonius looked down at the copy of the Septuagint
open before him—a compilation of the Torah and other
religious books by the ancient Israelites, translated into Greek
by seventy-two religious elders commissioned by King
Ptolemy II almost a hundred years earlier. Apollonius's version
had been hand-copied directly from the library of Alexandria.
Antiochus had since ordered all copies in the region burned,
but Apollonius had secreted his away, wanting to understand

his enemy better—what motivated them, and how they fought.

The Hebrew rebels had proved themselves organized and strategic in their objectives. They knew the terrain better. The Greeks' supply line was stretched, they were losing money, and fighting a defensive war on enemy land. Even if they managed to wipe these Hebrews out, Apollonius mused, who was to say more wouldn't readily take their place?

§

Admiral Kalisto looked off the bow along the horizon, scratching his beard. The day before they were to set sail for Antioch, convinced that the king and his army were cursed, Kalisto had, in an act of treason, departed from the Port of Sidon. He had taken the prized war galley and crew, effectively deserting.

His fortune lay on the other side of the ocean, he had decided. Neither he nor any of his men had been paid in months. He would pay the crew from the small chest of silver that had been stored aboard the ship. The silver alone would enrage the king, but the fact that Kalisto had also taken priceless nautical charts, and the ship, would likely send him over the edge.

Over the edge of what? Kalisto thought, with a mirthless chuckle. The man was already clearly over the edge! Kalisto didn't need the charts. He had sailed the world, serving in not one but two navies and shipping trade goods over four empires. He'd even sailed past the Pillars of Hercules toward the end of all things, into the unknown, and survived. What need did he have for maps? But taking them would spite the king, and that pleased him.

They had spent weeks in Cyprus and then longer in Crete before hearing rumor of other Seleucid ships in the area, presumably tracking them. Kalisto now felt the breeze on his face as the sun dropped in the west, mirroring its light on the dark blue horizon. He spat over the side of the ship.

There was a Greek trading post in Sicily where goods from Egypt and Greece were brought to barter with Rome. That was where he planned to head, a place where he could make some real money. Deep in Roman waters, where Seleucid naval ships would be unlikely to follow. Rome, everyone knew, was furiously buying up the entire Mediterranean Sea, having taken Sicily from Carthage thirty-five years earlier, and opening up importation from all over.

"Looks like a quiet night, don't you think?" His subordinate officer's words broke into Kalisto's thoughts.

"No. No, it doesn't," Kalisto answered, his expression thoughtful as he stared out at the horizon. Vague shapes coalesced slowly into two triremes—war galleys. And they were headed their way.

§

"Have you lost your senses?" Nabis exclaimed. "Thirty tetradrachm?"

The slave merchant shrugged. Business was good enough, and he'd seen the longing in Nabis's eyes. A little persuasion, however, appeared to be needed.

"Most of these Hebrew slaves have already been sold off to Greek soldiers or local colonialists," the slaver exclaimed. "I don't know why no one's grabbed this one. She's young and unsullied." He smirked, the lie coming easy. He'd had her himself a number of times, deciding only to sell her when he'd eventually tired of her. "Who wants to fuck a corpse?" he had sneered, disgusted at how she had lain there unresponsive, eyes unseeing. It had only taken a little pain to make her submit.

Noticing the beauty of the girl, and aware of the ways of slavers, Nabis assumed the statement was a lie. *You were there when we took Jerusalem. You saw the horrors.* Something about her reminded him of the woman he'd seen crucified in the square while the life poured out of her. He still had nightmares about it—her body naked, her arms dislocated, the weight of the infant's corpse hung around her neck dragging her down. This girl had the same vacant, broken look in her eyes.

"I'll give you fifteen."

The merchant scoffed. "I wouldn't sell a cadaver's cunt for fifteen. Twenty-eight."

"Twenty."

"Twenty-seven!"

"I can't go higher than twenty-four."

"Twenty-six?"

Nabis hesitated. Since his promotion, he had the luxury of an entire floor all to himself. Now he desired a slave to take care of menial tasks he didn't have time for. Besides, a slave would make him appear more distinguished to his peers and superiors.

"All right, twenty-six," Nabis said reluctantly, after a moment of hesitation.

The slave trader laughed inside his mind. *Fool!* he thought. *She'll lie there like she's dead. She won't fake pleasure even when you beat her. And she's skinny and sickly. Twenty-six tetradrachm! An unheard of price.*

Nabis reached into the small leather purse on his belt and counted out twenty-six silver coins with Athena's head imprinted on them.

§

"It's going to rain soon," Simon said, looking up at the darkening sky. "He'll be harder to track if it rains."

Eleazar stared toward a small ridge up ahead. A riderless horse had appeared and was galloping in the direction of the camp.

"That's one of ours!" Eleazar cried, sitting up high in his saddle. They charged after the animal. As they closed the distance between them, they knew: It was Judah's horse.

Simon tethered the runaway horse to his, as the rain began coming down in sheets.

"We'll never find him in *this!*" Simon shouted. A streak of lightning flashed in the distance.

§

Judah felt a raindrop land on his cheek. He was lying on his side near the brook, facing the patch of dark soil that was surrounded by grass. He had used his sword to dig the shallow grave that began to fill with groundwater. When he lowered her pale, stiff body, he had started to hyperventilate. He looked down at the corpse one last time, then filled the hole with loose black dirt. Falling down next to the grave, he wept. His hands and clothes were covered in mud. His shoulder-length hair fell to one side. He closed his eyes, listening to the water of the brook, wanting to talk to God. He wanted to pray, but he had nothing left to say.

§

Nabis sat at the front window of his apartment, looking out at the courtyard. He could see a storm moving south, but with the exception of a few clouds, the evening sky was clear.

You were lucky to get this place, with all these rooms, he mused to himself. Virtually all the adjacent housing belonged only to officers. The Hebrews who occupied the buildings before must have been wealthy. Who knew if they were alive now or dead?

Nabis looked over at the slave girl he had purchased earlier that day. She hadn't said a word to him the whole walk back. He told himself he had bought her because he needed a servant, and because his position in the army allowed him to do so. In truth, he knew it was mostly because he was lonely. In his heart, he admired the Hebrews, even though he fought them.

"What's your name?" Nabis asked her now. She stood, filling his cup from a pitcher of wine. She hesitated, as if she could not remember who she had once been.

"Abishag ... my lord." Her voice was as empty as her eyes.

Nabis looked up from the bench near the rectangular wooden table where his food sat. The meal had been good, and the wine to his liking.

"Sit. Please," he said, motioning to the bench opposite his. She flinched, fear in her eyes.

He found himself feeling sorry for her.

"Where are you from, Abishag?" When she didn't answer, he prompted. "Come now. Surely you speak Greek."

"I was born outside the southwest wall, near the Huldah gate," she said, in a tremulous voice.

Her Hebrew accent was soft and oddly pleasing. She looked no older than seventeen. He wanted to ask her more about herself, but her distressed manner made him think better of it.

"Please. Help yourself to some wine."

"No, thank you, my lord."

After an awkward silence, Nabis finally muttered, "Let me show you to your room." Abishag stiffened.

The second story of the square house had wooden floors that creaked beneath their feet. The master bedroom was extravagantly large, a fact that had delighted Nabis. The main living space featured a modest room across from his. There was no bed, but he had stacked several woolen blankets upon which the servant girl could sleep.

She followed him as far as the doorway but could not bring herself to enter the small room with him standing above her bed.

"Make yourself at home," he said, and she flinched as he stepped toward her. Then he passed, crossed the living space to his own room, and closed the heavy curtains behind him. With shaking hands, Abishag closed her own curtains.

Nervous, she lay down on the blankets, convinced that at

any moment her pagan owner would be back to force himself on her. She squeezed her eyes shut and willed herself not to weep. She could not block out the images of the slave merchant and the countless soldiers who had ravished her, the searing pain in her loins as she gasped before being silenced with a slap. She remembered her father's horrifying cries as a sword hacked through his neck, eventually severing his head from his body, and the screams of her mother as she was dragged away.

And now you're a slave to a soldier just like those who did this to you. For all you know, he could have been one of them. They all look alike. And you—your father's daughter—have to serve this pagan un-kosher food and strong drink, clean his house, and empty his chamber pot. You should kill him! So she thought to herself. But even if she killed him, where could she go? Her home was gone. Her family was gone.

She replayed all of it over and over in her mind, seeing again the death of her parents. Mercifully, sleep came upon her, freeing her—for a few hours—from the nightmare.

§

Through the pouring rain, the brothers rode up to the ridge and looked out on the darkened terrain.

"We're not going to be able to see anything in this," shouted Simon over the deafening sounds of the storm. "We could pass him, and we wouldn't know it."

"We'll have to stop and wait until morning," Eleazar called back.

Distant lightning flashed again across the sky. Shielding his eyes, Eleazar could just make out the figure of a man, rising to his feet near what looked like an overflowing stream.

"Look! There," he pointed. They raced toward the figure as the rain continued to pound them—relentless, as if berating them. The man looked up as they approached. Now they could tell it was Judah. The misery on his face said everything.

"She's gone!" he murmured helplessly. "Gone."

Jumping off his horse, Simon hastened over to Judah, putting a hand on his shoulder. "Brother, it was her time to go home."

Judah just hung his head.

§

The dawn was cloudy and pale, misted in fog. Most of the soldiers were still asleep. Mattathias stared at Judah as his three sons returned to camp. He couldn't tell him yet of the reports from their man in Jerusalem, that the Syrians were preparing to deploy their entire army to hunt down and slay every rebel. They must continue marching. In a few days they would be the farthest south they had been since first they fled, almost a year before.

Judah staggered forward, unsure if he would be able to continue to stand. He couldn't believe she was gone. His father put an arm around him. "I know," Mattathias said.

As weak as Judah felt, he still noticed his father's frail embrace. *He's getting worse,* he thought. *My world is crumbling.*

Chapter 19

ANTIOCHUS FELT THE icy pre-dawn breeze on his face, as the hooves of his horse trotted through the light snow. Behind him was his Agema Cavalry. He rode over the white earth near the eastern edge of the Syrian kingdom, on the border of the Parthian tribes, thirty miles from the river of Hari.

The small melee had happened less than an hour before. His scouts had spotted the band of Parthians around a campfire, and his men had attacked from horseback. Blood stained the fresh snow in blotches surrounding the dead bodies.

The cavalry had moved in front, in the direction of the skirmish. They had taken no casualties and weren't even sure if the men were Parthian militants, but that didn't matter. Their clothes were made of leather and fur. Their inner garments, made of thick cloth, came low around the ankles. Their faces were drained of color, and Antiochus felt very much like a god, looking down at their prostrate bodies.

The journey across the Seleucid realm had been tedious. He had rendezvoused with and taken command of the eastern army, continuing the march toward Parthia. His dynasty had ruled these people since Alexander the Great conquered Darius III at the battle of Gaugamela. When their king, Arsaces II, revolted, Antiochus's own father had stepped in to conquer them yet again. *Every twenty years or so, they need to be reminded who is in control*, thought Antiochus. Soon he would do to them what he had done in Jerusalem.

Now they were trying to rally under that animal

Mithridates and start their own kingdom. He would swiftly deliver them from such fantasies. They could not even agree upon their gods. Half of them worshipped the Greek deities but felt compelled to give them different names. The other half worshipped the Persian god Ahurra Mazda as the sole deity, not unlike the ardent Jews. As if there were only one god, the fools! Then there were some who believed Ahurra Mazda and Zeus were the same entity, but still believed in only one god. *That's why these people will never recognize me for who I truly am*, he told himself. *They will never willingly accept my authority—my divinity.*

The Agema commander approached and spoke. "My lord, these men we have killed could be part of a forward observation post. I respectfully request that, for the benefit of your subjects, you fall back with the main body until we know this area is secure."

"As you say," replied Antiochus.

A horse whinnied, and its rider looked about. The harsh wind had softened.

Another rider tensed, then stared at the line of trees ahead. There appeared to be an unnatural swaying of low brush close to them, within the forest shadows. He wheeled his horse nearer. As he approached, he could make out a man crouched low, covered by a cloak of foliage and branches. Before he could shout a warning, an arrow slammed into his chest, just below the throat, knocking him from his mount. Arrows filled the air from all directions.

Antiochus urged his horse forward and felt its legs buckle as the hail of arrows found their mark. The animal groaned with multiple arrows deep in its chest and crashed to the ground. Antiochus collided hard with the earth, pinned momentarily between the ground and the flailing animal.

An Agema rider galloped forward, javelin in hand, preparing to hurl it in the direction of the enemy. Then an arrow slammed into the soldier's side, tearing through his leather armor. He fell from his horse, and the javelin slipped from his grasp.

The volley of arrows ceased abruptly, as scores of men in Parthian dress dashed out from the forest, brandishing spears, axes, and swords. Antiochus looked up to see a Parthian standing over him with a sword above his head. Only the quick javelin from of one of his Agema bodyguards saved him from certain death.

Sliding his leg out from under the horse, the king was consumed by fear. As men fought all around him, he got to his feet and drew his xiphos from its sheath, lifting the blade just in time to block a blow from a Parthian battleaxe. The juddering impact knocked him off-balance and onto one knee. The man who had swung the ax loomed, enormous, above him. Before the attacker could swing again, a mounted Agema jammed his blade into the center of the axe-wielder's chest. The axe fell, and the man came crashing down on top of Antiochus.

"Protect the king!" he heard some of his men cry, as two riders dismounted and surrounded him.

"My lord, mount the horse!" cried another, fighting off a Parthian with his lance. Antiochus looked behind him as one of his men handed him the reins. He pulled himself into the saddle before he noticed that the soldier had an arrow lodged in his pelvis.

"Ride, my lord!" the soldier groaned, before dropping to his knees.

Antiochus kicked the horse, and it took off. Bodies lay on the powdered ice all around him. Men were clambering in the snow, struggling in hand-to-hand combat. Parthians continued to charge from the tree line. Racing across the ice, the king rode low, his chest as close to the mane of the animal as he could manage. An arrow whizzed past his ear, then another. Ahead, a Hetairoi formation bore down on them with fierce speed. He headed straight for the center.

The formation widened to surround him, then closed ranks again, continuing to bear down in the direction of the skirmish.

Four cavalrymen splintered off and turned to protectively encircle the king. His horse stumbled. Looking down, he saw two arrows lodged in its right shoulder. He kicked the horse harder as they neared his main forces.

Generals and commanders were ordering their men toward the fighting. Argyraspides were marching hastily on foot, their silver shields glinting as they held their immense sarissa spears aloft. Urion rushed out on foot from the supply party, protectively yelling after the king, who ignored him entirely.

Near the food supply carts, where the king's servants rode, Theophilus caught a glimpse of Antiochus, disheveled and panicked. The cook wondered whether, amid all the chaos, tonight might be the ideal time to exact vengeance and poison him.

§

Mattathias stared as the flush sunrise broke above the horizon. His eyes were sunken. The vomiting was getting worse, and he barely had strength to stand. *A strange thing life is*, he thought. *We're born into God's world, a descendent of Adam. We live and we die. I can't imagine it—how it must feel at the end.*

He didn't want to worry Judah or his other sons, so he refused to complain. He remembered how his wife had always complained about his never complaining. *"How is anyone to know something's wrong with you?"* he remembered her saying. She had been a good mother and wife, and he thought Adi would have made a good mother.

Poor Judah. Their success would lie heavily on his shoulders, and his alone. Gaddi wasn't a tactician, and Simon was unable to inspire and lead men, except in prayer. It would all fall to his middle son. *How to ensure Judah takes over when I'm gone?* he asked himself. *I don't have many of these sunrises left in the land of the living.*

And how would he tell Judah—still devastated about Adi and now about to lose his father— that responsibility for their cause now rested on his young shoulders? But Judah had to be told. According to informants in Jerusalem, Apollonius was, at that very moment, preparing to mobilize a force to destroy them. Mattathias knew in his heart he would not be there to lead or even to help in any way.

"The tumor inside your stomach is growing," the physician had warned. "If it enlarges anymore, the sickness will spread, and you will die. *Ratzon ha'El.*" God's will. Everything was according to God's will. Mattathias thought of the other nations—both strong and weak—that, over time, had nearly all been uprooted and destroyed—the Akkadians, the Assyrians, the Babylonians, the Jebusites, the Hittites. Israel had held itself together by the law of God, the *Torah* God gave Moses, the writings of the prophets, and a chronicle of their people. Would they survive this latest assault by the heathen, embedding themselves deep in the law and will of their God? Or would they grow unfaithful, and disappear from the earth? Whether Judah was ready or not, he must be warned of what was coming.

Mattathias saw the flap of Judah's leather tent open. His son emerged wearily, then came to sit down beside his father. Now was as good a time as any, the old priest decided.

"They're coming," Mattathias said. "They're coming from Jerusalem. The Syrians are preparing their southern army." Mattathias knew this was what Judah had hoped for all along. Every skirmish and raid they conducted, every engagement they took part in, had for its sole purpose the goal of moving the Syrian army north to meet them.

"We need to march south quickly," Judah exclaimed emphatically.

"I will go with you only as far as Modein."

"What are you talking about?" Judah asked, afraid to hear the answer he already knew in his heart.

"I'm not going to get better, Judah. The sickness is taking

me." Mattathias's voice broke slightly.

Judah had expected this kind of response, but still was taken aback by the bluntness of it. He felt a wrenching in his gut, a swelling in his throat.

First Adi and now my father, he thought sullenly. Why was God abandoning them when they needed the leadership and guidance of Mattathias now more than ever before?

"The army will fall to you, Judah. You will lead it when I'm gone."

"I'm a strategist. I can't lead men the way you can. Surely Simon, a priest who has the voice—"

"It must fall on your shoulders, son. You won't bend to blind idealism, or ceremonial piety over the fate of our people."

"What about Simon then, and Gaddi?"

"Your brothers will help you—help you administer and advise you. They will swear to it. But the command of the army and the destiny of our people, Judah, lie in your hands."

§

Seron, the acting governor, glanced up at Apollonius as the two walked down the citadel corridor, their sandals thudding softly on the stone floor.

"I need you to leave at dawn," Seron ordered. "Our last intelligence indicates the rebel militants are on the move, headed south. Your men will ride north to the Petah Tiqwa outpost, north of their last known position. There you'll join up with a regiment of Samaritan half-Jew mercenaries. Take your army south toward the main force I will be commanding. With luck, that will drive the rebels in my direction. When we meet, we'll coordinate our attack. The remainder of the army will mobilize and move in from the southeast, cutting off any chance for the rebels to escape."

"And if we're forced to engage with the rebels before that?"

"With your two-thousand men, I'm confident you can

destroy them. They number less than seven hundred. The rest of the army will simply be there to show the king we're doing all we can to quell these detestable whelps." Seron's eyes narrowed. "Under no circumstances is that to be interpreted as permission for you to track them on your own. This is not about *your* glory. I'm not taking any chances. I want our whole force in play to ensure there are no survivors. The next letter I send the king will be to inform him of the rebels' complete annihilation."

Can't share the glory, can you, you greedy bastard? thought Apollonius. *Of course you want all the credit.* Another inexperienced politician, presuming to give soldiers tactical orders. Mobilizing forty-thousand soldiers to take on seven-hundred men with no military training was completely absurd. With two-thousand men, Apollonius would have all the soldiers he would need to secure victory, but Seron needed his little demonstration of effort and insisted on including every soldier at his disposal.

Apollonius kept his expression blank.

"Yes, my lord," he said simply.

§

Laodice walked through Antioch, heavy with child. Her heart still ached for Naia, but now her thoughts turned to Theophilus. It brought a smile to her face when she thought of the poison she had entrusted him with.

"These are seeds from the castor oil plant," the old Assyrian woman had whispered to her. "Four seeds baked into the bread or a cake is sufficient to kill. Be patient. It can take up to five days to die from the poison. That will work in your favor, since it's harder to determine the cause. You have sufficient seeds here for a whole army."

Laodice smiled again, imagining Antiochus dying in agony. *I hope he writhes in pain,* she thought. *I hope he realizes he's been poisoned, and thinks then of my son, whom he killed.*

She would have to be patient. As she had informed Theophilus, they could not afford to strike until her baby came into the world. That would be in another four months. "My son needs to be born before news of Antiochus's death arrives here in the kingdom," she had explained. She prayed to the gods that the child *would be* a son. If not, she knew an aspiring noble or ambitious general would simply assassinate her and the infant and take the throne. If word of the king's death reached Antioch before her delivery, or Theophilus killed the king and her child was not born male, she would swiftly follow Antiochus into Hades.

Chapter 20

MARCHING SLOWLY INTO Modein, Judah breathed in the scent of vineyards and dates redolent of his childhood. He glanced down at Mattathias on the stretcher, whose pallor betrayed the great pain that now wracked his body. The stretcher had been lashed at one end to a horse and dragged in sharp, jarring movements along the ground, scraping two etched marks along the dirt road.

Only the day before, Mattathias had ridden near the front with Gaddi and Simon, and despite the grinding pain in his stomach, he would occasionally drop back along the column, rallying the troops and shouting, "For God and for Israel!" The men on foot would respond with a roar, raising their spears in the air. He had pushed himself too hard, however, and had fainted, falling off his horse. When his leg broke, it sounded like the bough of a tree snapping. Judah knew the men were worried. He could see their realization that they were losing their leader.

When they reached the house of Mattathias, Judah dismissed the men and told them to rest and take refuge among the townspeople, adding that any of them were welcome on their land. Out of the corner of his eye, Judah saw Simon and Gaddi whispering to each other. He wondered if Gaddi would use the double-portion law of the firstborn, established in the Torah, to legally take control of the army against his father's wishes. Had his father informed his brothers of his decision yet? Judah didn't know.

The house was uncharacteristically dusty, having lain

empty for so long. The wool mattress was missing, as was most the furniture. They made Mattathias as comfortable as they could. When he stirred, Judah held a cup of water to his lips.

"Try to drink, Father."

Mattathias gulped thirstily, then began to choke.

"Slowly, Father. I'm here. We're home now."

Mattathias nodded wearily and slipped back into unconsciousness.

"Go and get the physician," Judah told Eleazar, who had just returned with filled water skins. Nodding, his young brother disappeared again from the room.

§

"Sir?" Nabis asked in disbelief.

"Your unit will move north to support one of our outposts, but not you," replied Isadure, a ranking officer of the Jerusalem citadel.

"I don't understand, sir," Nabis answered.

"Orders from Antioch. General Lysias is stationing of a small group of Argyraspides here to train a new unit in their specialized methods and battlefield tactics. I've informed the commander of your own experience with the Silver Shields during the Egyptian campaign. He requested you be reassigned to assist in the training. They may not have long to learn their skills. If the problem with the Jewish rebels gets any worse, Lysias may march the whole army north to stamp out the bastards."

Nabis couldn't believe it. The Argyraspides! The unit was a source of his pride and brought him admiration from others, but he tried hard to remember how miserable he really was while in it. *Still*, he thought, *to wield a silver shield again and to stand next to men who knew they were the best fighters on earth!* That had its effect on soldiers. When men on the battlefield saw the Argyraspides leading the vanguard, they felt all the more confident that the battle was theirs.

But Nabis was conflicted. All the soldiers in his current unit he had trained and led. How could he just leave them now as they marched into battle for the first time? And Abishag. He took a slave thinking he'd be there for the duration of his enlistment, but if they put him back in an Argyraspides unit, they could send him off at the whim of some commander clear on the other side of the empire. Then he would have to sell her. *But I don't want to sell her,* he thought.

He didn't understand the hold the girl seemed to have over him. He treated her as kindly as any master ever should treat a slave. Still, her eyes were cold to him, and empty. He didn't know why his innermost desire was to make her happy, to give her some kind of restitution for the devastation his empire had brought upon her and her family. At his insistence, she finally had told him the story of how she lost her parents and siblings. Proudly fighting back the tears, she narrated the details with her chin held high, as if to defy him, his people, and all his Greek culture stood for. Listening, Nabis couldn't help but feel ashamed. The suffering she had endured moved him greatly.

"Sir," Nabis said. "I'm honored by the opportunity, but I respectfully request to remain with my men."

"It's not an opportunity," Isadure replied with a smirk. "It's an order. Eighty of the finest infantrymen in the region will be training under you and the other Argyraspides. Four of your own men are included in those to be trained."

Nabis's conflicting emotions kept him confused. Part of him still felt elation and the fulfillment of glory he had all but forgotten.

"That will be all, Nabis," Isadure said. "You are dismissed."

§

"He's waking up. Go get Gaddi and Simon," Judah ordered his youngest brother, Jonathan. Judah and Eleazar stood at their father's bedside. Mattathias had been coughing and wheezing all night and all morning. He had slept through the afternoon, and now the coughing had woken him again. Judah was anxious, not knowing whether he endangered their cause—endangered them all—by delaying the march.

Gaddi and Simon entered the room with Jonathan, and all five sons now stood around the bed. Although Mattathias was weak, he was lucid. He looked up at the worried faces gazing down at him.

"My sons," he said, "it's time for me to go the way of all the earth. I will give you my wish, and beseech you to keep it." Mattathias took a slow breath. "Continue to be sons worthy of me. Be ready to die for God's laws. Our bodies are mortal, and subject to fate, but our actions are immortal. Act nobly, and your name will live on with your deeds. I would have you in love with this kind of immortality."

Wheezing, he took another breath, and smiled up at his family. "Each of you, my sons, has your own strength. Honor and respect the strengths of your brothers. Simon is prudent and gives good counsel. Heed what he says in all things spiritual. Take Judah as general of your army. His strategies and courage on the battlefield are unmatched. He'll lead you to restore our nation, and bring vengeance on our enemies." Mattathias fixed his eyes on Gaddi. "Never resort to mercenaries, but admit to your army the righteous. That will augment your power. Remember the deeds of your ancestors."

He coughed, then took another labored breath. "These are my wishes. Now promise me," he whispered, "all of you, that you will fulfill them."

They nodded.

"I will obey your wishes," Eleazar said.

"And I," Judah responded.

"And I," both Simon and Gaddi repeated.

"As will I," Jonathan said meekly.

Mattathias began to murmur a prayer in Hebrew, blessing

them. When he had finished, he smiled, satisfied with life. Soon his face relaxed, and he drifted off again into sleep.

After a few minutes passed, Judah walked with Jonathan out of his father's house. He made a point of not looking toward the room he once shared with Adi. Outside, he gazed at the six-hundred-man force, almost all of which waited in groups on his father's land, near the brook. Suddenly he spied a rider galloping toward them.

"Judah!" cried the man, out of breath, rearing his horse. "Apollonius marches south with two-thousand men, and they're heading right for Modein! One of the shepherds spotted them on the march."

Judah turned to Jonathan. "Prepare the men to move within the hour."

Turning, Judah saw Eleazar stumbling toward him with his head down. He noticed there were tears in his eyes as he moved closer. He was shaking.

"He's gone." the young man murmured. "He woke up again and smiled at me, and then he just stopped breathing." Judah put an arm around his brother, who broke into sobs, burying his face in Judah's shoulder. Judah fought to control his own emotions in front of the men, swallowing the swelling in his throat. His brother's weeping added to the difficulty.

Suddenly, all the pain of losing Adi, and now his father, washed over him. He fought it back, with sheer force of will. *Not now, not now,* he chided himself. *You must be strong for your people.*

"*Ratzon ha'El,*" he said aloud. *God help me with what I must do,* he prayed silently.

§

"How long?" Apollonius barked, looking down at the Jew betrayer who had promised information in exchange for money and his life. Three columns of the Samaritan mercenary force guarded the flanks, holding their javelins at ninety-degrees.

"Three hours," the man said, swallowing hard. The Jewish man looked frightened, trying not to think of the three men with xiphos pointed at his back. He wondered if the men were Syrian or Samaritan.

"Three hundred and fifty left, you say. And they know we're coming?"

The man nodded.

"And their leader is dying," Apollonius added, with a slight smile, talking more to himself. He thought quickly. *If that scout made it through to Modein, that mob of stiff-necked fanatics will probably try to retreat to the east. If this dog is telling the truth, and there are only that many left, they won't head north and stand alone against my two-thousand men. With such small numbers, that would be foolish. They can't run south either, without risking being trapped between my forces and the whole southern army.* Heading west would also trap them. No, he decided, they'd head east. If he headed east now, over the pass of Wadi Haramia, he could lie in wait, and trap them in the Shiloh Valley.

If they suffered heavy casualties, Apollonius knew Seron would tell the king the general had disobeyed a direct order. That way Seron could escape blame and curry favor for himself. *But if I'm successful, suffer few casualties, and wipe out the revolt singlehandedly, I'll surely gain eternal favor in the king's eyes,* Apollonius mused. *I'll be restored to the position of governor, and Seron, that contemptible worm, will be disgraced. I'll never have another opportunity like this,* he thought, and felt his blood quicken in anticipation.

"What should we do with this sheepmonger, my lord?" The guard's words interrupted the general's contemplation.

The Hebrew began to tremble. "My lord, you promised me my freedom in exchange for—"

"Bind him. Take him with us as a guide," snapped Apollonius.

§

Mithridates stared down the mountainside from amid his scouting party at the fortified citadel of Heratas. The blistering-cold wind numbed his bearded face. He could see the Hari River from their position as he and his personal scouting party moved forward. He had taken Herat the year before and united the Parthian clans under his banner after his brother had died. He then took the Syrian fortresses and the Silk Road that led into India, and was now heralded as king of the Parthian people.

Parthia will be a sovereign nation, Mithridates promised himself, *not a puppet to the Greek dogs of Syria.* Antiochus had made too many enemies. Rome, Egypt, and now another uprising in Judea. Clearly, he had no idea how to deal effectively with his Jewish subjects, abusing them too harshly and putting them to the sword even after the violence had ended. Even Rome knew Antiochus and his Seleucid Empire were in trouble. Why else were they sending supplies and money to help Mithridates fight him?

Hearing that Antiochus was coming to personally lead the Syrian army, Mithridates had deliberately pulled back his host of mounted archers in a feigned retreat and let the Syrians give chase. Once the Syrians' supply line had become overstretched, Mithridates cut them off, enveloping their flanks with his cavalry and massacring the Syrian vanguard. It was an old trick liked by the Scythians, and he had executed it well.

Fondly, Mithridates glanced down again at Herat. They called Hari the "river of golden water." When Alexander the Great had taken Herat, he renamed it Artacoana. Before it was Greek, it was called the Pearl of Persia. Mithridates was determined not to let it fall into the hands of Antiochus, back to the Seleucids—not while he still breathed.

His men began cautiously descending the icy slope, alert to any sign of the Syrians his spies had reported were heading east.

Ice caked the Parthian king's beard, and the wind sliced through his leather garments. On his back was a quiver of arrows slung next to a short bow and, on his belt, his curved short sword. He longed for the warmth of a house and a stomach full of mutton—they hadn't eaten in two days.

Rumor had it that Antiochus was ill. The mountain pass was treacherous, but Mithridates knew that, if his spies were right and the Syrians were headed this way, this pass would be the most expedient place to launch a surprise attack against Herat before the city had a chance to fortify itself. Mithridates had spread his army thinly, harassing the Syrian lines. He had decided to lead a scouting party himself through the hills to find out whether they truly were in danger. But he saw nothing. He wondered how sick Antiochus really was. When he made it back to Herat, he decided, he would dispatch riders and order a full attack on the Syrian camp.

Chapter 21

THE DIRT-ROAD MOUNTAIN pass of Wadi Haramia disappeared around a bend amidst the rugged terrain. To the south, tall, dried brush covered most of the draw below. Over two-thousand Syrian soldiers and Samaritan mercenaries marched around the curve in the road in two single-file columns. Over their shoulders rested their spears, each the height of one-and-a-half men. Their armor, wicker rucksacks, and helmets were strapped across their backs; their shields were laced to the outside. General Apollonius rode toward the center, in between the two columns. To his right rose a stone ridge, ascending toward the peak of the hill they were climbing. His lower back ached.

"Sir! Look there!"

Apollonius wheeled around to see where his commander was pointing. Nearly three hundred yards ahead, he spotted twelve men crouching low. Having been caught in the open, they quickly melded into the high brush beside the road.

"Scouting party?" the commander asked. "Or just travelers, do you think?"

Apollonius looked hard. In the distant foliage, light flashed from glinting metal. "Those are spears!" he bellowed. "Apprehend them immediately!"

Three dozen Syrian soldiers darted down the road with their javelins outstretched, but to no avail. The twelve strangers had disappeared. Officers shouted to their units to prepare arms.

Half of the soldiers were ordered to strap on their armor.

The other half held their spears tilted away from the road—their armor and ration sacks at their feet. Sweat dripped from the men as half struggled to ready their armor. The runners were nearly at the place where the twelve had disappeared into the brush. Apollonius gripped his horse tightly with his thighs, his eyes scanning the ground foliage for any sign of movement.

Then, at once, the brush came alive, as men charged from behind the steep draw toward the outermost column. Half of Apollonius's men were still struggling to don their armor. The attackers lunged, their javelins impaling dozens of Syrian soldiers before they had time to react. Even those pulling security were caught off-guard, barely able to respond to the ambush in time to defend themselves. Scores of Samaritan men, many still in preparation, had spears and blades plunged into them. The Syrians and Samaritans struggled to defend themselves.

Within moments, the Hebrew rebels broke from the melee and retreated down the slope. Apollonius couldn't believe his eyes. "Fools," he sneered. "They're attacking from the low ground." They'd had the benefit of surprise, but this was abrogated by their botched tactical skills. He watched as his soldiers hastily created a wall of spears and began lunging at the fleeing Hebrews, who continued to fall back down the slope. *They've just killed themselves,* Apollonius thought, amused.

"Charge them!" he shouted. The rebels raced down the hill as the general repeated his command. A column of Syrians dashed forward in tight formation, their spears held before them at ninety-degrees as they descended upon the Jews.

"Push forward!" Apollonius yelled again.

Many of his men were still struggling with their armor, some giving up and joining the fight without it. The enormous line of his soldiers curved, concaving around the Hebrew rebels' flanks as Apollonius watched, eyes narrowed. He could taste his victory now.

Without warning, several hundred Hebrews, armed with

spears, leaped down from the rise just above Apollonius. The road was suddenly engulfed with men.

He charged his horse forward, ahead of their swords. Most his soldiers were down the hill and did not realize that far more rebels were closing the distance behind them than the number of rebels they were pursuing. *An ambush!* Apollonius muttered, incredulous. *We walked into a god cursed trap.* He wanted to shout for his captains to divide the columns and defend themselves from behind, but before he could get close enough to yell the order, a rock slammed into his wrist. The pain was sharp.

Apollonius looked up at the three Hebrews above him, with slings aimed at him. Another stone hit the side of his helmet, leaving him dazed, his ears ringing. He barely managed to stay on his horse. Another missile struck his horse, and the animal reared and threw him. Apollonius hit the ground hard with a blunt impact. He couldn't tell if he had broken his teeth, though he had. Rebels were racing down the steep hill, like an avalanche.

The general staggered to his feet. He had lost his helmet. He ran down the hill toward his men, trying to escape the attackers behind him. He wondered if he could make it to safety. One of his captains had ordered the columns to split. To the north was an open draw leading to a valley below.

A Hebrew *shofar* sounded, followed by another further afield, and then a third. In response, another hundred rebels, who had been concealed in the brush, rose and assaulted the southern flank. The Syrian soldiers looked about in confusion. There were rebels in almost all directions. They were nearly surrounded.

Syrian commanders down the line shouted conflicting orders, and the confused Samaritan mercenaries still had more soldiers facing the smaller force in front of them, than the larger one behind. Apollonius badly wanted to shout for his commanders to reorganize the lines and restore order, but he could not. The attacking Hebrews crashed into his ranks. In those fragile moments, the Samaritans made the choice whether to stay with their leaders or turn toward the inviting slope that offered retreat. Many discarded their helmets, dropped lances, and disappeared down the hill.

Apollonius drew his father's sword, feeling the familiar leather-wrapped gold hilt, and stood firm as hundreds of his men raced for the safety of the open space below. Judah, having anticipated this panic, had deliberately left the area unmanned to entice the enemies to break and flee. A violent clang of shields and swords erupted as the Jewish force that held the high ground slammed into the surrounded Syrian force. Men in droves now tunneled toward the draw in a frenzy, afraid their only avenue of escape would be closed off, every moment their last.

§

Judah had prayed for the safety of Joel, the mock informant, who had offered to pretend to betray the rebels' position. The idea had been Judah's, but he couldn't bring himself to order anyone to execute such a deed. Joel had volunteered. The danger was incalculable. Even if the Syrians believed the informant, they might kill him anyway just for being Jewish. Judah calculated that, if Apollonius were told the rebels knew of his position and strength, he would guess the Jews would head east to set up an ambush. The Syrians were numerous and, accordingly, over-confident. Judah's plan was simply to feed them the disinformation and take the least-used pass through the mountains, setting a trap for the Syrians on the narrow road over the hills at Wadi Haramia.

Everything had gone according to plan. He had baited and attacked the enemy, closing in from three sides and forcing the enemy soldiers into the narrow draw. His own men had performed the maneuver perfectly. With one hundred hidden in the high brush behind the drop near the road, he himself led four hundred from above the rise. The last group of one hundred, placed to the south, boxed the enemy in. His men were silent, quick, and lured the foe into pursuit, just as planned. His fighters retreated to the flat part of the slope, and when both Syrian columns foolishly followed, Judah gave the order to spring on them from the rise. But the battle was not over.

Judah parried a blow from a defending Syrian before lunging his spear into the man's jaw. Judah was instantly confronted by a young Samaritan in Syrian armor who held his spear uncertainly, unsure whether to hold his ground or move forward. Judah raised his lance and threw it with all of his might. The spear spiraled and embedded itself in the soldier's corselet. The man fell, and Judah continued to close the distance toward the enemy columns. Drawing his sword, he felt a shock wave pass through his hand and wrist as a sharp spearhead stuck his blade.

Jonathan traded blows with another Samaritan, who blocked Jonathan's spear with his Syrian shield. Jonathan aimed low and felt his weapon slice into his opponent's thigh. On the other side of the panicked Syrian force, Eleazar, Gaddi, and Simon emerged to hold the low ground, moving their men uphill to create the classic hammer-and-anvil tactic. More Samaritan men at arms began fleeing the battle, heading toward open ground.

Pushing ahead down the hill, Judah engaged an officer clad in gold armor. He suspected it was the general, Apollonius, whom he had heard much about. As he lifted his sword, the man's xiphos swung upward toward him, level with his eyes. Judah's round, bronze-plated shield came up automatically, deflecting the heavy blow. Without hesitation, Judah lunged, aiming low with his sword. Apollonius slashed at him, knocking the blade from its intended path. The general swung horizontally and Judah raised his sword, barely preventing his head from being taken off. Apollonius's blow broke Judah's blade in two. Judah grimaced and took a step backward, as he felt his opponent's blade slice across his forehead. Blood dripped into his eyes, mingling with sweat, making it difficult for him to see. He staggered on the steep slope, still holding onto the hilt with its sheared blade, raising his shield in time to block another deadly swing from Apollonius.

Judah felt his footing give way from the force of the downward blow. Sliding, he fell to one knee, barely aborting another heavy-handed swing. He felt fear for the first time, realizing that, although he was winning the battle, he was on the verge of losing this fight. His mouth was dry, his muscles fatigued, and all that remained was his elemental desire to survive.

Still on one knee, he deflected a stabbing blow toward his chest, which rammed his shield violently into his body. With all of his faltering strength, he slammed the shield down on the foot of his enemy. Bones gave way, and Apollonius bellowed in pain. Blood poured from the wound through the thin leather straps of his sandal. Judah lunged, the shield surging skyward, and caught Apollonius full in the face, the top of the shield striking his nose with a hard crunch. Losing their footing, both men fell forward, crashing to the ground.

Apollonius struggled to reach for his sword, but Judah hoisted himself and caught his opponent's wrist, pinning him to the ground. Judah knew Apollonius was stronger and that he couldn't hold him long. Judah brought his shield up and swung the edge of his shield down into the general's face, over his eyes, slicing deep into his skull. There was no scream. Apollonius went limp, then his body spasmed violently.

Slowly, Judah picked up the fine blade of his now-dead enemy and dragged himself to his feet to rejoin the battle, but it was ending.

The Syrian soldiers who hadn't yet fled or fallen were now outnumbered two to one and were quickly being cut down.

Judah stepped forward on shaky legs. His arms felt like they were anchored to his sides, the muscles strained and exhausted. He felt the pain for the first time in the palms of his hands, where his rough calluses had been torn away by the haft of his spear, which had slid in his grip. He also became acutely aware of the pain from all the scrapes on his legs and knees, and the gash across his forehead.

The hillside was littered with the bodies of the dead and dying. As he limped down the slope, a cry pierced the air, and his men looked up the rise to see Judah staring down at them.

"Glory to God and to Judah Ben Mattathias, theMaccabee, the hammer of God!" a soldier shouted. Shouts of elation echoed off the surrounding mountains. Everything seemed sharpened, to Judah's eyes. Amid the approving roar of the Hebrews, some began to chant.

"Maccabee! Maccabee! Maccabee!"

Judah raised the unfamiliar sword of Apollonius over his head and shouted back in a voice that sounded to him, oddly, like his father's. "For God and for Israel!"

Chapter 22

SERON SAT ALONE at the dimly lit table in the dining room of the governor's house. A bronze cup of wine and a plate of food sat before him, both untouched. He held his head in his hands, trying not to panic. Over five hundred dead! So much for Apollonius's reputation as a skilled tactician. There would be no hiding it now. Undoubtedly, the king would have already heard of the disaster and would realize Seron had been withholding information from him. *It won't matter if my dispatches arrive, because it will still be too late.* The king was not a rational man, as Seron well knew.

At least with Apollonius dead, Seron could blame him for everything. He sat up straight at the thought. *I'll tell the king his prized general was entrusted with scouting out their whereabouts and notifying me first, but he failed to send the news as ordered. It was all a vain attempt to gain glory for himself to restore his reputation and regain the governorship.*

Seron got to his feet and started pacing, his mind racing. *Who's left to contradict my report? I have no choice now but to send the whole army. I will leave nothing to chance. I'll divide my force, box them in, and make an example of them in the name of the king.* He exhaled heavily and reached for the cup of wine.

It had to work. His very life depended on it now. He would lead the host himself.

§

Kalisto stood on the bow of his galley as they approached the Syracuse port, feeling the familiar, comforting swell of the waves beneath his feet. He saw merchant ships docked, flying flags of Rome, Greece, and Carthage. Kalisto had narrowly escaped the two fast-moving war galleys that Antiochus had sent to pursue him, after a harrowing two-day chase. Tychon, the second admiral of the Seleucid navy under Kalisto, had been in command. Kalisto had trained him well, but not too well. When they were barely more than a stadion apart, close enough that Kalisto could make out Tychon's features on the deck, he briefly considered jettisoning everything he had stolen from the king that he'd intended to use to pay his crew—along with food and anything else they could spare—to lighten their load and increase their speed. He even planned to jettison the chest of silver. Then the gods intervened, and the winds abruptly changed. Kalisto had felt it on his face and immediately shouted orders to turn the ship.

The galley had caught the wind in its sails, heading into it, and whirled around so sharply it nearly dipped its sails into the water, immersing all of its port oars. Once the wind was solidly behind them, Kalisto charged the nearest enemy trireme at full sail.

The brass ram at the ship's bow sliced through the water and slammed hard into the hull of the enemy ship. Wood cracked with the crash of violent thunder, and both ships shuddered. As they drifted apart, Kalisto watched seawater pour into the other vessel's gaping hull. The rowers within screamed in desperation. Tychon was shouting orders from the deck, his face red with fury.

Kalisto knew that neither enemy galley posed them danger now. Tychon would rescue the crew and supplies off his damaged ship and leave just the oarsmen to drown. *Fortunately for me*, Kalisto thought, *the ship I rammed was the one with Tychon aboard.* Had it not been, Tychon would have abandoned the sinking ship, continuing his pursuit in the other trireme.

Now Kalisto's eyes scanned the peaceful harbor his ship was entering. He had joined the navy in a port not unlike this one. Back then, the island had been part of Carthage. He thought back to the day when he had experienced another narrow miss. That time the ship had been lost, devoured in flames. *It was so long ago,* he thought. *I was just a boy.*

The Second Punic War had been underway already for three years by the time Kalisto was born. Hannibal Barca, the charismatic Carthaginian leader and son of Hamilcar, had left North Africa for the Roman colonies in Spain with ninety-thousand infantrymen, twelve-hundred cavalry, and a sizeable number of war elephants. He conquered or allied himself with every tribe, from Spain through Gaul and across the Alps to Italy, defeating the Romans at every turn. Determined to halt him in his tracks, Rome, after suffering devastating defeats at Trebia and Lake Trasimene, had sent an army of ninety-thousand men—nearly double the number Hannibal had still remaining. Despite being outnumbered, Hannibal's forces surrounded the Roman army and annihilated them at the battle of Cannae.

Hannibal had kept his army in Italy for years, Kalisto recalled. The Romans, accepting that they couldn't manage to kill him on their soil, sent an army to his home in Carthage, where he was eventually defeated. *The man was a true soldier,* Kalisto thought.

Only twelve when his mother died, Kalisto had signed onto a ship as a deckhand for the Seleucid fleet, which was allied with Carthage at the time of Hannibal's retreat. Kalisto had seen Hannibal once, when the ship had docked. The fleet was headed east into hiding. The man had lost an eye and looked broken, defeated. Now Kalisto rubbed the burn scars on one arm, remembering. The ship he was on had gone up in flames just a few days later, during an engagement with Rome.

"Navy?" the harbormaster asked, studying his galley.

"No, we're private traders," Kalisto said smoothly. "I bought this ship in Cyprus from the Seleucid navy. It was nearly unsalvageable."

The harbormaster raised an eyebrow. "You must have excellent craftsmen. She looks solid. Neptune himself would have difficulty sinking her." He cast his gaze around the deck, trying to ascertain the intent of the activity onboard. "Do you have goods to trade?"

"No, just money to spend, and we're looking for work."

"Well, there's plenty of that to be found. You'll find the Roman traders provide most of the cargo vessel work around here. These days, they pay the best, too."

§

It was cold. Judah loathed the cold. The icy moisture of the predawn hours seeped through his clothes, making them cling to his skin. He never felt more demoralized than in the cold weather early in the morning. He sat up and forced himself to put it out of his mind. Sleeping on the ground out in the open certainly didn't help, but tents were in limited supply, and he had given his up after Adi's death to one of his soldiers who had a wife.

"That was foolish," Gaddi had said. "A leader must be held above the common soldier, and that includes the quality of his quarters. Father would tell you the same. He would never voluntarily lessen his status or approve the general of our army doing such. A leader isn't a servant," he added, pointedly. When their father was alive, Gaddi had often scorned Judah and Jonathan for marching with the men, while Gaddi and the other brothers, along with Mattathias, had ridden astride Syrian horses.

But Judah knew he was winning the loyalty of his men. He knew his men would die for him. There was already talk of making him king, which irritated Judah. They were calling him the Messiah, and he was no messiah.

"The Messiah will be of the line of David. The throne of Judea belongs to the descendants of King David," he repeatedly pointed out. "I am a Levite, the son of a priest. I am a military leader, nothing more."

Still, the people talked of it. Their recent victory had inspired all of Israel and, as a result, their numbers had doubled. The men didn't even call him Judah anymore. They always called him Maccabee.

Uncomfortable, Judah tried to redirect the title by referring to the army as the hammer, the maccabees. Men from all over Judea were traveling to join God's army and to fight with the maccabees, he would say. But despite his objections, the soldiers typically used the name of honor in reference to Judah personally.

As he wandered the camp, rubbing his arms to get some warmth, Judah thought of what the near future looked likely to bring. He hoped he could live up to his men's expectations. According to reports, Governor Seron had taken personal charge of the king's southern army, which outnumbered theirs tenfold. That army was better equipped and had superb cavalry and archers. Clearly, the king was now taking the rebels seriously, judging them a legitimate threat.

"Maccabee," one of the watchmen said, pulling himself up to attention as Judah passed by. Judah acknowledged him with a nod and continued contemplating.

Judah's hand rested on the sword he had taken from Apollonius. *An excellent sword,* he thought, his fingers caressing the leather wrapping. His thoughts turned back to Seron's army.

They'll be coming after us, so the battleground can be of my choosing, he thought. *If I position my men up a steep-enough hill, their cavalry will be of no use and their archers of limited benefit.* He could set up a defensive position as a diversion, then have the enemy march their phalanx into a narrow valley, where their twenty-foot spears would be of no use, and bombard them with arrows and rocks, before attacking their phalanx formations at an angle, using the slopes as leverage from which to attack. The enemy would not be able to maneuver. If his men could maintain the high ground, it should work.

Then, if they kept fighting, kept winning, they would be able to push the Syrians out of Judea altogether. The Israelites would once again be free to establish a government of their own, and rule themselves.

After ensuring the security measures of his camp, Judah returned to his blanket and lay down on his back, hands clasped beneath his head. He missed Adi terribly. The sudden thought of her brought back memories of his father's funeral. After the battle at the Wadi Haramia pass, they had returned to Modein to attend to the wounded and to bury Mattathias at their family's tomb. Afterwards, they had to wait several days so they would not be "unclean." As written in the law, they had ceremonially purified themselves from the blood of battle with water, and after the required days of waiting, finally were ready to move on.

His mind returned to his strategizing. *Where to fight,* he wondered? He thought of the maps they had captured, deciding to look at them come first light. He would have to plan carefully and plan well. There was no room for error. If they lost the upcoming battle with Seron, it would all be over for them.

§

Theophilus tried to appear inconspicuous in the king's kitchen tent. He sorely missed the palace life. He missed Laodice. His heart yearned for her. His chest felt restricted whenever she entered his thoughts.

He surreptitiously touched his purse, wherein lay the precious castor beans. For weeks he had intended to use them, but fear had stayed his hand. Once he had managed to crush some of the beans atop a dish of chicken and vegetables that had been intended for Antiochus, but then word came down that the king had already taken ill. Apparently he was ranting, far wilder than before, and refusing food and drink. The servants whispered that their master had finally gone irrevocably mad.

He would not stop shouting about his divinity and how he would destroy every last Jew, Roman, and Parthian.

News had come of another uprising by some priest in Judea, who was attacking outposts and murdering soldiers, and that had apparently set the king off.

After serving up the poisoned chicken dish, Theophilus was terrified that the king's taster would take ill in the following days, casting suspicion on the kitchen staff. However, the taster seemed fine. It was only after two of the dogs that traveled with the army died, that Theophilus realized the taster must have tossed the poisoned meal to the animals. *Had anyone made the connection?* he wondered.

But now the king was eating again, and Theophilus was ready once more to mix the castor beans with the food. He might get caught, but he had to take the chance. He would die for Laodice, he decided. She would know that, right up to the very end, he had protected her, and she would love him all the more for it.

Theophilus added spices and a sprinkling of ground beans to the king's soup that evening. *Laodice, I love you,* he thought, as he stirred the mixture. *And when they kill me, I hope my name lives on in your mind forever in painful remembrance of me. And that, because of what I do here, you will be set free at last and find some peace in this life, and know that you were loved.*

§

General Lysias—viceroy in the king's absence—stood on the castle parapet. As the sun set in the distance, he stared down onto Antioch. The city had been celebrating for the past two days, as Laodice had given birth to a son, who according to his father's wish had been immediately named Antiochus. The infant was healthy, and the people rejoiced at the birth of an heir to the throne. *If indeed he would ever inherit his throne,* Lysias mused. Heirs to the kingdom seemed to change rapidly of late.

The king's subjects had all but forgotten even the memory of Demetrius, the original heir, long presumed dead. *But is he dead?* Lysias wondered. Rome had insisted upon Demetrius as a hostage in order to keep the previous king, Antiochus's father, under their control, but the boy had perished while in Rome's captivity. If Demetrius had not died, if the Romans still had him, they could wait for the right moment to secretly reveal to Antiochus that the true heir, his rival, still lived. That would give them power over the king as it had given them power over his father. Antiochus could then negotiate with Rome to continue holding Demetrius hostage, or perhaps to kill him. It would be a brilliant political stratagem, and Rome was known for such.

Lysias walked from the parapet wall to the roof ladder and descended to the palace corridor below. Even if Demetrius were still alive, Lysias knew his own loyalties would remain with the king. After all, Antiochus had recently appointed him viceroy over all Syria, chancellor of the empire, and accountable to no one but the king himself. Lysias was even guardian over the king's family in his absence. Antiochus had made Lysias arguably the second-most powerful man in the region, perhaps in the world.

If the king died while fighting now in Parthia, that would make Lysias steward king over the greatest, or second-greatest, empire on Earth. It was a heady thought.

He recalled Antiochus's latest dispatch. "Destroy Judea," it had said. "Make them pay. Kill all of them." Lysias grimaced. He had sent riders to deliver a letter to Governor Seron, instructing him to attack if he had not already done so. News was probably already on its way to the king, informing him of Apollonius's defeat.

§

"Hold it steady!" Nabis shouted to the column of men, their sarissas leveled in front of them. They held their spears two-handed, their shields secured by the strap around their neck and forearm. They lunged forward with the twenty-foot spears at the sound of his next command. "That's not your xiphos, and it's not a javelin. It's a sarissa, so hold it properly." Alongside the other trainers who had ridden into Judea from Antioch, Nabis was instructing the unit of new Argyraspides.

The trainees were motivated to earn their silver shields, and they learned quickly, training ceaselessly with every weapon available. To carry a silver shield was to be revered, almost as if a demigod of the battelfield.

Nabis remembered his own training—just as brutal, just as unkind, and just as effective. The shouts of the other instructors could be heard across the training ground.

Everyone knew of General Apollonius's death, and how his men had fled. Nabis decided to use this fact to spur his exhausted men to drive themselves harder.

"If Apollonius had been leading Argyraspides soldiers, do you think they would have fled?" Nabis asked in a moment of calm between battle drill and armor runs.

"No!" the men who had gathered around answered in one voice.

"Argyraspides do not retreat, and they never surrender!" he bellowed.

"Those cowards were mostly Samaritans, not Greeks. That's why they ran," another trainer added.

At moments like this, Nabis would listen to himself in disbelief. He never had envisioned himself as a leader and trainer, never had imagined himself doling out the same cruelty that had made his own life so miserable. What astonished him most was how the men on the receiving end of his cruelty responded with admiration, loyalty, and the desire to please him at any cost.

It's a strange thing that happens, Nabis thought, *how the people you make suffer begin to feel more respect and commitment to you, and self-contempt for letting you down. It happens right when they are at the physical or mental breaking point. You sit them down and talk to them softly, letting them have just a glimpse of the human side you've been keeping hidden. They take it as kindness that you aren't using the time to punish them for one thing or another. And you speak to them in a kind way, though patronizing. You tell them how cherished and special the goal they are pursuing is, and you give them back something they had lost and all but forgotten they ever had . . . pride. Then they'll do anything for you. Anything to keep from disappointing you, and then they are yours to mold as you see fit.*

He thought of Abishag and wondered whether she might look upon him with admiration and loyalty if he began mistreating her. Perhaps he was being too kind. He had never beaten her, had never taken her—never even touched her. *Maybe I haven't been mean enough to her for the process to work. I can tell she still resents me. I've been respectful, and still I can see the coldness.* But could he blame her? Her family was dead, and she was a slave. *It's the Seleucid Empire you serve that did it.* The house was always clean, the food cooked well. She had never given him an excuse to chastise her.

Nabis could hear another Argyraspides trainer shouting in exasperation to his men.

"Yes, we march. *So what?* The Hetairoi is there to support *us* and to protect *our* flank. The cavalry is too lazy to march. The whole army — cavalry, archers, all of them — are there to support *us*, to support the infantry. And you are training to be the most elite infantry soldiers in the world."

Chapter 23

THE ICY WIND howled through the hills. Sharpening his sword on a flat stone, Jonathan rigidly turned his thoughts away from the bitter cold, and how much he missed Modein. The mountain's slope encompassed a slight plateau, upon which sat their bivouac site, just below the final peak of the Gophna hills, which towered above them. He wondered when life would ever go back to normal . . . *if* it would ever go back to normal.

An older man named Benjamin Ben Joshua was conducting training in the distance, teaching many of the new recruits the fundamental blocks and attacks and how to maneuver as a phalanx. Simon appeared next to Jonathan and, without greeting, began hammering out the dents in his shield. In the battle, Simon's shoulder had been cut, and it aggravated him with every movement. This added to his already irritable mood.

"How long do you think all this will last?" Jonathan asked, peering up at the columns of men drilling with their spears. Judah had assigned the most experienced soldiers to do the trainings, showing the inexperienced Hebrew militants proper use of a sling, a sword, a bow and arrow, and how to ride. Then they would be integrated into units and rehearse battle drills.

Simon stopped hammering and shrugged. "Who knows?" His tone was gruff. His wife and children had gone to stay with his wife's family in Berea, and Simon had been irascible ever since. Judah had ordered the women and children to remain behind in the cities as the army pressed forward—something their father would never have done.

"If we want to be an effective army," Judah declared, "then we have to act like an army, train like an army, move like an army, and march like an army. We can't do that bearing our children on our backs and fearing for the lives of our women as we step into the path of danger."

There had been protests—fears that the Syrians would pass through the villages where their families were hiding and slay them all—but Judah was convinced they would not be distinguishable as the wives and children of patriot soldiers. Reluctantly, most of his troops acquiesced and found safe havens for their families. Those who refused headed back home with assurances that their decision would not form a rift between them and their comrades.

"Do you think Father would approve of going on and leaving the women behind?" Jonathan asked Simon.

"There are many things Father would not have done," the older brother growled. "I don't think Father would have dragged the men up this cursed mountain at this time of year, either."

Jonathan tried to focus his thoughts that seemed numbed by the cold. The air was getting brisker as the sun moved behind pale clouds. *Father's death is probably hardest on Eleazar,* Jonathan thought. Eleazar was the jovial extrovert of the family—always laughing, telling stories, cracking jokes. But Jonathan had not seen him smile once since Mattathias's passing. Jonathan wanted to ask Simon when he thought the fight would come, but realized Simon didn't know. After a few more minutes of working on his shield, the older brother grunted, then left without further words.

Jonathan felt cheerless. His thoughts turned to Sarah, the girl he madly loved. She was just sixteen—seven months younger than himself. She was the daughter of Levi, one of Judah's captains over fifty men. The first time Jonathan saw her, it was in the camp, a few months back. He remembered the way she looked at him—innocent, wanting, afraid of her own desire, her eyes lost in his. For days Jonathan passed by her tent just to catch a glimpse of her. Finally, she said hello to him when her father wasn't near. Nervously, he tried to talk with her, reassuring himself that he was desirable, too—that he was Jonathan Ben Mattathias, son of the priest and leader of the rebellion. Before he left, she had asked him to walk with her the following evening by the stream. He had agreed.

That next evening, they had walked alone. That would have been considered improper by most of the community, and surely by her father, had he known. This walk was followed by other walks and meetings … all clandestine, many of them in the night.

Jonathan was amazed by her, and felt an ineffable churning in his heart. He felt pain remembering what she had confided in him: how her father had divorced her mother, who had moved to Jerusalem shortly thereafter, just before the Syrians attacked the city. He remembered the strain in Sarah's voice when she said she did not know if her mother was alive. Her father would never speak of her, and Sarah hated him for it. Jonathan, too, found himself hating the man, on Sarah's account, although he had never spoken to him.

The night before the men had left for raid on the Tephon garrison, when her father was away on a hunt and the camp slept, she had slipped out of her tent when her three younger sisters fell asleep, and met Jonathan near the stream. There on the banks they had planned to be together. Both knew it, but couldn't fully admit it to themselves. With effort, Jonathan had put the sin of what he was doing out of his mind, overcome by his passion for her. They were in the midst of a war and could both be killed at any moment. He had seen more people die that year than he had in all his other years combined. Life itself had become ephemeral, and Jonathan had no wish to delay the experiences and love they felt for one another, the love they so longed for, in hopes of a future they might never have.

Sarah had felt overcome, weak, loving—telling herself

Jonathan was nothing like her father—that this was good, because their love was good. Furthermore, she had no wish to beg the permission of a man who would undoubtedly scorn his daughter's wishes, no matter what those wishes were.

For moments they had stood together, transfixed in each other's eyes, unsure what to do. They knew where they should be, where they wanted to be, but uncertain how to get there. Finally, he kissed her, and they both sank to the dry, cold dirt. He climbed on top of her, and her head scarf fell to the ground. She felt his warmth through their clothes, and the pleasure began to rise, as he moved on top of her. Jonathan pulled her skirt up, and then the pain came—sharp, taking her breath away. She tried to hide it, but it became quickly unbearable. Her eyes filled with tears, and she started to panic.

Jonathan stopped in the midst of his satisfaction, the reality of it all suddenly returning. Their moments of tenderness were spoiled by the shame they now felt, as the guilt of their sin descended upon them. Sarah began to weep, feeling empty— exposed—prostrate in the dirt, like a whore. Then the thought struck her that perhaps she might conceive. Whatever would she do?

She asked if there had been any emission. Jonathan was too embarrassed to tell her there had been. She hadn't known there would be blood and so much pain. Finally, Jonathan calmed her down, and they walked back together to the camp, each of them feeling separate and alone.

The next day Jonathan had departed to raid the Tephon garrison. On his return Adi had died. After that came the death of their father. Jonathan asked himself if it were all God's judgment upon him for sinning.

Now Jonathan longed only just for the sight of Sarah, his heart aching in remembrance. The words of Moses came to him in a flood of guilt: If anyone deceived a virgin that was not betrothed, and lay with her, he must surely take her as a wife to himself. And if her father should refuse, and not consent to give her as wife, the sinner must pay compensation to her father according to the amount of the dowry of virgins.

There had been no time, however, Jonathan argued to himself, to right the wrong. His brother's decision to dispense with the women and children had ensured that. He swallowed. He hoped he had not left her with child. He would marry when they returned, if she would have him. That much he promised himself.

Jonathan jumped, startled when Judah dropped down beside him on the log, where he was sitting.

"Didn't mean to alarm you." Judah was smiling.

Jonathan noticed he had cut off his long, wavy hair.

"Why did you cut your hair?" Jonathan asked, surprised.

"I figured it was time." The shorter hair made Judah's thick brown beard look fuller. Jonathan had been trying to grow his beard out, but little hair would grow, and that made him feel insecure. He had been teased by friends and even Eleazar because of his sparse facial hair. Gaddi had once told him that he'd be mistaken for a Greek or a woman on the battlefield. It was embarrassing, but his father had said not to worry, that his beard would grow in after a few more years.

Now Jonathan looked up at Judah. He didn't know how to tell him about Sarah. He would soon have to do it, though, since Judah would have to arrange the dowry.

His gaze traveling to the men drilling with their spears, suddenly Jonathan longed for a normal life. A house, like his father had, near a brook … Sarah for a wife, and children. He could even become a priest, like Father or Simon.

"What has you so happy?" Jonathan asked, since Judah was still smiling. Jonathan had not seen that smile since Mattathias's death.

"Nothing in particular," Judah replied. "Joel and some of his men found a beehive in one of the trees down the slope. We'll have honey with our bread this evening." Joel had won renown for himself after volunteering to pose as a traitorous shepherd to the Greeks, providing Apollonius with the disinformation that led to his defeat. It was a wonder that Joel escaped with his life after that. He had been made a captain over one-hundred men after the incident. Though an excellent leader, Joel was also boisterous and comical. Jonathan had heard him arguing with one of his men, whose old horse had collapsed on a patrol down the slope. "The horse wouldn't have died," Joel had teased, "If you weren't riding him as hard as the Greeks ride their boys." The statement had ushered in a plethora of sardonic comments about the femininity of Greek men and their unwavering compulsion to sodomize their boys.

"Joel had an idea, by the way," Judah went on. "He suggested that all the commands on the battlefield should be given in Hebrew from now on, to confuse the enemy."

"No one speaks Hebrew anymore," Jonathan scoffed. "It's only used for religious ceremonies. What's wrong with Aramaic? The enemy doesn't understand that either. They speak only Greek."

"There are enough of them who might understand. Joel's right. We need to be cautious. And there are enough people here who speak Hebrew. Simon speaks Hebrew, you speak some. I even speak a little," he chuckled.

"It just strikes me as potentially confusing. You're asking them to speak a language other than their own in the heat of battle, when they have enough to think about trying to survive and kill the enemy."

"It can be done," Judah replied. "I want you, and the men under you, to start using Hebrew commands during battle drills. Soon it will be second nature." Judah put his hand on Jonathan's shoulder, wondering if his brother were really mature enough to command the hundred men he had put under him. *Jonathan is never far from your side,* Judah reminded himself, reassuringly.

"I'll appoint some men to train you first, and the captains of ten and fifty that are under you, so you can learn some of the basic commands. Hebrew isn't that different from

Aramaic," Judah added, slapping Jonathan on the back as he got to his feet. "Anything to confuse those Greek bastards."

What a complete waste of time, Jonathan thought, as Judah walked away. *It will just confuse everyone in the middle of battle.* Left by himself, Jonathan felt his melancholy returning as his thoughts again went to the girl he loved. *If I pay Sarah's dowry and marry her, I will be within the law, and will justify myself before the Lord. God, let it be so.*

§

The clouded sky cast a pall on the evening as Nabis strolled down the streets of Jerusalem toward his home. The insurgent attacks on Syrian soldiers had increased of late, and rumors spread that soldiers would be brought in to be quartered within the new citadel if things got worse. Even in these seemingly tranquil surroundings, Nabis never went out without his armor, sword, and shield. Torture of various Jewish families had provided little satisfactory information on the identity of the culprits. *You can't rule by fear forever,* Nabis thought, turning into a narrow alley. Ahead were three Jewish men, headed in his direction. Their eyes met—facial expressions unapologetically hostile. Nabis's hand shifted to his xiphos. He felt a bead of sweat roll down his hairline as the men strode toward him. He tensed as they parted, passing on either side of him. He glanced back and relaxed slightly when the men continued on, ignoring him.

After a ways, Nabis arrived at the terrace of four connected homes that housed his apartments. He ascended the wooden creaking stairs to the second floor and at last walked in through the door.

The main room was dim, and no candles had been lit. He could see no sign of Abishag and assumed she wasn't there. The curtains to her modest quarters were drawn. He stepped forward and slid them open. To his surprise, the girl lay prostrate on the floor, an open scroll at her head. Her face turned toward him, and she looked terrified.

He suddenly felt enraged. She had been praying—worshiping the Hebrew god. He bent down and grabbed the scroll. It was written in Hebrew, the words meaning nothing to him.

And what was he to do now? This slave was in his home, breaking the king's law. She could be killed for such a transgression. He could lose everything if this became known. He looked at her in bewilderment, feeling betrayed. How could she put him in such a position? Confused and seething, he could not trust himself to speak.

He could see she didn't know how to react, but stared up at him in fear. The moment was still and lasting as he stared at her. Nabis stepped toward her, and she cringed, turning her face to the floor. A calmer inner voice interrupted his thoughts. *If it were my family that had been butchered and sold into slavery, how would I respond? What if she feels all she has to turn to is her god? The law takes even that from her—even her right to pray? Is that decent? Is that just?*

He was shocked at his doubts. *If anyone found out what just happened in this room, they'd take her away and kill her. If anyone suspected you permitted it, you'd lose far more than your position as an Argyraspides.* He would be locked in the dungeon, or sold into slavery. No—for supporting sedition and sanctioning a violation of the king's orders, they would execute him along with the girl. He could lose his life over this. And *she* had placed him in this compromised position.

Nabis breathed heavily, trying to calm himself. *If you don't kill her, you're leaving your life in her hands. If anyone hears of it, it will be your body hanging from a cross.*

His heart ached, and he knew he couldn't hurt her.

Abishag rose to her feet. Nabis could see the tears in her eyes; her hands were trembling. "Are you going to kill me?" The soft voice was surprisingly steady as she met his gaze.

"No," He responded in a cold whisper after a moment's hesitation.

"And what is to be my fate?" she asked in trepidation. "Please don't sell me," she begged suddenly, her voice frail.

Nabis was startled. She wanted to stay? He walked out of her room, still holding the scroll. He looked at it again before tossing it onto a table, then poured himself a cup of wine from the nearby clay pitcher. He sipped and sat down to ponder a faith that triumphed over a fear of death.

His father had been an ardent worshipper of the gods, especially of the Greek god Ares. His mother, a virtuous woman, preferred the temples of Athena. Nabis himself had felt nothing, since Egypt, when he had tried to pray, and had finally given up. He wasn't even sure if he believed the gods existed—a fact that certainly would have grieved his parents, had they known.

Some of the philosophers, like Aristotle, believed in an unmoved prime mover, a divine being, but the idea of licentious deities controlling the fate of men and waging war because of jealousy seemed more and more unlikely to him. He didn't know what to believe anymore.

Nabis grimaced in surprise when he felt Abishag's hand lightly touch his back. She sat down on the bench of the table next to him. She leaned her head on his shoulder. Nabis felt a warmth pass over him, and his heart quickened. The moment lasted, both of them lingering in the pleasure of the strange connection they felt.

"We have to burn it. If anyone were to find this here, they would kill us both."

There was a pause. He felt Abishag nod her head against his shoulder.

"What does it say?"

"It's in Hebrew," she whispered. "My Greek is not so good." She picked up the scroll, her hand taking hold of the coarse papyrus.

"My soul waits in silence," she translated haltingly, "for God only; from Him is my salvation. He only is my rock and my salvation, my stronghold; I shall not be greatly shaken. How long will you assail a man, that you may murder him, all of you like a leaning wall, like a tottering fence? They have counseled only to thrust him down from his high position; they delight in falsehood. They bless with their mouth, but inwardly they curse. My soul waits in silence for God only, for my hope is from Him. He only is my rock and my salvation, my stronghold; I shall not be shaken."

Nabis lost himself in her beautiful accent as she read.

§

The fog began to rise in the distance, the sun setting over the far mountains, the fading light catching the whiteness of the snowflakes as they fell. Urion felt the frozen earth under his winter shoes.

The camp was virtually empty, most of the king's troops having moved toward the front lines. The king had finally recovered from yet another lengthy, severe bout of disorientation. Perhaps it was the cold that affected his humors, thought Urion. Now the king was devoting his time to preparing his armies for their concentrated counterattack against Mithridates, whose cavalry had been repeatedly harassing the Syrian army.

We need to move forward quickly and take some of the Parthian towns, Urion thought, *or we'll run out of food and supplies. This place is a death trap.*

In more ways than one, he reflected. He thought of how the king's taster and one of the bodyguards had caught the head cook pulling out a mysterious container from his cloak and sprinkling the contents on a dish of mutton intended for the king.

The bodyguard had recalled the dogs that had died suddenly after he gave them some of the king's food.

"Eat it!" the guard had ordered. The cook, Theophilus, had refused, backing away, declaring himself unworthy to partake of food prepared for a king. "Eat it!" the guard roared again. Theopilus had tried to dart around him, in vain. Then he had grabbed a poker from the fireside and swung it.

The guard wrenched it away and struck the cook across the back of the head with it. Theophilus staggered, his hands fluttering as he fell to his knees. The guard dragged him to the fire and plunged his head into a cauldron of soup, holding him down until Theophilus stopped struggling.

When the incident was reported to the king, Antiochus had ordered the entire kitchen staff executed, including the bodyguard. The food they now were served was a far cry from what the trained cooks had prepared.

"Makes you miss the warmth of Egypt," Antiochus said, suddenly standing beside Urion.

"It does, my lord," his loyal advisor replied. "Perhaps in the future, you might arrange our wars to be held in more temperate climates." They both laughed, and Urion was relieved to see the king's improved mood.

"When Alexander died, he would have been wise to leave his kingdom in the hands of one man, not several," Antiochus mused. "All this bloodshed among ourselves . . . and all the while, Rome grows stronger. But Parthia foolishly tries to cut off our trade route from the Silk Road. If we lose our trade in the east, I lose my empire."

He continued on, conversationally. "Did you know it was Alexander himself who had Philip, his father, assassinated? Philip wanted to pass the throne to the younger son of his new wife. Alexander had fallen into disfavor after embarrassing Philip in front of an ambassador. Philip tried to kill Alexander that night, but he was too drunk to do it. They later reconciled and seemed to grow closer, but there was no talk of reinstating Alexander as heir. So Alexander arranged for one of Philip's former lovers to murder the king in public. Then Alexander killed the murderer to cover up his own involvement in the incident."

You'd never be able to prove it, Urion thought. *They couldn't prove it then, and they can't prove it now.*

"Sometimes one must do seemingly evil things to preserve the kingdom," Antiochus continued, philosophically. "Sometimes there is justification to be brutal, to do evil, to sacrifice for the overall good. In fact, it was my ancestor, Seleucus, who ordered the assassination of—"

His words were cut off by the eruption of not-so-distant thunder. But instead of fading, the sound grew louder. The king looked puzzled, then his eyes lit with recognition.

"Cavalry! They're attacking us from the rear!"

Urion froze as Parthian riders emerged from the mist and snow, bearing down on them, swords drawn.

Chapter 24

HOW IS IT that I'm headed back to this god-cursed part of the Mediterranean? Kalisto thought, staring at the clouds on the horizon. Back to Judea. The pig-fornicating Romans paid well, he mused. If someone had told him a month before that he'd ever be setting sail back toward the realm of the insane Seleucid king, who probably had more reward money on his head than someone would pay for Midas's golden cock, he'd have cursed the person for being a witless liar. But here he was. Without a doubt, the Romans did pay well.

Kalisto had been soliciting for cargo work in the trading companies of Syracuse when a young man had approached him after nightfall.

"They say you know the waters off the coast of Philistia well."

Kalisto tensed. He scrutinized the stranger. Was he an assassin, sent by Antiochus?

"I am being paid officially—you don't need to know by what government—but I need a captain who knows the seas and can get me where I need to go," the young man muttered.

A Roman, Kalisto decided.

"Good luck with that," he grunted and turned away.

"I'll pay in gold."

Kalisto halted without turning back around.

"I'll pay you half a talent of gold for taking me to Judea and, in a month's time, sailing me back here. I know who you are. We know about you, and we know you are no friend of Antiochus."

Kalisto turned and looked at the Roman, eyes narrowed. The man smiled slightly.

"You are the admiral who has taken a galley from the Seleucid navy, yes?"

Half a talent of gold to take two men to Judea? What by the name of the gods is Rome planning against the Syrians? Kalisto thought. They must need him desperately to offer such an outlandish sum. Kalisto harbored no love for the Romans, not since they'd set his first ship ablaze.

"Three-quarters of a talent of gold, and no less," he answered gruffly. And so the deal was struck.

Kalisto sold the Syrian galley, which would have been far too conspicuous, and bought a new Carthaginian-style vessel from a Cyrene shipmaker—perfect for war or for transporting cargo. Then he set sail with the young Roman official and one of his comrades. Both men had the look of soldiers about them. Pontius Fabius Æmilius was the name the young man had given, and Gaius Crassus Quintilanus was the name of his companion. *The Romans and their god-cursed names,* Kalisto thought, as his ship rose up and down upon the waves.

§

"Our intelligence reports indicate that the Israelite rebels are camped in this mountainous region here, in the hills of Gophna," Seron said, pointing to the map. His commanders were gathered around the table, studying the layout. "Our plan is to avoid a foolish disaster like the one Apollonius walked into. We will avoid these mountainous regions here and here, which are ripe for ambush, and will march up the coast instead, on open ground, where there will be no surprises. We will cut directly northeast here, toward Gophna, passing through Adida, Beth-Horon, and Tephon."

Seron stepped away from the table, pacing pensively for a few seconds. "I trust I don't have to remind you to keep your men in line. We can't afford attacks on the general populace or to be slowed by local insurgents. That could render us immobile for the battle to come. Unless the local peasants pose a direct threat, you take no action against them."

"Understood, my lord," one of the commanders murmured, as the others nodded.

"Our spies have infiltrated the Jewish force. They tell us their ranks have swollen in the months since Apollonius's defeat. We could be facing up to nine-hundred men. That's why I'm mobilizing the majority of our combat-ready soldiers and deploying four thousand. We'll take no chances. We must annihilate these rebels."

"And once we reach Gophna, sir?" asked a commander.

"We will divide our force into three. The vanguard will assault the mountain up the shallower incline on the western slope, pushing the Jews down the hill in one of two directions. There each of our two remaining elements lie in wait, forcing them to engage while outnumbered. Whatever direction they choose to flee, we'll have additional troops to close in behind. We'll wipe them out. Our cavalry detachments will wait in reserve, blocking off the open escape routes and roads, and ride down any rebels who slip past the main assault."

The governor walked to the door, and the commanders turned to face him. "There are to be no survivors," he growled. "No one escapes. This rebellion ends here, under me. The surrendering rebels all will be killed, including women and children, and the leadership will be crucified. I will personally lead the attack." His eyes on fire, Seron marched out of the room.

§

In the large tent, set up on the training grounds inside the Jerusalem citadel, Nabis sat eying the new Argyraspides—their prized, unused, silver shields resting upright against their shins, as if the soldiers were reluctant ever to let them go. *They probably don't even put them down to defecate,* he thought with amusement. Nabis still remembered the proud excitement he felt when he had received his own silver shield.

They had completed their training that day, and each one had, by now, drunk his share of ale and bore the mark of the Argyraspides tattooed on his shoulder. Nabis recalled the relief he had felt when the brutality of his training ended, and the honor of wielding the highly coveted silver shield. His eyes sought the men he had trained. Crinos was talking loudly with Orestes, both men eager soldiers. Eugenio and several others clustered about one of the other Silver Shield trainers, listening to war stories.

"Argyraspides! On your feet!"

The men leaped up and stood rigidly at attention, as the commander of the citadel entered the tent.

"Gentlemen, I am General Arillias, commander of the Jerusalem citadel under Governor Seron. Let me be the first to congratulate you on your notable accomplishment, making it through the toughest training in any army on any location on earth. I'm proud of all of you."

"Eleleu! Eleleu!" The men voiced the war cry in unison.

"Sorry to cut your respite short, but a main portion of the army here will deploy tomorrow at first light to quell this rebellion. I have requested that the Argyraspides accompany the main force."

At this news, the faces of the older soldiers remained placid, while the faces of the younger men, who had never seen combat, broke into anxious smiles.

"Tomorrow at dawn, we will march north on an undisclosed route, at which time you will finally put your training to the test."

§

od didn't intend for me to become a soldier, Gaddi thought,
resentfully. He didn't care for the disrespect his trainer—a
weapons expert considerably older than Gaddi, who had been
drilling him on the proper use of a spear—showed him. Judah
had asked Benjamin Ben Joshua to privately train Gaddi
and every leader he had appointed as a commander of one
hundred, and had put the trainer in charge of the archers.
Benjamin had been harsh with Gaddi, and now Gaddi was
licking his wounds.

I'm an administrator, not a soldier, he grumbled. *Father was
right. Judah should handle the military matters. Yet, as the eldest, I'm
entitled to a double portion of any inheritance. I should be ruling the
people, not Judah. He should be serving under me, yet I take orders
from him!*

Anyone with eyes to see should know they could not win
this war. Judah had just got lucky. He had surprised the Syrians
in an ambush, and now the men showered him with glory
like he was some kind of military genius—another Joshua or
Gideon. It was absurd. Now the Greeks—fed up—would no
doubt advance, careful not to get caught again in an ambush,
and they would destroy the Hebrew force. Judah's mythical
persona would be forgotten. Gaddi felt a wave of envy when he
thought of the name the people called his brother: Maccabee.

Some distance away, a Hebrew scout appeared, scaling the
final ridge to their camp. As he approached, escorted by several
guards, Gaddi could see he was out of breath. Alerted, Judah
strode toward the scout, along with a number of his leaders.
Gaddi scurried over as the scout gasped out his message.

"The Syrians ... they're moving the whole southern
army ... up the coastline ... headed this way! The governor—
Seron—is leading the army himself."

Judah thought for a moment.

"Gather your men," he said decisively to his captains present. "Prepare for battle."

A battle? What we need is an alliance, Gaddi thought with irritation. He remembered a conversation he'd had with an acquaintance of his—Marcus Cornelius, a Roman ambassador who had stayed in Jerusalem before the massacre, during the time when Gaddi would frequently journey there. They had since discussed an alliance between Rome and the Hebrews.

"If you can help us with soldiers, supplies, and weapons to overthrow the Syrians," Gaddi had said, "and help us to reestablish our own rule and authority in Israel, we would support Rome establishing a base of operations to prepare for any eastern campaign." That would be advantageous to Rome, creating a buffer between Rome and Syria. If the Roman Senate liked the plan, Gaddi would enjoy considerable personal gain in both position and reputation.

Rome wanted nothing more than for Syria to fall from the stage as a world power, solidifying Rome's own dominance over the world. Rome would not only be an ally, but would have Israel as a staging ground if eastern countries ever made war on Rome, Marcus Cornelius had said. "If the senate votes to do so, they will likely send an agent to coordinate getting you the supplies and soldiers you need to defeat the Syrians. They'll use this person as a liaison between us. In the meantime, we'd coordinate with our man in Jerusalem, Isaac Ben Zechariah."

Gaddi had caught his breath. Their own government! That was what they had been waiting for so long, to reestablish their sovereignty and the laws of Moses—freedom to worship how they chose, the freedom to be Jewish. "The senate will demand to know who will run this newly established government within Judea," Marcus Cornelius had continued.

"My father," Gaddi had replied, avoiding any mention of his father's illness. "He was chosen by the people to rule and to serve as commander of the army."

"And upon your father's death, who will take his place? It must be someone who remembers our assistance to you."

"Our rulers are chosen by vote, but after that, the rule is passed down through lineage. After my father dies, I will rule, and, after I am gone, my children. They will remember you always for your support."

That is how Gaddi would take control. When the Romans lent soldiers to support their new government, those soldiers would be at his own disposal. *The Romans will do what is best for Rome, and that is having me, on the throne— supporting Israel, the people, and the law, while furthering Rome's interests. Judah will remain in charge of the army, just as Father wished, and Simon will hold the office of priest. That should appease him. Judah's fate is to be a soldier, and to die in battle. But I—I will be king!*

סֵפֶר אַרבעה

Book IV
The Tumult

166 BC

"For they have sown the wind, and they shall reap the whirlwind."

~ Hosea

βιβλίο τέσσερις

Chapter 25

LAODICE FELT HER infant son's mouth tug against her breast. The shoulder of her extravagant, long red dress lay along her elbow. Though it was customary for royalty to utilize wet nurses, she had wanted to feed him herself. A soothsayer had told her that Gaia, the earth mother, joins a part of their souls forever if a woman nurses a child herself. Cradling her son, she glanced into the mirror catching a reflection of herself. She was painfully thin, like a common field worker, despite her efforts to put on weight.

Am I still beautiful? she wondered. The lines on her face looked deeper and her eyes tired. Thoughts of Theophilus entered her mind. Why had she not heard news? Had he betrayed her? No, she decided. If he had, then Lysias, on one of his many unannounced visits to check up on her, would surely have slain her.

She wondered if Lysias had told the king that his beloved spy, Aetos, had died—fallen drunk from the palace battlements in front of his subordinates. She wondered if the king would suspect what actually happened. In fact, she had spent an enormous amount of money to have the wretch killed. After luring him onto the palace wall, four of his men held him down and forced strong drink down his throat, holding his nose. As ordered, Aetos had been held by the legs, dangled upside-down from the parapet. The last words he'd heard were, "Queen Laodice gives you her best wishes," before he was dropped headfirst to his death. The body was almost unrecognizable, but according to the reports of the sentry who found him, both Aetos and his clothes smelled distinctly of alcohol. Laodice remembered his touch with only disdain now. What kind of a man would bed his queen, to lie to her and spy on her? The worm!

She was still undecided whether to execute the four assassins for the "incompetence" of letting their drunken superior fall from the palace walls. She needed to surround herself with loyal subjects who would unquestioningly do her bidding, so these men could be of value for future clandestine projects. Yet it was risky to leave them alive and knowing Aetos's death had not been an accident. Lysias might yet find out who was behind the incident.

§

Nabis looked ahead at the long column of soldiers winding around the road, kicking up dust that rose aloft in the warm air. The Argyraspides had been placed in the center element in order to aid the vanguard or the rear, should either one be ambushed during the march. Nabis glanced up as one of his men stumbled over a stone in the dirt road. The soldier regained his balance and continued marching, annoyed.

It had been some time since Nabis had been on a march as tediously long as this one. He tried not to concentrate on his feet's painful blisters. His leg muscles ached, his shins felt strained, and his back felt twisted under the weight of his silver shield, the twenty-foot spear, and the armor he carried on his back. *Think of something else,* he told himself. *Your men are hurting more than you are.* He had to be mindful not to complain. Everyone in the column looked to him to lead them. They were allowed to complain. He was not.

Nabis adjusted the weight on his chafed back. This march could have been made in ten miles, he thought, but Seron had taken every precaution possible, making it almost three times as lengthy. First they had marched west along the coast to prevent getting ambushed in the hills. Then they had moved north to their intended latitude, near Joppa, and then east.

The rebels will just run and hide, Nabis thought. They had got lucky with one well-planned ambush against Apollonius and a pack of undisciplined Samaritans. But there were over five-thousand Greek soldiers here. The Jews didn't stand a chance. According to latest updates, the Hebrews numbered in the high hundreds. Ambush or not, if they fought, they would die. No question about it.

Seron, ever overly-cautious, had divided up his forces into three elements. If one was ambushed, the others could still maneuver, close in, and destroy the rebels. So the Israelites would continue to do what they had been doing—running and hiding—and once Seron's host ran low on supplies, they would head back to Jerusalem again until the Jews' next pathetic raid.

"Stop!" The command echoed through the columns. "Twenty-minute rest!" The order traveled down the line of men.

Unstrapping his equipment from his back, Nabis placed his shield properly upright against the rest of his kit, keeping his spear tip out of the dirt, leaning it on top of his gear. Jason, another column leader, tossed his gear to the ground next to his. "My feet hardly have skin left on them," he complained. "My body feels like I was just ridden by a three-hundred pound Cyrenian harlot."

"And it looks like we have that peak to climb next," Nabis said, looking up at the steep ridge a few miles ahead.

"That's Beth-Horon," said Jason. "There are two villages, the lower one and the larger one, just above the slope there." He pointed further up the ridge line. "Chances are our commanders will order us to pass through quickly, and we won't stop. The place has some religious significance to the people, and we mustn't offend the locals," he added sardonically.

"It does make sense when putting down a rebellion not to try to incite a new one," Nabis answered.

"Are you a Hebrew sympathizer now?" Jason asked, with a chuckle.

"Get your gear on!" The order echoed down the lines.

"Twenty minutes my ass!" Jason moaned irascibly.

Nabis thought of Abishag. When he left, he had given her every chance to run away and try to find any surviving family members. He gave her money and charged her to keep his house in his absence, unsupervised. But though she could, she probably wouldn't leave. *If she does, I won't chase her,* he thought. She should be happy. He would not even report her missing. He would simply go to the registry and report her a freed woman.

A small smile came to his lips. Thinking of Abishag made him less conscious of his aches and his annoyance.

He hoisted his wicker rucksack onto his back and noticed how weary the men of his unit appeared.

§

Staring down the winding road that sloped past lower Beth-Horon, Judah, Eleazar, and a number of Judah's commanders watched from their concealed position on the edge of the upper city. The Syrian army marched out of the tree line below, toward the base of the ridge. From the edge of upper Beth-Horon, Judah could see the smaller city less than two miles down the slope, which changed from a subtle elevation at the beginning of the rise, to a steep inclined ascent.

"They can't see us?" Eleazar asked, uncertain.

"No," Judah replied. "But we can see them."

The city of upper Beth-Horon waited anxiously to see whether Judah and his men would withdraw or engage. This was the place where Joshua had defeated the kings of the

Canaanites and the Lord God had sent hailstones upon their enemies, killing far more than the Israelite army had managed to do. That battle that established Israel's dominion of the land of milk and honey. And here, Judah decided, they would make their stand. "They've divided their forces into three parts," he observed. "See that lead element?" He pointed at a mass of men far down the slope. "That's where Seron is."

"How can you tell?" Jonathan asked.

"It's the lead element, it has the most men, and Seron wouldn't permit another commander to steal his glory."

Judah was pleased he had decided to raid the outpost a few miles from Gapha, giving them ample supplies of arrows, bows, and new swords. They were ready for this battle.

"There must be more than four thousand of them!" Hadad, a captain of one hundred men, exclaimed. "Macacabee, we can still withdraw from this place. By the time that army makes the climb up—"

"We will fight," Judah said cutting him off.

"The men haven't eaten yet today. Is it wise to fight on an empty stomach?"

"See that part of the slope surrounded by high cliffs on both sides of the road?" Judah continued, ignoring him. "See how narrow that is?" He pointed to a spot about a mile below them, where the road passed through a cut with large stone ledges towering on either side. "I want our archers and men skilled with the sling concealed on both sides. I'll take six hundred of us and swing around the road behind those rocks, severing that forward element from the rest of the force. I'll cut the main body off from behind, and the rest of you will attack from the front downhill. They'll be boxed in so tightly in that choke point, they won't be able to use their phalanx. Once we attack, the bows and slings will fire barrages from both sides of the cut that rises above the road, down into the center of Seron's lead force. The rest of us will be positioned below near the rise, preventing the other two elements from reinforcing the forward echelon.

"Maccabee," Hadad interrupted nervously, "that forward echelon is over two-thousand men. Even if we manage to cut them off from the other two echelons, we'll still be outnumbered two to one.

"Fill your heart with courage," Judah said coldly, looking into Hadad's eyes, seeing the deep fear that gripped him. "Today we destroy the enemies of God, and your soldiers will look to you for courage and direction.

Judah's eyes passed over his ten captains. "Gather your men," he said.

Looking down the slope of Beth-Horon once more, everything around him became distant. He saw the choke point, the cut through the surrounding high rocks where he would launch the ambush. He saw the embankment where he would hold off the other elements from reinforcing the main body. He pictured it in his head; he could see it all at once like a vision, or a distant memory.

Judah began to pray silently. *Deliver our enemies into our hands, Lord, for Your name's sake, for the name of your chosen people. Lord, hear the prayers of your people, and remember the covenant of Abraham, Isaac, and Jacob. Remember your covenant with David. These people come against us not just as conquerors, but they come blaspheming Your name, and desecrating Your temple. Today, I ask for victory against Your enemies, and restoration of Israel, Your people.*

Turning around, Judah could see the gathering multitude of nearly a thousand men, most of them on one knee, keeping a low silhouette as they waited anxiously.

"Will we fight, Maccabee?" asked one of the captains of fifty. He was a strong man of distinction who commanded respect among the soldiers.

"We will!" Judah answered. A slight murmur rose among the men, and nervous whispers began traveling through the ranks.

"My General," the man continued. "How can we? They outnumber us five to one! We've been fasting all day; not a man here has had a single thing to eat."

"It's easy for the many to be hemmed in by the few," Judah replied. "For in the sight of God, there's no difference between them." He raised his voice, projecting it to all soldiers in the vicinity. "It's not the size of the army that determines the victory. Our strength comes from heaven. These soldiers have come against us today to destroy us and our families. We fight for our lives, and for our laws. God Himself will crush them before us!" His voice grew quiet, as every ear focused on his words. "Do not fear them, because today's victory belongs to the Lord."

§

Nabis shielded his eyes from the dust kicked up by the men marching ahead of him. The brutality of the climb, after a tedious march, had become excruciating. They had passed the lower city a mile back. All about him, the soldiers struggled, each lost in his own world, trying just to keep moving. Nabis glanced up the turning slope at the upper city, over the crest in the distance, and then back toward the ground, willing himself forward. His legs felt stiff and began to buckle under him.

He had already marched by twelve men who had passed out, or couldn't continue on. It was odd, Nabis thought … the people of the lower city had cleared the streets, which was normal, but as the soldiers left, he had looked over his shoulder and seen children's faces peeking out of the windows, watching the army as they climbed. It gave him a strange feeling of foreboding.

Nabis was jolted from his thoughts by sudden shrieks, and distressed cries that erupted up ahead. He knew the sound. The forward echelon, about a mile up the hill, was enveloped and under attack where the road narrowed. The columns were hemmed in on all four sides. Arrows and stones rained down on the formation from the overhead ledges. The rebels were to their front and rear and even at this distance, Nabis could see men dying.

By the gods, he thought. *They just appeared out of nowhere!*

"Don your armor! Now!" The order was passed down. Nabis repeated it to his men as he stripped his pack from his back, strapped on his own armor, and assembled the two sections of his sarissa with the coupling sleeve. "Get ready to move!" he shouted.

"Argyraspides! Argyraspides to the front!"

Nabis moved his column of men forward, many of them still frantically strapping on their armor and grieves. He looked up the slope and saw a host of waiting rebels between them and their forward element.

"Move! Move!" a commander shouted. "Those are *our* men getting killed up there! Stay in formation, but jog! We're the first ones in. Form up! Form up!"

The Argyraspides formed a narrow phalanx the width of the road. Nabis and his column were four ranks deep—shields against their forearms, sarissas balanced in both hands.

"Break through their enforcements on that embankment," their commander ordered, "so the other units can attack from the rear. Let's go!"

Trudging up the steep incline, Nabis tried desperately to ignore the muscles in his legs as they screamed in protest. There still was half a mile to climb. His mouth was so parched it barely could open and close. For the first time, he wondered if he would make it or would pass out and be trampled by the soldiers marching behind him.

"Keep moving!" another commander shouted, as the troops slowed. Nabis looked up, and what he saw filled him with horror. Half the Syrian soldiers trapped were already dead. Screams filled the air as arrows and stones bombarded the center of the formation.

The road grew sharply steeper just two hundred yards from the Israelites, who waited as the exhausted troops approached. Hundreds of brown faces, surrounded by ragged hair and thick beards, looked down on the Argyraspides. Nabis was startled to see Syrian sarissas in their hands, pointed at the Greeks who were lumbering toward them. He could hear but no longer see the battle happening above the crest.

Archers suddenly appeared overhead, in between the spearmen, drawing their bows and firing into the Argyraspides phalanx. Most of the arrows were deflected by shields and armor; just eight men fell, mainly from the first two ranks. Nabis moved forward in the phalanx, the pain in his legs long-forgotten. Bodies began falling all around him as another wave of arrows descended only fifty yards from the embankment. His unit was being decimated—the men he had so carefully trained falling before they could even get close enough to fight.

He remembered in despair that their own archers who weren't with the forward element, were at least a mile behind them. The phalanx was disintegrating, indecipherable orders being barked over the dispiriting sounds of death. The world around was an incoherent cloud of war. What remained of the phalanx pushed forward, closing the distance to less than fifty feet from the defending crest. The Israelite archers drew their arrows again. The final barrage was almost directly in front of Nabis's men. Every arrow was devastatingly effective. Then it came just as Nabis had known it would. The Hebrew warriors lowered their spears and charged.

Chapter 26

"BUT IT'S WINTER," spluttered Tigrines, a Parthian chieftain. He stared at King Mithridates, incredulously. "You want us to invade? Now? We've just driven Antiochus away from our borders."

Mithridates shook his head. Were his chieftains simpletons?

"We haven't driven him away. He's merely regrouping. When the snows melt, I guarantee he will cross the river with his army and reestablish his dominion." Mithridates shifted his weight in his chair and looked around at his war council, seated inside the tent. The large fire, fueled by horse dung, did little to dispel the chill in the air.

"Your Majesty," Tigrines said with a haughty tone, "your father was king of his tribe as was his father before him. Both were forced to pay tribute to the cursed Syrians. When we united the tribes and elected you as king over all, it was because you promised to free our people from Seleucid control. You have done so, but this—this is too much! If we attack in the midst of winter, we'll sustain mass casualties just from the march. And we'll be moving further away from shelter and our supplies."

"You're thinking from the perspective of the old style of warfare," answered the king. "An army as mobile as ours need only take supplies from the dead enemies we leave in our wake. The Syrians have been unable to catch us!"

Tigrines looked at Mithridates in disbelief.

"We've given you kingship over the tribes. What more do you want, Your Majesty?" he asked, irreverence in his voice.

A dynasty, Mithridates thought, contemplating whether to kill Tigrines. He wanted an empire, like Cyrus the Great. Once the Seleucid threat was gone, he was convinced the chieftains would turn on him to reestablish their tribal autonomy.

"I want what's best for our people," he said out loud. "So, come dawn, I will take my army on horseback, ride west for Media, and attack the king of the Syrians."

The chieftains' voices rose as all began talking at once. Mithridates closed his mind to the babble.

§

Kalisto watched with amusement as Crassus, the Roman companion of Fabius Æmilius, ran to the side of the ship, leaned over the edge, and vomited. *At least this time he made it to the railing,* Kalisto thought. They had been traveling on the seas for almost a month, and Crassus was still puking up his meal every day, wasting his food like a pregnant woman. Kalisto adjusted the levee of the helm, a contemptuous look on his face. Crassus looked up, his pallor green, as Fabius approached. The tide was picking up, and Crassus could feel the waves as they slammed into the hull.

"More stomach trouble?" asked Fabius.

"I'm going to die of sickness before we ever reach land."

"We'll dock at Crete in a few days, and you'll get a short reprieve. From there, it's a short journey to Judea."

"Look at that bastard Greek," Crassus groaned, glaring at Kalisto who made no attempt to conceal his disgust. "Do you think he suspects?" He winced as bile began rising in his throat again.

Fabius shrugged.

"He may have his suspicions. I don't think he cares one way or another. He's no friend to the Seleucid king, not now, and they would likely see him dead."

"We're deep into Seleucid waters."

"He knows these waters well. He was one of their admirals, after all."

"This is probably a waste of time. Even if we're successful—"

"We've been charged by Gaius Popillius Laenas himself to accomplish this task," Fabius reminded his companion.

Crassus clutched the rail as his stomach rode the waves. "Do you think we'll be back in Rome by early next year?"

Fabius shrugged again. "It depends on how long it takes to seek out these Hebrew rebels, assuming their rebellion hasn't been suppressed. If it has, we'll head home. If it hasn't, we'll meet with their leader and arrange to supply them with coin and arms. Rome wants wars on the Syrian border, wars without Roman soldiers. The Syrians are a threat to the republic."

"My fear now is that we'll be among those asked to come back to deliver the arms and equipment," Crassus groaned. He pulled himself up over the rail and heaved, his vomit mixing with the green of the sea.

§

Judah sat back and relaxed, surrounded by his brothers and his remaining commanders, who dined with him at the table outside, within the stone walls of the house's courtyard. The people of upper Beth-Horon had welcomed the patriot army, vastly relieved that the immediate threat of Syrian persecution had been eradicated. The town's rabbi had willingly opened the doors of his own home to Judah and his brothers.

After pillaging the abandoned supply line of the Syrians, the Hebrews had enough food to feed the army for at least a week, and had far more Syrian spears and swords than men to wield them.

They had lost two hundred men, but volunteers from both lower and upper Beth-Horon more than offset the losses. They had been fortunate, Judah reflected. Amazingly, he himself had escaped without a scratch. He had been at the front lines with his spear, the Gentiles fighting like a diseased dog, and he didn't get a single cut.

Judah had led Jonathan and his men, crossing behind the rocks on the steep slope behind the road and the sheer drop below, into the valley. Judah had been worried someone would fall—not only for the needless loss of a man, but because a scream would have given them away. There they had waited until they heard the first element of Syrian soldiers pass them up the road before swinging behind them, cutting off their rear. They had cut off the forward element just in time for Eleazar, Gaddi, and Simon to attack from above with their force. Joel had taken his hundred men and broken off to hold the embankment below, to prevent the reinforcements from getting behind their ambush.

Judah remembered seeing Eleazar, Gaddi, and Simon's men attacking from the front. Their lines had wavered and undulated for a few long moments when the Syrians tried to push forward through the trap. It had been Eleazar who managed to re-fuse the forward lines. Joel and his archers, before charging into the fray, had killed off the Syrian reinforcements marching up the steep rise. And then it was over. The whole contingent below crumbled, while the other two elements broke. Syrians ran down the hill, abandoning their equipment. The people of lower Beth-Horon came out and threw rocks, attacking the scattering soldiers as they ran through the city in retreat. The rear element at the base of the hill was just as disorganized—retreating in four separate directions, abandoning their supply carts.

Of Judah's brothers, Jonathan, the youngest, had suffered the most: a mere broken nose where he had been hit in the face by a soldier's shield. *This victory is God's,* thought Judah. Still, he was taking no chances. He'd positioned several hundred of his men in lower Beth-Horon to keep an eye out for Syrian reinforcements.

Meanwhile, it felt good to rest, to sit here in the home of the rabbi and casually converse with his brothers and commanders.

"So who was it? Who got Seron?" Eleazar asked, yawning. They were all exhausted.

"One of Levi's men," Judah replied.

Jonathan looked up at hearing the name of his beloved Sarah's father. He knew he must speak to Judah about her soon, and must beg him to arrange their marriage.

"One of the archers took down his horse," Simon put in. "Either Seron's horse rolled on him, or his men trampled him when they tried to fall back. Seron sat there, choking on his blood, mumbling, "I'm the governor, I'm the governor," as if that would save him. One of Levi's men shut him up and took his head off with a single blow."

Judah drained the wine in his cup. "It's time we got some rest. Thank you for your hospitality to me and my men," he said to the rabbi and his wife, who were seated at Judah's right hand, having given up their place of honor at the head of the table.

"You are always welcome in my home, Maccabee," the rabbi said with a nod.

Judah glanced up at the night sky and rose from the table. He walked inside and down the hall toward the room arranged for him.

"Judah?" Jonathan fell into step with his brother. "May we speak?"

Judah turned a weary eye toward the youth, about to insist he wait until morning, but Jonathan's expression stopped him.

"I need your help," Said Jonathan earnestly. "I know it's not the time, but I want to ask you to pay a dowry for Sarah."

"Sarah?" Judah looked confused. "The daughter of Levi? Levi's Sarah?"

"Yes."

Judah was surprised. He didn't even know that Jonathan desired her. Judah suddenly remembered a conversation he had with Levi and said, "You know she's gone to live in Geba with Levi's sister and her family, yes?"

Jonathan nodded.

"Jonathan, I'm afraid Levi has already accepted a dowry from another man, someone close to her age whose family owns good farmland and a vineyard." Jonathan stared at Judah in shock. "Levi mentioned he missed her betrothal ceremony, but wanted to be there for her wedding."

"You have to stop the wedding!" Jonathan blurted. "Make Levi break it off!"

"I can't do that! On what grounds? I could never ask him to do such a thing!"

"You can, you can do that!" Jonathan insisted, his eyes filling with tears. "You will be king one day, over all of Israel. Everyone says so. He would not dare disobey you. You must. You have to order him to break it off!"

Judah placed his hands on the younger man's shoulders.

"Jonathan, I'm a general of the army, and only a general. God promised the throne to King David's children, a lineage that is not ours. To wish or say otherwise would be blasphemous. I have no authority to tell Levi what to do with his family. I'm sorry," he added, as Jonathan began to shake.

"Pay him off, then. Give him a higher price!" Jonathan cried, desperately needing a different answer. His thoughts screamed. *You've lost her! She's gone!* The words bore into his soul. He felt as if his legs would collapse. "Pay a higher price for the dowry!"

"Jonathan, Levi has given his word as a man of honor to this family. How would it look if he were to break his covenant between them?"

"I don't care!" Jonathan groaned. "I need this, not just for her, but to be right in the sight of the Lord."

"What are you talking about?"

Jonathan looked away.

"Sarah and I, we … *I've* lain with her." His self-incriminating voice was no louder than a whisper.

The confusion fell from Judah's face, and he looked at his brother, horrified.

"Jonathan, what have you done? You could be stoned for this! You've robbed Levi of his daughter and dishonored your own father's memory."

Judah closed his eyes in thought. *You should have gotten Eleazar and Jonathan wed, or at least betrothed, long ago,* he chided himself. *Father would have done so.* Since Mattathias's death, what with all the fighting, he hadn't had time to deal with what felt like trivial matters. They could be ignored no longer, and no longer were they trivial.

He opened his eyes and looked at his brother. "Get some rest. I'll think on this. Don't mention this to anyone else, do you hear me?"

Jonathan nodded, his expression miserable.

What should I do? Judah wondered, as he lay on his bed. *The boy is lovesick, as anyone can see, but what a shameful way to act!* Levi was one of Judah's commanders. What if word of this spread, here among the army, among of the Lord's faithful? They would demand punishment. *I am not Solomon,* Judah thought, closing his eyes and feeling overwhelmed. *What would the Lord have me do?*

§

Antiochus sat near a crackling fire within the confines of his tent, the icy wind howling outside. He signed his name to the letter intended for Lysias, demanding to know what he was doing about Judea. He felt helpless so far from the capital at Antioch, and was beginning to wonder if he had made the right choice, appointing Lysias as viceroy. Had he also overestimated the prowess of the beguiling little worm, Seron? The fool had to act. Antiochus had left his kingdom in the hands of incompetents, and he needed to know what was happening in Judea. He began to wonder if Lysias would be able to control that cagey bitch of a queen, with her incessant manipulation and schemes.

Though the army had pulled back to the west for the duration of winter, Antiochus had ordered, just yesterday, a full-scale assault along the Parthian-controlled villages north of their position. The cowardly militants had retreated east, abandoning their camps and villages to be pillaged by his army.

The king's eyes traveled to the corner of the room, in front of his bed, where a dark Parthian youth and a young Parthian girl sat back-to-back, bound together. They were gagged and naked. Fear was in their eyes, and the boy was shaking, which Antiochus enjoyed. He rose from his chair and walked slowly over to them. The girl glanced away submissively; the youth began weeping.

When the weather lifted, Antiochus would launch another attack and break the Parthian militants once and for all. Then he would return to Judea, but this time rather than desecrating their temple, he would tear it to the ground. He would then do what his incompetent subordinates were failing to do, and depopulate the entire region. He would systematically deploy his army to every single village and town and massacre every male of military age. He would kill the old. The women and children would be taken to various parts of his empire, perhaps even Parthia. Over the course of time they would lose all ties to their homeland, and within a generation, they would forget even their national identity.

Antiochus slowly ran a finger down the youth's cheek, smiling, seeing him convulse in fear. He walked over to the fire and drew from it a glowing barb that had been heating in the embers, and once more approached the pair.

§

Nabis collapsed as his companion let go of his arm. The shoulder pain was excruciating. He looked down at the arrow that had punched through his corselet an inch below the collarbone. His lips were cracked, his face ashen. As his troops were decimated, Orestes and Eugenio, two of his soldiers, had dragged Nabis down the mountain, avoiding lower Beth-Horon, whose inhabitants were attacking the retreating Syrians. From their position nearly a mile away, Nabis could see the few of their men that still survived, scattering in panic.

They found an abandoned supply cart with a mule attached, and began to travel west until they reached a small coastal region controlled by the Philistines, a remnant of an ancient naval people descended from a Greek island. They had been at war with Israel for hundreds of years until the Hebrew King David ended their strength as a military threat. Annexed and relocated by the Babylonians under Nebuchadnezzar, a scant few of the people remained.

In the hours that passed, another hundred Syrian soldiers made their way there. "Did any of our men make it?" Nabis muttered, as they waited for the physician.

"No," Orestes replied, "not from the Argyraspides. The whole army was scattered."

The doctor arrived. The physician was old, skinny, and toothless, with faded eyes. *If the arrow doesn't kill him, this man will,* Orestes thought.

"Help me loosen his armor," the old man said, in his native tongue.

None of them understood him. Exasperated, the physician began yanking the armor off of Nabis, who gasped in pain. As he began to lose his grasp on consciousness, he found himself praying. Not to the gods of his parents, to Ares or Baal. He was praying to the god of Abishag, the god of the Hebrews. He was not sure how to pray, or if his prayers would insult this god, but his prayer was a plea only to see Abishag once more before he died. He felt a searing pain as the physician clamped down on the arrow head with a heavy iron tong, and then Nabis felt nothing.

Chapter 27

LYSIAS BROKE THE king's seal on the letter as the courier silently slipped out of the room.

Lysias,

Word has reached me of the annihilation of two thousand of my army under General Apollonius. I have had enough. If the Israelites won't conform to Greek religion, customs, and way of life, they are to be put to death without delay. Order Governor Seron to put down this rebellion. Mobilize my entire western army. I order you to destroy every Hebrew town, and kill every Jewish man, woman, and child that you find. When I finish putting down the Parthian barbarians, I will join you to finish off any remaining Hebrews. Judea is to disappear into the ashes, never to be remembered or spoken of again.

Antiochus, Son of Zeus

Lysias dropped the scroll to the floor. Kill all of them? Seron had already set off to put down the rebellion with more than enough men. General Lysias had given Seron strict orders not to harm any Jewish bystanders, so as to avoid promoting further resentment and rebellion. And now Antiochus wanted him to mobilize the entire western army? It would take months of marching to get to Judea, and Lysias was certain that, by then,

Seron would have already killed off the rebels and staunched the uprising. Lysias was supposed to be keeping an eye on the treacherous queen, or had her husband already forgotten? If Lysias had retained any doubts about the king's sanity, they were now gone.

There was a knock on the door. "Enter!" Lysias barked.

"My lord, another courier is here," said the servant who stepped into the room. Lysias snapped his fingers, annoyed, and extended his hand to receive the letter.

The seal was from the Jerusalem citadel. Finally, some good news! He broke the wax seal, anticipating word of victory.

General Lysias,

Governor Seron has been slain and his forces destroyed or scattered. We require immediate troops and supplies. There is dispute among the leadership as to who will succeed Seron, and we now are at risk of losing Jerusalem and falling under siege here . . .

Lysias threw the scroll across the room. "Send for General Nicantor and Gorgias at once," he shouted, as his servant scurried out of the room.

This is too much, Lysias thought. *The gods have turned their backs on the empire.* He bent, picked up the message, and finished reading it. He swore. If the kingdom fell, it would be the end of the empire of Alexander the Great.

§

"FOR THE CHILDREN of Israel," the drover said, willingly relinquishing one-tenth of his oxen to Simon.

"Thank you, and may the Lord bless you and your house for generations," Simon answered. He signaled his men to begin the drive south toward Mizpeh, where Judah and his army were camped, just eight miles from Jerusalem, and the march began.

Simon remembered living in Jerusalem as a child, before their father moved them to Modein, and the sin that permeated the city of David. He remembered why his Father wanted to leave. Jerusalem had become tainted by Jews who tolerated or supported the Syrian ways. The laws of Moses were overshadowed by Greek philosophers who openly denied the words of the prophets. Worse were the Sadducees—a new sect, an off-shoot of the Hellenists, who denied the afterlife, even though Sheol was a key tenet of the Hebrew faith. *Judah will have these idolaters and the Sadducee scum to contend with,* Simon thought miserably. *Self-hating sons of Jacob and traitors to their own people!*

He turned his thoughts to the camp. The army had grown substantially since the battle at Beth-Horon. Their victory had garnered nearly a thousand more men, and every day, every town and village they marched through, brought new volunteers. With all these men came the need for more commanders.

Judah had arranged a marriage with the daughter of a recently promoted commander named Abner, a wealthy and capable commander of one-hundred men. Abner had promised his daughter to their brother Eleazar. Simon thought absently of his own wife and children. He missed them, despite how bitterly he had left things with his wife, leaving after a heated argument. He thought of his eldest son, who he had named "Mattathias" after his own father. The boy would want to join the fight soon, which would add to Simon's wife's indignation. *He'll be sixteen in just a few months,* Simon mused. He should be married soon as well, and so should Jude, his middle son. John, his youngest, still had time.

Simon's thoughts strayed to the strange tension between Judah and Levi, one of the commanders of one hundred. Judah had approached Simon and asked him to follow, to act as witness to a matter he wished to discuss. Simon was initially caught off-guard at the strangeness of the request. After the two walked to the training ground, where drills were being conducted, Judah had asked Levi if he would dine with them. Levi had assumed that all of the commanders would be present, until Judah announced, "I wanted to discuss a personal matter of great importance."

"Oh," Levi had answered. "What of?"

"You mentioned before that your daughter, Sarah, was recently betrothed."

"She was. She celebrated the *kiddushin* last month. Why do you ask, Maccabee?"

"I had in mind to join our two families. I have always respected you as an excellent commander on the battlefield, and I know you are someone I can trust. As it stands, whoever I decide to marry to my brothers, I will have to scrutinize the true intentions of the arrangement."

"Maccabee," Levi had answered with a smile, "I am honored to hold such high esteem in your eyes, but the arrangement has been made. The family has already paid Sarah's dowry, and the contract is binding. Perhaps one of my younger daughters."

"It will be some time before either one of them comes of age," responded Judah, "and Jonathan is at an age where it is appropriate that he marry. In addition to a more substantial dowry price, I will offer double the amount to the family who paid for Sarah's betrothal, so that what they paid will be returned to them."

"I will have to think on this," Levi had said skeptically. "The family is an old neighbor of ours. Sarah might be heartbroken if I were to break it off and offer her in marriage to a man she hardly knows."

"Perhaps you should speak with her and see how she feels about the prospect. Jonathan has told me that he observed Sarah in the camp before we moved it to Gophna. He said he would not be displeased with the arrangement. Maybe Sarah would feel the same."

Levi's face looked noncommittal. "I will think on it, which is all I can promise," he had answered.

But Simon knew his brothers. He knew it must have been Jonathan who put Judah up to bartering such an outlandish proposal for Levi's betrothed, unattractive, dark, and far-too-skinny daughter. Judah had always looked after Jonathan, even as children when Eleazar had tormented him.

"It will be sundown soon, Rabbi." Malachi's voice broke into Simon's thoughts. "Will we make it to Mizpeh before Shabbat?"

"Let's hope so. It's only a few miles away. If we don't, there will be a lot of hungry men."

"We could glean," Malachi suggested. "There's a field up ahead." According to Mosaic Law, orphans, widows, and others in need were permitted such charity—feeding upon grain that was left on the ground after reaping, or fruit left after harvesting.

They passed a vineyard where the men found ripe fruit fallen. The owner, who was supervising his workers at the wine press, waved as they passed by.

"Yes. Let's glean," Simon ordered. "Stay clear of the vineyard. We don't want the oxen to crush this man's vines.

§

"We should avoid the major highways," Nabis said to Orestes and Eugenio. His face was still pale. It had taken him the better part of two weeks to build his strength enough to travel. His companions had stolen three horses from a wealthy Hebrew in the area, and they left the coastal Philistine village armed only with two short swords. They had discarded their uniforms in favor of local dress, trading their armor to local Philistine villagers to help avoid detection.

After the physician had removed the arrow in his shoulder

and cut away the infected skin, Nabis developed a fever and didn't wake for two days. Orestes feared his lungs would fill with fluid, but the third morning the fever broke, leaving Nabis lucid but still bedridden for nearly another week. It was three weeks before he was well enough to travel.

Nabis was anxious to return home, to find Abishag. She filled his thoughts and, although he had left her sufficient funds to cover his absence, he was worried she might have taken the money and returned to her own people. With the rebel Israelite army now camped in Mizpeh, they needed to approach Jerusalem from the south, adding to the distance they must cover. If Abishag was still there waiting for him to return, he would set her free, or if she wished to remain his servant, take her to someplace safe, far away—Ephesus or Athens, perhaps—to escape this eternal conflict. Nabis had no intention of returning to his post in the army. He wanted to make a new life for himself.

Their horses plodded along the road, as Nabis sat lost in thought and Orestes and Eugenio gossiped.

"There's no doubt they're planning to lay siege to Jerusalem," Orestes argued.

"They don't have sufficient strength to take it—not yet anyway."

"But their ranks are swelling," Orestes countered. "If our reinforcements don't arrive soon, they will attack, surely. The city is sacred to them."

"Reinforcements are coming though," Eugenio answered. "The Philistines told me Antiochus ordered a mobilization of the entire western army."

"Good," Orestes declared. "Then that will be the end of the Hebrew people. There will be no mercy for them now. The king will want this whole region knee-deep in their blood."

"It's unfortunate," said Eugenio. "They're not a bad people, just stubborn to the core."

Nabis listened idly. He shifted his weight uncomfortably.

Unnoticed by his companions, the horse they had stolen for him was not fully broken. It was still skittish and cumbersome to ride.

Feeling a sharp internal pain, Nabis slumped forward.

Orestes spoke, noticing his behavior. "Sir, how are you tolerating the ride?"

"I'm all right," Nabis replied.

"We can make camp here if you would like to stop."

"No," Nabis answered quickly. "Let us keep moving forward." He dug his heels into the flanks of his horse, controlling it by the reigns. *Stay strong,* he told himself. *You can die once you reach Jerusalem, after you see Abishag and set her free.*

It is all right to stop and rest, another part of him argued. *Your men are committed to you. They will not think less of you.* The pain intensified, but Nabis swallowed hard and cleared his mind. He jabbed his heels into his horse's flanks once more. All conversation ceased as Orestes and Eugenio rode hard to stay with him.

§

Abishag walked up the rough, uneven, cedar stairs to her home. In her hands was a heavy clay pitcher of water. She walked to the well every day for water to fill her washbasin and, each time, made sure to come home with enough water to fill his, in case Nabis surprised her with his return.

She glanced at the sky. The sun was descending toward the western horizon. *I'll be late,* she thought, with a start. Leaving the full pitcher on a table, she rushed down the stairs and through the alleyways toward the street. In the weeks since Nabis had left, she had been secretly attending an underground synagogue. The group met covertly to hear a rabbi teach from the Torah. It was getting riskier, because his popularity was growing. If the Syrian military discovered a synagogue, they would crucify all of the attendees to set an example. Abishag had seen the members of a congregation hanging in the square from crosses, no more than two weeks before, under armed guard. Above the rabbi's not-quite-dead body was posted the reason for their execution. An unraveled scroll, part of the Torah, was nailed to the man's heaving stomach. She had moved cautiously through the streets, past the crowds of onlookers.

Now, to her left, she saw a group of Syrian soldiers, eating. She hid her apprehension, keeping her head down as a cacophony of shouts arose from some merchants in the square.

As she walked, she thought of Nabis. He should have returned by now. She had been careful with the provisions and money he had left her. But what if he never returned? The money would not last forever. She had heard tales of a great fight between the Israelite freedom-fighters and the Syrians. The rabbi had confirmed it. He said the Syrian dogs had been beaten badly, giving new hope to their people, that God had sent Israel a savior, a great military leader named Judah Ben Mattathias of Modein, who some were calling Maccabee, the Hammer. The rabbi claimed the soldiers of the Gentiles, the armies of the devil, were slain at Beth-Horon, and fell where the armies of Joshua had defeated the Canaanites.

Abishag felt conflicted. She loved her country and her people. She wanted them delivered from the Gentiles. She wanted Israel to rule itself, and she wanted freedom. At the same time, she prayed fervently that Nabis was somehow safe. Despite her coldness and hatred in the beginning, he had shown her nothing but kindness. He was to her, gentle—treating her more like a beloved sister than a slave. He had never beaten her. He had never violated her. He asked for things instead of demanding them. He looked her in the eyes when he spoke. He insisted she eat the same foods she prepared for him.

She thought about how different her life might have been with another master, and shuddered. If he were to die, she would be sold again, most likely to someone who would starve and beat her. He had even caught her worshiping her God. She had been convinced he would beat her then. Instead, he was curious, asking her questions. She had never known a man like him. She stopped suddenly as a new thought occurred to her. What if he came home with a wife? Would her life change then? Perhaps he would marry someone as kind as himself. She wondered what it would be like to be married to Nabis, and felt herself blush. She remembered the scene just before he departed. *He almost looked at me as if he loved me,* she thought. *Like a husband looks at his wife.*

She laughed to herself at the absurd idea. A slave becoming the wife of her owner! What madness! *Do you have feelings for him?* she asked herself. *Did you not find yourself attracted to him, even desiring him?* She bit her lip and kicked away a stone in her path. *No,* she told herself, lifting her head and straightening her shoulders. *I just felt sorry for him, and for who he is.* She refused to give in to foolish mental ramblings. But her heart sped up as she thought of him.

She scurried around a corner and down a dark alleyway. Pausing, she looked up and down the alley before descending a set of stone stairs. She didn't spot the two men eying her from further down the street, tucked as they were into a doorway. One was tall, with hazel eyes, and could pass for either Greek or Hebrew. He had a wide, jagged scar that ran from the right side of his lip to the left side of his chin. He held himself like a soldier, but was dressed in common clothing. The shorter, corpulent man beside him had curly hair and was sweating profusely.

"Who is she?" the taller one asked.

"The slave of an Argyraspides soldier who lives in the western quarter. He's out with the troops.

"I hate when people act liberally with their slaves, treating them like house guests, educating them."

"Apparently she's been coming to the synagogue ever since he left."

"You said he's an Argyraspides?"

"Yes, one of the Silver Shields."

The taller man pondered this. "They're all dead," he said.

"What?"

"The only Argyraspides unit in Judea was wiped out at Beth-Horon almost a month ago."

"Then I guess when it comes time to crucify them, you won't have to compensate him for the loss of his property."

"Compensate?" the taller man responded with a snort. "He should have kept a closer watch on his slaves. In fact, if he weren't dead, he'd be lashed and demoted for her actions."

"When do you plan to expose them?" the shorter man asked, a smile on his face that reminded the taller man of a begging dog.

"That's none of your concern." His voice was cold as he handed over a small purse of coins. "For your silence, as well as for the information. You Sadducees have proven useful. Fortunately, the king does not revile your sect of Judaism," he added, knowing the king would not be able to discern the difference if his life depended on it. "You're the only Jews who study philosophy, listen to reason, and don't get caught up in the words of Moses."

The other man pocketed the purse with a solemn nod, his expression concealing his reaction to his companion's ignorance. Moses was the only prophet the Sadducees actually *did* listen to.

Chapter 28

ELEAZAR SMILED AT the beautiful veiled woman standing before him. Deep-down he wanted a life of peace, a wife and children, and now he was to be married. Behind him stood Judah, and the father of his bride, behind her. Between them, the priest—his brother Simon—performed the ceremony and witnessed the *ketubah*, the oath of the bride and groom.

For months, Eleazar had not thought of Elizabeth, the young girl of Modein with whom he had been in love. When he left home, he had been heartbroken at leaving her, hoping they would one day reunite and marry. The parting had hurt him more deeply than the near-fatal cut he received across his stomach the day they began the revolt, but his feelings for Elizabeth had grown cold over time. When his father died, he stopped thinking of her altogether.

When Judah said he had betrothed Eleazar to a beautiful girl, the daughter of a wealthy property owner, Eleazar was glad.

Now the entire city of Mizpeh was in a state of celebration because of the wedding festivities. Eleazar looked over at Judah, who could see the happiness on his brother's face. Then trepidation gripped the groom, as he wondered what would be the bride's reaction at seeing the grotesque scar across his abdomen. He began to feel anxiety over the fast-approaching night they soon would share. What if he did not perform satisfactorily?

At that moment, his bride looked up into his face, casting him a glance of such admiration and innocence, that all his fears vanished.

The noise of the assembly grew quiet, and the wedding ceremony began. In spite of himself, Judah felt his mind drifting to the battle that soon would be upon them. *You need to fight this war lawfully,* he told himself, *like Gideon. People will tell you you're crazy, that you're risking your army and limiting our force, but I'd rather have God's blessing and five-hundred fearless men by my side than a thousand cowards, without the Lord's blessing, who will run away out of fear.*

Fear was contagious. It infected everyone around and could destroy a whole army. Judah knew that. He recalled how the Lord commanded Moses, saying "Whoever has built a new home and has not dedicated it, or anyone who has planted a vineyard and has not eaten of it, or anyone who is betrothed to a wife and has not taken her to his bed, he is to be dismissed from the army and sent home." Then, according to the law, officers were to ask their men who was fearful and fainthearted. They, too, were to be sent home and excused from fighting. Those were the precepts Gideon had followed.

Gideon was a judge of Israel who the Lord chose to free his people in days of yore. Before battle, he reduced his army of twenty-two thousand to ten thousand, but God commanded he reduce it still further. Time and time again, Gideon did this, until his army consisted of only three hundred of his most elite soldiers. This was so the people would know it was God who was their deliverer. With his three-hundred men, and using unconventional tactics, Gideon had destroyed the huge Midianite army and had freed Israel.

Judah's mind returned to the present when Simon, leading the wedding ceremony, spoke the *sheva brachot,* the seven blessings. *Jonathan, too, will be married soon,* Judah thought with a smile. Levi had decided in Jonathan's favor upon learning, to his surprise, that Sarah vehemently favored the change in bridegroom. So despite his reluctance, he had offered the slighted family financial compensation, and also his second daughter, who would be of age within two years. After much bitter discussion, the other family had finally accepted.

§

The three riders approached Jerusalem, the horses struggling and the riders not much better off. They hadn't found water since the night before, and even that shallow waterhole was nearly dried up. The day was hot, and the sun beat down relentlessly. The half-broke horse which Nabis rode grew increasingly irritable and unwieldy. Still Nabis refused to complain.

Their conversation had all but stopped hours earlier, in an attempt to conserve energy. Finally Eugeino said, "I wonder what state the army will be in? I'm sure they'll be happy to see us. They won't believe their eyes. They'll think we're shades from Hades."

A half-dozen miles outside the city, they spotted bits of an ancient stone wall that looked like remnants of a tollbooth from the Ptolemaic Dynasty. All that remained of the wall rose four feet on either side of the road. Up ahead, on one side, a figure sat perched, watching their approach. Two others leaned against the wall, conversing. Nabis and his comrades exchanged glances.

"Do you think these men are going to give us trouble?" Orestes mumbled.

Nabis forced himself to sit up straight, wincing as pain shot through his chest and shoulder. "Let's hope not. Just keep moving past them. They look like Israelites, so if they stop us, we're Carthaginian travelers passing through on our way north."

Nabis was acutely conscious that, of the three, he was the only one without a weapon. He was in no condition to fight and felt vulnerable. All three kept silent as they trotted forward. A stocky, bearded man jumped off the wall into the single lane, barely big enough for a cart, and blocked their path.

"Who are you, and where are you going?" he demanded in broken Greek, his expression unpleasant. His two companions by the wall seemed not to notice the riders. Then two more men appeared from behind the wall, each bearing a spear.

"We're travelers from Carthage, just passing through," said Orestes. "We came through Egypt and are on our way north." He spoke casually, as if this were a friendly exchange.

"Not unless I say so," replied the man, who gestured toward Nabis. "What's wrong with him? Is he sick?" When no one answered, he spoke again, in scornful amusement. "Hand over your money purses, and get off your horses."

"Now!" he barked. The men with the spears slowly moved forward until they were flanking Nabis and his friends. The two others, who had been resting against the wall, now stood with drawn swords, blocking the road in front of them.

"We don't have any money," said Orestes.

"You lie!"

"You're a Jew," Nabis said, keeping his voice low. "One of the chosen, and you're robbing people on the side of the road, like common thieves?"

"You think every Israelite is religious?" the man grunted. "Get off your horses!"

Nabis had an inexorable feeling that whether they had money or not, they weren't intended to leave that place alive. "Very well," he said.

He wheeled his horse around and made as if to dismount. Remembering how unbroken the animal was, he pulled as hard as he could on the reins and spurred the beast hard. He felt the horse's hind legs rise, as its hooves slammed into the abdomen of the one of the men brandishing a spear.

A melee erupted. Nabis was flung from his horse, landing hard on his injured shoulder. Eugenio reached for his sword but couldn't pull it free before a spear caught him under his arm, penetrating his chest. His assailant tore out the spear, readying to strike again, but Eugenio slid slowly off his steed and went down into the dirt with a hard thud.

Orestes wrested his horse around and slashed at the ringleader with his sword, slicing a deep laceration across his forehead. The man drew away with a groan. Orestes reared his horse, turned, and hacked away at the next assailant. "Nabis!" he cried, trying to hold the last three back.

In a dreamlike state, Nabis stood and looked around for his horse, which had taken off at a run. He saw that the man his horse had kicked was inert, curled into the fetal position. With a glance at Eugenio's unmoving body, Nabis staggered toward Eugenio's horse and mounted it. Spurring the animal, he galloped away from the city, Orestes close at his heels. Nabis felt the blood of his reopened shoulder wound soaking through his tunic.

§

"When we land," Fabius Æmilius said to Crassus, "our agents should be waiting." His fingers touched the silver medallion around his neck, the symbol that would identify him to the agents he was to meet. He had been instructed to find his way to a certain tavern near the shore, where a code would confirm the identity of the agents.

"The Seleucids will have soldiers on the docks for customs," Crassus said, nervously.

"We tell them we're Carthaginian slave traders, here to trade to Sicily. The Syrians love the Carthaginians because they harbored Hannibal all those years."

"Eventually we tracked him down," Crassus grinned.

"Unfortunately the coward poisoned himself rather than be taken alive by Roman troops."

"Can you blame him? Skipio should have killed him in Africa when he had the chance. Too bad it was all before my time." The men watched as their ship drew closer to the Joppa harbor. "Where are we supposed to be buying the slaves from?"

"Jerusalem," said Fabius.

Kalisto came on deck, his face cleanly shaven. The horrific scars on his arms kept anyone from studying him for too long.

This is a dangerous place for him if he is discovered, Fabius thought, suddenly understanding Kalisto's reluctance to remain in port.

Kalisto strode toward them. "How long am I to wait here for you?"

"It should not take us more than a month. Then we will give you new bearings."

"And if you don't return?" Kalisto growled.

Fabius met his hard stare. It was a legitimate question. "Make it two months, and then you may go where you will if we have not returned. Among the cargo crates below you will find half your pay."

Kalisto knew that. "And the other half?"

"It's in Sicily, waiting for you."

The galley slowed, as the oars weighted idly into the water, braking the ship. The rowers hoisted their long oars up into the vessel, and the deck hands lowered the sails. Others prepared ropes as the ship glided slowly toward the long pier.

The galley had been docked only for moments when a short, officious-looking man approached the vessel, a soldier on either side of him.

"Who is captain here?" he called in a nasal voice.

"I am," Kalisto answered.

"State your business in Judea," the dock official snapped.

"Trade."

"In?"

"Slaves."

"Where are you from?"

"Carthage." Kalisto stepped to the ship's gangplank, nearer to where the dock official was standing. A casual glance confirmed the presence of several groups of soldiers scattered around the docks.

"Any passengers?"

"None but galley hands in my employment."

"You're exporting?"

"Yes, sir."

"Then you had best be careful. There's been some unrest."

So the rebellion hasn't yet been put down, Fabius surmised. At least it wasn't a wasted trip.

"We need to search your vessel."

Kalisto nodded and moved to one side, permitting the men to board.

Fabius suddenly thought of his gladius, which was down below with his gear, and wondered if the Roman blade would give them away if discovered. *I'll say I traded for it in Sicily, from a soldier who had deserted,* he decided. He wished he had it on him. He had nothing more than a thin dagger sheathed beneath his cloak.

The soldiers swept through the ship, examining the rowers, the personal quarters, and, of course, the storage area below. They examined the barrels of wine and molding food, throwing open crate after crate to inspect the contents.

One crate, incredibly heavy, stopped them in their tracks. They wrested it open to find it filled to the brim with Carthaginian gold coins. The harbor official's eyes narrowed. Fabius stiffened. The soldiers stood, shocked, none of them ever having witnessed so much treasure in one place in their lifetime.

The harbormaster gave Kalisto a suspicious look. Kalisto shrugged as Fabius stepped forward, inching his hand toward his concealed dagger.

"You have to buy slaves with something," Kalisto remarked.

"You know, there's a tax for buying exports of this ... this quantity."

Fabius gave him a conspiratorial smile.

"I'm sure we can come to some arrangement."

§

Nabis collapsed into a cracked and dried-out ditch, near the hamlet on Jerusalem's outskirts. The city's southern wall loomed just over a mile away. Both of their horses were dead. Nabis's steed dropped shortly after their escape from the bandits, having been wounded during the melee, without him even knowing it. Orestes' horse had fallen an hour later, after they both tried to ride upon it. Neither they nor the animals had drunk water in almost two days. Now, although it was dusk, the day's heat remained, radiating off the parched earth.

"We're almost there," Orestes gasped. "I'm not sure I can make it." His lips were cracked, his eyes red.

"We have to keep going," Nabis answered. "It's not far. We'll find a well in the hamlet outside the walls." The pain in his shoulder had settled into a steady dull throb.

They helped one another to their feet, and trudged onward.

§

Abishag filled her pitcher with water from the well and, hoisting it in both hands, turned to go home.

"Shalom," a man said from behind, startling her. "May I help you with that?"

She eyed him suspiciously. He didn't look Greek or Jewish—maybe a mix. She couldn't place his accent. He spoke more like a Syrian, yet his Hebrew was fluent. He had a thick scar across his chin.

"Thank you, no," she said, taking a step back and lowering her gaze. She walked as quickly as the pitcher would allow, anxious to put distance between them.

"I am a friend of Rabbi Samuel," the stranger said softly, almost in a whisper. She hadn't realized he was keeping pace with her.

She turned to face him.

"I've never seen you before."

"I don't attend the synagogue," the man replied, "but I am a friend of the rabbi. He has asked me to warn everyone who does attend ..."

Abishag thought of the crucified bodies she had seen, and of her friends at the synagogue. Were they in danger? She gave the man a frightened look, but he smiled at her reassuringly.

"I could use your help. The Syrians are planning another massacre of the city. I need to know what people you know—apart of the congregation—who can be trusted, so we can provide protection to them before the Syrian soldiers strike."

"We meet tomorrow," she blurted. "Should we—"

"It is still safe to attend," he said, and she relaxed a little. "We just have to make sure the entire congregation is there so we can warn them, along with anyone else who can be trusted. Rabbi Samuel has been in contact with the Maccabees, the army of the resistance just north of here, in Mizpeh. They are planning to take the city before the Syrians can attack," he whispered. "Jerusalem will once again be ruled by the sons of Jacob!"

"I ... I only know a few people I can truly trust."

He prompted her for their names and locations in the city. Though he saw she was conflicted and apprehensive, he read her naivety well. Those who would not be at the synagogue the following day would have to be hunted down after. The man carefully remembered their names and the locations Abishag gave him. He repeated the information, confirming he had it all memorized.

No one will leave that synagogue alive tomorrow. Not even her. What a waste, he thought, noticing her beauty and youth.

"Stay indoors this evening," he advised, "and speak to no one until you reach the synagogue tomorrow. Secrecy is paramount!" She nodded, and gripped the pitcher hard, feeling her arm muscles starting to ache. With a furtive look around, she turned away and scurried home.

§

When Nabis awoke, his head was pounding, and the room was dark. Orestes was shaking him.

"Nabis, wake up! What happened to us? We're in some Israelite's house."

Nabis vaguely remembered how Orestes had collapsed as they neared the first houses of the hamlet. He had tried to lift him back up on his feet, but fell to his knees beside him. Then he had leaned his back against his comrade's prostrate body, and gave himself up to the inevitable darkness.

A tentative tap on his good shoulder had caused him to open his eyes. Gaging from the descending dusk, they had lain there an hour or more. Nabis looked up to see an old woman standing over him with a clay jar. She looked hesitant, perhaps fearing they might be Syrians. She offered them a drink, and Nabis had taken the water gratefully. "Thank you," he had choked. He poured water into Orestes's open mouth, jolting the man into semi-consciousness, and then drained the rest of the jar himself. He suddenly felt light-headed, disoriented. The world seemed to spin around him, and his ears rang. He slumped back down and everything went dark again.

Now inside the stranger's house, Nabis propped himself up on his elbow and peered around, his eyes slowly adjusting to the dim light. Vaguely, he recalled an old woman giving them water. Had she brought them to her home? The two men crept out of the house without waking anyone.

They staggered to the nearest well. It was dark, an hour before sunrise, Nabis guessed. Both men drank deeply and washed their faces as Nabis told Orestes what little he remembered.

"We look like beggars in these filthy clothes. I'm amazed anyone helped us at all."

They began walking toward the city walls.

"I'm sure all soldiers have been confined to the citadel," Orestes said. "We should probably go there first." The massive citadel, called the Acra, loomed just south of the temple mount. The Acra was positioned there strategically to overlook the security threat the temple hill presented.

"You go," answered Nabis, avoiding his gaze. "I want to get something from my house first."

"Shall I go with you?"

Nabis hesitated. If Orestes reported right away, they might come looking for him. But if Orestes came with Nabis, he would immediately know that something was amiss. Nabis could not take Abishag back to the soldiers' quarters. He must quickly find her and leave the city. He knew he would never put on a soldier's uniform again.

"No, go on ahead," he said. "It's safer if you report directly."

"What if something happens to you while—"

"Don't mention me. Or tell them you went on ahead and I plan to join up with you shortly." They walked along in silence for several moments.

"Where's your family from, Nabis?"

"My father was from Sparta."

"My father was in the army of Antiochus III. His father served before him, and his father's father, all the way back to Alexander's army. I've had family fight in every war the empire has ever waged. I guess I was destined for soldiering," Orestes said proudly. "I had an ancestor who was a young Macedonian. He fought in the Persian invasion and went on to become the right-hand man of Seleucus I. At least, that's what my father said."

"Is your family still alive?"

"My parents are dead. I have two married sisters. My brother died in Egypt three years ago when the army took Pelusium. What about you?"

"My mother is alive. I don't know if my father is. He was sick when I left for the army. As soon as I enlisted, after my training, I was sent to Egypt. I never heard what happened to him." Nabis looked thoughtful. "Your brother died at Pelusium?"

Orestes nodded.

"I was in that battle of Pelusium," Nabis said, recalling his first experience of combat and the first man he had ever killed. He couldn't believe it had only been three years. It felt like a lifetime ago. "Was your brother a Silver Shield?"

Orestes shook his head. "He was in the cavalry. They said he was hit by an arrow and broke his neck when he fell, but he would have died even if he hadn't fallen. It was better that way, quicker." Orestes sighed. "At least when the king abandoned the Egyptian campaign, we held on to Pelusium, so my brother didn't die for nothing."

Yes, he did, thought Nabis. *They all did.* It was all for nothing. Pelusium was taken from Egypt by the Persians four-hundred years ago, just as they had taken it from Ptolemy. *Nothing of substance changes; the world goes on,* he mused. *One century mimics the previous one. This generation forges the ideas of the last. People live and die. They control and are led. They eat, sleep, and procreate, and in the end, whatever rich king rules is ultimately covered by the same earth as his slaves.* Nabis recollected the words he had heard an elderly Hebrew man once cry out in the streets: *All is vanity. There is nothing new under the sun.* Nabis felt a flash of anger. No longer would he risk spilling his blood so some fool could get richer or expand his kingdom. Nor would he help to kill a whole people because they merely wanted the freedom to worship their own God. From this point on, he would be his own master. And Abishag would have her freedom.

Nabis wanted to say something to Orestes, but he knew what the man must be feeling, and his pride in being a soldier, a Silver Shield. His honest thoughts would accomplish nothing but only cause him confusion and anger, so Nabis kept silent.

Chapter 29

LYSIAS WALKED THROUGH the halls of the palace at dawn in deep contemplation. One of his spies had intercepted a letter addressed to the queen. The missive was from Rome, and Lysias had ordered the man who carried it to be killed.

How can this be? Lysias wondered, his mind reeling. *We assumed the boy had died in Rome years ago.* By now, the boy Demetrius was a man. He had been offered as a trade by the previous king in exchange for the king's captive son, and Rome had complied. Since then, no news had been heard of Demetrius, and he was long presumed dead.

Lysias glanced again at the letter in his hand. The ramifications of this piece of paper would shake the kingdom. Antiochus had only become king because Demetrius's younger brother, next in line for the throne, was judged too young to rule independently. Antiochus had maneuvered himself into ruling jointly with the child. Of course, now the boy had died mysteriously, leaving Antiochus with full claim to the throne. At least until now.

He read the letter again.

Dear Mother,

I am alive and well here in Rome. Until now, I have been unable to write you. I have tried and failed. If this traveler brings you my letter, reward him well. He has been a good friend to me, and I have put all the trust I have in him to bring this to you safely. Roman officials have informed me, if Antiochus continues in a way that overly threatens the interests of Rome, they will release me in hopes that I will create a civil war. They assume I will try to reclaim my throne, now usurped by my uncle, your husband. For now, I think they prefer me to be a threat rather than truly wish me to be released.

There are friends I have here that can try to get me out, but I need a great deal of money for this to be accomplished. I must bribe people to book me passage on a ship and must purchase the service of mercenaries. Even in Rome, there is word of the disastrous state in which the supplanter has left the beloved empire of my grandfather. Send money, and I will restore the empire to greatness.

Your son, Demetrius Soter, rightful King of the Seleucid Empire

Lysias held the parchment to a candle flame and watched until the letter was reduced to ashes. Now that the king had sired his own infant son, Laodice's days were numbered, as far as Lysias was concerned. The queen must be slain to protect the king. As soon as the boy was out of swaddling clothes, Lysias swore to himself, he would take care of that treacherous whore.

§

Abishag rushed to the synagogue as quickly as she dared, without drawing attention to herself, knowing the importance of this meeting. Secrecy was paramount, the man had warned. She was late, having spotted from her window what might have been a Syrian soldier dressed in common clothing, in the square outside. She knew she couldn't leave until the man left. He'd lingered so long, she feared she would miss the service altogether. Once she was certain he had disappeared, she had rushed downstairs, making her way through the housing district, through all the twists and turns. Out of breath, she was relieved when she saw the alleyway ahead that led to the synagogue entrance, where the secret meetings were held.

As she drew closer, she noticed, to her shock, Syrian soldiers standing just inside the alley, forming a perimeter around the synagogue basement. Inside the isolated space, soldiers emerged from the synagogue, dragging out bodies. She pressed herself against a building and watched in horror. She recognized those bodies. Another one was tossed atop the heap, blood pouring from the neck. It was the rabbi. The soldiers were laughing and talking among themselves. Abishag tried desperately to draw air into her chest.

She walked forward, avoiding the alleyway. Turning to look down another street, she observed two men following at a distance. A quick glance told her one was the supposed Syrian soldier she had seen outside her house. She fought to keep the tears from spilling over. On one side of the street, she noticed a crowd gathered around a group of popular merchants' tables. She stepped into the mass of people to disappear in the crowd.

The soldier and his companion quickly moved, trying to catch up, but Abishag had vanished in that throng. She moved past the shop tables in a daze; the voices were a chorus of indistinguishable shouts in her ears. She walked through a different alley that emptied onto another street. *How did this happen?* she kept asking herself. *Oh God! How did this happen?*

She looked about and thought of her friend, Adah, who lived with her husband nearby. She would seek sanctuary there. Although a devout Jew, Adah was too afraid to ever attend the synagogue. Abishag hoped she was home. She moved down another crowded street, and rounded another corner. She looked behind her again, but no one seemed to be following.

In front of her, another crowd was gathered in the street. It parted to let someone pass, and Abishag froze. Smoke was pouring from Adah's front door. Adah and her husband lay crumpled on the ground outside their home, their blood mingling in a pool about them. Adah lay, eyes open, in front of her doorway, having been stabbed repeatedly, while her husband's severed head lay near his ankles.

What is happening? the voice inside her head screamed. *Why Adah? Why her husband?* They never even went to synagogue, not once since the oppression began. They had been so careful. She approached in shocked disbelief. The inside of the house had been burned out, and smoke still smoldered from the bottom floor of the stone building.

Then the scarred face of the so-called rabbi's friend—the man who had offered to carry her jar— flashed in her mind. She remembered she had told him about Adah, and had given him names of other Jews who were faithful. Abishag kept walking, no longer able to hold back the tears. They were all dead—all dead!—and all because of her stupidity. That man she had trusted—the one who looked like an Israelite-Greek mix, he must have been a Syrian, or he was giving the Syrians information for money.

Oh God, what have I done? Guilt tore into her consciousness. She felt numb, like she was spinning, unattached to the earth. She had told the stranger the identities of people who trusted her. She had repaid that trust by handing them to their executioners.

Abishag trembled violently—terrified to remain where she was, and terrified to set off in any direction, lest she be followed. She had to leave Jerusalem, but how? Where could she go? North, she decided. North, where the patriot army had taken control of some of the cities surrounding Jerusalem. It might be safe for her there. But she would need to return home first. She remembered the money Nabis had left. She would take it and make her way from the city as best she could. *Oh*

Nabis. Would he understand that she had not run away from him, and had not stolen his money, but had fled for her life?

At length, taking multiple detours, she arrived at the courtyard terrace outside the building that housed Nabis's second-floor apartment. Seeing no one around, she hurried toward the stairs.

Abruptly, she stopped—her breath halting, her legs freezing as if of their own volition. The air in the courtyard grew still as she stared at the man with the scar across his chin. He emerged between her and the stairs, just three feet away. Her heart pounded. She turned around and sprang for the courtyard entrance.

In a split second, a hand reached out and grabbed for her neck. She crashed to the ground, her thigh hitting the leg of a long wooden table. Her back felt twisted. She was dizzy. She turned herself over and tried to stand, but the man grabbed a fistful of her long hair, snapping her head backward. He breathed heavily onto her neck. With his other hand, he gripped her wrist, as she stared up into his hate-filled eyes.

Her heart was racing out of control, her mind in a frenzy. She had been in this place before with the slave monger when he made her feel like an animal, defiled inside. She knew what this man wanted from his telling look, but she wouldn't be made to return to that hell.

The man laughed a knowing laugh, confident of his prey, and slightly loosened his grip. Suddenly twisting nearly free of his grasp, she clawed at his eyes and raked her nails across his face. He reeled in pain. Bringing her heel down on his foot, she darted for the street entrance. Then something snagged her arm.

Reflexively looking back, she saw a flash as the man backhanded her hard across the cheek, knocking her to the ground. She tried to look up, but his fist came down on her other cheek. Numb, her head spinning, she tried not to lose consciousness. Her attacker grabbed her garment now and heaved her by it, rending the seam, leaving her breasts exposed.

With a last surge of strength, she brought herself up and kneed him in the groin, but her blow was feeble. He only swore and tightened his grip, reigning a multitude of blows across her face. Blood flowed down her face and chin. She couldn't move. The man stood over her trying to put himself past the pain, catching his breath, his eyes and cheeks red and beginning to swell from the fingernails she had dug into him.

But her groans of fear and pain only aroused him. He hated her for that—that he could be aroused by a wench of such a vile race. He hated her for the dignity she had before displayed. He wanted to see her debased.

He kicked her hard in the stomach. That made her choke, arousing him further. He pulled the leather belt from his waist and tossed his sheathed xiphos heedlessly onto the table, preparing to take her.

Suddenly he felt himself flung forward into the support beam of the stairs. Someone was slamming his head into the beam.

Abishag looked up from where she lay, nearly paralyzed on the ground. It was Nabis.

Weak as he was, a rage surged up inside the soldier, filling him. He clenched his fists and beat the attacker in the face. Nabis heard the man's nose crunch beneath his knuckles. The rapist broke free, and they exchanged blows. Nabis was the shorter of the two, and the other man lunged, clinched hold of Nabis, and forced him to the ground. Now in control, he pummeled Nabis's cheeks and forehead. Amidst the blur of the foray, Nabis reached for a rock that lay along the walkway, almost out of his reach.

He swung this into the other man's temple, sending him whirling backwards. Falling against the table, the assailant reached for his sword belt. As Nabis rose, still clutching the rock, the other man jerked his blade free, slashing horizontally at Nabis's waist. Nabis jumped back, the blade barely missing him. He threw the stone at the man's head, but the man lifted his xiphos, and it deflected the rock.

Nabis dashed forward, tackling his assailant and controlling his sword arm. A bench overturned as they both crashed to the ground. Nabis's shoulder wound reopened, and blood soaked his garment. As the enemy grasped his sword, Nabis took hold of his wrist and brought his own elbow down hard, pummeling the other man's collarbone. The bone broke, and the assailant's body went limp at last.

Listlessly, Nabis leaned on his elbow, tossing his sword away. The rapist groaned, trying to sit up. With all the strength Nabis could muster, he kicked the man in the jaw. The attacker's head snapped back sharply and lolled to the earth, motionless.

Nabis breathed a sigh. Suddenly, Abishag's arms were around him. She was sobbing. He pulled his cloak over her bosom, covering her. They remained there together a long time before they finally made their way, stumbling, into the house, Nabis holding Abishag tightly.

Chapter 30

THE DISSONANT SCREAMS terrified the slaves, who fled in trepidation. "Tie him down!" Urion shouted as he and the other three bodyguards forced Antiochus to the ground. The king sounded like a snared beast. His face was red with the exertion of the struggle. His eyes were once again frantic, sinister, with an unnatural gleam. The bodyguards proceeded to tie him to the bed frame in his tent.

Urion had guessed that another bout of madness would soon take the king, and had warned the guards to take care that he didn't hurt himself. *What more can be done?* Urion thought despairingly. *We've done everything possible to try to balance his humors.* It was happening more and more frequently now, the madness. Maybe it was punishment for the sin of desecrating the Hebrew god's temple. It was strange that two days before, when the king heard the news of Seron's humiliating defeat, he didn't even react, as if he didn't comprehend the report.

Early this morning Urion had awakened to the horrifying sound of an animal's wailing screams. Stepping from his tent into the snow, he saw the king outside wearing nothing but a loincloth. He was torturing his own horse.

He had used his xiphos to slit open the animal's stomach, and its entrails were hanging. It had collapsed to the ground. Antiochus was laughing as he hacked away at the fallen animal's limbs. Urion stood in disbelief at the ghastly scene, the horse still alive, struggling to hold onto life. After a couple moments, it stopped fighting back and went limp. Antiochus let out a guffaw and began cutting into his own arms. He seemed unresponsive to his own pain and just stood there, fascinated by his own blood dripping into the snow.

"Call for the king's physician," Urion had murmured to one of the servant boys. "Wake the king's bodyguards." The bout of madness Urion had forecast was upon them. Now there was nothing to be done except to restrain the king until it passed.

§

"Did you talk with her about it?" Judah asked Simon. The army, camped outside Mizpha, was busy training in combat exercises, physical workouts, and maneuver drills.

"Of course we've talked. She's done nothing but nag."

"You should marry him off to a beautiful young woman, one he'll fall in love with. He'll be more reluctant to want to jump into battle. How old is he now?"

"Only two years younger than Jonathan," answered Simon.

"Those are the years that count, that truly make a difference. I'm sure he has an idealistic, romanticized view of war. The reality . . . is much different."

"Try telling that to a boy."

"Well, marry him off anyway, and he'll be exempt from battle."

"You're really serious about that, exempting all engaged men, and anyone who claims to be frightened?" Simon asked skeptically. "Even as a priest, I can tell that could hinder our numbers enough to make the difference between winning and losing a battle. And what was it you told us? If we lose a single battle, we've lost this war. If people were honest at all, every soldier would admit he's fearful and walk away."

"God must have known what it would do to the minds of men, being given the choice to fight or leave in shame. For those still choosing to fight, after the self-affirmation of courage, there's no excuse to falter in battle," replied Judah.

"You can be fearless and still die," Simon said with a snort.

"Look at all those his age—no longer boys, but not quite men. No sense in any of them. That's why his mother won't stop nagging me, and as soon as he joins the fight, his brothers will want to join him, too."

A moment passed before Simon continued. "Do you ever think about remarrying?"

"I don't have the time, even if I wanted to." Judah tried to mask the pain with a smile.

"Well, if you do, you can be the one to deal with the children."

My child is dead, Judah thought grimly. *She is waiting for me in Sheol, with Adi. I'll never marry again. I love her too much for that.*

He often felt his heart spasm with physical pain when he thought of Adi and the way she died in his arms. At times he would remember a special moment in their marriage that would make him smile—the excitement of meeting each other, the first time they made love on their wedding night—both of them nervous and so unsure, that funny incident at the wedding when Adi's mother fainted. After a few moments of peace, he would be brought back to the reality of it all, that in this life he would never see Adi again. It hurt to remember, but he couldn't bear to allow himself to forget.

But you're at war, he thought. *Could you have done all this with a wife and child to take care of?* The Lord gives, and the Lord takes away. Blessed be the name of the Lord. He just had to trust that God would reunite him with Adi and his daughter in the afterlife.

"So how far away did the riders say the Syrian army was?" Simon asked, already knowing the answer, wanting to change the subject.

"Less than a month's time, and they'll be here."

"Who's leading them?"

"Three generals," Judah answered. "Despicable men. They served Antiochus in Egypt, and were there when he desecrated the temple of God. Ptolemy, Gorgias, and Nicantor are their names—each one worse than the other, and each leading their own division of soldiers."

"You *know* we can't just hide in the hills and attack at our own whim anymore," Simon answered. "Our force has grown too large, and we'll be too easy to track. We can run only so far, then sooner or later, we'll have to face them."

Judah stopped speaking as a thought entered his mind. *That's what the enemy also thinks,* he realized. A little smile crossed his lips, but he said nothing. Judah knew this army would stop at nothing until they found him. They would eventually locate his base of operation at Gophna or find his men in one of the cities like Mizpha, that sheltered him, or on the move in the open. They were deployed for a single purpose, and that was to destroy his force. They wouldn't quit until they ended the national movement and stamped out the idea that was now on everyone's lips: the sovereignty of Israel. Judah couldn't attack head-on against such a sizable force—he would be annihilated. However, he could divide them.

§

Fabius shifted uncomfortably in his saddle. "How long is the journey to Jerusalem?" he asked. He had been looking forward to being on land after so much time aboard ship, but found he was weary after such a long journey.

"Only ten miles from here," answered Diomedes, the man who had made contact. Anticipating the arrival of Fabius and Crassus, he had posted his servant at the docks to watch for sight of them: two foreign strangers wearing silver medallions. Diomedes had waited for months, and finally they were here.

Athenian by birth, Diomedes was the son of a Roman ambassador and a Hebrew girl whose family had moved to Athens to trade goods from the East. They had married against her father's wishes. After the ambassador's assignment had ended, Diomedes' father took him and his mother back to Rome. Diomedes had benefited greatly from experiencing both cultures, receiving an education in philosophy and in Roman and Greek religion, and learning to speak Hebrew, Greek, Latin, and several Aramaic dialects fluently. The former ambassador converted to Judaism, and Diomedes became well-versed in the Torah and the writings of the Hebrew prophets.

After two years of service in the Roman army, Diomedes was asked by the legatus of his legion to travel to a place on the Seleucid border where his mother's people were from. The legatus had heard that he spoke the local dialects well. There, he procured information about Syrian movements, activities, the local populace, and their political sentiments. It was he who had tipped off the Roman officials during the Syrian invasion of Egypt, permitting Rome to halt Antiochus's advance, scaring him off with a single ambassador and a small cavalry unit.

The fact that Diomedes could pass for Greek or Hebrew allowed him to intermix and procure information easily. It helped that he had relatives in the area to introduce him to the local community. He was frequently seen at the synagogues, abating any suspicion among the Jews. He had, on more than one occasion, helped orchestrate the assassination of individuals at Rome's behest. After four years at this post, he had received word that two Roman agents would be arriving at the harbor of Joppa. Now he was to take them to Jerusalem, where they would meet with four other agents, and from there travel north to meet the leadership of the Jewish resistance.

"How far is this Mizpeh place, where you say the rebels are?" Crassus asked Diomedes as their horses loped along.

"Not a day's journey from Jerusalem."

"I don't understand. Why are we wasting our time going to Jerusalem if the rebels we're supposed to meet are in Mizpeh? Why not just head straight to Mizpeh?"

"Orders," Diomedes said, turning slightly in his saddle. "The men you will meet in Jerusalem will apprise you of the local situation in order to better your negotiation skills."

"Jerusalem is not in revolt?"

"No. Jerusalem is the regional stronghold of the Syrians. They built a citadel there to house all their troops. But the rebel army is just eight miles to the north. Reports have it that the largest Syrian force ever to pass through the region is on its way to put down the revolt. The rebels may count six thousand, but this force is easily five times that size."

"What do the locals think of that?" Crassus asked, glancing at Fabius.

"Their sentiments are with the rebels," Diomedes replied, "but understandably, they're afraid. It was just a few years ago that the Syrians murdered half of Jerusalem's population, and the city is under total tyranny. They hunt down locals rumored to be worshiping the Hebrew god and murder anyone remotely associated with, or suspected of helping, the rebels."

"They kill them just for worshiping their own god?"

Diomedes nodded, his expression grim.

"There's one man responsible for the savagery. He was appointed by Urion, an adviser to Antiochus and a former slave, as I understand. The appointee's name is Isokrates. He has a distinguishable scar across his chin, and like myself, reputedly can pass for either Hebrew or Greek. This has enabled him to infiltrate various Hebrew groups. He runs a network of spies and informants who tip him off to the religious and to the rebel sympathizers. Many of his informants are, in fact, Hebrews."

Fabius and Crassus exchanged surprised looks at this bit of information.

"The Hellenistic Jews and the Sadducees, sects of Judaism that don't adhere to traditional beliefs and who embrace Greek customs, have no love for those who stick to the traditional ways," Diomedes explained. "Isokrates pays them blood money, so they are happy to betray their neighbors."

He cast Fabius a pointed look. "Should Rome maintain an interest in this region, it would benefit our cause if this Isokrates were either handed over to the rebels or killed."

"What can you tell us of Jerusalem's defenses?" Fabius asked.

"They're not good. The soldiers don't trust the Israelites at all and are unconvinced of their own ability to quell an uprising. Most of the army's strength is concentrated at the citadel. I believe that, if the rebels could successfully lay siege to the city before that massive Syrian force arrives, they might be able to take control of Jerusalem. I don't know how they can manage that, though, as it's only about three weeks before they get here."

Fabius and Crassus mulled this over.

"When we reach Jerusalem, I will take you to the house of a prominent Hebrew, Isaac Ben Zechariah," Diomedes continued. "He will furnish you with more details of the rebel force, the size of their army, and the state they are in. He also can tell you all about the famed Judah, the one the people are calling the Maccabee. He is a skilled tactician and their leader."

"This Isaac—he is trusted by this Judah? He speaks with authority?"

Diomedes hesitated. Isaac had, in fact, been approached by Judah's older brother Gaddi, who was clearly stung by the fact that his father had passed him over in favor of Judah leading the army. He had hardly been subtle in his attempted maneuverings to secure Roman support. Diomedes was sure his goal was to see himself on the throne with Judah subject to him. No one who knew anything of the rebel army had any illusions who the leader was, the man who the Jews felt had been chosen by their god. Clearly, it was Judah, and that was the man who would rule, at least until a descendant of David could be placed back on the throne.

"Isaac has spoken with Judah's brother Gaddi, who proposed the idea of Roman support," Diomedes answered. "I'm not sure how much he has shared with Judah. I believe he hopes for you yourselves to make the proposal, to convince Judah of Rome's support of their victory over the Syrian army."

Fabius was silent. If the rebels were destroyed in a massive engagement with the Syrians, Roman support wouldn't do them any good. *Perhaps,* he thought, *I should wait until the Syrian army arrives and see which way the gods decide before I return to Rome with my recommendation.*

Diomedes' horse whinnied as a bearded man suddenly stepped from behind a short stone wall and walked into the road, blocking their path. Seemingly out of nowhere, four other men appeared. Before the riders could react, two of the strangers moved behind them with spears in hand. The bearded, stocky man standing in the road had a fresh cut running across his forehead.

"Those are beautiful animals there," he said in accented Greek. The Romans remained unresponsive.

"Who are you, and where are you from?" he demanded.

"We're Carthaginian traders on the way to—"

"*Carthaginians!*" the man interrupted with a smile of mock amusement, grinning at his compatriots, shaking his head. "Everyone's a Carthaginian. Hand over your money and get off your horses!" Fabius and Crassus looked at each other. One of the men moved in closer, his spear tip coming uncomfortably close to Fabius's head.

"Now!" the stocky man roared.

Without warning, Fabius gripped hold of the spear poised at his head, and with his free hand, unsheathed the gladius concealed beneath his cloak. In a single motion, he swung his blade into his assailant's neck.

§

Dressed in drab clothing, appearing as local travelers, Nabis and Abishag moved past the soldiers that guarded the city gates. She rode the mule Nabis had purchased the day before, and he walked alongside her. They had spent two weeks traveling from various locations within Jerusalem, staying at local inns, trying to appear as Jewish foreigners.

Nabis and Abishag had wasted no time escaping. Nabis had dyed his blond hair black with a crushed senna plant, cropping his wavy curls short. He began to let his beard grow, coloring it every few days, knowing they would ultimately have to pass the guards at the city gate, who would doubtless be on alert. He hoped that having Abishag at his side would help his disguise.

At his insistence, they posed as husband and wife, but Nabis had also insisted on sleeping on the floor at whatever inn they stayed for the night. This distressed Abishag. On the fourth night, when he again made preparations to do this, she refused to allow it. "It's unfitting for a master to sleep like a dog while his slave sleeps like a queen," she had told him.

He tried to explain how she wasn't his slave anymore, and that she was free. At first she mistook this for disfavor. Abishag was on the verge of tears by the time he was able to explain that it was because he cared for her that he was giving her her freedom. Then when her lips touched his, he realized her tears were for another reason. She had been overcome. The tension had subdued them both, and they no longer could hold themselves back, falling into one another's arms. Pressing against her with every passionate kiss, Nabis felt the warmth of her legs around him, as her dress slid up around her thighs.

Regaining control, Nabis stopped to say what he felt he must. "You are no longer my slave," he told her, trying to slow down his heart and control his breathing. "You are my wife." Their eyes locked, and each looked deeply into the other's soul. In that long glance, she conveyed everything she felt in that moment—the love in her heart, the gratitude, the intense longing for him. She let him take control of her, dominate every moment, and for the first time in her life, she gave herself willingly.

Abishag was smiling, remembering their lovemaking, as they slowly moved toward the city gates, but Nabis, aware of the danger, was focused on the guards. Fortunately, the sentinels were few at this hour, and none of them recognized Nabis.

As they stepped outside the city, Abishag squeezed his hand with a smile of happiness, and Nabis uttered a sigh of relief. But he knew their problems were only beginning. For one thing, he still could be caught—a deserter from the army. For another, the accomplices of their assailant, whom he presumed to be dead and a spy, could be looking for him. They had to get away from Jerusalem. They had some money to live off of, but they had to get clear of the areas controlled by Seleucid soldiers. They would travel north.

Angry with himself, Nabis remembered the man he had struggled with in the courtyard. *How could you have just gone upstairs for your money and left, not checking to see if he was dead or alive?*

He had walked away telling himself the man was dead, but he knew better than to assume things without checking. In his heart, he knew the man might have lived, but he had seen enough bloodshed, had killed enough people. Maybe he just didn't have the stomach for it anymore. Maybe, he told himself, he never did. *That son of a harlot was trying to rape Abishag. I should have made sure I killed him.* But even if the man was dead, whoever he had worked for surely was looking for Nabis, wanting retribution.

Abishag looked down at Nabis with glittering eyes. She smiled at his altered appearance. He looked even more handsome to her now—almost Jewish.

Nabis gazed back at his woman and felt his heart stir. A warmth passed through him. He had to look away before he felt he no longer could.

Abishag turned to see the city of David growing smaller behind them. Nabis felt his sword at his back, concealed beneath his cloak. "We'll need to be careful," he said. "There are bad men on these highways."

No sooner had he said that, than he remembered the

incident weeks before when he was almost robbed and killed. Then he realized where they were standing. It was the exact same place where the incident had occurred.

Abishag gasped. There in the dirt were strewn bodies of the dead, around a short wall on either side of the road. Before the stone wall was a spear with a head on it.

"How could people do such a thing?" he heard her say, covering her nose and mouth, trying to look away. Nabis stared at the head atop the spear and recognized it as the leader of the band that had tried to rob him. He noticed the cut on the man's forehead that Orestes had inflicted. Dust clung to the pale skin, and the stench of exposed rotting organs assailed his nostrils. The bodies must have been dead for hours. He saw another man dead that he recognized—the one his horse had kicked when he escaped. There was a gash in the stomach, and the entrails protruded from the side. They were all there, and all dead—his attackers.

"Nabis?" Abishag said, still covering her nose and mouth. Nabis realized he was still staring at the decapitated head in front of him. He pried his gaze away and once again focused on the journey before them.

Chapter 31

"THEY CAN'T JUST ambush us," Nicantor explained. "This is a different army. Nor can they face us on open ground. We command an army of more than five times their size."

The fire inside the tent was warming them against the cold that the enlisted soldiers had to face outside. Around the fire was the high command of the officers' corps.

"Still," Gorgias interjected, "we should avoid narrow passes like that fool Seron walked right into, repeating Apollonius's blunder."

"It's likely we'll get into a few small skirmishes, maybe an actual engagement," he added. "Of course, they'll lose these small fights because they can't win against our numbers. Then most of the rebel force will scatter and leave us to our work of ridding the land of their horrid race."

"But first, Jerusalem?" Ptolemy confirmed.

"Yes. The city is in a precarious state. We'll reestablish control, then make it our base of operations for destroying the rebels."

"My scouts say there's a road outside of Emmaus that's more favorable if we wish to avoid mountain passes and potential ambush points."

Nicantor let Ptolemy's comment hang in the air for a moment because he was thinking. He thought of the six-thousand men the rebels had banded together. He thought about this leader they had named "The Hammer." He thought about what the rebels would do next. They might pathetically rally their untrained band of rogues and face them. An army of dilettantes, but Nicantor had over thirty-thousand professionally trained soldiers, and more held up in Jerusalem. *You can't beat numbers,* he said to himself. *Faith and nationalism will get you only so far. In the end, it all comes down to military capabilities and the size of the army.*

"All right, gentlemen, that concludes our meeting," he finally said aloud, "unless anyone has something further." After a moment, he added, "By this time next week, we'll be dining in Jerusalem." *That is, if you'll work together instead of sabotaging each other to try to impress Lysias and the king,* he mentally murmured to himself.

"Good evening," Nicantor said with a smile as they all filed out to go to their own warm tents.

§

"Am I to understand you are the rebel leader of the army?" Fabius asked, inwardly surprised at the man's youth.

"Bring our guests food and wine," Judah said to one of his soldiers. He nodded to Fabius and gestured for them to seat themselves.

Judah's face broke into an unexpected smile, making him seem even younger than his modest years. "So, my honored guests, what brings you to my country?"

"Like yourselves," Fabius began, "Rome has good reason to despise the Seleucids. They have waged numerous attacks on our allies, and are openly preparing for war against us. There are many in Rome, in the senate, who have heard of your plight, of your struggle for freedom and independence. Rome believes that an alliance between us would serve both our interests."

Judah said nothing. So Fabius pressed on.

"The senate would consider sending you money, supplies, provisions, and weapons."

"What about men?" asked Judah.

Fabius hesitated.

"I am afraid that, while we may be able to provide training for your soldiers, Rome would not agree to part with its own troops in order to supplement yours, at least not yet."

"Tell me. What does Rome expect in return for all this generosity?"

"It would be enough to aid an ally and see an end to the Seleucid threat, both in the Western Region and against our people. We would," Fabius added, "enjoy opening up trade between Judea and Rome."

Judah's eyes narrowed slightly. He leaned forward.

"What we're fighting for is freedom, the freedom to be Jews, to worship our God the way we want, to rule ourselves according to *our* laws. What guarantee do I have that, once the Syrians pull out of Judea, we won't be subject to Roman law, Roman influence?"

"Rome's official policy is non-imperial." Fabius replied emphatically. "We have no interest in expansion and conquering countries and mingling in foreign affairs. We are a republic. Our war policy is strictly defensive. The only lands we have taken are Sicily from Carthage, and that was done solely to protect ourselves, and some small outposts on the border of Gaul— to protect us from the barbarians of the north. The Seleucids threaten us just as they threaten you, so an alliance could prove mutually beneficial."

Judah sat back, thinking. This was what Gaddi had proposed: an alliance with Rome to save their cause and the lives of Jews everywhere. He looked up at Fabius and Crassus. These men claimed Rome had no imperialistic designs, yet Roman power and influence continued to grow, affecting the whole region. Carthage had diminished, and now Rome dominated the whole western part of the world. Judah only had this man's word to rely upon, that Rome would not subsequently try to conquer and rule Judea. They could be trading one form of oppression for another. *Politicians forget,* Judah reminded himself. *They never remember history.* A time could easily come when this alliance would be forgotten or set aside. Judah reminded himself about all the admonitions in the scriptures that warned against relying on foreign powers, and in trusting in alliances rather than in the Lord God. He knew his father would never have approved a foreign alliance.

Judah regarded the men. Their countenances exuded military discipline. He had heard that Roman soldiers were excellent warriors. A pressing thought interrupted his observations. *Accept the help. Right now. What choice do you have? If Rome one day encroaches on our freedoms, we'll give them the same kind of war we're giving the Syrians.* His people would just have to inspire their descendants with the conviction and faith they would need to always fight in the name of liberty against anyone who would take it away, be they Greek, Persian, or Roman.

Fabius cleared his throat. "Unfortunately, our offer comes at a most inopportune moment," he said. "If we had met a year ago, you would already have had Roman supplies and arms at your disposal. Now you face one of the largest forces ever gathered, practically at your door. Once they reinforce the garrison at Jerusalem, you'll never take the city, and the whole paradigm of how you've conducted this war will change."

Judah did not reply.

Crassus, studying Judah, analyzing his every word and expression, spoke before thinking. "But you're not planning on letting that army reach Jerusalem!" he said, his shock apparent.

Judah just looked at the Romans in silence.

Words were spilling out of Crassus's mouth almost involuntarily, as he tried to read Judah's mind, "You plan to attack their force?

Judah's face remained unresponsive, but the look in his eyes and his silence were almost an acknowledgment.

"An army that large? But that's not possible. That's insane. It would be suicide.

§

Outside the tent, Isaac Ben Zechariah waited after taking the Romans to meet Judah. He saw Gaddi pass by, looking interested and giving a nod.

It had been Gaddi who was his contact. Gaddi, who had been the primary advocate of gaining Roman support, *but he has alternative motives,* Isaac told himself. *He wants to make himself king.* Isaac felt Gaddi had been corrupted by a covetous eye. The lust for power was more tempting than the lust for wealth or fornication. Gaddi had been passed over, as God had favored Jacob over Esau, and David over the sons of Jesse's older children. Gaddi had been passed over for his younger brother Judah. And Gaddi thought he could use Isaac Ben Zechariah to help the Romans barter a deal to support him being king. *Once the Romans realize no one will support him and that the strength lies in Judah, there'll be no hope for Gaddi,* Isaac thought. *Judah is the ruler God gave to Israel. Anyone can see that. At least until a descendent of David can be placed back on the throne.*

Chapter 32

HE HAD ONLY been sleeping an hour when Judah woke from his slumber to see Eleazar standing over him. "Judah," his brother said quietly, "the scouts have just returned." Judah sat up on his mat, instantly awake. "It's happening, brother, just as you said it would. The Syrians are dividing their force."

Eleazar grinned. The stratagem had worked. Judah had foreseen that once the massive Syrian army made camp near Emmaus, with twenty-thousand infantry and ten-thousand cavalry, there was but one way to defeat such a force, and that was to divide it. He'd therefore had his men leak disinformation among the local populace, in hopes it would reach the ears of the Syrian generals.

"The scouts said Gorgias, one of the Syrian generals, is preparing to depart their camp, with five-thousand infantry and one-thousand cavalry," said Eleazar. "They plan to attack our camp later tonight."

Judah knew they had only a matter of hours. "Wake the men," he said. "Have them assemble at once, but leave the campfires burning."

§

Gorgias saw the fires of the distant camp illuminating the darkness of the night. For two days he had argued in favor of a night attack, after his men had forced information from local shepherds about the size and disposition of the enemy host. He had also discovered the amateurish location of their camp—on low ground, against enveloping hills.

"We keep falling into these same traps," he had complained. "We are forced to meet the fight on the ground of their choosing, at a time of their choosing, and always when we least expect it. *We* should be the ones doing the choosing. The only way to counter these tactics is to emulate them."

Nicantor, the ranking general, had finally agreed to this unorthodox nighttime raid, granting Gorgias sufficient men to wipe out the rebels, while still retaining most of the army in the Syrian camp, twelve miles away from the rebels' location.

"Silence from here on out," Gorgias ordered softly, as his soldiers moved through the dark, hours before dawn. Now just a mile in the distance, the camp of the Maccabees was visible, glowing with the embers of hundreds of dying fires piercing the blanket of the moonless night.

"I want your men to charge down from that slope," Gorgias said, turning toward the cavalry commander and pointing to the shallow hill overlooking the camp on his left. "We'll wait for your charge and, once you engage them, the infantry will attack forward from here." The phalanxes would form a wedge to charge into the center of the camp.

The cavalry commander ordered his men to dismount and move as quietly as possible toward the hill. Gorgias marched his men forward just far enough to be able to gauge the cavalry attack when it came. He could hear the heavy breaths of his men, the soft muffled clinks of spears and armor. A soft breeze blew across the rocky desert.

The silence was suddenly shattered by the thunderous charge of a thousand Syrian horses coming down the hill.

"Forward!" Gorgias cried, as he watched the Syrian cavalry tear through the camp's flank. The infantry scurried forward as cavalry soldiers began upturning tents. Fires exploded into sprays of sparks, illuminating the night sky.

Something wasn't right. It took a moment for Gorgias to realize that, in the chaos, no rebels had appeared. The camp was empty!

He swung around, desperately searching in the darkness, his vision impaired by the light thrown up from the fires everywhere.

"There!" One of the commanders shouted, pointing to the hill. Men were dashing up the slope, away from the camp.

"After them!" Gorgias screamed. Even then, he knew this was not a six-thousand-man army. Where were they?

§

From atop the ridge near Emmaus, Judah stared down at the sleeping, massive Syrian camp spread out below. He hoped that the two-hundred men he had left behind in his own camp, to lure the Syrians into the hills, had made it away safely. Judah had marched all the rest of his men on the back roads northwest through the night, knowing Gorgias would travel southeast on the main road that led toward Mizpeh.

Judah had divided his force into three. Jonathan and Gaddi would attack the huge Syrian camp from behind with fifteen-hundred men. Simon and Eleazar would flank them with another fifteen hundred, while Judah and the remaining three thousand would charge from the front.

Their enemy's sparse palisades and fortifications looked weak. They had been so overly confident in their numbers, Judah thought in disgust, that they hadn't even bothered to set up proper defenses.

Seeing that his army was ready, he nodded. He felt the rush that always hit him before a battle. The predawn air was cold, and the anxiety that gripped him added to the night's chill.

The man beside him raised a twisted ram's horn to his lips and let out a long, low rallying note. Like a roar of lions, the men shouted, "The help of God! The help of God!" A chorus of shouts echoed off the hills as the Israelite horde charged the sleeping Syrian camp at full run.

Brandishing a spear, Judah led his men forward, running

down the slope over a small embankment. He saw the Syrian night watch turn and flee. Half-asleep soldiers emerged from their tents in confusion, clad only in their night garments, as the Hebrews swept in and mercilessly slaughtered them. They were being cut down before they knew what was happening. Judah plunged his spear into a Syrian who had on nothing but a sword and a loose-fitting short cloak.

Tents were overturned, and hundreds of bodies littered the ground. Joel cut loose the string of Syrian cavalry horses, scattering them into the night. Most of his force stayed in a line as they smote their way through the camp. Once they reached the center, they met a more formidable resistance by soldiers who had had time to don their armor. General Nicantor raced around at the rear of the camp, furiously trying to form a single large phalanx to counterassault. He had gathered almost two-thousand men, but the rest of the camp was in complete bedlam.

A wave of Syrians charged Judah's position. He parried an oncoming spear and countered it, plunging his own into the man's chest so ferociously that it punctured his armor and pierced him straight through the back. Judah tried frantically to extract the spear as another attacker stepped forward, but it was stuck in the dead man's swelling flesh. Drawing the sword he had taken from Apollonius, Judah blocked his attacker's thrust barely in time. Joel's spear found the attacker's stomach before he could strike again. Judah swung his sword, cracking the soldier's skull open. Blood sprang from the wound like a fountain.

Judah heard a ram's horn to his right. Simon and Eleazar were charging into the camp's flank. Judah and his men pressed forward, as resistance markedly lessened. They advanced to meet Eleazar and Simon's force and together they waded through the endless maze of tents. They emerged from the far side of the camp, as if into a clearing.

There confronting them was a colossal phalanx of infantrymen, two-hundred men across and thirty ranks deep, standing with a precipice at their back. Throughout the foray, Nicantor had managed to organize nearly six-thousand of his soldiers, armed and armored. Sarissas out, they now marched forward, determined to retake their camp.

Judah's force froze at the spectacle. The massive machine of metal and flesh, illuminated by the dawning sunlight, marched relentlessly forward, every step closing the short distance between them.

Judah noticed that the enemy formation stretched and subtly crested toward its center. He thought of a favored tactic of Hannibal Barca, who would have his center recede somewhat in order to envelop and trap his opponent with his flanks.

"Attack the flanks," Judah said softly, as if thinking aloud.

"What?" shouted Eleazar.

"Attack the flanks! They can't maneuver in that large of a formation!"

The massive phalanx was less than a hundred yards away.

"Follow me," Eleazar commanded his men. He darted forward at the head of nearly one-thousand Israelites, feigning an attack toward the center. The charging Hebrew host suddenly changed direction, toward the right, slamming into the wing of the phalanx, isolating its end. The enemy formation, clustered tightly together, could not break free.

Joel cut left, with over a thousand men behind him. Judah signaled to Benjamin Ben Joshua, the old man who had trained many of the men and who now was in charge of five-hundred archers and sling men. "I want that center bombarded with arrows!" Judah yelled to him.

The archers lined up and took aim. Judah knew that at such close range many of the arrows would punch right through the enemy corselets. They nocked arrows, drew, and on Benjamin's signal, shot straight into the ranks. The forward lines staggered, and men fell.

The wings of General Nicantor's formation attempted to face their attackers, causing the phalanx to undulate and fracture. Arrows continued to find their marks, but the archers were running out of arrows quickly, and the phalanx was almost on top of them.

Judah signaled the man with the shofar, and the ram's horn rang out two short bursts. Another shofar answered, trumpeting from behind the enemy phalanx as fifteen-hundred men, led by Jonathan and Gaddi, descended the slope like a swarm of locusts, shouting and brandishing their weapons. Like the waves of a violent sea, they swept into the rear of the Syrian formation, shattering it.

The lines were finally broken, and the Syrians, no longer confident of their numbers, dropped their spears and shields and took off at top speed toward the one small opening in the Israelite lines. Nicantor bellowed for them to return, then changed his mind. Seeing his army disintegrate and no point in sacrificing his own life, he drove his heals into the flanks of his horse and galloped after his men.

Judah, jubilant, led the charge on the heels of the retreating Syrians, knowing full well the highest rate of casualties inflicted in battle was always on retreating armies. Several of his men remained behind to deal with those Syrians who still held their ground.

Judah chased the fleeing Syrians down the slope, the Hebrews massacring hundreds, until, at last, he shouted for them to stop. They still had General Gorgias to contend with, as the two-hundred Hebrews who remained behind in the rebel camp were no match for Gorgias and his six-thousand soldiers. Knowing the fight was not over, Judah moved his men back to the edge of the Syrian camp.

"Gather the spoils!" he ordered. "Burn down the camp!"

The Hebrews set fire to the cleared-out tents, and smoke arose in the morning light.

§

Gorgias gazed down at the blazing Syrian camp, and what was left of Nicantor's army retreating in panic, disappearing into the distance. Gorgias had lost nearly three-hundred men, not to mention forty horses, to strategically placed Israelite archers in the hills, surrounding the abandoned Israelite camp. An hour's fighting proved what he had begun to suspect: that these rebels were a mere portion of the Jewish force, a decoy. Fearing the worst, he had ordered his men to return to their own camp as quickly as possible. His fears were now confirmed: Nicantor's soldiers had been attacked and put to flight.

Seeing the Israelites arrayed in a defensive position behind the smoldering camp filled Gorgias with despair. He could see from the Israelites assembled on the slope opposite, that they were ready for another clash of arms—waiting for him, hoping for him to attack.

"March the men for the coast," he ordered, wheeling his horse around, his expression grim.

§

Judah watched as Gorgias' men turned and began to march away, the enemy camp burning before him.

"Should we pursue them?" Joel asked.

Judah shook his head.

"No. Tonight begins the Sabbath. The Lord has given us a great victory. We will honor Him and observe Shabbat."

Behind Judah, the rest of his force was arrayed. Seeing the Syrians under Gorgias turn for the coast, they let out a cry of victory. As the shouts died, the chants began softly at first, then grew louder until the sound seemed to shake the earth beneath them.

"Maccabee! Maccabee! Maccabee!"

סֵפֶר חָמֵשׁ

Book V
Hanukkah

165 BC

"Proclaim ye this among the nations; prepare war; stir up the mighty men; let all the men of war draw near, let them come up."

~ Joel

βιβλίο Πέντε

Chapter 33

THE CHATTER OF voices reverberated through the thermopolium, where food and ale were being served. Inside the restaurant, here in the heart of Rome, patricians (the aristocracy) ate at L-shaped counters. Outside on the veranda, they ate and drank at tables, conversing. Fabius could hear the conversation at a neighboring table about *Hecyra*, Terence's new play.

"Egypt is in turmoil," said Ovidius Tiburtius, a corpulent magistrate who served at the behest of the senate. "Ptolemy is here—in the city, in exile. His brother took his throne, and the country is on the verge of yet another civil war."

Next to Fabius sat Crassus, listening intently.

"Thank the gods the Seleucid Empire is in chaos," the man continued expounding, "since now would have been their perfect opportunity to strike. Popillius Laenas and the senators wish to continue our policy of repressing the Seleucids, as they're still our biggest threat." He took a sip of his wine.

Here it comes, thought Crassus.

"This means we'll send you back to this Maccabee we've heard so much about and conclude our treaty. Once they agree, we'll start shipping the weapons, horses, equipment, and money."

"Yes, sir," Fabius replied with a nod.

I knew it, Crassus thought, indignant. *We're being ordered back to Judea.*

"About the rebels," Tiburtius asked. "Do you think they would stand a chance without our weapons, supplies, and coin?"

"They may," Fabius replied, after a moment of thought. "I saw them fight at Emmaus. Their leader is brilliant, and they have the spirit and will to win. It was six-thousand men against thirty thousand, and still they were victorious. I've never seen anything like it. It would have humbled Scipio Africanus."

"Trickery on the battlefield," Tiburtius answered, contemplating the ignobility of savage warfare.

"We will wait until we hear word, of course, before we send you back to conclude the treaty."

Tiburtius knew the senate didn't care about the freedom of the rebel foreigners. They cared about creating havoc for the Seleucids. And they could still release Demetrius to create a civil war if they had to. The Romans could even give the little shit weapons and money to buy mercenaries to start his civil war, and then take the whole region back from him.

"What do you mean, 'wait until we hear word?'" Fabius asked.

"Lysias has departed Antioch, personally leading an army of sixty thousand, to destroy the Maccabee and his rebels."

Fabius and Crassus were taken aback.

"You didn't know?" Tiburtius asked, surprised. "The army left some time ago. Lysias will arrive in Judea soon."

Fabius and Crassus were speechless. Sixty-thousand soldiers! The number was incomprehensible.

"It changes the dynamics of it all, doesn't it?" said Tiburtius. "The rebels can't stand and fight, not against sixty-thousand men, and not even if they had twenty thousand of their own, which they don't. If Maccabee is the master tactician you say, he'll resort to evasive maneuvers. Lysias will reinforce Jerusalem, which still has not been taken by the rebels, and the Israelites will never be able to take it back. But they can evade and continue in their savage, unorthodox tactics, chipping away at Lysias's army, costing the Seleucids lives and money. Lysias may very well end the rebellion with his sixty-thousand men, but either way, the rebel presence weakens the Seleucids immensely."

"Why then shouldn't we leave at once with the money and supplies?" Crassus asked, disturbed. "It could make the difference between—"

"No," Tiburtius interrupted, raising his hand from the table. "I want to hear what happens once Lysias reestablishes a stronghold. He's either going to end the rebellion quickly, or it will be a drawn-out conflict. There's no point in sending money and an envoy to a rebellion that doesn't exist, so we will wait."

Crassus couldn't believe it. He felt despondent. These people were fighting for liberty—fighting incredible odds with their lives at stake—and the senate didn't care. *They're playing politics,* he thought.

"Your ship and that captain, the former naval officer," Tiburtius asked. "Would he be willing to sail back to Judea if need be?"

"He'll want more money," Fabius answered grimly.

In the days he had spent in the Israelite camp, Crassus had come to know Maccabee well, though he enjoyed the company of the youngest brother, Jonathan, more. Although youthful, Jonathan was affable, and spoke to Crassus in confidence about his woman, whom he was engaged to marry—about all that was between them and their religious observance. After Judah defeated Nicantor at Emmaus, Jonathan had finally married her. Crassus recalled the strange wedding ceremony he observed.

He remembered telling Jonathan in a discussion afterwards, "I'm sure the Hebrew God is real, but it doesn't make sense that there is only one. How can one god control all the elements? Heaven and earth, the sea and the underworld?" But who really knew? Perhaps it was the case.

He had listened to Jonathan explain the story of their people and their god. Jonathan had told him how the Israelites escaped from Egypt as slaves, and afterwards the rule of judges and then kings. He had told him of the Israelite wars with the Edomites, Philistines, Assyrians, and Babylonians . . . how his people had been taken to Babylon as captives in an event called *The Diaspora,* resulting from a policy the Babylonians and Assyrians had of removing conquered peoples from their land and relocating them to another part of the empire, to cut land ties in hopes of preventing any revolts. But later, Israel was released from captivity by Cyrus the Great, the Persian conqueror of Babylon.

Crassus had also told Judah and Jonathan of his own people's history, how Rome was founded by two brothers, Romulus and Remus, descendants of Aeneas, a surviving prince of Troy. As children, at least according to legend, the brothers were nursed and raised by a she-wolf. He left out the part where Romulus murdered Remus and made himself king.

Crassus had gone on to explain how in the beginning Rome was ruled by kings for hundreds of years, until the rule of the seventh king called Tarquin, who, after raping a noble woman named Lucretia, was deposed by a great man called Lucius Brutus.

Brutus set up a constitution of magistrates elected by the people to represent them, and two elected consuls with the power of veto, who were the highest authority, except in time of national crisis. Then one man would be voted to the office of *dictatore,* having supreme authority for no more than six months before having to relinquish his power back to the consuls and the senate.

Crassus had relayed the story of Cincinnatus, the retired Roman consul elected to the office of *dictatore* in order to save a Roman army trapped and cut off by warring Aequians. He told how, after the victory, which was almost immediate, Cincinnatus could have held onto power because he had the love of the people, but sixteen days after his nomination, he abdicated the post and went back to his plow, like a true, freedom-loving Roman. Later, he was again appointed *dictatore* to stop a rogue politician who tried to make himself king.

Cincinnatus prevented this, then once more returned his power to the people.

"So you can see," Crassus had proudly explained to Judah and Jonathan, "Romans sympathize with your struggle against tyranny. We hate kings in general. Romans are true republicans, committed to freedom, and power in the hands of the people."

Now Crassus couldn't believe it. The politicians were considering abandoning their commitment and oath of friendship, which he himself had been ordered to offer to Judah on behalf of Rome. And now, at the very moment the Israelites needed it most, the Romans hesitated to help.

§

Hebron is seldom this docile, Naomi thought, *seldom this desolate.* She walked toward the only market she thought might still be open. Heberon was a city on the border of Idumea and southern Judea with a multinational population of both Israelites and Idumeans. Since the Hebrew army's advancement toward the southern Judean border, the Idumean population, loyal vassals of the Seleucid Empire, had fled further south. Most of the Jewish residents had already fled as well, traveling north because of rumors that the massive Syrian army was headed straight for their city.

Naomi was twenty-two years old and had three children. After the victory at Beth-Horn and the Jews' new hope that God would restore Israel to freedom, Naomi's husband, Jesse, had decided to follow what his heart had long yearned for. He would depart his family, go join the Maccabees, and fight.

Naomi remembered those nights before he left, the screaming and crying making her sadness all the more bitter. When he ignored her pleas not to abandon his family, her pain had changed to contempt. Still, Jesse had refused to capitulate.

"How are we to live righteously if we live as slaves?" he had asked. "How are we to be blessed by God when some who are capable of resisting, yet stand idly by, as the Lord is blasphemed by Gentiles? How can we call ourselves chosen if we abandon our faith and bend our knees to pagans and their idols?"

"Let others fight this war!" she had begged. "Let those without infant sons go and die. Do not leave your children, your family! We are helpless without you!"

"It is because of my family that I go," he had firmly and quietly replied. "I will not let my children grow up in a world where the chosen people of God are enslaved."

Despite the anger and pain, Naomi had been proud. Looking back, she knew he had done the right thing. She missed him greatly. Jesse had fought in the battle of Emmaus, briefly returning afterwards with his share of the spoils. It was more than enough to sustain the family for months.

Naomi could not leave the city now, in spite of her fears and the threat. If her husband returned, he would be unable to find her, and the open road was no safe place for a woman alone with small children.

Now the streets seemed vacant, with less than half the people on the streets as were usually out. She approached the market at the north edge of town. Getting near, she found a small crowd gathered around a young man who looked like he just had stopped running. He was perspiring heavily, trying to catch his breath. *Does he have news about the Syrians?* she wondered. She moved closer to hear.

"What do you mean defeated? Who's defeated?" an old man in the crowd was asking. The young man took a drink from a cup someone offered. He drained it, apparently still trying to catch his breath.

"The army is destroyed," he gasped as last. "Judah . . . has completely destroyed the Syrian army."

A wave of relief and wonder passed through the listeners.

"What? How?" multiple voices asked.

"We were tracking them down the coast for miles," the

young man answered. "Sixty thousand of them. Judah knew exactly where he wanted to attack. He waited until the army turned north toward the road that passes through Beth-Zur. He divided us into four groups in a place where the road descended into a narrow gorge. We attacked in two groups of one thousand each, along the enemy's flank. They were trapped with nowhere to go, unable to really mobilize against us. They seemed poorly trained—probably fresh recruits and mercenaries."

The woman who had offered him a drink, offered the cup again, and the young man again drained it eagerly. Wiping his mouth with his sleeve, he drew a deep breath and went on with his story.

"Judah had three thousand of us there, arrayed in battle on the slope above. Their phalanx in the gully tried to attack our uphill position, but we slaughtered them. Maccabee himself and Jonathan, his brother, were right next to me—fighting as if they were driven by the power of God."

A murmur passed through the crowd, and cries of "Glory to God!" When it grew quiet, the young man continued. "The forward Syrian phalanx broke and retreated right into their own lines, where the rest were still being attacked. The whole Syrian army went into a frenzy and took flight. There was a great slaughter, and the Syrians who didn't die fled toward the coast with their leader, Lysias. Judah had five-thousand men waiting in reserve, ready to attack the rear and turn the battle, but all the Syrians retreated before the force could even be used. I was sent here by Simon, the brother of Maccabee, to warn your city to be on alert for any Syrians who may flee in this direction."

The crowd broke out in an uproar of questions. Naomi wanted to ask if the young man knew her husband and if he was all right, but her words were drowned out. One man's voice broke through the cacophony. "What of Maccabee, and his patriot army?"

"Maccabee and the army are now marching on Jerusalem,"

the young man replied joyously. "He's going to retake the City of David. Our people will have their freedom!"

Naomi felt warm tears of relief running down her cheeks. She began praying that Jesse was still safe. People started singing and praising God out loud, and Naomi knew she would never forget this moment.

§

Judah, astride his horse, trotted down the southern road toward Jerusalem, his army—nine-thousand-strong now—trailing behind him.

After the battle with Lysias yesterday, he and his men had ceremonially bathed. They waited until this morning to head for Jerusalem. Outwardly, Judah looked austere, dignified, and collected, but inwardly, he felt ill at ease. *Sometimes it is hard to turn it off*, he thought, *the face you reserve for battle, the detachment from it all.* Was the fatigue of endless fighting and constant war at last getting to him? He wondered.

Judah remembered an argument that had erupted between him and Jonathan the night before. The quarrel had been pointless, caused by his own irritability. *Control your temper,* he admonished himself. *The whole nation looks to you now.*

He rode forward, appearing to the onlookers benevolent and kingly. In the distance he could see the Mount of Olives and where the valley of Kidron merged with the valley of Hinnon.

A procession of Jewish families waited and watched by the gray stone gate of the city. Cheering, they lined both sides of the road. Many were praising God. The faces of the young and old looked up at him, bright with admiration and gratitude. He had lived up to his name. He was The Hammer. Their leader had accomplished the unimaginable.

It's the army they should be admiring, Judah thought . . . the army, these patriots, the sons of Jacob, who had stood firm against hopeless odds, in the face of tyranny. News of their valor would spread through the world, telling all nations that Israel was free and would never again be trodden down by Gentiles.

Judah gazed at the city as he approached the valleys ahead. Beyond the walls, he could see the temple mount, and above it, the temple itself—the temple of God, the one place in the world where his people could look to remember who they are, and all God had done for them.

It was right there on that very spot, on Mount Morria, that Abraham adhered to the will of God, faithful to the point of sacrificing his own son—and he would have, if God had not intervened and prevented it. At that same location, the Lord promised Abraham his descendants would be as numerous as the stars in the sky, and in his descendants all nations of the world would be blessed. At that same place, King David had planned to create a house to the Lord, but God had said through Nathan, His prophet, "The Lord will make you a house. When your days are fulfilled and you lie down with your ancestors, I will raise up your offspring after you . . . and I will establish his kingdom. He shall build a house for my name, and I will establish the throne of his kingdom forever. I will be a father to him, and he like a son to me."

Because David was a man of war, the privilege of building a house for God was left to his son, Solomon, who built the temple, after David made the financial arrangements. Glimmering on that mountain, it stood as a symbol to all the nations of God's presence and His covenant with the people of Israel. It remained there until the day Nebuchadnezzar laid siege to Jerusalem for a third time, and leveled the temple along with the city, bringing the Israelites to Babylon in chains.

Seventy years later, Cyrus conquered Babylon. So impressed was he by the Hebrews that he ordered them released, giving them funds to rebuild their beloved temple. Reconstructed, the temple had then stood in splendor, atop its shining hill, until the day Antiochus defiled it, raising a pagan idol in the Holy of Holies, desecrating the altar with the blood of unclean animals, in the wake of his massacre.

Judah's scouts had informed him that every last Syrian soldier had pulled back into the citadel, preparing for a long siege, but the city itself was unprotected. Judah realized with awe that he was doing something only a handful of kings and conquerors had ever done in history. He was about to take the city of Jerusalem, and he was about to do it without a fight.

I wish Father could have been here to see this day, Judah thought with nostalgia. *I wish Adi could see us now. She would hardly believe it. But who knows?* he asked himself. *Perhaps she can.*

The first thing he would do is cleanse the temple, he decided. Every piece of furnishing, every article, would be purified. He would tear down the altar and rebuild a new one, cleansing the house of the Lord from all the unrighteousness the Gentiles had inflicted.

Then he would establish a new order. There were those who would make him king, but he would not violate the covenant that God had made with David and his offspring. One day a descendent *would* rise from the line of David and take the throne of Israel, and when that day arrived, *he* would support him. But he could not, meanwhile, leave the people in anarchy, without a leader.

It was the army that deserved credit for all that had happened. Still, it was he who was riding a horse at their head. It was he who they looked to for leadership. *I'll create a new order after the name of my grandfather, Hasmoneus,* thought Judah. *I'll create a ruling order, not a monarchy.* The title of king was reserved for the children of David's tribe. He and his brothers were sons of a priest, descendants of the tribe of Levi. They would lead and rule, until God sent them a king from the line of David.

Though Simon was the only practicing priest, Judah and his other brothers all had been trained as priests, or *kohan*, by their father. That was the custom for all male Levites, the direct descendants of Aaron, brother of Moses. Their training included practices in sacrificial offerings and an in-depth study of the scriptures.

The high priesthood, first held by Aaron, maintained no political authority in the beginning. That changed after the fall of the David's dynasty and the Babylonian exile. Now the high priest was an ethnarch—his religious authority expanded to include political authority.

The office had lain vacant ever since the last legitimate high priest, Jason, had fled to Egypt before Antiochus's massacre of Jerusalem. Seleucid's puppet, Menelaus, a man ineligible for the position because of his Benjamite lineage, had fled north to Syria. Now the people were crying for Judah to be king, to rule their land and reestablish their own form of government. But Judah would not violate the Davidic covenant. He could however, because of his training and lineage, rule through the high priesthood. He would simply make himself the high priest, and rule the land until a son of David would one day take the throne as king.

Judah felt peace in his heart with this decision. He knew his plan was righteous. It did not violate the Davidic covenant. He had the backing of his army, and the support and love of the people. Now political dominion over all of Judea was within his grasp. All he had to do was take it.

§

Laodice looked down at her son, Antiochus V, as he slept. The boy, although only three years old, already resembled his father. Laodice feared who one day he might become. The past three years of raising him had worn on her. She was still beautiful, though she felt constantly tired and like a prisoner in her own palace with the way Lysias kept such a close watch over her. With the exception of the king himself, she hated Lysias the most, and the idea that she would need to plot his death, to ensure her own survival, had occupied her mind for almost a year.

She had been grieved when rumor from the east had reached her ears of the cook Theopilus's murder by the king's guards. She had then contemplated killing Lysias, or even seducing him to turn him against the king, but she knew that wouldn't work. The hate they bore for each other was too deep, and the loyalty he bore for Antiochus was too strong. Besides, Lysias, like the king, was more partial to giving his affections to young men. Now Lysias was in Judea, and she hoped he would die there.

She walked into her room and opened her cupboard where the letter was hidden. She wanted to read it again. Three months before, it had arrived, the precious letter from her son, Demetrius. In it, he referred to an earlier letter that she could only speculate had been lost or intercepted by one of Lysias's agents. Her son was alive—Demetrius, rightful king of the Seleucid Empire! She felt overwhelmed, reluctant to let herself believe it. After all these years, after she had long since believed the lies of his death, he still lived, a prisoner in Rome.

He needs my help, she told herself. She could barely even remember him. He'd be all grown up now. It had been nineteen years after her father, in his cruelty, traded the poor boy to Rome for the release of that dung heap, Antiochus her husband.

Demetrius can take this throne, she thought. *He can kill Antiochus and Lysias and all those who have wronged me.* She had to help him. She would send men to aid in his escape, and bring him back home where he could build an army.

Suddenly a horrifying realization came over her. Her son Antiochus. One day he would be a man, and a rival to the throne. Demetrius would know this. *No,* she answered herself. *You will convince him not to bring any harm on his brother. He'll listen to you. He has to, especially if it is you who rescue him.*

She tried to push away any lingering doubt. How can a mother choose between her children when the life of one may mean the death of another? But her darling boy, Demetrius, was alive, and that was all that mattered. He was always such a sweet child. She was so young when he was born, only sixteen, and he was the son of her love, Seleucus, who when they were children, had protected her from the horrible Antiochus. For all she knew, it was Antiochus who had Seleucus killed. Everyone always assumed that Heliodorus, the minister, acted alone when he assassinated Seleucus. Perhaps Antiochus had put him up to it, knowing it would create an opportunity to for him appear like a hero by rallying support and taking the throne back. He didn't have to worry about Demetrius, as the boy was a hostage in Rome. By default, Antiochus became viceroy and ruler. After that, all he had to do was kill Laodice's younger son by Seleucus. He did so, poisoning him, and so the throne became his.

Tears came to Laodice's eyes as she remembered her grief when she realized her little boy was gone. She couldn't picture him living anymore. She could not imagine how he was when he was still alive, playing and laughing. The image of his dead body, pale and grotesque, was all she could remember.

I have to save Demetrius, she told herself. *He's all that's left of my beloved Seleucus.*

Chapter 34

NABIS TURNED THE lever of the creaking winepress, as the lid descended atop the square stone cavity in the earth. All around him were the sounds of celebration, the joyous cheers of the other vineyard workers. In that moment he thought of Orestes, who had pulled him from battle, saving his life. His friend must now be trapped in the citadel, Nabis reasoned—if he was even alive.

Nabis and Abishag had traveled north trying to get to the Port of Joppa, where Nabis had planned to book them passage to Ephesus, the last location where he had known his family to reside. He had enough money saved up for the journey, more than enough for them to get there and begin to establish themselves. Then suddenly, they were penniless. Their robbery came not in the form of brigands, but children.

As they passed through Gederah, Bedouin children had stolen their largest coin purse, which was buried deep in the satchel on their mule. The children took the money while their mother was begging for alms. Nabis had hardly noticed what the youngsters were doing as they galloped playfully about, their laughter mixing with their mother's supplications. He had been distracted when he opened the coin bag on his hip to give the women a tetradrachm. He thought he was being overly generous. She began praising him, thanking him for his kindness before quickly moving away.

The tetradrachm was more than enough to feed her and her children for over a week, but as soon as he had given it to her, she approached the next passerby to beg for money as well. Nabis had shaken his head baffled, wondering if she had realized the value of the coin he had given her. He noticed, too, that she wasn't keeping a close watch on her children as they gallivanted down the street in the opposite direction.

Later that evening at the inn in Gederah, he discovered he had been robbed. He still had the small money bag he kept on his hip, and the even smaller one laced around his neck, but without warning, most of their money had vanished. Nabis was furious, and Abishag was sad. She felt responsible for not noticing what the children were up to.

Nabis was in despair. What he had around his neck wouldn't cover their night at the inn, and what was on his belt wouldn't feed them for a week. Everything was gone.

Abishag was so taken aback and distraught at Nabis's ferocity that she somberly suggested he sell her to a slave trader for money, although she knew in her heart that would kill her. Nabis grew more enraged at this, shouting at her for the absurdity of the suggestion. He was shaken, trying to comprehend if she even understood love, or what marriage was, or what she meant to him.

Though he loved her, all he could show in that moment was anger and spite. Then she had wept, not knowing what to do or how to act, just wanting to make it better. At the sight of her tears, Nabis eased his petulance, trying to control the anger that engulfed him. She sat next to him, her hand on his back, her head on his shoulder. "*Ratzon ha'El*," was all she said.

"What?" Nabis tiredly replied.

"The will of God," she answered in Greek. She told him a story from the Torah, how Jacob the son of Isaac sojourned in the east, where he fell in love with a girl of his mother's kinsman, named Rachel. Jacob loved her so much that he offered to work for her father, Laban, for seven years—provided he would agree, in lieu of wages, to give him Rachel in marriage. After seven years of hard labor, Laban had then tricked Jacob, veiling his oldest daughter Leah, and substituting her as his bride during the ceremony. Distraught, Jacob then agreed to work another seven years to win Rachel as his second bride—which he did, and finally they were married.

Having two wives and two maidservants, which was customary at the time, Jacob had twelve sons. God gave Jacob a new name: Israel. The descendants of his twelve sons became the twelve tribes of Israel. Abishag's story calmed Nabis, or at least took his mind off the fact that everything he owned had been stolen.

The next morning Nabis walked through the streets, looking for the Bedouin woman or her thieving children, but there was no trace. The only help he got was from a Hebrew citizen who said, "Always be wary of Bedouins. They are habitual thieves—and good at it, too."

By the end of the week, they had made it to Hadid. Three days later, he sold his mule, which should have given them money to live on for a month, but as they tried to travel north on the Samarian border, the money began to dwindle. Finally, when there was only enough to last them a few more days, Abishag told Nabis that before the insurrection, there were members of her mother's family living in Aphek. The following day, to keep from hunger, they had gleaned handfuls of grain from a field. They made the journey to Aphek without one coin remaining.

Fortunately, Abishag's relations still resided in the village. Abishag told Mary, her mother's cousin, that Nabis was a Spartan trader whose father was an Israelite. She said they had been married in the past year, that he was in Judea to help supply the patriot army, but that all of his goods were stolen, leaving them impoverished.

Abishag couldn't believe she was capable of lying to her family like that, but she couldn't tell them the truth. She couldn't tell them that Nabis was a Syrian soldier and she had been his slave. The truth would be more shocking than the lie. If they found out that Nabis was a Syrian soldier, not only would they not help them, they might try to kill Nabis.

Mary's husband, Zebulun, owned a vineyard. He said he would put up the couple as long as necessary. If they needed money, Nabis could work on his winepress—an offer which Nabis gratefully accepted. Abishag had asked where their son John was, who was close to her age. Mary explained, with sadness, that he was killed at Beth-Horn fighting for the patriot army.

Weeks had since passed, while Nabis worked the winepress and helped in the vineyard. He could not help but worry that Zebulun might have figured out he was not of Hebrew descent. Every time Nabis and Abishag spoke, in the forefront of their minds was their need to conceal the truth. One evening Zebulun spent the entire meal raging about the evil Seleucid dogs and how, in the end, every one of them would be slaughtered and burn in Hades.

Early the next morning, Nabis and Abishag woke up to sounds of joyous celebration. A rider had passed through the town at dawn, bringing word that the Hebrew people were, at last, free. Eight days prior, Judah Maccabee and the rebels had been victorious in an enormous battle at Beth-Zur against Lysias. Judah had taken Jerusalem.

§

Everything seemed muted as the large stone slab fell off the side of the temple mount. Then the silence was shattered with an exploding crack as the piece of temple altar collided with the stones of the earth below. The thick, rectangular slab dashed into fragments on impact against the white rock, crumbling.

Judah stared down from atop the temple foundation. He had ordered the altar to be torn apart and destroyed. "I will not have the altar of the Lord shared with pagan gods, tainted with the sacrifice of unclean animals," he had said to his people.

The masons were nearly finished reconstructing the new altar. Judah stared across from the temple mount at the citadel, called the Acra, where every remaining Seleucid soldier was busy trying to improve the fortifications. He could see the soldiers stare from the fortress walls. Outside, Judah's men were besieging the citadel, surrounding it. His army was trying to locate the cistern that provided water to the enemy. The plan was to either close it off, or to use it to sneak men inside to open the fortress gates. Judah stood motionless as the workers cast another large slab off the side of the temple mount.

When they had entered Jerusalem eight days before, the Jewish force saw that the city gates had been burned. Clearly, the place was in a state of anarchy. When they came to the mount and ascended the stairs after ceremonially bathing, they found the temple walls covered in graffiti and licentious scribbling left by Syrian soldiers. The temple looked like no one had been inside it for years. Weeds grew through cracks in the floor. The walls were bare except for the dirt and cobwebs.

In the Holy of Holies—the back room that hundreds of years before had housed the Ark of the Covenant, the room the high priest alone was permitted to enter, and only on ceremonial occasions—there stood an atrocity: Antiochus's ten-foot-tall statue of Zeus. The naked idol was carved from stone, brandishing what once had been a chiseled bolt of lightning but now was a weathered stub.

You are the high priest now, Judah had told himself, taking hold of an iron sledgehammer. He had walked past the temple porch. To his right lay the collapsed table of showbread. He continued through the holy place where the altar of incense was. The veil shrouding the Holy of Holies was no longer there—just a gaping hole where the blasphemous pagan idol stood, staring down at him. Judah's heart churned in derision, He moved toward it until the statue was right before him.

Bellowing in anger, he then lifted the heavy hammer above his head, bringing it down on the idol. The hammer cleaved the ankle, breaking off the statue's leg at the knee. The idol wobbled a moment, off-balance, then came crashing forward, gravity and the temple floor cracking its limbs as it landed. The body broke into thirds, and the face slammed hard against the stone, its nose breaking on impact. Judah raised the hammer again and brought it down on the idol's head, dashing it to pieces.

Afterwards, his people swept the mess away, pushing the remains of the statue over the edge of the temple mount. Then they had begun cleaning, rebuilding, and refurbishing the temple.

They had found only enough oil in the temple to keep the menorah lit for one day, but it had stayed radiantly lit through the entire rededication process. Now it was the eighth day, and the menorah still shone brightly. Some of the more mystic soldiers and masons proclaimed it to be a miracle. This morning, Judah had announced that today worship would once again commence. "Henceforth," he'd said, "in the years to come, for eight days of this month of Kislev, we will celebrate this rededication, this illuminated festival—this *Hanukkah.*"

Now, as Judah stared out from the temple mount toward the citadel, he realized how close to the brink of obliteration they still were. He knew the Syrians would return. Now that he had fractured Seleucid control not just within Judea but the region, the empire would perceive him even more as a threat. For all the tyrants knew, Judah was on the verge of uniting every surrounding nation against them.

"How long do you think they can hold out?" Jonathan asked, approaching his brother, seeing him stare at the citadel. The masons pushed another stone slab over the edge of the cliff. It crashed below with a thunderous bang.

"If we can't get to their water cistern, who knows—a year maybe," Judah answered.

"Word is spreading that we've won our freedom. All the surrounding countries that relied on the Seleucid Empire to keep order, and keep us oppressed, are panicking. The Idumean cities are levying conscripts because they heard what we did to the Seleucids."

Idumea was a region south of Judea inhabited by the descendants of the Edomites, the offspring of Isaac's twin brother, Esau. Edom had always had animosity toward Israel, until David conquered them. Later, when Babylon subdued the region, most of the Edomites were relocated, but a small remnant remained and migrated south of Judea, calling the place Idumea.

"I knew they would," Judah said. "After the festival, I will send men to fortify Hebron, to ensure they don't attack our southern cities out of pure fear."

"Do you really think they will?" Jonathan asked.

"I hope not," Judah responded, sick of fighting and sick of war.

"Maybe they'll see that if we can defend against an empire like the Seleucids, then—"

"They'll take that as weakness on the part of Seleucids, not as strength on our part."

The silence lingered a long moment.

"I wish Father were here to see this," Jonathan said. "He would have been happy."

Chapter 35

"THEY ARE ALL gone," Mithridates said in a low voice to Phriaates, his brother, as they rode out of earshot from the cavalry force at their back. "Every voice of opposition, every political opponent— I've not left one alive. No voice that would dare to speak up among the old tribes is left with breath to protest my domination of our people. All submit to me now."

Phriaates nodded, at last understanding the sudden absence of many of the Parthian chieftains. "Now we expand west?"

"I've secured the trade routes to the east, and before us lie forest and desert. I will carve out of this world a region for our family, my children, and for our tribes."

"And how far will we go?" asked Phriaates. "We can't chase Antiochus all the way to the ends of Persia, can we?"

Mithridates gave a sardonic smile and patted the side of his horse. "Babylon," he answered. "I'm going to take Babylon. I'll create a new era of Parthian rule, where Parthia is esteemed as one of the world's great empires. Babylon is the key. It always has been."

"Antiochus is trying to raise money in Persia, but he's also gathering soldiers," cautioned Phriaates. "We don't want to overstep our supply line too far."

"Brother, have you not yet realized that our enemies *are* our supply line? I will take from that swine his land and his kingdom. For years, he has treated my countrymen with malice, hoping to make us his puppet. He is the embodiment of evil. One only need look at what he did to the Jews.

Phriaates listened to these words with wonder, awed at the extent of his brother's audacity and ambition.

"He worships his many gods," Mithridates went on. "We worship the Mazda, and for all I know, the Hebrew God and Mazda are one and the same. I will take everything from Antiochus, because he is weak. Even after all the torment he's inflicted, he still cannot hold onto Judea, any more than he can hold onto Parthia. The time is right to take his kingdom from him and build an empire for our people out of the ashes of his own."

§

Naomi heard the shouts through the curtain of her open window. "Stay here!" she ordered her three young children.

She hurried down the steps into the street. All around her, people were running frantically north, through the main housing quarter. Finally she recognized the husband of a friend. "What's happening?" she cried out, instinctively afraid for her children.

"The Idumeans—they've attacked the southern wall!" the man cried. "The soldiers Maccabee sent couldn't hold them. They're all dead! Stay in your home! Hide!"

"Wait! Where are you going?" she called, but he was already running away with the crowd. *God protect us,* she prayed. She had heard from one of the patriot soldiers, whose home was in Hebron, that Jesse was alive and with the army in Jerusalem. She had asked herself why he could not be here. Now she was glad he wasn't.

She ran up the stairs to her flat, as a woman down the street screamed.

"What's wrong, Mother?" the youngest boy asked as Naomi came through the door. The two older children trembled, too afraid to say anything at all.

She bolted the lock.

"Nothing, sweetheart," she answered tremulously.

§

The sun rose in the east, and the cool air blew in from the balcony of the old Syrian governor's palace. Judah thought with contentment how well the rededication had gone. After the altar was rebuilt and the inside refurnished, the whole city had celebrated, and sacrifices were again being offered to their God.

Most of the Hellenistic Jews had fled south with the Sadducees, afraid of what the mass influx of Mosaic Jews pouring into the city might do to them. Out beyond the temple, most of Judah's men camped, surrounding the citadel. He had sent troops to start a garrison at Beth-Zur, and armed men to Hebron. He also had ordered the masons to begin rebuilding the wall of Jerusalem, which had fallen into disrepair due to the neglect of the Syrians.

For the first time since he could remember, he had slept in the warmth of a bed. He missed Adi, and how she made him feel. The bed reminded him of her absence. He found it hard to believe that in one day he went from living on the plains, sleeping on a blanket in a tent, to a palace. *Is this how David felt going from a sheepherder to nobility?* Judah wondered, as he moved toward the comfortable chair to sit.

Abruptly, Eleazar barged through the door. "Judah!" he cried, his face distraught. "The Idumeans—they've attacked Hebron. They also ambushed our troops on the road who were headed there to protect the inhabitants."

He handed Judah the letter. Judah stared at it coldly, not wanting to read it. *I knew this might happen,* he thought to himself. He had prayed it could be averted. Why was it only the children of Israel who had no right to live? Why would the world not leave them in peace? *We're no longer subjected to a Seleucid tyrant, so these fools attack us for it. Why do they hate us? Why is it us alone that the world insists on destroying and blotting out from the light of the world?*

Then he remembered a passage from one of the books of Moses where God said to Abraham, "I will bless those who bless you, and the one who curses you I will curse, and in you shall all families of the earth be blessed." Well, the descendants of Edom, the Idumeans, had cursed his people's name this day, making war on the Jews for no reason. Judah would make sure the Idumeans were cursed in turn. He would indeed now become the hammer of God, bringing vengeance for the Lord's sake, and for his nation's sake, because the Jews, too had a right to exist.

"Assemble the men." he said dispassionately.

"But the citadel, the siege!" Eleazar answered. "That is how the Idumeans *want* us to react!"

"*Assemble* the men," his brother repeated.

סֵפֶר שִׁישִׁי

Book VI
Judah

164 BC

"Behold, all those who were incensed against you shall be ashamed and disgraced; they shall be as nothing, and those who strive with you shall perish. You shall seek them and not find them— those who contended with you. Those who war against you shall be as nothing, as a nonexistent thing. For I, the Lord your God, will hold your right hand, saying to you, 'Fear not, I will help you.'"

~ Isaiah

βιβλίο Έξι

Chapter 36

"HE'S DEAD," THE physician said. The room full of guards and servants let out perfunctory, loud lamentations. Antiochus lay with his eyes partly open. Everyone had known he couldn't hold on much longer. He had relapsed into his madness once more upon learning the Hebrews had destroyed Lysias's army and had taken Jerusalem. He was depressed for days after that, then violent. Then came his total split from reality.

For three weeks, Antiochus didn't know who or where he was. He lashed out at everyone he saw, and spoke in indiscernible phrases that made no sense even to the mediums and priests. There were those in the army who suspected he was cursed by the magi, the Parthian spiritual leaders, or by the god of Israel.

Then, when everyone thought he was on the verge of death from malnutrition, Antiochus emerged from his delirium. He was himself again, and the inner corps of leadership felt a glimmer of hope once more, but still the king would not eat. Urion tried to reason with him, as did his slaves, concubines, and lovers, but to no avail. He remained bedridden. He looked like he had aged twenty years in a single month. His eyes were sunken, and his cheekbones protruded. His skin looked like wax. His now-thinning hair became white. His teeth began to rot and fall out.

On the last day before he lost his ability to speak, the king ordered Urion to bring in Philip, one of Antiochus's male lovers whom he had arbitrarily—in a fit of rage—made a general. Philip was passive by nature, and his mannerisms were effeminate.

"I'm dying, Philip," the king proclaimed from his bed. Urion had noticed that the supposed general had tears welling in his eyes. "But when I'm gone, *you* will be king," he croaked weakly.

"What?" Urion blurted out, in disbelief.

"When I die," Antiochus gasped, ignoring Urion, clasping his crown to his chest. "You are to rule in my place, until my son is of age."

This is insane, Urion had thought. Did the king not realize he had already appointed Lysias as viceroy? This would start a civil war among regent kings! Or was the king so displeased with Lysias's defeat by the Hebrews, that he no longer wanted him to rule?

The king reached out with trembling hands and bestowed his diadem on Philip, who burst into tears as he received it. Urion thought about grasping the makira sheathed on the belt of a bodyguard and running the soft, feeble general through. *He's unfit even to bear a spear in war, let alone hold a command as general, or be a king!* Urion shouted inside his own mind.

After Philip finally departed the room, sobbing, Urion tried to talk to the king, hoping he would listen to reason, hoping he had some faculty of mind remaining, but the effort was useless. Antiochus waved Urion away. The next day the king could no longer speak, and for two days after, he lay propped up on his bed, silently staring at everyone around him. His generals and servants remained by his bedside. On the third day, he finally stopped breathing.

Urion knew that night they would build a massive pyre, put coins on his eyes for the boatman, and set the body alight. He knew in the morning General Philip would announce the abandonment of the Parthian campaign and take the remaining army west to march on Antioch, in order to take the throne that had just been given to him.

§

Judah stared up at the tower of the Idumean fortress of Akrabattene. Archers shot down into his ranks as his men trudged forward. Two runners, brandishing torches, darted ahead of the formations. Both hurled their oil-filled skins, along with their firebrands, upon the tower's gate. The dead were strewn on the open ground beneath the tower. Rocks were being dropped from the battlements, and one dashed down upon one of the runners, mangling him.

Judah could see the doors burst into flames and the surviving runner fall back to the lines as Benjamin and his archers took aim toward the embrasures. The fire erupted quickly, and the army waited, transfixed as the flames consumed the thick dried wood of the tower gates.

After Judah had left Hebron, his men were attacked by Ammorites who had allied themselves with Idumea. Both nations had a lasting hatred for Israel. The Ammorites, originally from the kingdom of Ammon (later called Amathus) just east of Samaria, were the progeny of the incestuous relationship between Abraham's nephew, Lot, and one of Lot's two daughters. According to the story, both sisters had made their father strong drink and, after he drank it, seduced him. Each one conceived. The oldest gave birth to Moab, whose descendants occupied the area east of Judea. The youngest gave birth to Ammon, whose offspring inhabited the area just to the north of Moab.

Judah had left one-third of his force in Jerusalem under Jonathan, who oversaw the siege of the Acra citadel. Gaddi, Simon, and Eleazar came with Judah to deliver their people from the assailing nations. The leader of the attacking Ammorites, named Timothy, not only had a compulsive hatred for Jews, but was being paid by Lysias. When Judah entered Hebron to refortify the city and to bury the countless dead, he had seen the devastation written on the faces of his soldiers. It made him sad and furious.

Jesse, one of Eleazar's men, had dropped to his knees in the street, overcome at the sight of his wife's ravished corpse lying next to their dead children. "Naomi," he sobbed uncontrollably. "This is my fault. I should have been here."

Judah understood his grief, the realization of finality. He came forward and put a hand on Jesse's shoulder. There was nothing he could say that would help. He only hoped his presence might be a comfort.

The next day, on the open plains, Judah and his soldiers had engaged a coalition of Idumeans and Ammorites, led by Timothy. Judah had decimated them. The survivors fled to the east, leaving the Idumean cities undefended. Judah laid siege to Jazar, and after he had burned it to the ground, moved south to the surrounding villages. In every town he attacked, first he offered terms of peace. When these were not accepted, he gave his men strict orders not to harm the women or children. He remembered what God had commanded Moses: "When the Lord your God gives it into your hand, you shall put all its males to the sword. Only the women and the children and animals and all that is in the city, all its spoils, you shall take as booty for yourself."

After Judah took the Idumean villages, he turned toward the city of Akrabattene. The tower was their last stronghold. Judah had hoped that those on the inside had been foolish enough to build a barricade of wooden debris behind their thick cedar gates.

Now that the fire was bursting forth from the kindling gates, it was clear they had. Those inside began to panic as smoke started billowing through the embrasures. Judah and his brothers held back, waiting to see if the fire would die out or continue to climb. Soon, the arrows stopped as those inside the tower fled in search of escape. The fire expanded, and the wooden staircase of the tower ignited, as did the surrounding internal beams, turning the whole tower into a furnace. Flames crawled up the outer stone walls, turning the tan stone black with soot. In the end, those who moved back toward the crest of the tower made the choice to leap, or burn alive inside. Within twenty minutes, the screams had ended, and no one was left alive.

§

On the hillside, a rider sat atop his horse eating an apple he had picked from a nearby tree. The sun rose bright just above the distant hills, the thin rays of dawn pointing toward the city of Heshbon, just ahead. The morning was quiet, the air cool, but the day would soon be hot. Heshbon was a city with high stone walls that lay just east of the Jordan in a land known as Tob. The inhabitants were mostly Jewish, and the rider knew that this was why he was there.

Hearing a rustling of grass, he threw what was left of the apple onto the ground.

"No sign of anyone?" asked Timothy, his general, appearing from behind him.

"No, my lord," the rider answered.

"Any word from the army of Maccabee?"

"Just rumors that he's still in Idumea, ransacking every town and village there. I heard he burned down Jazar and killed every male inhabitant, only leaving alive the worthless women and children, who will probably all starve to death without their husbands."

"I heard the same. Apparently he laid siege to Akrabattene as well," Timothy replied, thinking one less Idumean city just meant fewer nuisance Idumeans. He could not care less if they *all* died. The men, the women, the children—it made no difference to him, and shouldn't to any other Ammorite. Though the Idumeans weren't putting up much of a fight, they offered a pleasant distraction, keeping the Maccabee in the south while his weak younger brother remained in Jerusalem.

And I am here, Timothy thought. Here beside this Jewish city that encroached on Moabite lands. Moloch would make them great and bring his vengeance upon the Israelites and their false god. He would wipe them out, starting with the cities west of the Jordan and moving west, pushing the descendants of Jacob into the sea.

They are a morbid people, he mused, *cutting their phalluses to commune with their god. How absurd. They keep their laws and rituals so observantly, looking down on everyone not of their race. They have the hubris to believe that God chose them. Their venomous traders profit from selling their goods to foreigners, making more money than any people should, while the Ammorites just grow poorer. They've plagued our people for hundreds of years, but their time has passed.*

People would be worshiping Moloch hundreds and thousands of years from now, but the Hebrews and their god would be forgotten. They'd tried so hard to wipe out the name of Moloch from existence. The Jews had warred against Ammon because Moloch demanded human flesh as a sacrifice. Did they really believe a god would be happy with the corpses of lambs and goats? Fools! Moloch required a firstborn child to his fires, not a worthless ram. How insulting to offer something of no value. The Moabites could worship Chemosh, and the Philistines, Dagon. Those in Tyre and Carthage could worship Baal, but none of them were superior to Moloch, least of all the Hebrews' Yahweh.

Behind the embankment, out of sight from the city, Timothy's army waited. "We are almost ready," he told the rider, who nodded and kicked his horse, moving back into the ranks. This was the perfect hour and place to attack. The Jews would still be asleep, or at least not yet alert. Even if awake, the enemy would have poor visibility, with the sunrise being in their faces.

Timothy thought back to the previous weeks when he led the coalition against Maccabee. The Hebrews had got lucky in their placement of men and the angle at which their reserve force hit his lines, but he knew it was *only* luck. Maccabee's little tricks would not work on him a second time. They were too easy to see through.

If his scouts had only informed him that Maccabee's reserve was on his left, it would have been different. His men had outnumbered the Jews. The war would have been over. It was the fault of the scouts, but probably, in the long run, for the best. Maccabee was busy burning down Idumea, and Timothy was busy burning down the Israelite border cities. In the end, Ammon would go unscathed. Then they could take lands on both sides of the Jordan and put an end to the Jew dogs and their usurpation of Canaanite lands. When it was over, the Syrians would owe them, and the Ammorites would grow and become their equal in time.

Timothy nodded to his general, and the command was given. The Ammorite soldiers began moving forward, over the crest. Soon they broke into a jog, and approaching the gate, they began to run. The man on the eastern watchtower wasn't even at his post, and the man guarding the gate hadn't noticed the band of Ammorites until they were almost upon him.

Chapter 37

JUDAH SAT UP in a cold sweat, trying to remember the details of his dream, willing himself to cling to the fading impressions.

He remembered he was clad in armor along the banks of a stream, a waterfall thundering in the distance. Upon a stone embankment, midstream, stood a man. Judah had waded toward him, wondering about his whereabouts, anxious to find his soldiers. The spear in his hand, strangely enough, was a Roman pilum.

"Judah, what are you leaning on?" asked the man when Judah reached him. He took the spear in both hands and broke the thin iron shank from the lower wooden section. "You see?" said the man. It's nothing more than clay." Judah watched as the iron shank contorted and dissolved in the water.

Suddenly Adi was there on the bank, flailing her arms, calling for him. Judah had rushed toward her, but the man called him to come back and hear what he had to say. Then the stream became a tumultuous river, and he lost his footing, sinking under the weight of his armor.

Through the murky depths, he saw his father reaching for him, but when he broke the surface, his father had transformed into the man in the middle of the stream. Then Judah saw Adi's pale body lying still in the shallow grave, partially filled with groundwater, by the stream's edge where he had buried her.

He remembered the dream completely now. He told himself it was nothing, and rose to find water to wash his face.

Simon entered into the tent. "I see you're up. Half a day's

march, and we'll be in Jerusalem," he said with a smile.

Judah yawned. "Good morning to you, too. Let the men sleep twenty more minutes, then have the night watch wake the others."

Judah walked from his tent and found a bucket of water. He still felt upset from the dream. *What did it mean?* he wondered.

One of the dogs they kept in the camp to warn of enemy presence, lifted its head, alerted at Judah's movement. The animal came over and sat beside Judah as he washed. Such dogs, called *kelevs*, were common to Israel and prevalent in the area. Still kneeling, Judah petted it behind the pointy ears, and the dog cocked its head, panting happily. Judah stood up, looking at the rays of the rising sun, feeling better.

Before the sun came over the horizon, the army had reached Jerusalem. There they were greeted by crowds as returned heroes. Judah's mood was bright. The damage they had inflicted upon the Idumean towns would completely debilitate their neighbors' aggression for a time. He knew the Ammorites had returned north to regroup. It was unlikely they would have the strength to continue a campaign anytime soon.

By noon they had completed the march back to Jerusalem. Judah returned to the governor's palace. After bathing and dressing, he heard a knock at the door. "Enter," he called, and Jonathan stepped into the spacious room and embraced him.

"We already heard what you did to the Idumean cities," said the younger man, with a smile.

"How are things here with the siege?"

"We found the cistern that supplies the citadel with water, but there's no way we can get to it. It's an older one cut off by three other channels and supplies the rest of the city with water. It would take a year to dig another channel to divert it, and by then, they will all be starved out anyway."

Judah thought a moment, tired and wanting to sleep.

Unexpectedly, Simon and Eleazar entered through the open door.

"Judah," Simon said, extending a scroll he held in his hand. Judah noticed the seal was broken, and that Simon must have read it.

"It's not good."

Judah had already gathered as much by the grim expressions his brothers bore. He took the brown rolled parchment and read.

To Judah, the Maccabee, protector of the Hebrew people. From the faithful descendants of Jacob who have fled to the stronghold of Dathema. The Gentiles around us have gathered together to slaughter us. Timothy, the Ammorite, is leading their forces. Many have fallen, and all our kindred who were in the land of Tob, numbering more than one thousand, have been massacred. The enemy has captured their wives for their soldiers to ravish, and their children for slaves. We beg you to come while there is still hope and—

Gaddi burst through the door, and Judah looked up.

"Judah!" Gaddi bellowed. "A messenger from Galilee!" Accompanying Gaddi was a man in his late twenties, with torn clothes and dried blood on his face.

"Maccabee, my lord," the man said in a tremulous voice. "The people of Ptolemais and Tyre and Sidon and all the Gentiles in Galilee have gathered together against us, to annihilate us! They're sweeping through the northern cities, massacring every Hebrew in their reach. I barely got away myself!"

We're being attacked on every border, thought Judah. Every neighboring Gentile nation was gathered against them, their hatred for Israel uniting them. "This is too organized, too timed." Judah said. "It's as if the whole world, in unison, has proclaimed that the descendants of Jacob have no place in the land of the living. They need money for this, which means that the Gentiles are arming their warriors with Seleucid weapons, paid for with Seleucid gold."

"My God!" Gaddi lamented. "We can't fight the whole world . . . not all at once."

"We can," Judah responded after a moment. "And that is exactly what we'll do. Simon, you, Gaddi, and Eleazar, take for yourselves three-thousand men and head north to evacuate the Hebrew population from every refuge, city, and village. Bring them back here, to Judea. If you encounter the Gentile armies, destroy them."

"And you?" asked Eleazar.

"Jonathan and I will go to Gilead. I will find Timothy, kill him, and rescue our brothers under siege at Dathema."

"Maybe I should stay here in Jerusalem," suggested Gaddi nervously, seeing his opportunity. "Someone has to remain and make sure the siege at the citadel is successful." Gaddi knew if he managed to sack the citadel while Judah was away, he'd be able to buy all the loyalty and support he needed with the riches housed there in the Seleucid treasury.

At that moment, Judah saw something in his brother. He didn't want to believe what his instincts were screaming.

"No," Judah replied. "I need you with Simon and Eleazar in the north. Joel and Azariah will take charge of the siege and the soldiers who remain here."

Judah could see the rage and disappointment in Gaddi's eyes, though Gaddi tried to hide it. *How unquenchable is the lust for power,* Judah thought, *but you yourself know this. You feel it, growing within you every day. Could you give it up now? You say you are weary of fighting, but would you give the power and glory to another?*

§

The hull of the ship slammed down hard against the wave. The trireme rocked almost onto its side, nearly capsizing, and the bow crashed forward into the sea, jetting back up as water washed across the deck. At the stern, Kalisto piloted the helm. The oarsmen tried in vain to keep the ship balanced against the tempest. There was no moon, and the only refuge of light was the occasional lightning that illuminated the bleak sky.

Another wave pummeled the trireme, making the whole galley shudder. Below deck, Crassus vomited into a wooden bucket. He looked ashen. Sitting up, he tried to brace himself against the bulkhead as the ship was tossed through the sea by the cyclone.

"I knew we shouldn't have traveled across the world at this cursed time of year!" Crassus shouted over the noise of the wind.

"Orders," Fabius said, a tinge of fear evident in his own face. He looked up, seeing the water dripping rapidly from the deck overhead. Everything around him was wet. He began to contemplate the possibility of the ship being dashed to pieces, and what death by drowning might be like.

"No one travels distances this time of year—nobody sane," Crassus bellowed. "I told you those hypocrites would pick us to go back and deliver the treaty. We could have traveled in the proper time of the year, but no—the vipers waited 'til the Jews already had won the war before committing to anything."

"The Seleucids will be back. Even if Antiochus is dead, Lysias won't let that defeat stand. Nor will anyone who sits on the Seleucid throne. They *will* be back, and the Jews will need our money and arms to win."

"Like they did before we arrived? Hah! We're only doing this so those greedy, power-mad Roman senators can build an alliance. They think that will help them invade the eastern kingdoms and forge their way into their trade routes. We're simply *using* the Jews. Don't you know that?"

"The safety of The Republic may depend on our ability to attack those kingdoms before they attack us. And we need those trade routes!" Fabius answered defensively.

"What a barrel of horse dung! And another thing. We're never again sacrificing a god- cursed thing, not even a pigeon's rotting scrotum, to Neptune ever again!" Crassus remembered the sacrifice to the gods that almost all Roman soldiers made before a long journey.

"You shouldn't slander a god in his own domain. It's foolish," snapped Fabius

"We should have tried worshipping the Hebrew God. Maybe then we'd have kept dry!" The boat slammed down again, creaking and rattling. Crassus began laughing, sardonically. Kalisto could hear the faint sound of the argument over the wind that seemed to cut right through him.

A wave washed into the side of the deck, almost knocking Kalisto off his feet. *Concentrate!* he scolded himself. *You can't lose it here.* One wrong move, and they'd all be dead. The sky lit up with a bolt of lightning. The bow, still rising and falling, slammed against the sea floor again. The rain picked up and stung mercilessly against his skin.

If he survived, he would return home, Kalisto decided. He would see where they burned the plague-diseased bodies of the villagers. His wife's sister lived in a neighboring village. Perhaps she was still there and could tell him more of what happened. It had been so long since he'd been back. Although his family was dead, he now knew he wanted to return.

A wave kicked underneath the ship, and for a moment Kalisto was staring straight up at the sky. Then the ship came crashing down once more, jarring him to the core. Yes, he would go back, for certain. He would go back if he lived.

Chapter 38

"HOW MANY ARE they?" Judah asked.

"I can't be sure," the Nabatean chieftain replied, sitting in a circle composed of Judah's high command and the elite among a Nabatean tribe. Shadows from the campfire flickered on Judah's face.

The Nabateans were an Arab nation whose capital was in Petra. They held oasis lands over which crossed many trade routes of countries that hated each other. The Nabateans had first established their settlement in Petra, near Edom, when Nebuchadnezzar took Israel and relocated the captive people to Babylon. The Edomite remnant moved to the grazing land south of Judea, which they named Idumea, and the Nabateans moved in from the east, taking the abandoned Edomite lands and creating a stronghold there. They were known for carving their palaces into the rock faces of sandstone canyons. Unsuccessfully and numerous times, the Seleucids had tried to annex them, which was why the Nabateans were so willing to help the Israelites now.

"They killed thousands of people in Gilead," the chieftain explained. "Many of them have been shut up in Bozrah and Bosor—in Alema and Chaspho, Maked and Carnaim. These cities are all large and strong, making it difficult for the Ammorites to take them, but Timothy has positioned all his men, besieging each city. Tomorrow he plans to take all of them at once. With the number of men he has in place, he *will* take them."

Lord, Jonathan prayed silently. *How can we defend six cities at one time?* How could they decide which ones to let fall and which to save from annihilation? Maybe some of them would hold out on their own. "Which ones have the most fortified defenses?" Jonathan asked the chieftain.

"Bozrah and Bosor. But not one of the cities will last another day. Most of them are already in the hands of the Ammorites. Only a stronghold or fortress remains for each, where the remnant has fled. By now each remnant is weak and out of food. Some may be without water. Tomorrow they all will fall."

Jonathan looked at his brother, trying to read him. He could tell Judah was planning something, calculating and weighing his options. *I wish I could be like him,* Jonathan thought, *the way he just knows what to do, the way he can manipulate our enemies, snaring them in their own plans.*

§

Three men dashed across the patio in front of the marble stairs that ascended to a veranda. They move quickly, trying to avoid detection by the Roman guards. They could hear the Latin words of the dinner party guests of the host: Senator Lucius Servius Vibius. The three had considered dressing in aristocratic clothing, but decided dressing as servants would be safest.

Senator Vibius was known as a man of the people, a true *populares.* The plebians loved him, and he often spoke of social reform to help the lower classes. In fact, he believed little of his own words. He only talked reform to keep the commoners on his side. Inwardly, he abhorred the lower class. Often he hosted parties like the one he was hosting tonight. Rome's wealthiest were invited, and they always arrived bringing lavish gifts, ensuring that any social reforms would be sure to leave their interests untouched.

On the veranda, bordered by marble columns, the talking was loud. One of the slaves dropped a silver platter holding a pitcher of wine. No one seemed to notice. The men moved around the back, away from the party, where the servants prepared food. Trying to appear inconspicuous, they entered a hallway, where, as planned, they met their contact, a eunuch named Marius. They had promised to give the young slave enough money to buy his freedom and entry into any class of society he might choose.

Marius had waited for the conspirators in the servants' quarters. "We have to be quick," he whispered. "He should be in his quarters for the party's duration, but guards and servants keep an eye out for anything unusual."

The men followed Marius through the empty cavernous room. They moved up the stairs to the bedrooms. To their right they saw what appeared to be the large bedroom of the senator. They moved in the opposite direction down the hall. Marius pulled out a key, unlocked a door, and looked around frantically to see if any servants or others were nearby, but all was silent.

In Rome, when a dignitary was taken as a political hostage, it was common practice that he not be kept in a dungeon like a criminal, but as a house guest of a prominent Roman family or the family of a politician. This policy served two purposes. First, it maintained diplomatic relations with the enemy kingdom. Second, it reduced the likelihood of escape, because Roman nobles—having a vested interest in keeping foreign hostages captive—were less prone than others to accepting bribes in exchange for a hostage's freedom.

"Where's his guard?" one of the conspirators whispered to Marius.

"I paid him. He's pretending to be sick."

The men pushed open the door. Inside was a man in his twenties, standing and reading a scroll. He looked up with a bewildered glance.

"Did the senator wish me to make an appearance?" he asked in Latin.

"Demetrius?" one of the others asked in Greek.

"Yes?"

"Your mother has sent us to get you out of Rome."

"She received my letters!"

"Yes, but we don't have much time! We need to leave this moment."

From a cupboard, Demetrius grabbed some papers and tucked them under his garment, then quickly followed the other men down the hall. All eyes scanned the lavish surroundings for any guards or servants.

"Side door," muttered Marius, altering their direction.

They walked past the kitchen without attracting attention from cooks or servers, and reached the house's back entrance. Opening the door, they found themselves face-to-face with a very surprised Roman guard.

Before the guard could react, one of the conspirators drew a dagger from under his cloak and drove the blade into the man's throat, silently dispatching him. The little group moved hurriedly toward the tree line, away from the house.

"We won't have long before someone finds him," Demetrius said, as they stopped a moment to catch their breath behind a screen of foliage.

"What's your name?" he asked the man who had killed the guard.

"Bacchides," the conspirator replied.

"We have horses waiting," one of the others said, gesturing to move forward.

"And how is my mother?" said Demetrius.

"None of us ever spoke with her," Bacchides answered. "Her messenger hired us."

Deep in the woods they found the horses where they had left them, their reins tied to tree branches. The five men mounted their steeds.

"We have to make the harbor before first light, or we'll never make it out of here," Bacchides whispered, spurring his horse's flanks.

§

It was dawn, and the air was cool. The dew of the morning had left the plains damp. Judah could see that the gates of Dathema were still shut, the walls not yet breached, but the battle had begun. He noticed at once that the number attacking the city exceeded ten-thousand Ammorites. He also saw that the arrows being fired at the attackers were few. *They must be almost out,* Judah thought. The Ammorites were moving siege engines toward the wall and were almost there.

Judah looked at his officers and his brother. "Fight today for your kindred. Our brothers and sisters are in there," he said, "fighting for their lives. If we fail them, they all will be dead by sundown."

He gave the signal, and the shofars sounded. Judah's army let out a deafening shout, charging over the embankment toward the rear of the enemy.

The night before, his soldiers had killed every Ammorite man in the neighboring city of Bozrah. The heathens were eating their fill, growing drunk with wine and enjoying the spoils of the Jewish town. The last of the Israelite survivors, held up in the fortification on the other side of the city, prepared for the final assault. Judah had rescued them, adding almost a thousand new men to his ranks. Afterwards, taking the plunder with him, he had burned Bozrah to the ground, then marched the army through the night on to Dathema.

Now, before Dathema's walls, Timothy rode astride his horse, pushing his fighters forward. He looked about and noticed the men behind him were moving to one side, away from the city walls.

He wheeled his horse. To his consternation, a screaming multitude of Israelite soldiers were charging the rear of his position. He sat there in dismay, incredulous.

Suddenly the gates of Dathema opened, and the eight-hundred Hebrews poured out, assembling in formation in front of the city walls. *They're attacking,* he thought, enraged. They were in front and behind him. For a brief moment he wondered if he could defeat the men in front and gain access to the town, but there was no time. His foot soldiers behind him were breaking from the lines and fleeing in panic as fast as they could. Few were fighting. The multitude was charging him, and it was only moments before they would be upon him.

Without a word to his men, Timothy kicked his horse and took off at a gallop, following his deserters. The five-thousand men who were left behind without any horses had no time to escape, but were trapped between two Israelite forces with no remaining leadership. Both Hebrew elements slammed into the Ammorite formations almost simultaneously.

Judah thrust his spear into the neck of an Ammorite man, whose face contorted into a shocked grimace. The Ammorites tried desperately to fight but in their confusion quickly faltered, their thinning lines compressing and deforming.

Someone stabbed at Judah with a spear. Judah raised his shield just in time to save his life. The leaf head kept driving forward slicing into the side of his waist, beneath his armor. Jonathan could see his brother wince, but Judah ignored the pain, returning the blow to his attacker.

A spear tip slammed into Jonathan's shield. He used all his strength and momentum to lunge his spear through the flimsy leather armor his attacker wore.

The lines were intermingled. Both sides of the Hebrew forces surrounded and enveloped the surviving Ammorites, who continued to fight. In moments, only the wounded Ammorites were left breathing. Over eight-thousand Ammorite bodies were littered outside the city. Some were killed standing their ground, some as they attempted to retreat. Judah knew most of them were not dead but that over the next few hours and days, almost all would die from their injuries.

Jonathan stood in front of his brother, their men re-forming.

The men of Dathema sent up a euphoric shout in joy for the salvation of their lives.

"You should have the doctor look at that," Jonathan said, gesturing toward the blood now dripping from Judah's waist and down his thigh.

"Not now. Gather those who are still able to march and hold a spear. We must save Maapha before it's taken," Judah replied.

Jonathan looked dumbfounded. *We're going to take three cities in one day?* he thought to himself.

"Judah, the men are exhausted. At this rate they won't even be able—"

"We're leaving at once," Judah interrupted.

"Alright, Maccabee," Jonathan answered, letting Judah know he was obeying as a subordinate, according to their father's wishes, while disagreeing with the order. *The men can barely stand,* Jonathan thought. Judah was wounded, and defending another besieged city that day could only be foolish *huspa* that would get every one of them killed.

Judah dismissed Jonathan's reaction. He didn't have time nor energy to enumerate the reasons why Maapha needed saving despite the risk of their exhausted army. Judah believed he understood the army's limitations, but he had faith in his men. He felt the pain in his side where the spear edge had sliced through. Jonathan was right about one thing: he should see the physician. The wound needed dressed and possibly stitched, but there was no time if they were to save Maapha.

Chapter 39

THE VILLAGE OF Arbela flushed in contrast against the blackness, as the village burned to the ground. A mile away, the Israelite army made camp against the Sea of Galilee to the east. The flames of the village illuminated the night sky, reflecting in the dark waters.

"Bring him in," Simon said to the two men, who proceeded to drag the general of the army of Sidon forward into their large tent. The man's hands were tied behind him and his ankles bound. He wore stained armor over his foreign clothes. Inside, they shoved the man to his knees, and the two guards directed their spears toward the prisoner's neck.

Simon, Eleazar, and Gaddi stared down at the man, who glared back at them with brazen eyes filled with wordless hatred. He despised them, not because they had virtually destroyed his entire army, or because they had captured him, but because they were Israelites, Jews. He tore his gaze away and stared straight ahead, accepting his fate.

"Why did you attack our people?" Simon asked calmly, looking at the man. Simon nodded to his men, who stepped back, redirecting their spears upright.

"We were at war with the Seleucid Empire, not Tyre or Sidon or the Gentiles of Galilee. Why would you attack us? What harm have we caused Sidon?" The man ignored his questions. "There was a time in the past where Israel was an ally to Sidon."

"We were never your ally!" the general burst out. "We used you when it suited us." The man glared intensely, emotion pouring out from of his voice. "We have always hated you. We *will* always hate you! Now, and a thousand years from now, we will hate you. You and your god! You can't hold on forever. You and every Israelite is a descendent of a slave—unworthy to hold any land, least of all the lands encroaching *our* borders. Every one of you will be a slave again. We will fight for years if we need to, but we won't stop until your entire people are dead, and with you, the memory of your god."

Simon, Eleazar, and Gaddi all looked at each other, amazed at the venom the Phoenician spewed forth.

At the entrance of the tent, a soldier appeared. "Sir, an urgent letter from Jonathan. I think it's about Maccabee and the army in the south."

Simon took the scroll, ignoring the general, and broke the seal, reading aloud for his brothers to hear.

To my brother Simon,

It would seem now that we are at war with all the world. The Philistines have also declared war against us, thinking us weakened. So Judah marched on Azorus and put it to the sword, ordering us to tear down their altars and graven images to false gods and burn them with fire.

Simon paused. *The Philistines, too,* he thought, dismayed.

"What of the Ammorites? What of Timothy?" Gaddi asked impatiently.

Simon continued reading.

The Philistine army was destroyed before us, and the towns surrounding Azorus we burned to the ground. In the days prior, we defeated the Ammorites at Dathema and rescued the inhabitants of Maapha. The following day, we marched on, then took Chaspho, Maked,

Bosor, and the other cities of Gilead. Afterwards, Timothy gathered his forces and encamped opposite Raphon, on the other side of the river. Judah sent men to reconnoiter the camp. They reported back that all the Gentiles had amassed an enormous force—made of Idumeans, Ammorites, and Arabs—on the far side of the river. Judah ordered the whole army to cross the river at night, and we destroyed them there on the bank, where Judah killed Timothy, their general.

Then we tried to return to Jerusalem, by way of Raphon. The only feasible approach was through Ephron, but the city was fortified and held the road, making it impossible for us to pass. The men of the city shut us out and blocked up the gates with stones. Judah sent them a cordial message, requesting permission to pass through their land to get to Jerusalem. He assured them that not one of their inhabitants would be harmed, that we would simply pass by on foot. But they refused to open the gates, and responded to our message with contemptuous insults.

Then Judah ordered the city besieged, and we fought against them all that day and throughout the night, and the city was delivered into our hands. We destroyed every male by the sword, and razed and plundered the city before passing through, over the slain, bringing the women and children with us. Then we crossed the Jordan into the large plain that borders Beth-Shan.

Judah kept rallying the laggards, and encouraging the people the whole way until we came to Judea. When we arrived, we went up to Mount Zion with gratitude and joy, and made burnt offerings, because we had not lost one refugee and had returned in safety. Then we set out again to face the Philistines.

Unfortunately, in our absence, Joel and Azariah took the remaining army out of Jerusalem and attacked Jamnia, where the Seleucid general Gorgias was camped. Gorgias and his men came out of the city to meet them in battle, and Joel and Azariah were routed and pursued to the borders of Judea. Two-thousand Israelites fell that day.

Simon remembered how Judah had given Joel and Azariah specific orders not to leave the city to engage the enemy under any circumstances. *Fools,* he thought.

Two thousand Israelites fell that day.

Judah's orders are that you complete the evacuation of the northern cities and return to Judea in haste. With their losses, the Philistine army is now completely ineffective, so tomorrow we will march again for Jerusalem.

Your brother, Jonathan Ben Mattathias

Simon stopped reading. He noticed that the Phoenician general, still on his knees, was looking around distressed, like the news of the successful campaign in the south was physically wrenching.

Gaddi took the letter with irritation. "It sounds like Judah turned every country surrounding us into a bloodbath."

"You won't continue to be victorious." the Phoenician spat. "Baal will leave your lands decimated, and the—"

"Kill him, *please*," Simon said to his men. The guards grabbed the general by the arms and dragged him from the tent, his lips quivering as he barked profanities in his native tongue.

Simon sighed. "We still have cities in the north to liberate and Israelites to save before we can return home," he said to his brothers.

§

It was hours after sundown. Nabis walked through the vineyard, not wishing to return to the home where he knew that Abishag's cousin and her husband, Zebulun, eyed him with suspicion. It had became apparent to Nabis, when Zebulun would add emphasis to certain words, when he spoke of the *Greek dogs*, while peering at him, that Zebulun suspected him.

They had to get out of there. Nabis felt like slave. The man had promised money for his labors in the vineyard, but paid him only with food and a roof over his head. At least Abishag was safe, Nabis reminded himself. She acted like she wanted to be happy there, but he knew, in truth, she was as worried as he.

The previous night Zebulun's eyes had burned with hatred. It was the anniversary of the death of his son, whom he lost at the battle of Beth-Horn. Nabis feared his life would be in danger if Zebulum finally made up his mind that Nabis was, indeed, Greek.

The region was in chaos. The Israelites there, who first rejoiced upon hearing the news of the retaking of Jerusalem, were griping and losing faith now that the Phoenicians from Sidon and Tyre were attacking their northern towns. Zebulun was constantly saying, with a bitter shrug, "It's only a matter of time until they come and kill us all. What can we do?"

Nabis looked up at the almost-full moon. From the opposite side of the vineyard, a rider emerged suddenly at a full gallop, coming straight for him. He was only a hundred yards away, then fifty. Then the man fell from his horse and tumbled onto his side, in between the hedges. Nabis darted forward. The stranger remained motionless. The horse stepped forward a few paces, then halted.

Arriving at the man's side, Nabis looked down at him. The man was curled on his side, with two arrows protruding from his back, one which had broken at the haft when he tumbled. Nabis crouched low to see if he was still breathing. He observed that the armor and clothes looked Phoenician, but the weapon was Syrian. The man's chest was rising and falling in fast, shallow breaths.

"Who did this to you?" Nabis asked.

"What? You're a Greek?" The hurt man gasped, wheezing. "Thank the gods ... A Seleucid?"

"Yes," Nabis whispered.

"I can tell by your accent. I am Phoenician." he croaked. You're a soldier?"

Nabis nodded.

"Of course. Why else would you be here in this dung heap, among such a people?" The man began to cough, hacking badly. Nabis could see in the moonlight the blood accumulating at the corners of his mouth.

"I don't have long. On my horse, in the satchel, are six bags of silver."

Nabis's eyes lit up.

"Your people and mine are allies against the Jews. I was charged to bring the money to our camp, ten miles north. We were attacked by the army of the Maccabee. That silver *must* reach camp, or the governor can't pay his soldiers, and the army will starve."

"Maccabee is here? In Galilee?"

"No," the man grimaced, his breathing growing shallower. There was the whistle of air being sucked into his chest, and Nabis knew his heart must be beating fast, trying to compensate for the loss of blood. "His brother ... our army was defeated at Galilee where I was wounded and ... and ... I ... was charged to—"

"Is someone chasing you, someone who knew you had this silver?" Nabis asked.

"Shot me . . . doubled back . . . lost him, I think." The man's head tilted, and a passive look came over his face. His eyes looked cloudy and vacuous in the moonlight. Nabis shook him, but there was no response. Nabis had seen the look before, and knew that he was gone.

Glancing around, Nabis listened for sounds. All was silent. He stood and walked to the horse that was lathered with sweat. He quickly rummaged through the saddlebags and felt with his hands the silver the stranger had spoken of. He got on the horse and rode some distance, then dismounted behind some foliage, listening to make sure he had not been followed. Then he removed the six bags of silver, laying them out on the ground in the moonlight.

He opened one, in disbelief at what he saw inside. There was more money than he could make in ten lifetimes working as a soldier. This would do far more than get him and Abishag to Greece. He would be able to buy a palace when he got there. *I can't be seen with all this,* he told himself. He would take a little silver with him and bury the rest in the olive grove outside of town. When he and Abishag left for the harbor, he would come back for the buried portion. He knew he had to let the horse go, or it would raise suspicion.

§

Judah sat resting with a thick wool blanket wrapped about his shoulders. "You shouldn't drink wine," Jonathan said. "Not when you're sick."

"I'll be fine," Judah replied, pouring wine into the silver cup. Judah had come down with a fever a second time since the battle at Dathema, where he received the wound that pierced his side. The first time was just days after they had liberated the last town from the Ammorite siege. The physician had drained the wound multiple times, and cut away at the infected skin, and the fever left after only two days. Then it struck a second time when they battled against the Philistines. The wound had to be reopened and drained once more. This time the fever had lingered for over a week and still showed no signs of abating.

Even while sick, Judah made a practice of donning his armor and walking through the ranks so his men could see him. They thought of him as indestructible, and their attitude on the battlefield reflected that. He wanted to maintain their morale, but the ritual was proving increasingly daunting. The walk took everything out of him. He knew he couldn't let the men see. Their leader must not appear weak.

Judah felt weary, beyond the tiredness caused by the sickness. He knew that even after all this war and destruction, after hamstringing the armies of every surrounding nation, he still had the revenge of the Syrians to contend with. Soon he would have to face them on open ground. *You should build a cavalry,* Judah thought to himself. It would give the army mobility and allow them to feign retreat while luring the still overconfident Syrians into a trap.

Judah's force had a few-score riders he used as scouts, but he needed a formidable host of horses. Trained with good riders, on open ground, a cavalry's speed and momentum could crash into an enemy's formations and roll their lines, allowing the opposing army to flank or get behind the enemy's position. Mules were the common means of transport in Israel, for most purposes. The rugged terrain was dangerous for horses, causing them to easily break their legs, but for military purposes, the animals were invaluable. Judah knew that in the flatter coastal regions, he could find enough steeds to purchase to easily build a cavalry of a few thousand riders.

Judah took another drink of his wine, then coughed long and weakly. Jonathan looked at him, worried. He thought about their father, and how quickly his health had deserted him once he fell from his horse and broke his leg. Though

Mattathias's condition was already in decline, after his fall he was as good as dead. *The flesh is weak,* Jonathan reminded himself, and *by the sweat of your face you shall eat bread until you return to the ground, for out of it you were taken. You are dust, and to dust you shall return.*

Judah noticed Jonathan's morose expression. "Stop worrying about me, brother," he chided. "It will take more than this wound to put me in the grave. Can you lead the siege against the citadel for a few days, until I'm back in shape?"

"Of course," Jonathan replied, sounding confident, but deep-down questioning his own abilities. *I don't know if I can ever do anything the way Judah does,* he thought. For so long, he had wanted to be like his brother. But Jonathan knew they were different. Judah was so ruthless, almost merciless. Jonathan thought about the towns they laid siege to. Judah had killed every single man who wasn't a Hebrew. He had ordered them slain, even after the cities surrendered.

Ephron had been the worst. Judah had been furious that they wouldn't let them pass through their lands. In some way, Jonathan could sympathize with those Gentiles. It was their city, their own people, but the army had meant them no harm. Judah took the refusal as another insult against Israel, then butchered every man in the city and still passed through, burning the place to the ground in his wake. Jonathan couldn't be like that, nor did he want to be. This was his only conflict with Judah—a hero, in his brother's eyes, in every other respect.

While he could be brutal, Judah was remarkably compassionate with the old and young Hebrews they had rescued. He had slowed the whole army on the march for one old woman, and often went through the crowd, encouraging the weak and elderly. He had inexhaustible patience with them, it seemed. When everyone else had wanted to hasten back toward Jerusalem in a rush, Judah insisted on moving at a speed that was comfortable for the refugees. Jonathan had never seen such a display of compassion and love for one's people. Judah even gave from his own money to those who were forced to abandon their homes and belongings, so they would not enter Judea destitute. And although Judah had slain all the men in the enemy cities, he did obey Mosaic law: he spared the women and children, bringing them to Jerusalem, where they would live as servants in the homes of the Jewish citizens.

Jonathan pondered the dichotomy of the man who was his brother: loving and ruthless, strong and empathetic, giving and methodical, compassionate and unforgiving, devout and deceptive, righteous and vengeful . . . loved and feared. One thing above all else characterized Judah: he loved his people, his country, and the Lord God.

Jonathan remembered in the heat of battle how Judah had found Timothy, the Ammorite general, as he attempted to retreat for a third time. There at the edge of the river bank, Judah fought with him until the man's strength had spent itself. Then Judah beheaded him. *God help me lead these men until Judah is recovered,* Jonathan prayed.

Judah watched Jonathan, as the younger man silently brooded. Judah was pleased. He knew that underneath the blustering, Jonathan was unsure of himself, despite the fact that Judah and everyone else had confidence in him. Over the past year, Judah had watched his brother become a man.

"Sleep well. I'm going to bed," Jonathan said with a sigh. He longed for the touch of his wife, who was quartered in apartments on the other side of the governor's palace. Judah smiled, and Jonathan left, closing the door behind him.

Judah thought about Sarah and the role he had played in making her Jonathan's wife. He didn't regret his part in shaping the outcome, despite the guilt he had felt in manipulating Sarah's father. *No, not manipulating,* Judah told himself. He had merely influenced Levi's decision so his brother could make things right. *Be honest with yourself,* another part of him said. *You did manipulate Levi and his decision, and if you had to go back, you would do it again.*

Judah coughed bitterly, feeling cold, and walked to the window. He thought of the journey back from Bosor. There had been a young woman among the people they had rescued at the stronghold. She had looked at him with eyes that conveyed attraction, admiration, intrigue, and infatuation, all in a single glance. He immediately noticed her when they rescued the survivors of Bosor, and she noticed him, before she even knew that he was Judah, the Maccabee.

On the road, she had been one of the many people in a group he had stopped to encourage and give hope to, as they neared the City of David. Later, after they crossed the Jordan, she had stumbled. He had been there to pick her up. He remembered the softness of her skin, her warmth, and her smile. He remembered the way his heart felt when she looked into his eyes that time, knowing who he was.

He had placed her on his horse, and let her ride beside him while he walked. They had conversed for some time on the road back to Jerusalem. Her name was Martha. She was a widow whose husband, a Bosor merchant, had been killed by the Gentiles in a property dispute the year before. She had no family left. He remembered the pain in her eyes when she spoke of her history, and felt sorry for her. She and her husband had not had children, and she was alone in the world.

Judah had asked Simon's wife, who was living in a house formerly occupied by a Syrian magistrate, if Martha could stay with them for a time, and Simon's wife had agreed. Judah thought of stopping by to see how Martha was and how Simon's family was doing. He wanted to see the woman again, to look into her eyes and feel that same warmth he had felt while on the road to Jerusalem. But he had decided against it.

He felt guilt over his attraction to her. He missed Adi. *You can't tarnish the love you had,* he thought. *Her memory is all of her you have left, and you can't diminish it. You've promised yourself there would be no other wife.* But he was the high priest, and ruler of Judea. If he had no offspring and heir, who would rule when he passed on? Didn't he owe his people a son to rule in his place after he was gone?

To complicate matters further, it was unlawful for a high priest to marry a widow or a divorced woman. He was allowed only to marry a virgin.

For the first time, Judah seriously contemplated who would take his place if he were to die. Not Gaddi. One of his other brothers perhaps? He sat on his bed and coughed again, feeling very cold.

§

Entering his chambers, Jonathan glanced at Sarah, who sat on the bed, waiting for him. He smiled at her tenderly.

She stood and helped him remove his cloak. He sat down exhausted, and she drew near, caressing his arms softly.

"How's Judah?" she asked, seeing the worry on his face.

"Not well," he answered, staring toward the wall.

"It will be all right."

"I hope so."

She leaned toward him, and their lips met.

"I love you," she whispered.

He ran his fingers down her cheek, and kissed her again.

סֵפֶר שְׁבִיעִי

Book VII
The Spy's End

164 BC

"He who has overcome his fears will truly be free."

~ Aristotle

βιβλίο Επτά

Chapter 40

DEMETRIUS STOOD AT the bow of the galley, gazing out at the gray clouds low against the horizon. The cool breeze swept across his face. "Not the best time to cross the great sea," he heard Bacchides, one of his rescuers, say. "There are many storms this time of year."

They had driven their horses from Rome to the harbor, where the men indeed had a ship prepared and waiting. They all boarded in haste. Demetrius was glad to see Rome fade into the distance. He had been there for over eighteen years, and in that time had lived in four different households. The senator had always treated him like a freed slave, a second-class citizen.

He remembered bitterly how he had come to Rome. When he was young, his grandfather, the great king Antiochus, had traded him for his uncle. His father, Seleucus, had done everything to try to sway the reigning king's mind, to the point where the king nearly denied Seleucus his position as heir and threatened to disinherit him. Finally, Demetrius was taken and traded. Rome wanted the son of a future king, someone of the royal line, not the runt uncle, who would never inherit the throne. And the old king wanted his son back, so the trade made everyone happy. Except for Demetrius and his parents, of course. Demetrius remembered the look on his uncle's face when they made the switch at the harbor. His uncle had smiled at him.

Demetrius's father had promised him that he would somehow bring him back home. If it took him every coin in the treasury, he would bring him back once he became king. When he did inherit the throne, Seleucus wasn't king long enough to free his son, though he started the negotiations. Through treachery, Antiochus became king, and Demetrius was forgotten about. Demetrius had heard stories of Antiochus poisoning his young brother. Roman politicians sometimes gave him reports they had heard from their spies. They told him of Antiochus's abuses and of the rape of his mother. Demetrius knew it had resulted in the birth of another child.

When he heard the wretch Antiochus had died, Demetrius was disheartened. He had wanted to do the honors himself. Afterwards, he assumed Rome would release him, but they said they'd rather have a boy ruling Syria than a man, so in Rome Demetrius had remained, until now.

As he stood on deck, looking out at the lowering sky, Demetrius contemplated all that Antiochus had done to squander the wealth and reputation of the Seleucid Empire. Everyone felt the great kingdom's best days were behind it now. His grandfather, despite his cruelty and all his faults, still kept Syria strong. Now Mithridates, the Parthian, was invading from the east, seeking to establish an empire of his own, taking more and more Seleucid lands. Philip, an upstart who Antiochus had arbitrarily made viceroy, and Lysias the other viceroy, were about to war with each other, while the empire just grew weaker. This furthered the opportunity for Mithridates to take still more of their lands. *I'll wait until Philip and Lysias rend each other apart, and then I'll make my move,* thought Demetrius.

Bacchides, the man in charge of ensuring the heir apparent's escape, leaned against the ship's railing. He was a lean man in his mid-forties, with thinning hair and a stone-hard gaze behind his strange blue eyes. "Did you sleep well, my lord?"

"I slept free, for the first time since I can remember," Demetrius replied with a smile.

Bacchides looked out at the sea.

"Why were you chosen for this?" Demetrius asked.

"Ten years ago I was a ranking commander of the Hetairoi, one of the elite cavalry divisions."

"I know my own military," Demetrius snapped, feeling a little insulted.

Bacchides ignored the remark. "I was passed up in rank by one of my peers, who made every effort to destroy my career, so I took my talents elsewhere."

"Then you did this only for money?" Demetrius asked, rancor in his voice.

"As a patriot," Bacchides answered coldly. "The reasons I fell out with the military were political, a question of loyalties. After your father's assassination, I refused to give my allegiance to Antiochus."

Suddenly it became clear why Laodice, his mother, had chosen this man to rescue him. He was a prior commander of the greatest cavalry force on earth, a devoted follower of his father, a political enemy of Antiochus, and he had been reduced to a cheap mercenary. He was loyal, had nothing to lose, and everything to gain.

"I will take back the throne of my father," Demetrius said sullenly.

Bacchides did not respond.

"And I will take care of Judea. The most disgraceful of my uncle's many blunders. Defeated by a pack of armed monkeys on foot. Once I'm king, that will be the first humiliation I rectify."

"You need that land," Bacchides said at last. "It's the last buffer zone between us and the Egyptian worms."

"I won't let a band of uncultured religious bigots, who squabble over everything, fracture my empire because of their belief in some intolerant deity. Their leader, Judah, the one they call "the hammer," bested every Syrian general. So my fool uncle sent more generals for him to destroy. The solution is clearly to assassinate Judah. Rebellion over. Chop off a beast's head, and the body *will* die."

Bacchides said nothing.

§

Simon's body swayed back and forth as his horse trotted slowly down the slope, toward the village of Aphek. He led the columns of over two-thousand warriors and many Jewish families and refugees. The people had taken what little option they had and followed Simon, as he gathered the Hebrews in the north, before the area became overrun with hostile Gentiles.

Simon was tired of traveling and tired of the road, but Aphek would be the last town before they hastened back toward Judea. He knew if they ventured farther north they would walk right into the heart of the Phoenician territory, and all would be lost.

Some of the refugees were of military age, but most were women, children, and the elderly. Their march south was slow, and if the armies of Tyre and Sidon maneuvered rapidly, they doubtless would overcome Simon's company. The refugees ate more than Simon's soldiers. One more town, and then they had no choice but to return to Jerusalem. They had saved a lot of people, but it was not enough. *Ratzon ha'El*, prayed Simon. *God, protect the sons of Israel we cannot save.*

Simon wondered if Judah had returned yet to Jerusalem. After Joel's botched attack against the armies of Gorgias, the Seleucids would be building an army solely for the purpose of invading them. *Thank God for Antiochus's death,* Simon mused. The Lord finally saw fit to punish the depraved wretch for his years of being a paragon of iniquity. Thank God the fool appointed a second viceroy before he perished, to challenge the power of Lysias. The Parthians were attacking the eastern empire, and the Syrians were losing not only Israel, but other lands simultaneously.

Simon contemplated how Judah seemed intent on accepting Rome's help. But Simon remembered his father's advice before he died. Mattathias had been apprehensive about foreign assistance and cautioned against such alliances. Simon also remembered the passage in Isaiah, where the prophet warned against trusting in foreign nations and commanded the Jews to trust in the Lord God alone. Other nations were pagan Gentiles and worshiped the same false gods as the Greeks, although they ascribed them different names. Simon distrusted all Gentiles.

Glancing down, he brushed some dirt off of his priestly garment. He was the only brother who dressed in the ritual garb. He and his brothers had all been trained as priests, but only Simon was a priest and rabbi by actual vocation. Though Judah called himself high priest, as a title of administrative authority, in truth he was an ethnarch ... a ruler who would not violate the monarchic office of the line of David.

Simon motioned toward Eleazar. "Have the men wait here on the outskirts of the town. There's no need to alarm the people. I'll take ten scouts and gather the citizens in the forum. I'll announce our intention to escort any Hebrew south with us to Judea."

"Will ten be enough?" Eleazar asked. "There are a lot of Samaritans in these northern cities. Some of them aren't too happy about what we're doing in the south."

"Fifteen then. The Samaritans fight like women. There are far more Israelites here than Samaritans anyway. Until we get to the forum, we will pass as local travelers."

Eleazar nodded. "Hopefully, most of the people will come with us," he said. He thought of the scores of families who stubbornly, or stupidly, had chosen to remain in the northern towns, knowing they would soon be overrun.

"Some people think no harm can come to them," Simon said. "The graves are filled with such idiots."

Simon turned his thoughts to the task ahead, as his fifteen scouts dug their spears into the grassy soil, keeping their swords concealed under their outer garments. They walked toward the village, passing by small homes on the outskirts of a large vineyard, surrounded by rich hills dotted with palm trees.

Galilee contrasted sharply with the barren sand dunes and dry mountains of Judea. *Soon we'll take the north back again,* thought Simon. *We first must establish our stronghold in the south. For now, we can't hold these northern cities.*

Moving through the hedges of vines, they approached a large barn where wine presses stood. Simon heard a disturbance ahead and, moving closer, sensed danger. The commotion grew loud. As they passed the barn, he saw seven men attacking someone curled on his side, trying to protect himself with one arm. His face was bloodied and stained with dirt. The men surrounding him were shouting and cursing. There were two men on the ground, incapacitated. Simon could only assume they had been injured in the brawl. Behind the group, was a beautiful young women in tears, shrieking, "Leave him alone!" She was being restrained by an older woman in similar dress.

Not understanding what was happening, assuming the man was being unjustly assaulted, Simon drew his sword from under his cloak. His men did the same.

"Stop!" Simon yelled in Hebrew. His baritone voice carried over the chorus of shouts. The men in the circle turned to look at him, startled by the fifteen men with drawn swords. "What's the meaning of this?" Simon bellowed.

"I am Zebulun!" shouted a man who seemed to be the ringleader. This is *my* land and my vineyard. Who are you?"

"My name is Simon Ben Mattathias, commander of the Israelite armies in the north, and brother of Judah Maccabee." This created a stir in the crowd.

After a moment, the man who called himself Zebulun said, "This man came onto my land, saying he was starving, with this girl, my wife's kindred." He pointed at the woman who had been shouting. She was looking at the man on the ground. There was worry in his eyes, affection and outrage in hers. "But we have learned my wife's cousin deceived us. This man is a Seleucid spy!"

Simon looked down at the man with new eyes. Though he had a beard, through the blood and dirt, his facial features and fair skin did look Greek. And his hair looked unnaturally black, like it had been dyed with senna plants.

"What proof do you have?" Simon asked.

Zebulun moved violently toward the young man and gripped the sleeve of his garment, tugging it with enough force to pull his victim off the ground. The sleeve tore, and the man fell. His exposed shoulder revealed a black tattoo in Greek letters with the mark of a Seleucid soldier.

"You see?" Zebulun hissed. "This is the mark of the Argyraspides, the Silver Shields. One of my workers spotted him roaming through my vineyard at night, meeting with a Phoenician soldier who escaped from a battle with your army just two days ago. The Parthian died, but not before he confided whatever message he was bringing to his contact here!" Zebulum kicked the Greek man in the side. "And this mockery has happened in *my* house!"

"Don't hurt him! It's not true!" the young woman cried. "He is not a spy. He's not even a soldier anymore!"

"Shut your mouth, Greek whore! We don't need the lies of a traitor who plays the harlot with Gentiles, who betrays her own people, *for lust!*" Zebulun raised his hand and backhanded the girl across the face, knocking her to the ground.

Enraged, the Greek tried to stand, but was held down by three of the men, who stood on his shoulders and chest.

Simon felt a pang of conscience, seeing the man hit the woman. He was not sure who was in the wrong here. He moved forward, and a vineyard hand stepped aside to make way for him.

Simon stood over the injured man. "Is this true, Seleucid? Are you a spy?"

The Greek did not respond. He was trying to break the hold of the men pinning him down. "What did the Phoenician tell you before he died?"

"We are going to stone him to death," Zebulun said with a bitter smile. The woman let out a shriek.

We don't have time for this, Simon thought. "Zebulum, you need to gather the inhabitants and head toward Jerusalem," he said. "It's no longer safe for Hebrews to remain in this region."

"I'm not a spy. I'm a deserter," the man on the ground uttered. "She's not a harlot. She is my wife."

The Hebrews in the circle murmured in outrage. Some yelled insults. Zebulun said to Simon over the din, "As long as this man has breath in his lungs, he can pass whatever message the Phoenician gave him. We have to stone him."

§

You can't fail this time, Lysias told himself, as he stepped into the palace map room for his meeting with the high command. The empire around him was crumbling, and the eyes of the world were upon them. They wanted to know if the Seleucid Empire would remain the great power it was or pass into obscurity—like Egypt, Assyria, Babylon, and Persia—only a shade of its former self.

Nothing lasts forever, Lysias thought, *but you have devoted your life to an idea, and that idea is the strength of the empire.* He never thought he would be king. But now the king was a child, and the survival of the empire was in his hands.

Lysias felt rapture at his newly acquired power. He was accountable to no one, answered to no one. He thought of Laodice and her brat. She had hurled insults at him the day before, when he ordered her to take her son and step onto the palace balcony, for the boy's subjects to see. "One day my son will stand before you, a grown man," she had crowed, as if she suspected that he was planning treachery. Which he was, of course. But the people must be made to believe their leaders were in unity, that there were no political divisions.

You must kill her, Lysias thought—her and her half-witted

prodigy. The little whelp wouldn't be alive by the time he was tall enough to stand up to Lysias's waist. It was too soon, though. It would look suspicious if the queen and the boy died suddenly after the king. The opinion of the peasants didn't matter, as the nobility held most of the wealth. But the nobility were less likely to spend their gold if they thought the empire was in peril, rendering them unable to tax. And if they thought it suspicious that the royal whore dropped dead so soon after her loving husband, there would be chaos. In fact, they might even point fingers at the new viceroy and accuse him of the queen's untimely demise, especially if her son died with her, or shortly thereafter.

Lysias strode to the table and looked down at the large map of the known world. Nicantor would be at their meeting as well as Gorgias. They must crush Judea. The Israelite insult would only be forgotten if they made an example of the rebels.

This time it would be different. No mountainous death traps or valley pathways. They would march down the coast and attack from the south, where the land was flat and open. The Jews had been weakened. Every surrounding nation had gone to war with Judea. Nobody liked the Israelites because they were rodents, abhorrent to civilized cultures. Antiochus should have torn down their temple instead of profaning it.

Lysias had employed the best soldiers of every nation on Earth for the campaign. He would have elephants—something the Hebrews hadn't seen. Judah's wily tactics would not work against *him*. Lysias had seen elephants slam into phalanxes, completely shattering them. He would retake Jerusalem, tear down that temple of theirs, and save the soldiers besieged in the citadel if it weren't already too late.

Then a calmer thought came to him. Antiochus was an ass, and his subjects had reason to feel outraged. Would it be so terrible to make peace? What if, instead of crushing them, he gave Maccabee money, and gave them all religious freedom to worship their own god? He could let them choose their high priest and rule their own country as long as they abided by Greek laws and paid their taxes. Not only might the Jews accept the offer, but if they saw Lysias as their benefactor and bestower of their freedom, the Jews might even fight for him against people who challenged his right to rule ... people like Philip.

No! He interrupted this train of thought. The world would see such capitulation as weakness, and a desperate attempt to control the borders. The empire would lose its pride and be attacked by every nation. Besides, the Jews had beaten them over and over again, and now they'd beaten every small nation around them. Why would they even consider an offer of peace? No, he decided. It must be complete destruction of Judea, their god, and their backward way of life.

Lysias fidgeted, glancing around the room. As always, he was early for the meeting. He thought of the weak Philip, to whom the deranged Antiochus had handed his crown. Lysias had gathered what was left of the soldiers—those who had not deserted or been killed—and was slowly attempting to recruit support for his claim to the throne.

He remembered the correspondence that Urion, the king's servant and advisor had sent, informing him of Philip's movements. Urion would be useful in the future. But from what he heard, Philip couldn't lead a trained dog. As soon as that moron had departed for the capital, Mithridates had ridden his horde all the way to the edges of Babylon. Now Philip was stuck in Persia until winter was over, desperately trying to recruit men and gain the support of the wealthy Persians, but failing. There was dissent among the officers, and Lysias suspected one of them would assassinate Philip, or his army would abandon him, before he managed to mobilize west.

The door opened, and General Nicantor stood in the doorway. He bowed low before Lysias, showing veneration to the man he knew was now the power behind the throne.

§

Diomedes walked into an inn on the west side of Hadid, a city on the outskirts of Samaria. He had been traveling for weeks on the trail of Isokrates, the commanding intelligence officer and henchman of the Seleucid Empire. Diomedes had instructed his servants to watch the docks for the two Roman agents who had shown up the year before. He anticipated their return for the finalization of a Roman/Jewish treaty, having received word long ago that they were on their way. But they did not arrive at the appointed time. *It was stupid to try to cross the great sea at this time of year,* Diomedes thought. He visited the docks himself every day for weeks, but still there was no sign of them. They should have planned ahead and waited a few months for calmer seas.

Some time back, he had received a directive to assassinate the man named Isokrates, or at least that was the name he was known by. Isokrates, identifiable by a scar across his chin, was an agent appointed by Antiochus's servant Urion, not only to procure information in the area but to hunt down the faithful Jews in the land who refused to adhere to Seleucid law. He was in charge of the entire network of spies within Judea.

Diomedes had been trying to catch up with this man for months when suddenly it appeared as if he had vanished. Diomedes heard the spy had uncovered an underground synagogue the week before his disappearance, and had killed everyone inside. Then there was no word of him. Later, Diomedes heard rumors that a Syrian soldier had killed him in a brawl over a woman. Another report claimed Isokrates was alive, merely had suffered a broken collarbone in the scuffle, and recently booked passage to Antioch, having been sent for by Lysias. In any case, Diomedes surmised that something had happened that caused the spy's inactivity, or perhaps his spy ring had been shattered when Maccabee took control of Jerusalem.

While waiting on the docks the week before, Diomedes

heard from one of his Jerusalem informants that three Syrian soldiers had escaped from the Acra, the besieged citadel, and were traveling north in hopes of informing a Syrian outpost about Maccabee's movements. Their plan was to beseech Lysias for aid, since those in the Acra could not hold out much longer. According to his informant, one of the three soldiers carrying this message was a tall man who had a distinctive scar across his chin, who could pass for either Hebrew or Greek, and whose left shoulder sagged slightly due to what looked like a broken collarbone that had not been properly set.

Diomedes posted a few of his men at the docks to wait for Fabius and Crassus, and headed north to try to catch up with Isokrates, if that was who this man was, at the next city in his path, Hadid.

"Are you looking for a room?" the innkeeper asked.

"I will take the best room you have available," Diomedes answered, having already booked a room in three of the city's four inns.

"The best room costs double," the innkeeper muttered.

"That will be fine."

"Do your horses or mules need tending? Or can I interest you in food or wine after your journey?"

"Perhaps later. I'm in Hadid trying to find my brother-in-law. I heard he might be traveling through. He's a tall man, who looks like he's not quite Hebrew or Greek."

"I'm looking at him," the innkeeper answered sardonically.

Diomedes feigned amusement. "This one has a large scar across his chin, and a damaged shoulder."

The innkeeper squinted, remembering. "I saw a man like that who stayed here two days ago. He had two others with him."

"Which way were they headed?"

"North, as I recall."

"Thanks. Come to think of it, I won't be needing that room after all."

The innkeeper looked surprised and was about to say something, but Diomedes walked out the door.

He's three days ahead of me. I'll have to hurry, thought Diomedes, mounting his horse. He reminded himself not to push so fast that he would be exhausted when they finally crossed paths. He would need his strength to fight the scoundrel. If that man was Isokrates that the innkeeper saw, he should be headed for Neballat, unless he already had moved on.

Chapter 41

ARROWS RAINED DOWN from the stronghold, as a massive barrage was returned from the archers below. "Fire!" Judah shouted. Instantly his battery commander relayed the order, and half a dozen oxybeles—massive crossbows that worked on torsion-powered ropes—released their large javlin-sized missiles over the wall of the citadel. Likewise, four large catapults lobbed heavy stones over the battlements. Judah had been trying intently over the past few days to break the will of the Syrians inside the Acra. He knew he didn't have much time left before Lysias launched another massive army against them. Then he would be forced to lift the siege.

Judah had slowly recovered from the infected wound. The physician had to drain it three more times before it began to heal, and the fever began to lift. He was pleased with Jonathan's organization of the siege works—positioning the men, inspiring the leadership, and boosting the morale of the entire army while Judah was bedridden. Now was the time to break into the citadel. He'd hit them hard for a week without letting up, and when he didn't think they could take anymore, he would offer terms for their surrender. He had to end this siege before the Seleucid Empire launched their forces and he found himself trapped between an army inside the city and and one attacking from outside.

The wall appeared misted by the quantity of arrows flying back and forth from the battlements, but the enemy appeared to be running out. Every day, the volleys diminished. Judah could see his army's siege towers roll closer to the walls, ready to let their drawbridges fall and unload men in an attempt, once more, to take the wall. Inside the siege towers, on every floor, were built-in, downsized oxybeles pointed toward the parapet of the fortress.

Suddenly, multiple drawbridges dropped onto the battlements, and Israelite soldiers rushed forward toward the defending Syrians, who knew they had no choice but to hold their ground or die. Judah saw men fall from the drawbridges and some make it over the parapet. Though his army inflicted casualties, they were soon overtaken, and his men were thrown from the side of the wall.

"Call the rest of them back," Judah ordered one of his commanders. "The siege towers will only cost us lives today."

He wished Benjamin was there. The old man he had put in charge of training his men and commanding his archers had passed away in his sleep the week before. He had put Benjamin in charge of building his cavalry, and in two weeks the fellow had managed to train and structure a mounted force of almost three hundred. Though three hundred wasn't enough to inflict great damage against the Seleucid cavalry, it was a beginning. Soon they would have a thousand.

Judah had also contracted masons to reconstruct the walls of Jerusalem and to fortify the temple mount. If they were overcome by the Seleucids, the temple was as good a place as any to make their last stand.

As the siege towers halted and began to reverse, there was silence from the citadel. The enemy just stared out at them in relief. *A month before they would have been shouting, taunting us,* Judah thought. *Their morale is weakened, and their spirit broken.*

§

Nabis tried with effort to peer through his blackened eyes, which were almost swollen shut. His nose was broken, and even after he tried to reset it, it curved slightly to the left. His broken ribs made it difficult to walk.

You have to keep up, he told himself, trying to stand up straight and stop limping. Six guards surrounded him and the other nine captives, who all were bound with ropes behind their backs and around each of their necks, fastening each prisoner to the next. The lead prisoner was tied to a mule, so if anyone startled the mule or hindered it, the animal would kick frantically, forcing them all to stumble.

Nabis reflected on the events of the last two days. After he'd buried the silver, he had told Abishag all that had happened. "This money is our freedom from this place and all this madness," he had said.

Abishag had sat listening, emotionally confused with the realization that she would be leaving the land of her people, the promised land of Israel, for some pagan country. She had no idea what to expect. All she knew was that she loved Nabis, and would follow him wherever he went. He was her husband. Though there had been no ceremony and no witnesses, he had declared it, and she had accepted it. She was his wife. Nabis saw the trust in her eyes, deeper than the confusion.

"But we can't sneak away without letting my cousin know," she had said. "They gave us shelter and food when we had nothing. We'll tell them your family sent money by way of a courier and that now we can make the journey home."

"They'll caution us to stay because of the Phoenicians to the north and Maccabee to the south."

"Would it be that bad if we stayed one more week?" she had asked, pleading with him.

"We can't," he told her. "The silver I buried could get stolen. We can't risk it."

Nabis hadn't known it at the time, but when the Phoenician rider had fallen in the vineyard, it had startled one of Zebulun's workers, who had snuck around the back of the barn near the presses to meet one of Zebulun's daughters. When the dying rider fell from his horse, the young man and woman were startled and rose to dress hurriedly.

Peering out to see what had made the noise, they saw a man standing over the fallen rider. The rider's body went limp after he breathed his last. Then the moonlight illuminated Nabis's face, and the worker recognized him as he rummaged through the saddlebags of the horse. The worker had labored alongside Nabis on the presses, and had never trusted the man. He didn't believe he was Jewish like he said.

Once Nabis rode away, the worker moved in and examined the fallen rider. He recognized him as a Phoenician soldier, and quickly concluded the man must have been there to give Nabis a message. He instructed Zebulun's daughter to slip back into her room, and once he was certain she was there, he knocked on the door to tell Zebulun all he had seen.

The following morning Nabis had planned to thank Zebulun for his hospitality and tell him of their plans to depart. "May I have a moment of your time?" Nabis had asked.

Zebulun gestured for Nabis to follow him, and as he walked toward the winepress, acting even more dour than usual, ten of the workers suddenly sprang upon Nabis. He tried to fight back but was beaten and quickly overcome. He lost consciousness, and when he came to, Abishag was rushing toward him, screaming. Zebulun's wife, Mary, grabbed her and restrained her. That was when the Jewish priest had appeared, and fifteen men with swords.

In the midst of the ordeal, Nabis had prayed—not to the gods of his countrymen, but once more, as when he fell wounded at Beth-Horn, to Abishag's god. He prayed to the God of the Hebrews. He prayed not for himself, but for his wife. *It would be justice if I died here in this way,* he thought, remembering Jerusalem and the woman crucified with her baby whom he was ordered to guard, *but if their God is just, he won't let harm come to Abishag.*

When Zebulun demanded that they they stone him,

Nabis could see by the priest's eyes that he was going to capitulate. "*Ratzon ha'El,*" Nabis murmured under his breath, remembering the word Abishag had taught him.

"What?" the priest had asked, an odd silence coming over the group. "What did you say?"

"*Ratzon ha'El! Ratzon ha'El!*" Nabis repeated, unsure if he had pronounced the Hebrew word correctly. "If I am to die, so be it, *Ratzon ha'El*, but don't harm her. If there is any justice in you, if the god whom you serve is good, don't harm her!" He gestured toward Abishag.

"She's done nothing wrong but take a husband who once was a Seleucid soldier, and who now worships your god and follows your ways." Nabis added this remark because he knew the Law of Moses prohibited marriage to foreigners who worshiped false gods, but also because a large part of him really did now believe in their god. He felt he could discern between truth and a lie, between right and wrong, and he could find no fault or flaw in the Hebrew teachings.

The priest paused, unsure how to react. "Tie up the Syrian and his wife. We'll take them with us to Jerusalem, and decide the matter there."

"Rabbi," one of his soldiers said. "Look, he's almost dead. He won't be able to walk. He'll slow us down. The decent thing would be to give him a quick death."

"No, he'll walk," the priest had answered.

Now marching toward Jerusalem, the opposite direction from where he wanted to go, Nabis wondered whether they would stone him there or release him. He knew they had taken Abishag, putting her in with the Gentile women they had captured. Nabis said a prayer that she was safe. Hazily in the distance, the city of Neballat began to take on form.

§

"How long until we're there?" Crassus asked Kalisito.

"Three days," he responded. The skies were cloudy, but the seas were calm.

The storm had blown their ship so far off-course that they had ended up shipwrecked on the island of Cyprus. The galley had slammed against the rocks, rolled onto its side, capsized, then sank against the reef.

Crassus and Kalisto and a few of the crew had managed to swim to shore. They never saw what happened to Fabius. *He must have drowned before he made it,* Crassus thought with remorse.

Men were screaming and jumping into the waves when he seized a piece of wooden debris and leaped into the water himself, using the wood to stay afloat and to brace his sword and the satchel containing Rome's treaty.

Crassus remembered how the waves had pummeled him. He kicked franticly toward shore, fearing he'd never make it. They all swam hard, but caught in a riptide, only kept moving farther away from land. Soon the shore was three miles away and growing more distant, but then the winds changed, and they started moving closer.

Crassus had never seen a storm so turbulent. After he and Kalisto crawled up onto the rocks, rain continued pouring down in the heavy wind. He asked Kalisto if he had ever witnessed a storm of that magnitude. Kalisto only answered with a shake of his head.

The next morning, only a remnant of the tempest remained on the horizon, and only a handful of their crew had survived. Crassus still had enough coin in his pouch to lease the use of a small boat from a village on the island.

In the boat now and once again headed toward Judea, he found his thoughts returning to the treaty, which he had almost died to save. It was inscribed on small bronze tablets. Encased in a glass cylinder was a parchment for the Maccabee to sign.

Crassus opened the satchel and read the Latin engraved on the tablets:

Good success be to the Romans and to the people of the Jews, by sea and by land forever: and far be the sword and enmity from them. But if there come first any war upon the Romans, or any of their confederates, in all their dominions, the nation of the Jews shall help them according as the time shall direct, with all their heart: Neither shall they give aid to the enemy nor furnish them with wheat, or arms, or money, or ships, for the duration of the fighting.

In like manner also, if war shall come first upon the nation of the Jews, the Romans shall help them with all their heart, according as the time shall permit them. And there shall not be given to them that come to their aid either wheat, or arms, or money, or ships during the duration of the fighting.

According to these articles do the Romans covenant with the people of the Jews. Concerning the evils that the Seleucid king hath done against them, we have written to him, saying: "Why hast thou made thy yoke heavy upon our friends and allies, the Jews?" If therefore they come again to us complaining of thee, we will do them justice, and will make war against them by sea and by land.

Crassus wondered what would happen after Rome no longer feared the Seleucid kingdom, with only one ally—the Jews—standing between combining their western and eastern provinces into one powerful, undivided empire.

Chapter 42

SIMON PLACED THE parchment over the campfire and watched the orange flames scorch through and blacken the paper. A thin flame spread across the page, leaving nothing but an intact sheet of ash, which curled onto itself, then broke apart into pieces.

He rubbed his arms to warm himself. It was cold here on the outskirts of the city of Neballat.

Eleazar approached the fire and sat down near his brother. *"Shalom,"* he said in greeting. Simon nodded in acknowledgment. "The messenger said there was a letter."

"Yes," said Simon with a sigh. "From Judah. Lysias is mobilizing an army of over fifty thousand—infantry, chariots, and cavalry."

Eleazar blanched, sudden anxiety gripping him.

"That's not all," Simon continued. "He has enormous monsters from the south, called elephants, which tower above the battlefield." Simon had never seen an elephant, but he had heard stories about their fierceness in war and how they could crush a man. They had hot tempers and shrieked howls that screeched above the noise of battle. Men and archers rode upon them and could shoot down from that vantage point. War elephants were armored, and could charge right into an enemy's infantry lines, shattering them.

He had heard how Alexander of Macedon's advance toward the eastern sea was halted by the Nanda and Gangaridai, tribes from India who fought with six thousand of the creatures, until

Alexander amassed an elephant force of his own and invaded, reaching farther than the Hydaspes River, where he founded two cities.

"The letter instructed us to send some men to the Nabateans," said Simon. "For a small fee, they've agreed to store a portion of our arms and gold in their treasury. Judah says we might need such a cache as a last resort, if it ever comes down to evacuating the army across the Jordan." Simon remembered how Judah had made an alliance of friendship with the Arab kingdom after they provided information about the Jewish cities that the Ammorites had been besieging.

"Judah must really be worried about this coming Syrian invasion," Eleazar replied, grimly.

"There are over fifty thousand of them coming," said Simon. "What's not to fear?" He contemplated a moment.

"You should send Gaddi to supervise the transfer of goods to the Nabateans," Eleazar murmured. "Gaddi has always been good at bartering."

"They'll probably steal our coins and use our weapons against us," Simon answered cynically, only half joking.

"Then there is this issue of the Seleucid spy who has been bedding one of the daughters of Israel. I should have killed him yesterday."

"I'm not sure I agree."

"If he *is* carrying a message, it could end the lives of hundreds of our men," said Simon. "We can't risk that."

Eleazar remained silent.

"He must have really beguiled her," Simon mused, thinking of the girl who the Syrian claimed was his wife.

"She seems to be truly in love with him."

"Maybe she's a traitor and is on the Seleucids' side."

"That's hard to believe," replied Eleazar. "She seems so innocent."

"With these spies you can never tell."

"We should interrogate her, and see if we can prove the

Seleucid is lying. If you kill the man and he's not a spy, you'll have his blood on your hands," Eleazar prompted.

"No, we can't risk it," Simon said dispassionately." Tomorrow, after the Sabbath ends, the Seleucid dies. I should have never hesitated. This is war, and in war there are high prices to pay."

God, Simon silently prayed, *guide my hand, and keep me from evil.*

§

Nabis awoke in the darkness of the camp, jolted by the nightmare. In his dream, he had relived the crucifixion of the woman he had guarded in the Jerusalem massacre, but this time it was Abishag hanging on the cross, with an unknown baby's corpse dangling beneath her.

Intense pain throbbed in Nabis's head and body from the beating of the previous morning. He tried to move, but his hands and feet were bound with ropes, and his neck was still secured by a long rope to the prisoners in front of him and behind him. His ears were ringing, and his teeth felt loose.

The cold air of near-dawn felt freezing and damp. He peered up into the darkness and saw two guards monitoring the perimeter, spears in hand.

I'm not going to die here, Nabis thought, with decision. *I'm not going to let Abishag die here.* Something was surging in him, the same passion to live that rose up in him at hopeless moments in battle. It was the same passion that onced earned him the Silver Shield.

He could feel the nearness of the other prisoners, bound so closely together. The man in front of him shifted when Nabis jerked awake, making the rope between them even tighter. Now he felt a wetness on his knees, and concluded by the smell that the prisoner tied behind him, unable to move, must have urinated on him in the night.

Nabis needed to escape. He considered his options. A rock—he needed a sharp rock.

He brushed his hands, bound behind his back, along the hard ground, moving slowly enough not to alarm the guards or awake the other prisoners. He found nothing. He felt a pinch in his side and moved his hands closer to it, realizing he was lying on a rock, but it was wedged too deeply into the soil for him to pry it free. Finally, at his thigh, he found a small, thin stone. Slowly, he curled his legs into his chest and began sawing away at the top cord of the rope that was securely wrapped about his feet.

This could take a week to get through, he thought. He stopped suddenly, hearing the faint whispers of the two guards. They both appeared to be young.

"How much longer are they going to be?" the first one whispered, in a complaining tone.

"Who knows?" the second replied. "Neballat is right there."

"You'd think they could find the brothel easily enough. We're not going to have time to go ourselves before first light."

"I think this whole idea was foolish," the other whispered back.

Nabis realized there were only two of them, instead of the four that were guarding them only hours before. The others had apparently left their post to visit a harlot in Naballat.

This may be the only chance you have to escape, Nabis thought to himself, as he inconspicuously began to saw again at the rope. In his heart, he began thanking God, the Hebrew God, who had answered his prayers after Beth-horn. Now, he petitioned once more. *Help me now,* he prayed, *and I will be your servant for the rest of my life. I will deny all other gods but you, for all of my days.*

Nabis continued his painstaking task. His hands were wet where the sharp stone had slipped and gouged the flesh of his fingers.

These people aren't trained, he thought. *The experienced soldiers are sleeping, and they ordered these boys to watch us, and they can't even do that. Don't kill them,* he told himself, *not unless you have no choice.*

"I think it was all a bad idea," the second young guard whispered, reiterating what he had already expressed. Both men were looking away toward the town instead of watching the prisoners inside the perimeter.

"Why are you so worried, Mattathias?" the other replied. "These prisoners are half-dead anyway, your father is the general of the army of the north, and your uncle is the Maccabee himself. Do you think a father is going to put his own son to death? Even if we do get caught, which we won't?"

The other guard moved closer to their small fire, still ignoring the prisoners.

Nabis felt the first cord of the rope give way and the binding around his ankles loosen. *They tied it wrong,* he thought. *They didn't weave the rope and fasten safety knots throughout the bindings.*

Slowly, Nabis shifted position and began working on the next rope, which was around his neck.

§

Only five men remained inside the tavern, as the languid night bore on. The owner was busy calculating in his head his expected earnings for the evening. Two of the souls who loitered were regular customers. Another, with the appearance of a vagrant, sat alone at a table, swaying drunkenly in his seat. The last man, a foreigner, sat with his back against the wall inside a tucked-away cranny, hidden by the shadows of the room. The man had been waiting for hours and had only sipped at a cup of wine.

The door of the tavern swung open, and three travelers entered. The chill from the outside brought a blast of coldness in. The door shut behind them, and they moved directly toward the man in the shadows.

"It doesn't shine, but in a tavern this late at night," the tall man with the scar on his chin said, standing over the foreigner, who sat calmly behind his table.

"And wine might still illuminate truth," the man replied, responding appropriately with the prearranged password he was given. The tall man sat down. His companions took chairs at an adjacent table.

"Isokrates, is it?" the man who had been waiting asked. The tall man with the scar nodded, and the other man continued. "From here I will pass through Sidon and book passage to Antioch, so what you say will be heard directly by the king himself."

"But the king is just a child," Isokrates said caustically.

"I refer to Lysias, the *real* king," the foreigner replied, noticing the sagging shoulder wasn't as misshapen as he had been led to believe by the description. In truth, the deformity was almost unnoticeable. "So what is this news?"

"First, the citadel can't hold out much longer. I just came from inside where I was healing from the injury you were just eyeing. They're starving now, and I barely escaped. Lysias needs to send relief, or they'll all be dead soon. Maccabee is attacking us daily with siege engines and artillery weapons he stole from us."

Isokrates paused as the tavern owner came around the fireplace and asked, "Would you like something to—"

"Wine," he said shortly. He waited until the innkeeper was out of earshot before he continued. "Tell Lysias that Maccabee is building a cavalry. Not to the size where it can be very effective, but he may try to use it as a trick on the battlefield."

The man across the table listened intently, his face stoic, but taking mental notes on every detail.

"By the way he's training his men, it appears he's preparing to fight in a pitched battle. There won't be any ambushing tricks based on terrain this time. The army now numbers some thirty-thousand men, and their morale is high. Maccabee has rebuilt the wall of Jerusalem and rededicated the temple, putting it back into practice as the center of Hebrew worship. He knows he faces a threat to his success and expects an attack on the temple. He's fortified the temple mount with catapults and barricades, preparing for possibly having to make a last stand there."

The innkeeper returned with the wine, and Isokrates took a long drink before he went on.

"So when Lysias does invade, he'll have to maintain a siege inside a hostile city, trapped within its walls. I've examined their fortifications. They'll hold out for a time. The religious fanaticism of these people may benefit Lysias, if he acts quickly. The Jews have a Sabbath year, which they observe by not tilling the land or harvesting grain or fruit. This is that year, so now they may face a food shortage. If it comes to a siege, Lysias has that advantage."

The foreigner nodded, understanding.

"Lastly," Isokrates continued, trying to ignore the belch of the drunken vagrant across the room, who was still swaying in his chair, spilled wine dripping from his clay cup into a puddle on the floor. "You'll want to sleep in the tavern tonight. The rebel northern army is camped two miles from here, with four-thousand men. You don't want to get caught."

§

Simon walked hastily toward the rear of the camp, an expression of consternation on his face. The campfires illuminated the grounds all around him. The night had become cold, and Simon could see the mist of his breath as it rose. When he moved past the tents and saw his son Mattathias, relief washed over him.

Simon had been awakened by one of his bodyguards. There had been a problem, and some prisoners had escaped. His initial reaction was horror. Was Mattathias all right? He had placed the boy on night watch, hoping the tedious drudgery of watching the captives would dampen his lust for being a soldier. Simon didn't want him near any battlefield.

Simon had sworn to his wife he would keep Mattathias safe. It wouldn't be long until his other boys, Jude and John, would also want to be soldiers. Jude was only fifteen. John was eleven, and had an inner strength his studiousness mostly masked. Quiet and reserved, he reminded Simon of Judah as a boy.

Simon strode to the camp's perimeter, where now some twenty men surrounded the remaining prisoners. Mattathias was sitting down with another guard, talking to someone standing over them. He looked disheveled, with a gash on his temple and a streak of blood down his face.

An officer, looking uneasy, stepped forward and addressed Simon. "Sir, three of the prisoners escaped. Two guards snuck off in the night for Neballat, apparently to visit a harlot. They haven't returned yet. We have scouts out looking for them."

Simon felt rage boil inside him.

"It looks as if one of the prisoners cut through his bonds with a rock, and crept up behind your son and the other guard, who remained at their post. Your son was hit over the head with a stone. The other man was beaten unconscious. From what we can gather, two other prisoners managed to escape afterwards, with no guards watching them."

Simon's heart sank when he examined the faces of the prisoners and realized who was missing. "The Seleucid spy? You're telling me the spy was one of those who escaped?"

"Yes," the officer answered.

"We have our scouts hunting two of them now, and our riders are in pursuit. They headed west for the hills. One, possibly the spy, stole your son's cloak along with his weapons. They're still trying to pick up his trail."

"Find him!" Simon demanded. "At all costs, find him!"

Why had the spy let Mattathias and the other guard live? Simon wondered. It would certainly have been safer for him if he'd killed them. And as badly beaten as he was, how did he manage to overpower two armed guards, even if they weren't paying attention, with their minds fixated on the lust of a woman?

Then he thought of it, angered that he didn't think of it sooner. "The girl! The one we captured with him?"

The officer instantly made the connection. "The women prisoners are being held at the other end of the camp."

"Get your men over there!" Simon commanded. "Now!"

§

Silent and alone, Isokrates slipped out of the tavern. The cold wind sent an instant chill through his body. Though he had advised his contact from Antioch, as well as his own two men, to stay the night in the tavern, he had work to do. He was focused on the new task his contact had given him.

Before the evening's conversation had ended, the man had reached into his satchel and pulled out a corked leather vial. "Lysias, *the king,* wants you to get close enough to Maccabee to have someone pour this into his food or drink," the man had said.

Isokrates had pulled out the small cork and sniffed the liquid inside. "Hemlock?" he asked. The scent was vaguely familiar from his past experiences dealing with the poison.

His contact nodded. "There's no pain, just a numbness that overtakes the body, followed by paralysis that starts at the feet, and a loss of speech. The paralysis moves up the legs through the body, over the course of thirty minutes—and then, death."

"I am aware how it works," Isokrates snarled, already plotting how he would get the vial to someone close to Israel's beloved new ruler. "I am surprised that Lysias—sorry, *the king*—didn't ask me sooner. I thought this order would have been given long ago."

The man hesitated, as if considering what he should say. "The two previous attempts failed because of chance incidents that prevented the poisoner from reaching the target," he replied.

Now Isokrates would need to hasten to Jerusalem. He hadn't made it far down the dirt road before a sound drew his attention. It was the drunken vagrant from the tavern. The wretch had stumbled out and was vomiting outside the tavern door.

Isokrates turned again, headed for the inn where he would remain until the army of Judah's brother passed by. He had left his men at the tavern with the Seleucid contact, as protection. He had to ensure his message succeeded in reaching Lysias.

Isokrates rounded a corner. The streets seemed abandoned at that late hour, except for two people huddled together under one long cloak, trying to keep warm as they passed on the other side of the road. They looked at him, a man and a woman. He wouldn't have taken notice except that there was an uncomfortable recognition in the man's face. He stopped as they continued in the opposite direction.

The man was moving like he was injured. Isokrates realized they weren't huddled because of the cold, but because the woman was helping to support her companion. Just as Isokrates was about to turn and continue on toward his destination, a light from a doorway illuminated the injured man's face. Isokrates recognized him even under the bruises and lacerations. It was that bastard who had broken his collarbone back in that courtyard, and the wench with him must be that Hebrew slut.

It had not taken Isokrates long to find out everything he could about the Argyraspides Silver Shield deserter, who lived on the second floor in the north quarter with his Jewish slave, in active violation of the king's law. His name was Nabis, and the man had almost cost him his life. Isokrates had interviewed everyone he could, seeking any clue to the deserter's whereabouts. He had spread the word among the ranks that Nabis was now a fugitive, an enemy of the kingdom, and if found, he was to be killed. He had spoken with a soldier named

Orestes, who claimed to have saved Nabis's life, when they had fought together at Beth-Horn. Orestes refused to believe that Nabis was a traitor. From all Isokrates could gather, Nabis had been a respectable soldier and trainer until he fell in love with his slave, who must have converted him to her foreign customs and illegal religion. Now, he was one of the enemy.

Isokrates couldn't believe his luck. He had searched everywhere trying to track the bastard's whereabouts. He could only assume the woman with him tonight was that same slave whore he had fought to protect. As the couple turned a corner down an intersecting road, Isokrates drew his xiphos from underneath his cloak and darted across the street, down a narrow alley.

Chapter 43

SIMON CHARGED FORWARD, leading forty men on horseback, into the town of Neballat. As they entered the hamlet, the dirt street transitioned into a neighborhood of poorly built homes, made of stone and mortar. Eleazar accompanied Simon at the head of the column.

Simon knew he would have no sleep that night. He was determined to apprehend the fleeing Greek. If he was who the farmer had said, he couldn't risk letting him escape.

Simon felt a pain in his hand where he had struck his son Mattathais in punishment for his transgression. He hoped the loss of pride had hurt more than the blow.

"You think you're ready to be a soldier?" Simon had asked angrily. "You can't keep control of three other men. You were complicit in their act of abandoning their post and duties to seek out a whore!" Before his son could reply, he snapped, "That's it, isn't it? You and that other simpleton guard had already snuck off to Neballat to have your turn at desecrating your bodies inside a harlot's room. Now it was their turn."

"No!" Mattathias exclaimed. "I didn't want to go at all. It was—"

"Then you're too weak and foolish to be leading men to their deaths." Simon's voice grew quieter. "You put this army at risk and endangered the safety of our people—not just our lives, but Israel itself. Did you know one man you were guarding was accused of being a spy, carrying information brought to him by a Phoenician? And now he has escaped."

"Sir," a man interrupted, entering the tent, "the guards who were keeping watch over the women prisoners—we found them unconscious and bound together. Two of the women are still there, but the Greek's woman is missing."

"Gather riders!" Simon snapped, staring at his son angrily. "We are moving armed into Neballat."

Now in the town, Simon planned to search the streets and enter every tavern and inn, asking if people had seen a man and woman passing through who met the description. *After I've killed the spy,* Simon thought, *I'll have the two guards who left their post to visit the brothel flogged in front of the entire army. My son will administer the beatings.*

They halted at the first inn of the city. Ten of the riders continued down the dirt road, sending thick clouds of dust into the air. Simon hadn't made it to the door of the inn when he heard the shofar scream from a short distance away.

Darting quickly back to his horse, he mounted it and galloped in the direction of the noise. By the time Simon reached the location, twenty of his warriors, still mounted, were surrounding four people in the street. One man was dead, with blood soaking through his garment into a puddle that appeared almost black in the night. There was a woman sobbing, and two men staring at the thicket of spears poised at them from every direction.

§

Diomedes contemplated the events of the evening. After so many weeks of fruitless search, so much had happened so quickly. He yanked open the tavern door and entered with his sword drawn. At his back were five men armed with spears. They weren't Roman soldiers, like he was used to working with, but Hebrews. The tavern owner looked up, startled, but before he could say anything, Diomedes yelled, "Through here!"

The soldiers hastened past the tables, down the hall to the sleeping rooms. At the first room, Diomedes stepped aside and nodded. One soldier kicked in the door, and three others pressed past the threshold.

The two men inside the room had little time to react. The first reached for his sword, sheathed on his belt lying on the table beside him. Before he could draw his blade, the soldiers had plunged their weapons into him. The first spear entered his chest, the second his stomach. The other man darted for the window but was impaled against the wall. He began screaming, the sharp leaf spearhead having skewered his pelvis. The blow with the butt end of a second spear silenced him.

Diomedes motioned for the soldiers to follow. They crept to the room down the hall, and again the soldiers broke through the door and leaped inside. This time, the window was open, and the room was empty. "He's gone," Diomedes said with annoyance.

The two men they had slain were those he saw entering the tavern with Isokrates.

When Diomedes had arrived in Neballat, he had asked at every inn, tavern, shop, and market if anyone had seen a tall man who could pass for either Greek or Hebrew, with a scar on his chin. No one had. At last, an innkeeper remarked he had seen a Greek waiting in a tavern, on the north side of town, just sitting in the corner by himself.

Diomedes had found the tavern in question, then took a seat staring at the wall. He noticed the man not only looked Greek, but also had a military bearing that was unmistakable. The stranger had no scar and therefore could not be Isokrates, but Diomedes suspected that the man had come here to meet with that fiend.

Diomedes had waited. When the tavern owner came to his table, he ordered a cup of wine and drank it quickly. Then quietly, he asked that his cup be refilled with water. Again, he drank it quickly, acting as natural as possible, and soon he began acting intoxicated. He slumped in his chair and began to sway slightly, giving the appearance of a common drunkard.

The whole time, remaining inconspicuous, he watched the foreigner who was drinking alone in the cranny beside the fireplace. He tried to gather as much information as he could, noticing small details like his satchel bag, his shoes, and his manner of dress—which was Hebrew, not foreign.

After an hour, Diomedes had switched to wine, but drank far less than he made it appear to those around him. He spilled some liquid on the table, and slouched staring at it, with a look that suggested he might, at any moment, vomit.

At length, the tavern door had swung open, sending a gust of wind through the room. Three men had entered, shaking off the chill from outside. Clearly, the man in the center was Isokrates. He held his shoulder awkwardly, though he still walked like a soldier. The scar was unmistakable. His companions took seats at another table, but Isokrates sat down directly across from the foreigner.

Diomedes kept up his act—appearing drunk, trying to listen, but seeming to pay them no heed. A few times he heard the words "cavalry," "Maccabee," and "citadel." Then he saw the foreigner hand Isokrates a leather flask, and he thought he heard the word "hemlock."

Is Isokrates planning on poisoning Maccabee? Diomedes asked himself. Isokrates had been doing all the talking. What information had he given the other man, who must be the contact from Antioch? Whoever he was, Diomedes decided, none of these people could be allowed to leave the town alive.

When the conversation ended, Isokrates had risen and headed for the door. The hour being late, it wasn't long before the foreigner walked over to the tavern owner—to ask for a room, apparently, because he was shown to the second room down the hall. A moment later, Isokrates' two companions were escorted to the first room, closest to the drinking area.

As soon as they were out of sight, Diomedes discarded his drunkard act and bolted for the door. Exiting, he saw Isokrates, just a few hundred yards down the street, turn back and look at him, startled. Diomedes instantly resumed his guise—doubling over, pretending to vomit. Isokrates had turned back around and continued in the direction he had been walking, then disappeared around a corner. Diomedes again threw off the act and ran in the direction of his target.

Reaching the corner and peering around it, he saw Isokrates gazing down the street at two people huddled beneath a cloak, one of whom seemed to be limping. Then Isokrates darted across the street and down an alley.

Diomedes followed. At the next corner, he peered around and saw Isokrates stealthily lifting his blade, preparing to strike an unsuspecting man. A woman screamed.

Diomedes ran forward, as Isokrates and the man began to fight. It was the limping passerby he had seen earlier. Isokrates must have recognized him from somewhere. The metal clanged as the two swung their swords. Both men were quick and appeared to be well-trained.

You don't know who this man is, Diomedes thought, *but whoever he is, he's probably on your side.* Then he felt uncertain. Just because Isokrates wanted to kill him, didn't mean the stranger wasn't a danger to him.

The fighting waxed fierce. Isokrates' blade connected with the other man's side, causing the man to almost lose his footing, but he kept on. The woman kept crying out, "Nabis! Run! Let's just *go!*"

The shorter man, whom the woman was calling Nabis, swung once more at Isokrates, who caught hold of the shorter man's wrist. In return, Nabis gripped Isokrates' sword hand, leaving both men struggling in place. Isokrates's strength began to overpower Nabis, whose face already appeared battered. The taller man's sword began to slowly turn, aligning its sharp point with Nabis's head. It inched closer.

Isokrates drove his knee into Nabis's side, where he had been wounded. He did it again. The shorter man groaned in pain, and his xiphos slipped from his grasp. All the while,

Isokrates' blade moved closer toward Nabis's eye. The woman, seeing the perilous state of affairs, struck out at Isokrates, reigning blows on his back and head with her fists.

Letting go of his enemy's wrist, Isokrates backhanded the woman across the face, sending her whirling to the ground. Seeing her fall, Diomedes was reminded of his own Jewish mother, and a wave of pain passed through him. Should he intervene? What would be the consequences?

Nabis used his free hand to grip the hilt of Isokrates' shortsword, trying to turn it away from himself. The blade fluttered slightly, and both men remained checked in place, their strength fully exerted. Suddenly, both fell, and Isokrates was on top of Nabis, his full weight upon him, as he once again attempted to move his blade into his antagonist's eye.

Then Isokrates, with his free hand, reached behind him. Diomedes thought he was reaching for a second blade, but he had clasped the small leather flask that the foreigner had given him. With his thumb, he popped off the cork, which dangled by the thin leather laced around the stem. Perceiving danger, Nabis released the sword hilt with one hand and clutched Isokrates' hand that held the flask.

Isokrates turned his wrist slightly, dripping the poison inches from the Nabis's lips. The droplets dampened the dirt beside his face. Isokrates once more rotated his wrist, again spilling the poison even closer, almost onto Nabis's mouth. The blade in Isokrates' other hand again inched closer to his victim.

"Nabis!" the woman cried out again, and suddenly Diomedes recalled the rumors of Isokrates, about his fight with a Greek who fought to protect a Jewish slave whom he had come to love. He remembered the name his informants had mentioned: the name this woman was shouting.

At that moment, the woman looked right at Diomedes. She saw his drawn sword. He looked into her eyes that petitioned so ardently for help, and he knew he had to act while he still could.

Diomedes could see that even though his face was turned to the side, the stem of the flask was now right over Nabis's mouth, and again Isokrates began to turn his wrist.

Stepping silently out of the shadows, Diomedes plunged his xiphos into Isokrates' back. Isokrates let out a roar and turned, slashing at Diomedes, the flask dropping harmlessly to the ground.

Isokrates stood suddenly, unaware of how badly wounded he was, and again charged forward, swinging his blade, with Diomedes' xiphos still lodged in his back. Diomedes recoiled backwards, narrowly missing the blow. Ashen-faced, Isokrates stood still for a moment, wheezing badly, then brought his sword above his head. Diomedes moved out of the direction of the blade and drew out a small dagger. Before he could again strike, Nabis, who had scrambled to his feet, picked up his sword, maneuvered behind Isokrates, and brought it down hard on Isokrates' shoulder.

Isokrates collapsed to his knees, making a sound of helpless fury, looking deathly faint. Diomedes would have finished him off with his dagger, but Nabis lunged his xiphos down into his enemy's chest. A hiss of air escaped the puncture wound, and blood began to pour from Isokrates' mouth and nose. Nabis stood motionless. Then he put his foot on his assailant's shoulder and wrenched his blade from his chest. Isokrates' eyes rolled back, he moaned, and his chest heaved its last.

Then Diomedes heard the abrupt, melodious squeal of a shofar, and looked up to see a rider charging them, spear in hand. It wasn't twenty seconds before scores of other riders charged around the corner, spears in position. Diomedes knew these men must be a part of Maccabee's army in the north. Surrounded, Nabis tossed his sword to the ground. Surprised, Diomedes recognized two of the men. One of them clearly recognized him as well.

"I've seen you before," Eleazar said, looking down from his horse at Diomedes.

"Yes, you have," Diomedes answered.

Simon glanced at Diomedes, trying to place him and to understand what had happened in the moments before they arrived.

"You're Rome's man, working with those foreign diplomats," Eleazar said. Simon, too, now recognized him.

"Yes," Diomedes answered, agreeably. "And you are Eleazar, brother of Judah the Maccabee."

"What is the meaning of this killing?" Simon barked. "Why are you with this runaway prisoner who was captured as a spy?"

"A spy? Oh, I very much doubt that," Diomedes responded disarmingly. "To the best of my knowledge, the man is a Syrian soldier—a Silver Shield who deserted his garrison months ago because he was caught letting his slave, who he had married in secret, worship in a synagogue. He had to flee because of this wretch before you." Diomedes pointed at Isokrates' corpse. "He was leader of the Syrian espionage network in Jerusalem. I have been tracking his movements, intending to apprehend or kill him, for some time."

Simon sat on his horse, his mind racing, unsure what to believe. What if this was a setup? The whole thing sounding unlikely.

"And there's more," Diomedes continued. "Three men are staying in rooms at the tavern on the next street. Two are companions of this man. One is an agent from Syria who carries information received from this Isokrates. He is bound for Antioch."

Simon listened carefully. "You can take me to these men?"

"I will."

"What of him?" Eleazar asked his brother, gesturing toward Nabis, who was kneeling beside Abishag with his arm around her.

Simon paused a moment before responding in Hebrew, "Tie him up and take him with us. He may be a spy or not, but either way he knows too much just to be let go. We'll decide in

Jerusalem where his loyalties lie."

"A very wise decision," Diomedes responded, also in Hebrew, which he had learned from his mother as a child. "But your inquiry will reveal the truth of my report."

"Take us to where the Syrians hide, Roman. If you have lied, your blood will be on your head." Simon said it in Hebrew, quoting the phrase in Levitical Law regarding condemned men.

Chapter 44

"SIMON WILL SOON be returning from the north," Jonathan said, as he and Judah walked through the files of soldiers that surrounded the citadel. Men were moving siege works back from yet another onslaught against the enemy stronghold. "The scouts said they have over forty-five-hundred refugees with them. They should be here tomorrow."

"Good," Judah replied.

"It's a lot of mouths to feed," Jonathan said, worriedly. "It's the Sabbath year. Most of the fields in Judea remain unsown and unharvested."

"It will also mean more men we can arm against the Syrians, for the coming fight," Judah answered.

The rumors of Lysias's plans to mobilize troubled him. This would be their decisive battle. The invasion would determine if they could truly win their freedom, or if they would be broken and once more enslaved to the will of a Seleucid king. If Judah broke their army before they arrived, if he could shatter their host, they would have a country of their own, a place they could call theirs, no longer ruled by Gentiles, but by themselves, by Hebrews.

But if he failed and their massive army did, in fact, enter Jerusalem, it would be over. Of the patriotic movement, only the idea would remain. Even if they survived, it would take ten years to regain their current momentum, if that were even possible. The belief the people had in him—the belief that they could rule themselves—would be uprooted forever, and Lysias's men would be so embedded in Jerusalem, they'd never be able to dispel them. Lysias wouldn't make the mistakes Antiochus made. In the end, the Jews would be taken in chains from their lands or massacred.

Judah wondered if Simon had done as instructed and sent men to store the gold and arms with their Nabatean allies. But if it came down to evacuating behind the Jordan, and relying on the Nabateans, all would be lost anyway.

Better to die as men, thought Judah, *and be remembered as heroes and patriots. At least then our deaths might yet inspire those who remain to take up arms, and fight for their freedom, with words of our deeds on their lips, and thoughts of what we did for our country on their minds.*

"The pagans can't possibly hold out much longer," Jonathan said, staring up at the citadel. "They have to be getting low on food by now. There are fewer and fewer arrows coming from the battlements every day."

"It's hard to say," Judah replied. "I've heard stories of people under siege who survived on the flesh of their dead for years. When Simon returns with all of his men, we'll array our whole force before the Seleucids to further demoralize them, and then we'll extend one last invitation for their surrender."

"I'm sure Simon will be anxious to see the rest of his family," said Jonathan. The remark made Judah think of Martha, who was still staying with Simon's family. In spite of himself, Judah had gone to visit her on many occasions. They often found themselves awkwardly staring at each other, not knowing what to say, each of them holding their glance just a little too long.

"And I'm sure Eleazar will be pleased to find out his wife is with child."

Eleazar's wife had conceived shortly before he and Simon took their men to liberate the northern towns of Israel. For over seven months they had campaigned in the north, but over four-thousand-five hundred Jews had been saved because of it.

I imagine he will," Judah responded, happy for his brother.

"The physician said she looks so big that she might be carrying twins."

"Does the world really need two more Eleazar's?" Jonathan asked caustically.

"*Ratzon ha'El,*" Judah said with a smile.

§

Looking across the valley at over fifty-thousand men who made camp in the shadows of the hills, Lysias thought to himself, *they do look impressive.*

He had never even seen a force of that magnitude at one location. It was larger than the army Alexander had used to conquer the world with.

The elephants were sequestered from the soldiers. The number of horses they had amassed seemed infinite, and they would press more men into service on their march south. The Phoenicians would join, the Ammorites, and more. *Judea will be a memory,* he told himself. *In a thousand years, they will say the land of Israel was a mythical place that never even existed.* The march would be long, but he would restore rule to their southern border and put an end to this troublesome tribe of people.

Lysias was ignoring the tedious details that General Nicantor was disclosing in his dreary, monotone voice. He wanted to yell at the man, "You see to the details. That's your job, but in the name of all the gods, speak with some brevity!" but he didn't. He nodded his head while tuning Nicantor out, trying to focus his thoughts on the coming battle where his force would face this Judah the Hammer, and destroy him.

The other fools could never win, because they don't comprehend the way the Maccabee's mind works, thought Lysias. The upstart would never allow the Seleucid army to reach Jerusalem without a fight, no matter how enormous they were. Judah would try to break them on the march. The people would rally to him, but they would falter, and when it was all over, the Jews would be destroyed.

"What?" Lysias said, his ears picking up something Nicantor had said.

"I said, how is the king?" Nicantor repeated.

"Oh, as good as a five-year-old child can be in this environment."

"Are you sure it's wise to bring a boy, so young, on a military campaign—especially when he is king of the empire?"

Yes. Not when I don't care whether he lives or dies, Lysias thought, but he replied genially, "He has to rule the empire someday. It's time he learns."

Now at least I can get him away from that bitch mother of his while he's still young and impressionable. She had told him, "One day my son will stand before you a man and make his mother proud." The way she said it, in her habitually arrogant and sneering voice, the words were clearly a threat. If he could teach the child some values, the boy would learn right from wrong and would see the wicked woman for who she really was. *If such as thing as right and wrong even exists,* Lysias mused. The philosophers and the pious claimed there was a distinction, but was such a concept just a product of human perception? Would killing that boy be any more "wrong" than a lion killing a goat?

Lysias's mind wandered to the message his agent had brought him from Isokrates in Judea. The agent said the Acra would not hold out much longer. Well, it would simply *have to* hold out until after the invasion. How could he could get supplies to the citadel without first invading the country?

The whole thing will be simplified if Isokrates succeeds in poisoning the Maccabee, he thought wistfully. The patriot army would then dissolve, and Jerusalem would fall into their hands like ripe fruit from a tree.

§

Crassus watched dreamily as the bow of the ship glided through the waters. He could feel the rhythm of the waves gently smacking the hull. He looked up wearily to see the Joppa harbor straight ahead. It looked different. This time there would be no harbor master, no Seleucid soldiers, no remnant of customs or government at all. Jewish fishermen went about their trade at will, with no one to order them about or take twenty percent of their catch at the end of each day as tax for their rulers.

Leave it to man to devise a brilliant invention like government, Crassus thought despondently. He glanced down at his satchel that held the treaty tablets and patted it protectively. It was a miracle they had made it this far.

Have I changed as much as this place has? he wondered. He thought of Fabius, his old friend, who was never short on giving guidance and always knew what to do, even in impossible situations. If he were here, Fabius would stop at nothing before completing the mission.

And that is what Crassus would do, because it was the right thing. Somehow he would find Judah again, wherever he was. He would give him Rome's promise. He would sail back to Rome, deliver his answer to the senate, then leave Rome for the north forever.

He already knew Rome would want him to return and act as a guide for whatever soldiers and arms they were actually willing to send. They wouldn't get their way, though. He would do something Fabius would never have done. He would take his uniform and burn it, buy a horse, and head for Northern Italy, where he would buy farmland, marry a woman half his age, and never look back.

The small ship slowed and eased into the harbor. The few men who had survived the storm jumped onto the dock with ropes. Crassus saw someone walking toward him with an air of authority and purpose. He gripped the satchel tightly and placed his other hand on his gladius. The man strode closer, and Crassus prepared to draw the blade. Then he saw the man's face, and relaxed in recognition.

"You're late," Diomedes said with a smile.

Book VIII
At the Lion's Gate

162 BC

"There is no man that hath power over the spirit to retain the spirit; neither hath he power over the day of death; and there is no discharge in war: neither shall wickedness deliver him that is given to it."

~ Solomon

βιβλίο οκτώ

Chapter 45

JUDAH WATCHED THE endless multitude of phalanxes move forward on the open plain toward their position. He tried to force the implacable thoughts from his mind, like the fact that if they lost this battle, Jerusalem would fall, and the brief period of freedom they had enjoyed would end. All they had fought for, all the blood spilt and lives lost, would be in vain.

He could see on the ascent above, the massed rectangular matrixes of men aligned up the shallow slope, converging on the left. Lysias had secured the hills, sealing off all avenues of approach from the high ground. Furthermore, the Syrians had placed themselves with the morning sun at their backs. Its piercing rays stabbed blindingly into the eyes of the Israelite army.

Spread out beneath the hills was a force made up of more armed men than Judah had ever seen. They were all marching right for them. In between their formations were contingents of cavalry.

Judah's series of connecting phalanxes formed a wedge, the center placed at the vanguard. Like the Syrians' own formation, the Jewish lines traveled the length of the inclined slope toward Judah's left. He had positioned his men with their backs against a shallow embankment, so the advancing sea of men would have to march toward them at an incline. Unlike the uniformed Syrians, the Israelites wore armor as diverse and unique as the men themselves and the weapons each brandished.

The rising tension was disquieting. The Israelite army seemed to collectively recoil at the shrill scream of one of the elephants as the beasts trudged forward between the clusters of enemy infantry.

On the other side of the plain, the handlers had poured strong drink into the animals' mouths, making the elephants drunk and irritable. The monstrous creatures had a square, walled carriage perched on each of their backs, strapped on by harnesses. Called a *howdah,* this platform bore four archers aloft, who braced themselves against the inner walls. In front sat an Indian driver, holding the creature's reins. Each driver kept a hammer and chisel on hand with which to sever the elephant's spinal cord, if the beast became uncontrollable.

Judah had remained sleepless the previous night, examining his armor, knowing the battle was upon them. He tried to contemplate what more he could do and what else could be done in preparation for the following day. After he could think of nothing else, he cleared his mind and began to sharpen his sword. His blade, which he had taken when he slew Apollonious, was already sharp, but doing the ritual quieted him and prepared his soul for the killing. It sharpened his heart more than the blade itself, desensitizing him against the fear and madness tomorrow would bring. Soon he found himself praying—not for his own safety or for a cessation of hostilities, but for his country, for the children of Israel, for the glory of the Lord's own name, which had been profaned among the pagans.

As expected, over the previous three weeks, Lysias had moved his army south beyond Jerusalem before rerouting north. He had attacked Beth-Zur, and massacred the city. The men Judah had placed there to hold off the army until they could be reinforced had not lasted three days before the siege engines breached the walls and the Syrians leveled it from its foundation.

Judah had moved his men south from Jerusalem, knowing with the shortage of food due to the Sabbath year they could not hold out against a lengthy siege. He knew he must stop Lysias's army before it reached Jerusalem.

The Hebrews had made their camp at Beth-Zechariah, toward the high ground. It was the last line of defense before the Syrians reached the city. *If I can't stop them here,* Judah thought, *my country dies before my very eyes.*

Judah had wanted Eleazar to remain in Jerusalem with his wife and newborn twin sons. For the first time since the death of their father, Eleazar seemed happy and at peace. But the younger man had scoffed at the suggestion. "Am I to stay in the city with the women and let my brothers do the fighting for me?" he had asked petulantly. Judah had eventually yielded, reminded of years before when they had hunted bandits in the Judean hills, both of them so young. He would have never believed back then that he would be leading the army of Israel in revolution against the Seleucid Empire, and that the only thing standing between oblivion and their freedom was he and his men.

Another scream from an elephant drew Judah's full attention to the impending battle. The enemy formations loomed menacingly. The elephants appeared mountainous as they closed the distance, mammoth tusks protruding from their faces. The pulsation of the synchronized marching grew thunderous in volume, and shook the very ground, displacing small pebbles and stones on the inclined rise. Judah could tell by their concave flanks that the enemy hoped to envelop them on both sides. He had counted on it, forming his men in a wedge just for that reason.

The details of the infantry units grew clear as they approached. Pacing behind them marched ranks of Syrian archers, readying nocked arrows. *They are almost in range,* thought Judah tensely, counting the seconds. From the front row of the forward phalanx, he turned his head and nodded to his signal commander. The commander raised his shofar to his lips, letting out a deep melodious bellow that smote the hillside. At once, the host of Israelite soldiers roared a salvo of shouts.

Forty feet above the slope at their back, Judah's men pulled away the sackcloth coverings that camouflaged all twenty-three torsion catapults they had emplaced. "Now!" Judah roared. Another loud note sounded from the shofar, and the men manning the artillery released the levers with resonating cracks, as the torsion ropes were discharged, sending sixty-pound rocks soaring at an arch into the sky, many crashing down into the farthest-flanking Syrian ranks. The lines of enemy were instantly broken as soldiers were mangled, screaming from shattered limbs. Every phalanx hit was halted and forced to re-form. The catapults were quickly reloaded as the Syrians drew in, still nearer.

Judah nodded again, and a different note sounded from a smaller shofar. Then the Israelite archers in the center of the wedge nocked arrows to their bows and took aim. Again, a barrage of heavy stones was released into the advancing lines of Selecuid soldiers. The men broke their silence and cheered as they saw a boulder slam into the face of an oncoming elephant, causing the beast to rear up, squeal, and fall dying to the ground. Once more the front lines of Syrian phalanxes were pummeled with the boulders, and arrows rained down into the enemy lines. Hundreds of Syrians were already lying dead or wounded, but the tide of enemy soldiers kept pushing forward.

A third time, Judah gestured to his signalman. Another melodious note was repeated throughout the lines. Suddenly, Judah's six-hundred cavalrymen, led by Joel, charged from the tree line at the base of the hills and galloped toward the nearest far-stretching wing of the Syrian horde. The cavalry crashed into the poorly defended flank of the phalanx. The lines broke, and the forward phalanx folded in on itself, causing the lead element to fall back in retreat. The pursuing Syrians nevertheless continued their advance, and the Israelite cavalry wheeled around and attacked the next element. Joel's two mounted columns hooked into a two-pronged charge.

Then, from the far tree line in the shadows under the hills which the Syrians occupied, a massive mounted force broke into a full charge, cutting around the far edges of their own infantry lines. Judah stood incredulous, as over ten-thousand horsemen began flanking the outer lines on his left, countering his own cavalry attack. The Syrian force billowed dust into the air like a wall of smoke, from the animals' earth-breaking hooves. The charge sounded like an earthquake.

Joel turned his men, re-forming against the assault. They appeared as a grain of sand being hurled into a tempest. The world seemed motionless and strangely silent, before the two unparalleled elements crashed into each other. The Hebrew light cavalry was consumed on all sides, while the majority of mounted Syrians did not even stop, but continued their onslaught toward Judah's lines.

Simultaneously, the center phalanx surged forward, and now loomed right before them. The elephants towered above the men, and then, they, too, made straight for their ranks. Jonathan, who was in the same forward phalanx as Judah, one column behind his brother, grimaced at the coming collision of the two battle lines. Simon and Gaddi, in charge of the left apex of the battlefront, braced themselves, about to be assaulted by the massive cavalry charge. Eleazar stood his ground on the right, waiting for the Syrian force to come into range. Arrows began to rain down on him, and Eleazar began to take his first causalities.

Judah saw the momentum of the elephant between the two advancing phalanxes aligned with his center. The beast was armored with a breast plate and had steel tips on its tusks. He heard a high-pitched scream, and the animal rammed into his front lines. Men were shouting, and his phalanx contorted, as the lines warped around the huge creature.

The elephant, crazed, was rocking its head violently from side to side, striking men with its massive tusks and body. Occasionally, an Israelite soldier would strike at it, and the beast would let out another of its high-pitched squeals. The archers who sat perched in the howdah began firing down from their vantage point at Judah's men. Then the enemy's infantry crashed into the already mangled Israelite lines.

Knowing his lines were at risk of breaking, Judah shouted for his commanders to move the formations back and reform, but they were already engaged. Each Syrian advance across their lines began with an onrush of one or several elephants, smashing their front ranks.

Judah plunged his sarissa into the breastplate of a Syrian soldier. Rending his pike from the man's body, he impaled the next Syrian who stepped forward to fill the other's place. He lunged again at another, when his spear was impacted by the wooden haft of a Syrian pike, redirecting his blow downward. Judah felt the shock through his hands and heard the shaft of the sarissa crack. He drew his sword, moved in between two rows of pikes, and plunged the blade into the soldier's neck, then slashed at the face of another, the blow striking under the helmet and through the eye socket. Judah could hear an elephant's chilling scream, and saw that one of his men had advanced underneath the animal and sliced through its Achilles tendon, causing the beast to stagger and collapse under its own weight.

On one side of Judah, the mass of Syrian cavalry plummeted into the left wing of the forward lines that Simon and his men defended. The Jews' twenty-foot sarissas halted the momentum of the first wave of mounted Syrians, who toppled over on their dying steeds. Soon Simon's men found themselves engaged, checked in place with the Seleucid heavy cavalry, which attempted to move uphill, behind the Israelite lines.

Judah could see Jonathan leading his column forward, replacing Judah's own front rank, as they exchanged places and the exhausted forward ranks moved to the rear. The fighting raged on. Moving uphill, back through the ranks, Judah saw the whole battle at once. To his left were Simon's men, trying to hold off the cavalry and prevent them from breaching the phalanx's rear. The oscillating rebel lines compressed against the Syrian ranks.

Above, in the hills opposite them, Judah saw the wall of his men, hemmed in upon the high ground. The Syrian phalanxes were marching around toward one side now, attempting to concentrate and overwhelm his left flank. Once they moved downhill and advanced toward their wing, it would be over. To his right, Judah saw Eleazar's soldiers, who had decimated the first phalanx they faced and were pushing their lines onward. *If we can overwhelm them on the right,* Judah thought, *before our left folds, we may be able to force them to retreat.* All his hope now rested in the brother he had almost left behind.

Just then another elephant slammed into Judah's center ranks and drove a wedge between his men. Shouts of panic rose in the air as Judah's soldiers tried to close in the gap, prodding the animal savagely with their spears. The Syrian phalanx wedged inward, driving into the opening that the elephant had created, and the thicket of colliding spears appeared endless.

§

"We can break them," Eleazar shouted above the bedlam. He had just destroyed another phalanx, sending its men into full retreat. "Push forward!" he shouted over the madness. The next Syrian phalanx closed in. Syrian pikes mingled with Israelite spears, and again men started falling in panicked, shrill shouts. The sound of shields obstructing steel was deafening. Eleazar sensed his men were overwhelming the Syrians, bolstered by the ecstasy of their momentum.

Then he saw an elephant charging their position. *I'm not going to let these fat, stupid creatures steal victory from our hand,* he said to himself. The Syrian left was thinning as most the men withdrew in retreat. Behind the charging elephant advanced another phalanx, waiting for the disorder the creature would deliver.

"We can destroy them here!" Eleazar shouted, in the rapture of battle.

"Now!" he yelled, bounding forward with his spear, charging the elephant in his path. His men reacted, following his lead, advancing behind him. The elephant swung its head to one side, its tusk slicing through the abdomen of one of Eleazar's men, eviscerating him.

Coming around to the beast's side, Eleazar took aim, as an arrow from one of the archers in the howdah whizzed past his ear. Eleazar drove his spear forward into the beast's chest. The elephant let out a wail, staggered drunkenly, and came crashing down.

The whole advancing phalanx of Eleazar's men shouted in elation, seeing the beast die. Those in the howdah, their bodies rattled, attempted to rise and escape, but were slaughtered.

"Re-form the lines!" Eleazar yelled, as the next advancing Syrian phalanx made ready to close in on them. But then the phalanx halted, seeing the death of the war elephant and the Israelite lines regrouping.

"What are they waiting for?" Eleazar muttered impatiently. Then he saw it. Another elephant was charging into their position as fast as the creature could run. The archers on its back were already firing arrows. *They don't learn!* Eleazar thought. *These creatures aren't* that *hard to kill!*

He strode out ahead of his formation and saw that this elephant bore the royal crest and was larger than the other he had slain. "Rear columns, follow me!" he bellowed, wanting to leave most of his phalanx intact. Again he darted right for the charging elephant. The distance between them vanished. He saw one of his commanders drop to his knees, an arrow shaft suddenly protruding from his stomach. Eleazar moved to the side of the beast, ready to strike, and without warning was engaged by two Syrian infantrymen running alongside the animal. He ducked, and a spear tip barely missed his head.

Levi, one of Eleazar's subordinates, thrust his spear forward, impaling one of the soldiers. An arrow flew into Levi's neck from an archer firing from the back of the elephant. Another

Jew parried the second Syrian, while Eleazar re-gripped his spear and threw it up toward the archer who towered above. The leaf-head lodged deep into the man's shoulder, sending him staggering backwards into the howdah. Eleazar drew his sword, moved beneath the elephant, and lunged his blade into its stomach. He quickly stepped backwards, and the beast screamed, rearing onto its hind legs. Then it fell, crashing onto its side.

§

From the front lines, Judah stabbed at the mass of armored men who continued to press forward. Abruptly, he felt a sharp pain in his thigh and he knew his leg had been pierced. Unhesitating, he returned the blow. Seconds passed slowly, and he felt a rush of lightheadedness. His hands tingled, and a wave of nausea clutched him. He could barely make out something that flashed at him, and suddenly, he felt his head snap backward, sending him whirling to the ground. Opening his eyes, he realized he had fallen. He could make out the trampled, churned soil and shod feet all around him. He stayed low, as the men behind him moved near, gathering about him, protectively. They lifted him to his feet.

A Syrian spear tip had gouged the side of his face, slicing a deep gash from his lower eyelid down his cheek. Judah looked around for his spear, but it was nowhere to be found. Then he realized his thigh was bleeding profusely. He wondered if the bones in his face were broken.

Now isn't the time to think about it, Judah upbraided himself. *You're alive and can move. That's enough.*

It took a minute, but once Judah gathered his bearings, he shakily moved behind the lines. From this vantage point, he saw that his right flank, their only lingering hope, that had been advancing so earnestly, was now in full retreat.

What's happened? he thought, dismayed. The left was

now collapsing into the center. Disoriented, he saw a runner approach. He recognized him as one of Eleazar's captains. "What's happening?" Judah tried to shout, but his voice sounded faint, and blood ran into his mouth. "Why isn't Eleazar holding the right?"

"Maccabee," the man said, looking confused and tearful. "Your brother, Eleazar, is dead!"

Judah stood speechless, overwhelmed.

"He was crushed by one of those monsters, after he slew the thing."

Judah stared at the battlefield, the whole world in chaos. His commanders were surrounding him, talking in a chorus of shouts, "What do we do?" "We need to reinforce the left!" "We need to fall back!" "Get on a horse and escape while you can!" But he heard nothing.

He looked at the battlefield and saw the Syrians' reserve phalanx pushing into his left to support the already overwhelming cavalry. His center was on the verge of shattering, and more elephants were advancing, slamming into his forward lines. He had started the battle with almost thirty-thousand men, and now it looked like he had less then fifteen.

"Retreat," Judah shouted. "Move the lines back up the hill until the Syrians can't advance without overextending. Then move the archers to the front to cover us."

Chapter 46

THE SUN WAS descending westward, and only the last rays of light shown over the misty hills. Hundreds of vultures filled the sky, circling above the battlefield. The bodies lay strewn across the scorched desert earth. The sand surrounding them was stained maroon and black. Lysias had smelled the rotting stench of battlefields before, the smell of aging death. The air was heavy and stagnant as swarms of flies buzzed around the corpses.

Lysias walked up the incline where the Israelites had placed the catapults, which they set fire to before their retreat. He hadn't expected it. He examined the smoldered Greek artillery pieces they had no doubt captured in Jerusalem. *Nicantor did well,* Lysias thought, seeing the general below on the open ground, giving orders to a commander. Despite his flaws, Nicantor was the best field commander and tactician Lysias had. His timing had been perfect when he ordered the cavalry charge toward the Israelite left flank. Even when the enemy's right began to gain ground, his deployment of the elephants broke them, as the phalanxes crushed their center.

Walking down the rocky slope, two soldiers dragged a dead Hebrew soldier by the arms and dropped the body before Lysias. The junior officer who accompanied them spoke. "Sir, we were told by one of the captured Jews, that this one here is the brother of Judah, the Maccabee."

Lysias examined the bearded man closely. He had a great deal of dirt in his hair and beard. His clothes and armor were disheveled, and dried blood had streaked down his nose and ear.

"What happened to him?" Lysias asked, staring in bewilderment.

"He was crushed by one of our elephants. He slew it, and the animal fell sidelong, rolling over on him. General Nicantor wants to know what you want done with the body, if we should deliver it to the Israelite leadership, as an act of courtesy or—"

"Decapitate it and put the head on a pike with the rest of them," Lysisas answered, irritably.

"*Courtesy,* toward these people? I'm not here to be courteous. I'm here to kill them all. *To win.*"

"Yes, sir," the officer replied. He departed, and the two soldiers dragged the body away.

"That goes for the prisoners too!" Lysias shouted after them. "We're going to start fighting a new kind of war." His voice trailed off. "And bring the king from his tent to see. The boy needs to learn what his empire costs."

Lysias saw Nicantor approaching, stepping over and around the littered corpses.

"Still," Lysias said to Nicantor, "one has to admire these Jews. They might have won if we had fewer men and cavalry, and no elephants. If their right flank had only held … Well, now they're in retreat. They've lost more than half their men, with nowhere to go but Jerusalem, where they will make a desperate attempt to hold it, but will fail."

"They're beaten," Nicantor replied shortly, suppressing the vanity in his voice. He hated the Jews and resented Lysias's words. The battle was won because of him—not because the Jews lacked cavalry or elephants.

"Yes, they're beaten," answered Lysias, "and what's better, they probably know it."

The Jews had little food on account of their Sabboth year, and now—on top of hunger—their spirit had been crushed. Faith in their god was surely dwindling, along with faith in their leader. All Maccabee's people would see was a defeat.

That would do more to kill him and to destroy the rebels than poisoning the man could have ever done.

"They will try to hold Jerusalem, and they will all die there," Lysisas said to Nicantor, smiling. "Once the rebels are put down, I'll tear their temple to the ground. I'll take the Maccabee's head and hang it from Jerusalem's walls, then lock the gates and burn the city down. Every last Jew will die."

Nicantor looked weary. "We should be able to make it to the city by tomorrow," he said.

"What were *our* losses?" his superior demanded.

"Fifteen thousand of our infantry—"

"And the cavalry?"

"Just over six thousand, and seventeen of the elephants."

"I thought it was only fourteen." Lysias said, perturbed.

"The last three are so badly wounded, they won't be able to even get out of this valley. They're putting them out of their misery right now. There are one or two more who may not survive their wounds either. We'll know in a few days."

Lysias shook his head slowly, angered by the news. "How many of the enemy dead have we estimated?"

"They're still counting. Around fourteen thousand."

They lost fewer men then we did, Lysias thought. *Whose victory was it, really?*

"War costs dearly, and it sometimes costs the victor a higher wage in blood," Nicantor murmured.

"A Pyrrhic victory," Lysias said, remembering the Greek king, Pyrrhus of Epirus, who ruled in Epirus and Macedon some hundred years before. He was considered by many, including Hannibal, to be one of the greatest military commanders who ever lived—second only to Alexander the Great, who was his cousin.

Pyrrhus had invaded Italy with a twenty-five-thousand-man army and twenty war elephants. He won the Battle of Heraclea, but at the cost of almost as many lives as the lost lives of the Romans he defeated. Then at the Battle of Asculum, Pyrrhus defeated the Roman army once more, but again it cost his army as many lives as the dead of the enemy. This rendered him incapable of holding onto the territory he had won. This irony had given rise to the phrase, *a Pyrrhic victory*. Pyrrhus had died in a skirmish in the city of Argos when an old woman dropped a tile from her rooftop, killing him.

That's how it happens, Lysias thought grimly. *A great warrior and king meets his death at the hands of a frail old woman wielding a roof tile. Do the gods have no justice?*

"How long until we're ready to move out?" asked Nicantor.

"We'll camp up on the high ground until morning," said Lysias. "Tomorrow we'll march on the city."

§

Judah couldn't feel the numbness in his face or the blood running through the bandage, down his thigh. All he felt was the sorrow of his nation's calamity and the pain for Eleazar. His little brother was dead. How could this happen? Why had God refused to deliver their enemies to them in battle, as before?

It seemed like a dream. It seemed unreal—the brothers standing before him, their eyes filled with questions and sorrow, looking to him for answers.

He staggered, and Jonathan caught him.

"You must sit, Judah, before you fall. Sit," ordered Simon.

Gaddi stood some distance away, staring out at the wounded.

Judah limped forward, grimacing in pain. His leg was swollen. "In Jerusalem we'll get a horse for you to ride," Simon said. "You're no use to anyone dead."

After they had broken away from the battle, they retreated all that night, knowing the Syrians would not advance until morning. The retreat was slow. Many of the men were injured, and many more who had left the battlefield alive, would die in a few days. Their life had not ebbed away immediately, but it would desert them soon, Judah knew. Their souls would depart them in the night, in a fever, or on the march, in exhaustion.

More than the weight of his brother's loss was the torment of losing the battle. Not because of the loss of pride, but because he had lost his country its freedom. Lysias would chase them down, lay siege to Jerusalem, and tear it asunder.

He thought of Eleazar when they were small, how they would pretend to be soldiers in David's or Gideon's army, playing with sticks as if they were swords. They would bicker and fight at times, but Judah still knew that deep down, Eleazar always looked up to him.

He thought of Eleazar as a man. There wasn't ever a more affable person, a more satisfied soul. He was always cheerful, even in the darkest of moments. Though Eleazar had changed after their father died, once he married and sired children, he had found peace again.

What will I tell his wife? Judah wondered. She had two babies to look after, and her husband was gone. Judah would make sure she would always be safe, and her children taken care of, as long he was alive.

You know the truth, though, he told himself. *You won't be alive much longer to take care of anyone.* He had to face the reality. His army was destroyed. In two days, Jerusalem would be in the hands of the heathens. Lysias would never let him live—not if he was captured, not if he surrendered, and not if he escaped. Judah could try to hold Jerusalem, in which case they would fight bravely and would all die there, or they could take to the hills, where the army would be hunted down and slaughtered. It would have been better to have died with Eleazar in battle.

"What shall we do, brother?" asked Jonathan, his eyes big with uncertainty.

"Leave me be," said Judah.

He needed time alone. He limped to the edge of the ravine. He tried to pray.

God, how could You let this come to pass? he prayed silently. *Does it please You to see Your enemies at the doorstep of Your holy city? Why did You let this happen? Have we sinned? I did all I could, but I could not save your people.*

Judah cleared his thoughts, as he felt the soft breeze, cooling his face. A soft voice seemed to answer somewhere from the depths within him. *They are not yours to save. They are Mine. Jerusalem is not yours to protect. It is Mine.*

At once, a serenity blanketed Judah. He knew now what they must do.

He opened his eyes to find Simon standing beside him.

"What now, Maccabee? Defend Jerusalem, or take to the hills, like the old way?"

"Neither—and both," Judah replied.

Simon looked puzzled.

"The city is indefensible. It's too big, with the few men we have, and completely unfortified. If we try, the people will all be slaughtered when it falls. But the temple mount is not too big, nor is it unfortified. We'll leave one-third of our force there, with all the food and weapons we can spare, and barricade it. We'll lead the other two-thirds up to the mountains, and send riders to have our Nabatean allies meet us with our arms and money that Gaddi stored with them.

"The Syrians won't be able to chase after us, not with such a significant force being left in Jerusalem, so they'll be forced to lay siege to the temple mount. When they do, we'll attack them from the rear. We'll harass them and bleed them dry of resources and soldiers. Maybe we can hold out until Rome sends arms and some men."

Judah remembered how he had signed the treaty parchment Crassus had placed before him. Even if Rome was true to its word, help would not arrive for a year or two. And Rome had promised to send arms and money, not men.

Judah sighed. The future was in the hands of God.

Judah glanced at Simon and saw the uncertainty, the question he could not bear to ask. It really wasn't a question, but a statement of truth: *We are defeated, aren't we?*

Yes. Yes, we are, Judah thought back at him. *But that's no reason to make it easy for the bastards.*

"Judah," Simon finally said, "one of Eleazar's men said the elephant Eleazar charged had the royal seal on it. Eleazar must have thought he was attacking Lysias."

"It doesn't make much difference now, does it?" replied Judah. "Get the men up. We have to reach Jerusalem by sundown and set up our defense on the temple mount as best we can. Then we will leave the city at once."

"I'm not going with you," Simon said firmly.

"What?"

"I will stay with those who defend the temple."

"I need you with me, Simon."

"I am a priest. I will stay with the temple," his brother repeated.

Simon was surprised, almost to the point of worry, that Judah was too weary and broken to argue with him. Judah's moment of serenity had passed, and he was thinking about Eleazar again.

He yelled at himself in his mind. *It should have been you charging those mammoth creatures. You trying to inspire the men to win, not Eleazar. He should never have died. He would be here now if you hadn't failed him. You let your men die, your brother die, and now you're letting Israel die.*

§

Cloaked, Kalisto walked through Palermo, the Sicilian city founded by Phoenician traders to barter with Syracuse. It was their last stop before they reached Rome, and they needed supplies. *Then, I'm done doing business for Rome,* Kalisto thought, *or any other government for that matter.* He had made enough gold off the god-cursed Roman vultures to last him three lifetimes. He'd take Crassus back to Rome, then return to his old village and offer sacrifices for his family in the afterlife. He'd buy a mansion on the edge of the sea, trade goods, and have others do the sailing for him. He would live lavishly and have his money work for him.

Kalisto saw a supply post and walked in, his mind still churning. He would be surprised if Crassus ever again set foot on a ship after this journey. The emissary had never been the same since they shipwrecked on that reef. Kalisto remembered how Crassus acted after Judah signed the treaty parchment. He had returned to the ship, appearing even angrier and more disheartened than usual. Kalisto wondered what was bothering him. Crassus should have been pleased that he'd accomplished his mission. But he had just had thrown down his water skins and satchel bag with annoyance and ordered Kalisto to cast off and head for Rome. After the ship left port, Crassus had stared at his Roman gladius, then tossed it over the side, watching as it disappeared into the vast green sea.

Chapter 47

"WE DON'T HAVE enough food to last us three weeks," Gaddi said to Judah inside the large tent. Jonathan involuntarily blanched, looking even more despondent. Staring into the fire, Judah bore a similar expression. With so many wounded, the march out of Jerusalem toward the Gophna hills had been long and grueling, and several days more of the same lay ahead.

Judah felt unnerved at the state he had left his men in, in Jerusalem. He had only had a few hours to help fortify the temple mount. He had supplied the soldiers who stayed to defend it with arms, equipment, catapults, and much of the little food that remained. Then he had helped prepare the barricade to hinder enemy use of the stairs that ascended to the temple.

He had hugged his brother Simon goodbye, feeling choked up, knowing he would never see him again. Not one of them would let themselves be taken alive, Judah knew. Not one of them would give up and let the Seleucids take the temple. He had promised they would come back to help, and would attack the Syrians from the rear, but both brothers knew the reality. They didn't have enough food to hold out that long.

My God, Judah prayed, *are we to obey Your commandments and starve for it? Are we to follow your laws, and suffer unto death, until Your people are no more?*

"What can we do?" Jonathan asked somberly.

"Send riders to the Nabateans and ask if they will trade us food for the gold we stored with them," Judah said.

Jonathan nodded and left the tent. Gaddi followed him out.

Judah sighed and thought about Eleazar. His wife had taken the news even harder than expected. He wondered if she would ever be the same again. He wanted to tell her it would be all right, but he knew it wouldn't. Tears streaming down her face, she had looked at him in rage.

"I am with child again. Do you know that?" she had screamed. "None of his children will ever know their father. And who will protect them now, oh great Maccabee?"

He had tried to tell her he would protect her and her children. She had scoffed and cursed. "Look at you!" she had yelled, pointing to the gash that would leave a long scar on his cheek, and at his limping leg. "None of you can even take care of yourselves! And *you* are going to take care of my children? *Because* of you, they are fatherless. Now Jerusalem will fall, and all of us will die!"

Jonathan and Gaddi stepped back into the tent, and the younger brother sat down again beside Judah.

"We've dispatched the riders, Maccabee," he said. "How long do you think those we left on the temple mount can hold out before they ... before they—"

"Starve to death?" Judah interrupted coldly, finishing Jonathan's sentence. He sighed again, and ran his hand through his hair.

"They'll be out of food within the week," Gaddi said bitterly.

"So there's nothing more we can do for them?" Jonathan said, gazing at Judah. Judah just stared blankly into the fire.

"Judah?"

"He doesn't have an answer. Can't you see that?" Gaddi spat. "Without some miracle from the hand of God Himself, every one of them is as good as dead."

§

ysias slammed his fist into the table, atop the open scroll he had just finished reading. The child king, Antiochus V, who lay on a cot some yards away, stirred in his sleep.

Perspiration rolled down Lysias's brow. He gritted his teeth in impotent rage. Outside, the Syrian siege works were in place, and his army encompassed the temple mount. The previous three days of onslaughts on the barricade had failed, as expected. Maccabee, before evacuating most of his men from the city, had fortified the mount with catapults, polybolos, oxybeles, and other artillery weapons that now lined the walls above the temple courtyard.

Yesterday, Lysias's men tried three times to storm the stairs toward the temple and breach the barricade. All three times, they took heavy casualties. They had moved their siege works to the west side of the temple, and were decimated by heavy barrages from Hebrew archers and artillery. Lysias was exceedingly conscious that most of the rebel force still tarried to the north, encamped in the hill country.

After providing relief to the starving soldiers in the citadel, Lysias had torn down most of the city walls to ensure his men would not be trapped and slaughtered in any of the city's tight quarters. His intelligence sources said that the older brother of Judah, a priest named Simon, had remained to defend the temple with the others who chose to sacrifice their lives for the cause.

Lysias' eyes again scanned the parchment from Urion in front of him. So the rumors about Philip's intentions were true. Lysias reread the words:

My Lord,

I was with the king when the life left him. As no doubt your sources have well nigh informed you, Antiochus, in his delirious state, appointed Philip—one of his most inept officers—as viceroy, negating your current position. I do not believe if the king had his full faculties of thought, he would have been so foolish to appoint such an incompetent man as his chancellor, and protector of the heir. It is because of this that I write you. Despite his numerous vices, the fool Philip has taken to heart the dying wish of his former lover, and moved his eastern army, which I am a part of, away from the Parthian borders in order to march on Antioch, in hopes of seizing the capital and taking control of the kingdom while you are away fighting the Hebrews.

The upper echelon of the officers' corps serving Philip is very much divided, to say the least. Almost half of the generals despise the man. Some stay loyal to what they feel was the last decree of their king. Others can be swayed. I can convince the group loyal to you to attempt to slow down the march toward the capital only so much. Within two, maybe three months, Philip's army will be in Antioch.

If you deploy your men at once, you may still have a chance to stop him before he gets there, but do not linger. If Philip takes control of the capital and gains the support of Laodice and the nobility, or other members of the royal family, while spreading his propaganda of the king's loss of faith in you, amid accusations of treason, he will rule the Seleucid kingdom as long as he is alive. Your only chance is to stop him before he reaches Antioch.

Faithfully,

Urion, Advisor to the True King

Lysias lifted the parchment to a candle on the table. He watched the scroll ignite, holding it as it slowly burned away. *I can leave my force here, destroy the Hebrews, and lose my kingdom,* he thought to himself. He could divide his force, leaving the possibility of victory in Judea and victory against Philip, or in probability, defeat in both. The only alternative was to abandon the Judean campaign and move his army, war elephants, and cavalry north to defeat Philip and retain control of the kingdom. It would mean abandoning the southern border to the religious rebel savages.

Maccabee would take control of all of Judea. He would set up a kingdom, and his people would love him for it. The Seleucids would never get this land back. Once it was gone, their borders would only further diminish. *But you have no choice,* he thought. *By this turn of events, this cruel joke by the gods, you have had victory snatched from your grasp.* The troublesome people finally on the verge of annihilation would now be left free to their own devices.

Lysias took a drink of the last of the wine in his chalice, and, in disgust, threw the cup to the ground. The whole region would be in absolute chaos. Rome would see the Seleucids as weak, and they would move in. If they did indeed have a treaty with the Israelites, they'd garrison their troops on the edge of the retracting southern border, and wait for a moment of weakness before attacking. Parthia had already swept west toward Babylon. The empire was being fractured on every end.

But the Jew's didn't know this, Lysias mused. *Judah doesn't know we are in a civil war.* The irony of it! As far as the Jews were aware, the Seleucids could lay siege to them for a decade. The rebels were holding out now, but in a month, it would have been over. Lysias didn't know how much food they had stored in the temple, but it could not last them more than a month. After that, the whole lot of them would have been dead. In two months, Lysias's men would have marched north, found Judah in the mountains, and slain him with the remainder of his soldiers. With just two more months, he could have brought the rebels to their knees. Now that chance was lost. Now everything would be different.

Lysias looked up to see Nicantor enter his tent, questions on his face. Lysias ignored him, stepped to the water basin, and began washing his face.

"We're not going to be able to break through that barricade until they're too hungry to pick up their spears," Nicantor said grimly.

The child king stirred again, still asleep.

"I know," Lysias replied.

"Fifty men died this morning," Nicantor said, kicking at a rock on the floor of the tent. "*Fifty.*"

"We can't afford one more," Lysias said stoically.

"What are you talking about?" Nicantor asked, finally noticing the distressed look in his superior's eyes.

"We must abandon the campaign and march for Antioch at once."

"What do you mean *abandon the campaign*?"

"A courier arrived. Philip is marching the eastern army toward the capital to take control of the empire."

"*Philip?* By the names of all the gods!" Nicantor cried. "How far away is he?"

"If we leave immediately we might be able to stop him from taking the capital."

Nicantor rubbed his forehead in agitation. He was thinking.

There was a long, silent moment before he finally said, "What are we going to do about Judea?

§

Simon strode past the barricade. His eldest son, Mattathias, and another guard, walked alongside him. Simon wore his priestly garb, with a convex sword, his kopias, sheathed on his belt. He walked down the gray steps toward the base of the temple mount. As far as he could see, surrounding them in every direction was the massive Syrian army. They were all in formation, motionless, waiting ominously.

At dawn, a messenger from the Syrian force had walked to the barricade alone, holding a banner of truce. He had relayed the message that Nicantor, commanding general under Lysias, wished to speak with Simon, brother of Judah Ben Mattathias and priest and leader of the temple mount resistance. Simon had been instructed to come alone to an empty courtyard between the base of the mount and the Syrian perimeter, where he was to meet with the general.

Simon descended the steps toward the clearing. He nodded to the others, who stopped and remained there, as he marched forward toward the courtyard. He wondered what to expect. Was this a trap to kill the leadership, and dishearten those who remained defending the temple? *What would be the point?* Simon pondered. The men wouldn't break anyway. Maybe rather than stay pinned down in Jerusalem, Lysias wished to offer terms. He'd offer them their lives, as slaves. If he were generous, he would have them swear fealty to the king and send them into exile, or have them live as hostages, but the only reason would be so he could move his men out of Jerusalem and attack Judah's army. Lysias wanted the mobility, and in exchange, he would offer them their lives so he could deploy his force while Judah was still weak.

He should save his breath, Simon thought. *I won't do it! Dishonor myself for a little more time on this wretched Earth? Betray my own brother, my country, and my father's memory, for what—to be a slave?*

Even more grievous, Simon realized he'd be giving the temple of God over to the Gentiles, who would doubtlessly defile it once more, or tear it to the ground like the Babylonians had done.

I'd rather die, Simon thought. *Every one of us would rather die. At least we'll make our lives count for something, and cost the Syrians twice as many soldiers as they take with them.* If his people saw their faith and remembered their name, it could renew their dedication to the cause and give Judah the much-needed time to rebuild the army—a chance to put up a fight. Simon wondered if Lysias knew his men had run out of food two days ago.

Approaching the courtyard, Simon saw a man dressed in ostentatious gold-and-black armor. He stood waiting for Simon, resting his hand upon the hilt of his sheathed sword. Simon looked around, searching for the trap, but the nearest Syrian phalanx was over a hundred yards away.

He moved closer, and the man's face came into focus. It was middle-aged, holding onto what small vestige of youth still remained. The deep lines etched into the brow were accentuated by the tired look in the eyes, and the stress of constant war seemed to have prematurely aged him. The day's growth of stubble on his chin was gray, as was the hair bordering his temples. In his eyes, Simon recognized the cold look of suppressed hatred, concealed prejudice.

"Nicantor, Supreme General of the Seleucid Army," the man said in a clipped voice. His posture was cavalier, his shoulders arched, indicative of Greek aristocracy.

"Simon Ben Mattathais."

"First," Niantor began, "I want to congratulate you and express my admiration at not only your brother's prowess on the field of battle, but your excellent ability in defending this ground that you and your countrymen find sacred."

"What is your purpose in requesting my presence, General? I hope you know that no bribes or offers of mercy will tempt us to betray our countrymen, or the house of our God." Simon's tone was curt. He wished to dispense with the obligatory cordiality and reach the point quickly.

Annoyed, Nicantor answered, "I wanted to ask if you have the authority to speak for your brother, who is, in fact, the unofficial leader of your ..." He didn't want to say "country." "Your *movement.*"

"That depends on what I would be speaking on his behalf for," Simon answered. "But if you ask for the surrender of my people, neither I nor my brother can give it."

"Actually, my king offers terms of peace between our people and yours," Nicantor said, swallowing his pride.

*"What?"*Simon asked, incredulous.

"We've come to the realization that the hostilities between us are probably all due to a misunderstanding on our part. Furthermore, all of the enmity was the result of the policies of the former king, Antiochus IV, and in no way reflect the desires of the much wiser, current king, Antiochus V."

Simon remained speechless, wondering if the man had lost his wits, or if they were all truly taking arbitrary orders from the five-year-old king.

"The king has decreed, if you maintain the integrity of our southern borders, we will return to a new reduced standard of taxation. You may worship your god, give sacrifice to him, read your scriptures, perform ceremonial circumcision of your infants. You may even live by your own laws."

Simon said the only thing that came to his mind. "And the rule of our people?"

"Your country may be ruled by the high priest, your brother."

Simon stood in stunned disbelief—trying to search for meaning, or some kind of artifice that he was convinced he must be overlooking.

"So do we have terms? Can you speak for your brother and his people?" Nicantor asked impatiently.

Simon searched his mind, his thoughts spinning. "Yes," he answered. The word sounded like he was surprised he was speaking it.

Looking up, he made eye contact with Nicantor. "But how can we be sure you will keep your agreement?'

Nicantor held out a small scroll. "These are the king's terms. You will find the king's signature and Lysias the viceroy's signature, guaranteeing them. So, are we agreed?"

"Yes," Simon said hoarsely. "Yes, we are," he repeated more loudly.

"Good," Nicantor said. "The king will be pleased. We'll begin to move our army north this afternoon."

Simon watched as the general strode away. Then Simon returned in bewilderment to the stairs of the mount, where his son and the other guard were waiting.

"What happened? What did he say?" Mattathias demanded.

"I believe … I believe we just won our freedom."

"What?"

"Get ready to ride to Judah's camp … *to inform him* … that we've just won our freedom."

Book IX
Blood for Blood

161 BC

"In peace, sons bury their fathers. In war, fathers bury their sons."

~ Croesus

βιβλίο εννέα

Chapter 48

ANTIOCH WAS FLOODED with Syrian soldiers, returned from the battle. The guards who lined the promenade stood motionless, gripping their spears upright. Lysias opened the doors to the palace, the child Antiochus walking beside him. They had paraded him upon their return, publicly attributing to the boy the victory against Philip. Among the entourage, Nicantor followed behind, as did the king's bodyguards and Urion.

Lysias remembered when he told the child king that they must hasten home from Judea because an evil man wanted his throne. He had sat the boy on his knee and tried the best he could to convey to the child that this is what *he* wanted. It was what was for the good of the kingdom. The Hebrews—who the boy had been taught were bad—were no longer bad now, but were their friends. The child accepted this and was happy he would see his mother again.

Lysias, now in the palace, was far less excited than the boy at the prospect of seeing Laodice once more. For all Lysias knew, she could have been supporting Philip against him. *I constantly have to circumvent her ploys,* thought Lysias, *her endless impediments and grabs for power.*

He knew she'd never stop trying, but her son would not be her puppet. He would not allow it. *I'll have to kill her before the year ends,* he thought. *She's too much of a threat to keep alive.* Enough time had passed since Antiochus's death. People would not suspect treachery, if the deed were done properly.

The previous week had been daunting. Lysias had succeeded in making the march north before Philip could reach Antioch. The victory had been costly, but absolute. Through coordination with Urion, Lysias had co-opted many of the generals in Philip's army, making victory for Philip impossible.

Fitting, Lysias thought, *that Philip was disemboweled by one of his own men.* It happened in the farthest rear echelon, behind the battle. When Lysias had finally reached him, the imposter was still alive—pale and screaming in terror, desperately trying to fit his intestines back inside his body.

Now Lysias was brought back to the present by the boy. Antiochus, the child king, was skipping through the palace at a trot, pretending to ride a horse, mimicking the cavalrymen he had seen in battle. He was making noises that apparently were what a five-year-old thought riding sounded like. The boy stopped in his tracks, recognizing this part of the palace that a year before he had called home.

"Will I get to see my mother now?" he asked excitedly.

"Yes, you will," Lysias said with a smile, having grown somewhat fond of the boy in the year they had been on the Hebrew campaign. Glancing into the queen's chambers, Lysias saw they were empty.

"Where is the queen?" he asked one of the servant girls.

"She is in the throne room, my lord," the girl replied. Lysias nodded and moved down the hallway, thinking it strange that Laodice would be there.

The throne room was the location the Seleucid kings used for meetings with foreign heads of state, diplomats, or top advisors. Sometimes nobility would be invited, but seldom would a woman have any business there.

The throne room—long and rectangular—had hanging upon one its stone walls, an enormous map of the empire. In the center of the room stood a long cedar table bordered with chairs. Ten feet away, on a small platform, stood an elaborate throne, adorned with gold and jewels.

Through the open doors, Lysias and the child king peered inside. Laodice was standing there, dressed in an elegant purple gown. Haughtily, she strode toward them from the back of the room. Although he despised her, Lysias could not deny the fact of her beauty. It was an attraction that he carefully concealed. Watching her march toward him, he found it strange that she seemed to be ignoring her son, whom she had not seen in almost a year. Her eyes were only on Lysias.

Prepared for another contemptuous verbal sortie, Lysias stepped through the door. Nicantor, Urion, and the bodyguards followed him into the room.

Then he heard a muffled disturbance in the hallway behind him. "Now!" came the shout from someone concealed within the chamber.

Instantly, a multitude of spears tips were poised in Lysias's direction. Twenty soldiers, hidden along the inside wall, closed in on him and his small entourage. Turning back toward the door, Lysias saw more soldiers on either side of the hallway, blocking any chance of escape. The men brandishing spears were armored in Syrian uniforms. The child began crying for his mother, but he was held in place by a soldier.

"What is this?" Lysias tried to shout, but his words were choked off when he was grabbed by the neck, as another soldier clutched him by the arms from behind. An eerie silence fell over the room, and all, save the crying child, fell deathly silent.

Laodice continued to walk toward Lysias as if nothing out of the ordinary were occurring. Behind her was a young man, apparently a noble, but Lysias hardly noticed him amidst all that was happening. The soldier who had seized Lysias pushed him to his knees. Another man unsheathed Lysias's sword, jerking it away from his body.

Laodice moved in closer, and the room grew even more still. "I told you that one day my son would stand before you, a grown man," she said, smiling triumphantly. As she moved to the side, the young man behind her strode forward. Dressed in majestic armor, he appeared to be in his mid-twenties, with fair skin and black hair.

Suddenly, Lysias realized who this was.

"Demetrius." The nearly forgotten name escaped from his lips.

Demetrius looked down and nodded in acknowledgment. Lysias wanted to ask how this had come to pass. How King Seleucus's forgotten son, who had spent his whole life in Roman captivity and had long been presumed dead, could have somehow escaped, and swayed the loyalty of dignitaries and generals. But Lysias did not ask, because he knew the answer. Laodice was standing right there. *If only you had killed her when Antiochus had died,* he lamented to himself.

"My father was murdered in this room," Demetrius said calmly, still looking down at Lysias. "He had promised to pay for my release from Rome, but was killed before he could do so. His death was orchestrated by the very man you spent your entire life serving, whose son you are still serving," he said, looking over at the whimpering child.

"I served the Seleucid Empire!" Lysias said emphatically. "And I am of royal blood. I've devoted my life to—"

Lysias grimaced as Demetrius slowly drew his sword from its scabbard.

"By conspiring to help Antiochus poison my little brother, and keeping my mother a captive in her own palace?" replied Demetrius.

Lysias almost looked surprised as Demetrius put the sharp point of his blade to the side of his neck. The young man kept it there a still moment, enjoying the confusion he knew the older man felt. He looked into Lysias's eyes, then drove the blade downward through the base of his neck into his chest cavity, until the hilt pressed against the entrance wound. Lysias choked blood, and his eyes rolled back in agony. Blood jetted from his neck like a fountain. The viceroy slumped over on his side, heaving in tremors.

The child king began screaming. Nicantor stood beside the fallen Lysias, his legs shaking. Demetrius stepped in front of him. "I have a question for you, General," he said, wiping the droplets of blood off of his face. "If you answer it correctly, you may yet be spared."

"Yes, my lord," Nicantor said, swallowing hard, looking at Lysias, who was still writhing beside him.

"Do you wish to live?"

"Yes! Yes, I do."

"Good. I need excellent tacticians." Demetrius turned to two of his men. "See to it that Nicantor takes his oath of allegiance publicly." The soldiers acknowledged the order and escorted the general from the hall.

"And of me?" Urion asked pleadingly.

"Oh, dear Urion. I have not forgotten you. I remember how you served my father when I was a child." Demetrius nodded to one of his guards at Urion's back. Without warning, the guard dragged his blade across Urion's neck, cutting his throat. Falling to his knees, Urion clutched at the wound. The guard forced Urion's hands away, and continued slicing back and forth, into his neck.

The terrified child king, paralyzed by fear, screamed even louder than before. The guard who was holding him tightened his grip.

"Take him out of here. I don't want to see it," Demetrius snapped.

Realizing her elder son's intent, Laodice began screaming. "No! You swore! You swore you would not harm him!" Her voice grew shriller. "You swore he would live in exile!"

The child's terrified pleas for his mother grew louder, too. Demetrius held onto Laodice's arms, ignoring her cries, as the men dragged the screaming boy from their midst. His cries became muffled on the other side of the wall. She heard a sword being drawn from its scabbard, and then there was silence.

Demetrius let go of his mother, who, teary-eyed and shaking, backed against the wall. She covered her mouth with her hands, her breath coming in gasps. Demetrius nonchalantly walked to the front of the room, ascended the platform, and sat down upon the king's throne.

§

Moving the surface soil aside from the freshly dug hole, Nabis searched for the satchel through the dirt, where he had buried it months before, under the tallest olive tree. Abishag looked over his shoulder. They both were breathless with anticipation. Nabis probed something solid, then realized it was only a thick tree root. He dug further, suddenly doubting if this was the right tree.

It was dark. Are you sure? he asked himself. *Think!* But this tree had to be it—the same odd shape, tilting form, twisted branches. It was the biggest tree in the grove. How could he be mistaken? Or had someone stolen his treasure?

Nabis pressed his dirt-stained hand against his forehead. He looked up at Abishag. Her eyes were shining back at him with love. *She doesn't even care,* he said to himself, his frustration mollified. *She only cares because I care.* He thought back to all they had been through.

Nabis knew he owed his life to the man who had come to their aid from out of nowhere, the night he had been attacked by the thug he had once saved Abishag from. He owed the man even more for explaining to the priest that he wasn't a spy. He'd never seen the fellow before, but the stranger seemed to know Nabis somehow.

He could tell the priest's soldiers wanted to kill him. He could see it in their eyes, but the small amount of doubt the stranger created must have stayed their hand, and Simon had ordered him bound and taken back to camp.

Nabis recalled how the next evening, at sundown, the Hebrew guards led him by a rope to a tent. Inside, the priest, whom he learned they called Simon, was sitting at a table eating goat meat. "Leave us," he had said to the guards. A moment of silence followed as Simon chewed a bite of his food. Then he asked, without looking up, "Where are you from, Greek?"

"Ephesus," Nabis had replied anxiously. "My father is from Sparta, but moved from Argos to Ephesus after it fell to Rome."

"How long have you been a soldier?"

"Over seven years."

"And how long have you been a spy?" Simon looked up abruptly and stared into Nabis's eyes.

"I'm not a spy. I told you that. I left the army over a year ago. I've been trying to travel north since then, to return to my family."

"Then please tell me, if you would, why nine witnesses claim you were seen speaking to a Phoenician messenger?"

"The Phoenician escaped from a battle near Galilee," Nabis had explained. "Our paths coincidentally crossed, just as he was dying. He had arrows lodged in his back. He expired on the property of my wife's kinsman, the place where we were staying."

Simon's eyebrows lifted. "And what did this man say before he died?"

"Nothing." Nabis lied, not wanting to tell him about the money. "He was incoherent, and didn't know where he was."

"And the woman you call your *wife*." He drew the word out emphasizing how misbegotten he believed their marriage to be. "How did you meet her?"

"She was a slave, at market in Jerusalem, and I bought her."

Simon blanched when he heard this, inwardly seething.

"Her family was killed in the massacre. I thought I could help her."

"And why did you buy *that* slave? A beautiful young girl ... how long was it before you began exercising your sexual rights over her?" Simon was trying to control his anger. He hoped he could kill the pig and not feel guilty for shedding a man's blood. "One night? A week?"

"I never touched her when she was a slave. Not until I freed her and proclaimed her to be my wife, and she the same to me."

"Your *wife*. Under whose law do you think that contract of marriage is legitimate? What witnesses were present for your heathen marriage to one of the daughters of Israel? And I find it hard to believe your story. What was your true purpose in buying her? You bought her to bed her, and she, in the folly of youth, became infatuated with you. That's what happened, isn't it?"

"No!" Nabis responded angrily.

Simon wanted to believe the man was lying. He wanted to believe he was the pig he hoped him to be. He wanted to be justified in killing him, but there was something in Nabis's voice, and his eyes, that made Simon question his assumptions.

"Maybe, maybe not," Simon said, "but I will ask these questions of your *wife*, and if her story is different from yours, you both will be stoned."

Nabis was about to speak, but Simon shouted, "Guards!" When they entered, he said, "Get this Gentile out of my sight."

A guard then gave the rope around Nabis's neck a yank, and led him out the door.

There had been other interrogations. During the day, the army always marched south, away from the direction where Nabis wished to go. He was always surrounded by soldiers, but when night fell, and the Jews made camp, Simon would summon Nabis to his tent for further questioning.

Nabis didn't know exactly when the change happened, but sometime during the journey south, Simon began to believe him. One evening he asked about Nabis's father. He asked what battles Nabis had fought against the Hebrews. To the prisoner's surprise, Simon listened impassively, and was interested in Nabis's point of view of the Battle of Beth-Horn.

Nabis showed Simon the large, asymmetrical scar that bordered his shoulder and chest where he had been shot with an arrow, the wound further mangled by the physician when the arrow had been removed. Simon, ever the priest, inadvertently taught Nabis of the Torah and the writings of the prophets. Though Simon still remained detached, and ostensibly indifferent, Nabis clung to his words, and to the hope his change in demeanor seemed to promise.

As they approached Jerusalem, Simon ordered that Nabis be unbound and free to walk the camp. He was even allowed to see Abishag for short periods of time. Only one guard was placed on him after that. Nabis wondered if it was a test.

Four miles outside Jerusalem, nearing dusk, Simon approached Nabis with a saddled pack mule. Beside the animal walked Abishag. Simon handed Nabis the reins and said, "You are free. Go your way. I hope you find your family and what you are looking for in this world." Simon handed him a sealed scroll. "If you are stopped by any God-fearing Hebrew, this should keep you safe. If you are stopped by your own people, well ... *Ratzon ha'El.*"

Nabis was dumbstruck. Nevertheless, he didn't delay. He only held Abishag a long moment before helping her onto the mule and walking out of the Jewish camp.

Nabis and Abishag made their way north once more, gleaning off the land to stay alive. Even though everywhere food was in short supply, Nabis was surprised at how charitable the people were whom he encountered. Only twice was he refused the right to glean from people's property. Both he and Abishag felt grateful to be alive, and that somehow God was providing for them.

They stopped in a village, and Nabis found work with a half-Samaritan family who supplied local masons with brick and mortar. While working in the quarry, Nabis heard that the whole northern army once again was invading Judea and making its way toward Jerusalem. Then came word of Judah's defeat at Beth-Zechariah. The news weighed heavily on Abishag, and Nabis saw doubt and fear on the face of every Hebrew man in the village. Every day the news grew worse, and soon they heard that the Hebrew force was divided, some taking refuge in the hill country, while others were trapped in Jerusalem, besieged on the temple mount. The locals grew still more disheartened.

Nabis knew he had to get himself and Abishag out of this country. The fighting would never stop and the war would never end. Now, Nabis had saved enough money to retrace their journey as far north as Aphek, where Abishag's kinsman had nearly stoned him. After refusing to accompany the Hebrew army south to safety, Zebulun and his family had remained in the village. Nabis often asked himself what he would do to Zebulun and the others who had attacked him, once he reached Aphek again.

En route, Nabis had heard news that the Seleucid army was falling back and a settlement had been reached between Maccabee and Lysias. At first, Nabis didn't believe the rumors, but then he saw the retreating army as he and his wife traveled north.

One day, during their journey, Nabis stopped inside a supply shop. Across the room he saw Orestes, his comrade in arms who had saved his life at Beth-Horon. Orestes was with several other soldiers, trying to buy any kind of shoes they could find, but he failed to notice Nabis.

The man looked gaunt and lethargic, like he had been starving. Nabis almost didn't recognize him. He looked like he had aged ten years, and his eyes were sunken into his boney cheeks. Nabis wanted to say something, but couldn't bring himself to explain why he had abandoned his position in the army, when the army was in such need. Orestes must have been in the siege at the citadel for all those months, waiting for relief. He would never understand why Nabis had deserted. A part of Nabis hoped Orestes would recognize him, but Orestes's eyes looked glassy, his uniform was tattered, and his armor was rusted. He probably wouldn't recognize his own mother if she was standing right in front of him.

In fact, Nabis had to question if the man really was Orestes, or just some ragged, worn-down soldier who had similar features. He finally decided it was Orestes—but this was the man he had trained to be an Argyraspides soldier, who had carted him from the slope of Beth-Horon to Philistine lands and found a physician to dig the arrowhead out of his chest. He couldn't face someone so loyal and say that after all their suffering in this eternal war, his friend had left him and all their comrades to their fate because of a—what, a woman? Because he no longer believed in the nobility of the Seleucid cause? Because he sympathized with the Hebrews, who just wanted the freedom to follow their own laws and beliefs? Because he didn't have it in him to butcher innocent people? No matter what the excuse he would give, this man before him who once looked up to him, would never understand.

Nabis walked out of the store, without buying what he had come to purchase. "They didn't have it," he said to Abishag outside.

She smiled at him playfully, but then realized the alteration in his countenance. "What's wrong?" she asked.

"Nothing," he replied, trying inconspicuously to move away from the crowded shop.

"Tell me," she petitioned, afraid of whatever might be causing him anxiety.

As they departed the town, he had told her all that had happened and all that was on his mind. She took his hand in hers and kissed it. "You did what you knew to be right," she said. "Maybe this man …"

"Orestes," Nabis interjected.

"Maybe he would understand, and maybe not, but it doesn't matter. All that matters is that you did what was right."

He held her gaze, the two of them looking into each other's eyes as they walked north on the road outside of the town. Nabis held the rope of the mule that walked behind them, and one arm was wrapped around his wife, protectively.

When they finally had reached Aphek, they learned the land had been scorched and that most of the inhabitants, including Zebulun and Abishag's cousin, had been killed by Seleucid soldiers. They heard from the few survivors that her uncle, trying to defend his family, had been pulled from his house, tied to a horse, and dragged over rough terrain until he was unrecognizable. It took him three more days to die. Nabis felt indifferent when he heard the news.

They didn't stop, but immediately had walked west to the grove of olive trees where Nabis had buried the money he had taken from the dead Phoenician. His heart had raced as they drew closer.

"Someone must have dug it up," Nabis now said in frustration, pulling himself up from the wide hole he had dug. Abishag looked despondent, more for his sake than because of the money. Nabis knelt next to her, feeling hopeless.

After a silent moment passed, Abishag asked, "What would you have done with the money if you had found it?"

"First, I would get us on a boat headed toward Ephesus and try to find my family," Nabis said, wondering if his father might still be alive, knowing by now it was doubtful. "Then I thought I might use some of it to help build a synagogue."

Abishag looked at him, touched.

"There are some Hebrew families in Ephesus," Nabis continued, "but as far as I know, they have no formal place where they worship. And then I would build you a nice house overlooking the sea." He smiled at her. She leaned her head on his shoulder, simply enjoying his presence.

After a few long moments, Nabis got up to retrieve his shovel from the hole. As the shovel touched the dirt in the far corner, he thought he saw something move underneath it.

"What was that?" Abishag asked, surprised.

Looking down, Nabis could see a thin strap of leather, covered in loose soil. He pushed aside the dirt with his hand, then tugged at the strap. His old satchel broke free from the soil, and Nabis was incredulous with joy. Then the satchel dropped open, revealing a plethora of shiny silver coins gleaming in the sunlight. Ecstatic, Nabis and Abishag looked at each other with shining eyes.

Chapter 49

JUDAH WALKED WITH Martha along the dirt road that wound above the slope overlooking his home village of Modein. The evening was warm, with the retreating sun casting rose and gold into the sky behind the olive trees. Grapevines lined their path, and a wall of piled stones bordered the grasses on one side.

Judah had been taking care of Martha as well as Eleazar's widow and children. When they had arrived in Modein, Gaddi had insisted on taking their father's large house as well as one-third of his land, stringently exercising his rights as the eldest to inherit a double portion of their father's possessions. As far as Judah was concerned, he could have them, as long as Judah had a place where he could support Eleazar's family and help out Martha.

After Simon had negotiated the evacuation of the Syrian army, Judah had returned to Jerusalem, giving orders to rebuild the city walls that Lysias had torn down. He had established the *gerusia*, an administrative body ruled by elders from his ranking army officers, to handle the needs of the people. Over them he had placed Jonathan, who reported to Judah himself.

Afterwards, he and Simon had returned to Modein with Eleazar's family and Martha. Weeks before, Judah had sent word to have three houses built, two on his father's land and one on land he purchased on the opposite side of the brook. One of the homes was to be for Martha, one for Eleazar's wife and children, and one for himself near the brook's edge. All three were larger than their father's old house, which Gaddi insisted on having.

"How long will you stay in Modein?" Martha asked as they walked, surveying Judah's new land that lay beneath them.

"I'm not sure yet," he answered, glancing at her tentatively. "There's no immediate need for me to be in Jerusalem. Smiling, he changed the subject. "Are you happy with your house?"

"Yes," she said with an answering smile, looking down at her feet for a moment. "It's the nicest home I've ever lived in."

Judah was pleased. After a moment, Martha stopped walking and gazed out at the rosy sphere now almost half-buried beneath the horizon.

"Why are you doing all this for me?" Her voice was low. "There are many widows in Israel. Why me?"

"I'm not sure," he answered, gathering his thoughts. "I only know it's what I felt I should do. It's what I wanted to do."

Martha resumed her walking, then added in a teasing tone, "You know, they'll think I'm your mistress."

"Do you think I care what people think?"

"You *are* the high priest of Israel. Perhaps you should."

"*Perhaps* you shouldn't concern yourself with other people's opinions," Judah admonished.

"Does that include you?"

"Of course not."

She was about to ask why, when he said, with a mocking tone of conceit, "After all, I'm the high priest of Israel."

Martha smacked his shoulder, rolled her eyes at him, and began walking faster. His heart stirred at her touch. He hastened to catch up, enjoying her voice, her words, and her presence.

"You *are* the high priest," she said, stopping once more, and standing closer to him than before. "But you have no sons to take over for you when you go to sleep with your ancestors." She meant the words as a playful taunt, but she could tell by his involuntary grimace that the words somehow had hurt him.

"Forgive me," she said quickly, as he looked past her. "I didn't mean it like that."

"It's all right."

"No, I *am* sorry," she said earnestly. "I know you lost your wife years ago and haven't ever remarried."

How, she wondered, *can this leader, who I've seen lay waste to whole cities, who has been at war since he was barely a man, who has killed countless people, feel so much, and act so human?*

Judah swallowed hard, looking down at the road beneath his feet. "She died in childbirth, with our daughter."

Martha lightly placed a hand on his shoulder.

"I never thought I would remarry."

Martha began to speak, but stopped herself.

"No, it's all right," Judah assured her, rather insincerely.

"If you ever do remarry, would you seek a political marriage, to help strengthen Judea?" With her question, the mood became somewhat lighter.

"No," he said emphatically. "I would marry for me."

Martha bent her head to hide her pleasure at his answer. She knew how much she was attracted to him, to his personality, to the way he looked at her. Her heart skipped whenever she saw him looking at her.

Now he was standing so close. She looked up into the serious eyes, past the horrid scar that marred his face. To her, even the scar was beautiful.

They held each other's gaze for a moment, and she inched her body a fraction closer to his. He leaned forward, and pressed his lips to hers.

§

"What can we do about Judea?" Demetrius asked Nicantor, as they watched the chariots race around the arena from their seats in the royal scaffold. Laodice was there and Bacchides, the man who had aided Demetrius's escape from Roman captivity. Bacchides had been reinstated as general after helping to organize Demetrius's takeover of Antioch. Other dignitaries sat nearby, and below them were rows of stone seats where hundreds of spectators watched. The weeklong celebration was in honor of King Demetrius's acquisition of his rightful throne.

"Ah yes, the Jews," Nicantor sighed. "Lysias made a truce with them before we departed north." He leaned toward the king, trying to elevate his voice above the crowd while still remaining quiet enough that others could not hear his remarks. "Though he granted them liberty with the so-called freedoms they sought, the Jews are still part of your realm, my lord. They are responsible for maintaining the southern border."

"I know all this," Demetrius replied, irritably. "But it *looks* disgraceful. I don't much care for what the usurper's puppet has done." Demetrius looked up as a chariot swerved around the corner of the stone divider inside the arena, almost crashing.

"What would you have?" Nicantor asked.

"I *want* victory," Demetrius answered matter-of-factly. "The whole thing looks shameful, and my primary intent is to restore glory to the Seleucid kingdom. If we don't create the perception of glory, actual glory will most definitely not remain."

"I hate the Hebrews as much as anyone," Nicantor replied. "It was my men they killed. But starting an unprovoked war, not even a year after we offered them peace, does not look good to the surrounding kingdoms, or to the kingdoms we rule. It gives the impression that we will attack anyone for anything, and that we don't honor our word."

"I never gave *my* word," Demetrius remarked.

"Nevertheless, we need a plausible reason to go to war. Even Rome, who rumor has it is in the process of building an alliance with the rats, will see it as nothing more than a dishonorable lashing out at a people we no longer are at war with."

"Then we must have the appearance of legitimacy, and make it look like it is they who are inciting violence, once again rebelling against their sovereign," said Demetrius. "Despite your many faults, you are the best tactician we have, Nicantor. You are also the only one of my generals who has beaten their leader, Judah, on the battlefield. But the fact that these insurgents are still alive and that we had to cower and make peace with them is disgraceful."

The king's words were cut short as a chariot smashed into the side of the wall. The horses continued running at full gallop. The chariot rolled onto its side, a wheel breaking off, kicking up sand and dust. Again the chariot slammed into the curving outer wall of the arena and came to a halt. The driver lay motionless inside, his body drenched in blood.

After the cheering died down, Nicantor began again, confident in his knowledge of the Hebrews. "There is a man among the Hellenistic Jews in Jerusalem. He is very influential amongst the people there who are not staunch religious fanatics, who actually want a superior Greek culture. His name is Alcimus. During the war, he was one of the most useful informants to Isokrates, who was then the head of our intelligence network, before he was mysteriously slain. The man is a Levite, one of the Hebrew tribes that make up the heretical priesthood there. That's one of the problems your uncle, the usurper, had in ruling these people. He never learned to distinguish the difference between the religious extremists and the Hellenized Jews who are tolerable, and students of Greek philosophy."

"What are you getting at?" Demetrius interrupted, trying to wrap his mind around the complexities of the foreign culture.

"In our treaty with the Jews, we declared the high priest will be the authoritative power in Judea. He must be of the Hebrew tribe of Levi, as is Judah, or you will instantly have another rebellion, which is what started this whole thing in the first place."

"All right."

"So what I propose, your majesty, is that you simply replace the high priest." Nicantor paused a moment, for effect. Demetrius stared contemplatively at the floor. "Replace the high priest with Alcimus, or someone like him, who favors Greek customs, who would obey our wishes and, in fact, be a loyal vassal. This will instantly cause division among the staunch religious, but not enough to cause revolt, as long as we don't interfere right away with their religious freedoms."

"Go on," Demetrius said, listening closely.

"Then you empower your new high priest, as discreetly as possible, to hunt down and eliminate all of his political opponents and the influential echelon of the Maccabean supporters, as well as Judah himself and his brothers. With their leadership wiped out, the people will either fold to our will, abandoning their barbaric religion, or more likely, they'll rise up against the new high priest, violating the terms of the truce that they themselves agreed to, thereby profaning their rule and the rights of the Jewish people." Nicantor drew the next words out, emphasizing his lack of sincerity. "This would give us no choice, of course, except to go to war."

Demetrius smiled, understanding the scheming mind of his general. "Send for this Alcimus. I think I would like very much to speak to him regarding the future of Judea and the office of high priest."

"He's here in Antioch, Your Majesty, with some of his supporters," Nicantor replied. "He has actually requested an audience with you to discuss these very subjects."

§

Kalisto walked through the small village on the ridge, a mile inland from the cliffs that overlooked the sea. There were people in plenty, but Kalisto did not recognize anyone. All of them were new. They must have moved in after the plague wiped everyone else out. He saw a tent with a table outside, piled with fish. The fisherman had a scale and weights to price the fish for buyers. The air was sultry. The trees and flowers were in full blossom. Kalisto's graying beard was fully grown out again. The cloak he wore concealed the burn scars on his arms. Over his head he wore a soft leather hood.

I've seen the world, he thought, *every miserable part of it, but nothing reminds me more of the gods' injustice than this village.* He hoped for one person—just one—whom he would recognize, who could tell him where his family's ashes fell.

He turned along a dirt trail, now muddy from the rains of the previous day. His shoes stuck and slid as he pressed forward.

Then he found it. There before him was the house he had built for his wife. Inside, where once he had seen his children growing up, stood a strange woman in an open window, cleaning. A man appeared beside her and stared out at him. Kalisto pried his eyes away and turned onto the trail leading back to the main road. Who knew how long the people had lived there? He was not about to make an issue over who owned the wretched house. As far as he was concerned, they could have it. Kalisto just wanted to leave this cursed town. Coming here had been a stupid idea.

Outwardly, the town had not changed much in the thirteen years that he had been away. He looked at the faces of the villagers, but still saw no one he recognized. He should have been here when the plague hit. It was unfair that his wife, Cassandra, had to die with their children, alone. While she suffered, he had been wasting time transporting supplies, helping the Macedonians with their pointless war against Rome. Cassandra ... he had trouble even thinking the name. He could hardly even remember what she looked like now.

"Kalisto!"

He thought he heard someone say his name.

"Kalisto!" It came again, and he turned to see a middle-aged woman approaching, dressed in ragged clothes. At first he did not recognize her.

"Helen?" he asked in his raspy voice, looking at the sister of his wife.

"How can it be? You're alive!" she murmured.

"I've come to visit the resting place of my family, and offer sacrifice to the gods over the place where the plague took Cassandra and the children."

Helen looked confused.

"Do you know where their pyres were?"

"That was over ten years ago!" Her words came harsh and accusing. "You haven't returned in over ten years, and you come here now?"

"I've been making my living by the sea. It's a hard life, but the only life I know," Kalisto replied defensively. "The dead were not in need of me."

Helen looked incredulous at his words.

"I wasn't *ready* to come back," he added quietly. "I didn't think I could face this place after what happened."

"It's been over a *decade*. And you didn't think—"

"There was nothing left for me here. I didn't even guess that you were still alive."

She stood there, looking insulted.

"Helen, when you're the king's admiral and naval advisor you can't just—"

"They're alive!" she interrupted, with disdain.

"What?"

"Your family didn't die when the plague struck. We all left for the city when the first people began getting sick. You know how cautious Cassandra can be," she said with a shallow smile. Kalisto stood there in silent disbelief.

"She waited for you for *seven* years," Helen began again, her voice on the edge of tears. "For seven years she would walk to the cliffs and look out to sea for your ship, but you never came! Everyone told her you were dead, that you weren't coming back, but she wouldn't listen. Six years ago she met a merchant, and finally agreed to marry him."

Helen could see Kalisto's pain at these words. "With how long she waited, you'd think she was Penelope waiting for Odysseus. But life isn't a story," she said, wiping a tear off her cheek.

Kalisto tried to speak, but the words came out broken "The children?"

"Your boy took up your trade and is part of the crew on a cargo ship. Your daughter died last year of the fever. There was nothing more we could do for her."

"*Last year* ..." He could have had time—twelve, thirteen years—all so much time. He turned and headed back up the road, toward the edge of town. Helen called after him only once, but Kalisto could hear the insincerity laced through her words of beckoning.

He moved along the foliage-lined trail toward the cliff where, years before, he would gaze out, hearing the call of the sea. Now he braced himself against a stone outcrop that overlooked the water. He stared out at the ocean that had always held such an allure for him. All these years living the wrong life, chasing after the wrong pursuits. He had built his life on meaningless ambition.

He saw his ship harbored below, which had more Roman gold and silver aboard than he could manage to spend in three lifetimes. *I've made my fortune, but I'm an old man now,* he thought. *I can buy anything now, but I have nothing. I abandoned what mattered. I made my riches helping the very people I fought against in my youth.* He then realized something that deep inside he must have always known: that possibly his family could have survived. He had simply chosen to believe they were dead, reaffirming the belief daily, perpetually morning a loss that did not even exist. Until today.

All the time wasted. A lifetime wasted. He collapsed into the dense foliage, along the side of the road. He stared out at the sea, and for the first time in over twenty years, he wept.

§

S imon barged through the door. "Don't you knock?" Judah asked in annoyance.

"Judah," Simon said, ignoring his complaint, "Word came from Antioch. They're proclaiming that you are no longer the high priest of Israel, and that the office has been handed over to another. They're proclaiming all throughout Jerusalem that a Hellenist Levite, named Alcimus, is now the acting high priest. He entered the city with soldiers this morning and had some of our officers in high positions murdered."

"What about Jonathan?" Judah asked, rage building inside him.

"He managed to escape. He's riding here with his wife and some of the men, but he sent a rider ahead. The troops didn't know whether to attack Alcimus or not. He was announcing before everyone that he is now the high priest, saying you are dead."

"Dead?" Judah asked, amazed.

What is Demetrius trying to do now? he wondered. Clearly, trying to strip him of his authority, but more was at play. He was hoping to spread Greek influence by planting his puppet on the seat of power. But no, that was not all. Demetrius wanted more. *He's young and unproven, but he knows what he's doing. He's got to know how I'll react, how the faithful sons of Israel will respond. He wants a war, and he wants it to appear like we started it.* Judah's thoughts were churning. *But you don't supplant a leader, tell people he's dead, and then leave him alive to delegitimize your claim.* Obviously, they were coming for him.

"Gather what men you can. They're on their way, if not already here. We'll meet Jonathan en route. We need to send riders throughout all of Judea to reassemble the army. Tell them the war isn't over."

"Many of the men will come," Simon said to Judah, who was already strapping on his sword and packing his satchel. "The problem is most of the men have gone home over the past few months. Convincing Hebrews to fight Syrians is one thing, but convincing them to fight other Hebrews may prove difficult. I don't think many will understand what's really happening here. Also, our right to worship hasn't been attacked, so many of the men who previously risked their lives may not care, as long as they can worship in peace."

"Well, we'll have to make them understand it's a different tactic to accomplish their same goal. It's the same enemy and the same war. Send Gaddi and some of his people to contact the Nabateans. We'll need the arms and money we stored with them."

After Simon departed, Judah mounted his horse and rode to Martha's house. Workers were plowing the field on the neighboring lands. Dismounting, he tied the horse's reins to the thick branch of an olive tree, and walked down the path that led toward Martha's dwelling. On the way, he passed by two young men who had the appearance of resting laborers who worked the nearby field, but then he felt their eyes on his back. His own eyes shifted toward the ground, looking for any movement of shadows around him. He felt uneasy as he turned the corner along a stone wall, approaching Martha's door. He knocked.

"Judah!" she said happily, opening the door wide. Then she saw the grim expression he bore. "Judah, what's wrong?"

"Demetrius has appointed a new high priest, and they are telling the people that I am already dead."

Martha put her hand over her mouth.

"What's going to happen?" she asked.

"I have to leave. They will try to make their lie the truth. My brothers and I are leaving at once. We have to gather the army again and enter Jerusalem with enough strength to put down any Hellenistic subversives who have managed to take hold of power."

"Should I—"

"You should stay here," Judah said. "Take care of Eleazar's wife and children. Simon's family and Jonathan's wife will remain here, too. I wanted to let you know before—"

"Thank you," she said, gazing into his eyes with love and

reverence. Judah held that gaze for a long moment. Then he forced a smile, turned, and walked back up the path.

As Judah came near to rounding the corner again, he once more felt uneasy. He realized how much the manner of those two young field workers had bothered him. No, it wasn't their manner, exactly, but something else—his own instinct for recognizing concealed danger. An intuition, so often ignored on account of social mores and the fear of overreacting—an intuition that, if acknowledged, could sometimes make the difference between life and death. He had learned to listen to that voice over the years.

Judah was not surprised, but still felt a shiver down his spine as he rounded the corner and saw the two men still waiting there. As he drew near, he could see the expressions on their faces. He noticed that the younger man looked anxious, but the corners of his mouth turned upward in a smirk. *The bastard is looking forward to this,* Judah thought.

The second man's eyes darted to the side, making contact with someone else's. Judah turned his head and saw a third man, emerging from behind the tree where Judah had tied his horse. This man was gaunt, fortyish, with a pockmarked face, thinning hair, and a hard look in his eyes.

Abruptly, all three men closed in. Judah hadn't notice the fourth, who moved out from around the wall directly behind him.

Chapter 50

NABIS SHIFTED HIS weight forward, striding uphill. He led the mule, which Abishag rode, by the rope. Behind her saddle rested several large bags, one filled with Phoenician silver. Unlike most of Galilee, the region they were crossing was mountainous and rocky. The air was hot and dry. Neither Nabis nor Abishag had eaten much since the night before, and they both were feeling the onset of fatigue.

They still had three leather skins of water remaining and knew they soon would be nearing the city of Adashim. Two days before, they had crossed a place called Har Megiddo, passing through the Jezreel Valley, where hundreds of years before the wicked queen Jezebel, a devout worshiper of Baal and persecutor of righteous Jews, was cast from her window by her eunuchs and left outside the wall to be eaten by wild dogs.

"What harbor will we travel from?" Abishag asked.

"We'll journey up to Narbata, then west to the harbor of Dor, where we'll book passage on a ship to Ephesus."

"And what if your family has moved?" she inquired.

"Many of my mother's relatives lived in the area. It shouldn't be difficult to find them."

"What is Ephesus like?" Nabis could hear the apprehension in her voice. He knew she had never been far from Judea. This was the farthest north she had ever traveled, and the idea of leaving her homeland for a Greek city, where she would be a foreigner, must be somewhat terrifying. But he knew she would live anywhere as long as it was with him.

"It's beautiful, and bigger than any city in Israel," Nabis said encouragingly. "Outside the city there are green rolling hills, and rivers that lead to the sea." He looked up and smiled at her.

"Why are you looking at me like that?" she asked, smiling back.

"Like what?" he asked, still smiling, appreciating her beauty and sweet nature. He continued forward, trudging up the slope, the sweat rolling down his brow.

Reaching the top of the incline, Nabis looked down. At his feet lay a body, facedown in the dirt. Abishag let out a startled yelp. Nabis could smell the stench of the corpse, reeking as if it had been rotting in the sun for some time. He turned the body over. It was covered from head to foot in wrappings, but not the wrappings of a common shroud.

"Should we bury him?" Abishag asked, covering her nose.

"Who would leave a body out in the open like this, and not even cover him with stones?" Nabis asked, kneeling down.

"Don't touch him with your hands!" Abishag whispered. "It's unclean."

Despite her warning, he reached out and pushed away the veil that covered the face. Abishag let out a scream, and Nabis recoiled. He thought he was going to vomit.

Under the shroud lay a woman's body, covered in putrid lesions dripping pus, clear fluid, and blood. Her lips had rotted away as well as the gum tissue beneath. Half the skin on one side of the nose was gone, leaving exposed cartilage. What was left of her face was misshapen, and the tissue around one eye had disappeared.

Abishag let out a blood-curdling scream as the woman's hand shot up and gripped hold of Nabis's wrist. Her almost unnoticeable shallow breaths turned to heavy gasps. Nabis tried to whirl back, his heart racing. The woman attempted to say something, then fell back, her arm limply dropping to the earth. Nabis now noticed there were two slits in the shroud, for eyes, which he had not noticed before. The smell of rotting flesh was not from a dead man, but from a woman who was rotting alive.

Paralyzed in fear, Abishag was unable to say a word. Nabis stood up and looked down the hill, fixing his gaze upon stone huts in the distance. There were people, like the woman before them, shrouded in cloth, walking about.

"It's a leper colony," he said, his heart still pounding. All the veiled bodies in the valley below looked up at him eerily.

"Let's leave here," Abishag murmured, her voice trembling. Nabis stared down at the people. "Please, Nabis," she whimpered, agitated.

§

Simon walked into his house after telling Gaddi all that had happened. He just needed some provisions, for he knew there was no time to spare. "Where's Mattathias?" he asked his youngest son, John.

"Gathering the men," John answered.

Simon nodded. With a sudden pang of anxiety, he remembered the agreement he had made with John about what age he must be before joining the army. Despite his best efforts to delay it—John, too, would be wielding a weapon in battle within two years. He was almost fourteen now—sharp for his age, willful, and ambitious. Simon thought it interesting how different the personalities of his children were, and how young they were when those personalities took shape.

In some ways Simon found John stronger than even his older brothers, his moral character already very much grounded. The boy was so different from Mattathias. Simon thought it a weakness that most parents lacked the ability to objectively judge their own children. They all wanted to see the best in them, or more likely, they saw what they wished to see.

Are you so different? Simon asked himself. But yes, he was different. He saw his sons for what they were, he decided.

Mattathias, the eldest son, by no means lived up to his grandfather's name, though perhaps that would change one day.

Jude was moral, but timid and unsure of himself. He habitually followed his fool of an older brother.

But John—now he was a son to make a father proud. Simon recalled how two years before, John had asked, "If you are older, Father, why is Uncle Judah in charge of the army?"

Simon had explained such was the wish of his own father, and that Judah was the most gifted of all the brothers in battle and in strategy. Simon's role was to lead the army spiritually.

"Does that mean I can lead an army, even though my brothers are older than me?" John had asked.

"Perhaps," Simon had answered with a smile, seeing the ambition already kindling in the boy. "If that is what you want, who will stop you?"

Now Simon brought his attention back to the matter at hand and began packing provisions. In a moment, he would have to explain what he was doing to his wife. She was ignoring him, and he glanced over at her coldly. They had grown so distant over the years. She stared back—not really seeing him. He knew she hated him for not keeping their children out of harm's way and for putting his brothers' every wish ahead of their family.

Simon looked away, wondering how much time he should waste trying to explain what was happening in Jerusalem and why he had to leave. *It doesn't really matter,* he told himself. With her shallow understanding of politics, her eyes would glaze over and her mind would wander after his first few sentences. *I'd have better luck explaining it to my horse, though the horse might actually care,* he thought with irritation. He decided he'd simply tell her that Mattathias, Jude, and himself would be gone for a time. Then, seeing her cold gaze, he decided to say nothing at all.

Thank God I wasn't born a woman, specifically that woman, he thought. She grew more vexing by the day. She'd used to be beautiful. There was a time when she had enjoyed their marriage bed. Now, neither was true.

Suddenly a figure appeared in the shadow of the doorway.

Simon reached for his sword, then realized it was Mattathias. Instantly, Simon knew something was wrong.

"Father," Mattathias said, moving inside. "Judah was attacked."

"Attacked? How badly is he hurt?"

"There were four of them. If we hadn't been riding up the slope at that very moment, they would have killed him."

"He's alive then," Simon said.

"He received a bad cut across the chest, and a lesser one on his neck."

"Just because he's not dead doesn't mean they haven't killed him," Simon muttered, remembering how many men he'd seen die after battles from infected wounds.

"He's on his way here, Father. Some of the men are with him."

Mattathias felt pleased with himself that he had reacted so quickly, charging Judah's four attackers before they were even completely upon him. But Mattathias had a vague memory of one of his fellow riders charging forward even before he did. And Judah had already killed two of the attackers before he and his companions could reach him. By the time they had descended the slope, Judah was on the ground, badly wounded, with the other two assailants ready to finish him. Still, Judah sprang back to his feet, determined to defend himself.

Mattathias had looked upon Judah in growing admiration. His uncle didn't even act as if he had been wounded. He had blood soaking through his clothes, and a gash on the side of his neck, but he moved like he felt no pain at all, prepared to continue the fight. *I hope one day I can be like that,* thought the young man, *and have a reputation like his.* He envied his younger brother, Jude, for sharing their uncle's name.

Now, with an entourage of armed men surrounding him, Judah approached Simon's house. Judah moved through the soldiers, who stepped aside, then stood guard outside the door.

Judah clasped his brother's shoulder and walked inside, the physician following.

"They almost made their propaganda come true," Judah said, as he sat down in a chair with a groan, his body still animated from the adrenaline of the fight.

"Clear the house out!" Simon barked at his wife and children, who all began quickly heading for the door, except for Mattathias. Simon noticed Judah was not wearing his armor.

"You should have known better than to go anywhere alone," Simon said, annoyed.

"As you say." Judah shifted uncomfortably, as the physician cut away at the top portion of his garment. A sharp pain stabbed his chest with every breath, but the gash in his neck hurt the most.

Judah recalled the look in the eyes of the first attacker, who had emerged from behind the tree where Judah's horse was tied. He could tell the man knew how to kill but had not expected the feint when Judah deflected his blow, afterwards inflicting a deep gash between his assailant's upper ribs. At once, the three other assassins were upon him. He heard a man closing in from behind, but one of the two at his front, dressed as a field worker, dashed at him. Judah swung his blade, hacking across the man's face, before turning to stab the man in his back. As he turned to face his enemy, the assassin sliced across Judah's chest, while the younger man, now behind him, swung his sword, bringing it down violently upon Judah's neck, sending him sprawling. *The fool hasn't sharpened his blade,* Judah thought. *If he had, it would have taken my head off.*

Then all at once, Hebrew horsemen had borne down on the attackers. Judah looked up at the assailant whose face he had cleaved, rending the jawbone. The man stood there in shock before staggering and collapsing to his knees. One of the riders crashed into him, trampling him, while the other riders hewed down the remaining two with their swords.

Simon looked at Judah as the physician stitched the wound in his chest with a sharp curved needle and a long strand of horse hair. "You should be dead," Simon uttered. "Going out to visit Martha, with no guards, not even wearing armor—could you have been more foolish?"

"Apparently God doesn't want me dead yet," Judah said, wincing as the physician tightened the thread.

"*Do not put the Lord your God to the test!*" Simon said, quoting Moses, with an angry tone in his voice. He looked outside and saw the sun was setting. "We'll have to sleep here tonight," he muttered. "Already it's getting dark."

§

"I'm surprised they showed up," Bacchides said to Alcimus— the Demetrius-appointed high priest—as they watched the mass of Israelites crossing the open plain on foot below. "There are about sixty of them."

"I don't think they'll offer your men much of a challenge," Alcimus answered. "These old men are mostly scribes, but they make up the influential elite of the Hasideans, the religious and political party that supports Judah as high priest."

Bacchides could see an old man with a walking stick heading the group of approaching people. He walked with a distinct limp.

"Of course they won't be a challenge," Bacchides replied. "My men will have to make some sport of it."

"As long as it's done," Alcimus said. "If these old men die, the Maccabees immediately lose about a third of their political support and structure."

"I wonder if it's even necessary. They're all here, aren't they? They jumped at the opportunity to talk of peace as soon as rumors of Judah's death began circulating."

"Hopefully, he *is* dead by now," Alcimus said, "but I know my own people. They are not Hellenistic. They are devoutly religious, and will always side with whoever takes the role of high priest and represents it with sincerity and nationalism. They may side with us now, when they think they have no choice but to save their own necks. But believe me: at the first chance, they'll put their full support behind the strongest religious radical who promises to overthrow Greek influence."

"If I wasn't trying to *start* a war, I might give them the benefit of the doubt," Bacchides murmured. "But because the king wants war, and nothing starts revolts like butchering a mass of unarmed old religious men, we'll do what we have to." Bacchides wondered if Alcimus actually believed that Demetrius cared about consolidating power behind him. Bacchides knew better. For Demetrius, Alcimus was only an excuse to go to war, to regain the integrity of their southern border and the honor worthy of the Seleucid kingdom.

Alcimus, you are just another puppet, Bacchides mused. *But at least you know what you are. You don't really believe in your god, and you know exactly what the position of high priest truly is.* Bacchides understood there was nothing religious about it. "High priest" was simply another title of power—like "governor." All the religious trappings merely lent the position authority in the eyes of the simpleminded Jewish populace. Ultimately, the post was a useful ploy in the hands of the empire to keep the Israelites obedient to the real powers that be.

"In just a moment, they will see what Greek influence really means," Bacchides added out loud.

Bacchides turned around and stared at the three-hundred cavalrymen behind him. They kept low, laying their horses down behind the rolling hill that offered concealment. Each man was lightly armored, equipped with a spear and kopis.

Bacchides could now distinguish the faces of the men in the small crowd approaching them. He jerked his arm upward, signaling. The horses rose, and the cavalrymen dropped seated into the saddles as the horses stood.

As if the realization struck the advancing elderly men all at once, they paused momentarily, then scattered in all directions. Mounted troops poured over both sides of the shallow hill into the gorge below, engulfing the crowd. Bacchides could see the first javelin drive into the back of the old man with the walking stick, who tried in vain to hasten away from the riders. Bacchides looked over at Alcimus, who was smiling exuberantly.

Chapter 51

"THIS WILL HELP with the headaches," Laodice's servant said, handing her a small silver cup. "It will keep you young, too, Your Majesty."

Laodice took the chalice, poured the liquid mercury into her mouth, and swallowed—the taste sending an involuntary shudder through her body. She glanced in the mirror. She could not help but notice that her face seemed to be frozen in a perpetual sneer.

Across from her, on the balcony, Demetrius was pacing. "It's not that I don't agree with you," Laodice said, continuing her conversation with him, "but don't you think Parthia is a greater threat?"

"Parthia is on the other side of the empire," her son answered. "It may be as great a threat, but Judea is right here on our southern border, and I won't be foolish enough to make war on two fronts, like my uncle. The Hebrews first, and when they've been crushed and there's stability, then I will destroy Mithridates' hordes to the east."

"But the Parthians are conquering lands all the way to the edge of Babylon," Laodice said, putting her fingers to her forehead, where she felt the pain. Since her son Antiochus's death, she had suffered sleepless nights, and when she did sleep, she had nightmares. Most of the time, she told herself that the child had not really been killed but just taken into exile, that the sounds she heard were only those of Lysias and Urion dying. She imagined the boy safe and alive on some Greek Island. When she was honest with herself and acknowledged his demise, she rationalized that it was for the good of the empire, that he gave his life honorably for his kingdom, as would any Seleucid king.

"The Hebrews are no different," Demetrius replied. "Their leader has subdued and conquered every surrounding nation, and all at once. If they had larger numbers and weren't at war with us, they'd be able to hold onto those regions."

"Even if you manage to get the Hebrews to revolt, it will take months for word to get back to us, and months to deploy Nicantor with his army to destroy them."

A shrewd smile crossed Demetrius's face. "I deployed Nicantor with an army to Judea weeks ago, shortly after I sent Bacchides to appoint Alcimus high priest."

§

"Judah has only managed to rally six-thousand men," General Nicantor said to Bacchides inside his tent. "But more are joining by the day. You and that fool Alcimus killed off all of those Hasideans. Then you butchered all of those religious Jews and left them in that pit outside Jerusalem. I don't imagine the Maccabees are too happy about that."

"The city is more divided," Bacchides said defensively. "Alcimus managed to get many powerful people to defect to our side."

"You do *know* what they're saying?"

Bacchides looked at him blankly.

"That Judea was more justly judged under the rule of a Seleucid king than it would be under a pawn and traitor like Alcimus."

Bacchides smiled, amused.

Nicantor sighed. "You will return to Antioch, your mission accomplished. Alcimus will flee, and Judah will march on Jerusalem and take the city back, not knowing that we are directly to his north. When Judah gives chase to Alcimus to avenge his countrymen, he will be heading directly toward us."

"If you can keep your location a secret," Bacchides interjected.

"Once he's out of the city I will deliberately make our presence known, and the size of our force. Then I will offer to meet him, like I did his brother, to discuss a peace agreement."

"Peace?" Bacchides asked, in surprise.

"The king wants Judah alive, to be taken back to Antioch in chains, for a *very* public and *very* painful execution. The rest of the army will be destroyed or melt away. Then I will burn their temple to the ground once and for all, and Alcimus can be high priest and kill as many of his fellow Jews as he wants to," Nicantor said in disgust.

Nicantor despised Alcimus as much as Bacchides did. *The incompetent fool,* he thought. *Alcimus failed to kill Judah when he was all alone—even with the help of four hired thugs. How does someone botch that?* Could no one else see the irony of appointing someone head of a religion who was trying to *wipe out* that religion?

§

Mounted on a dark red steed with a black mane, Judah stared north toward Jerusalem. Simon and Jonathan sat astride horses beside him. Gaddi had already left, with two-score men, to retrieve their stockpile of weapons and money stored with the Nabateans.

Behind the three brothers marched seven-thousand men, with two-hundred cavalry. Their mounted scouts traveled ahead of the army, reconnoitering possible threats and securing potential danger areas and ideal ambush sites along the line of march.

"I want to move quickly," Judah said to his brothers. "Alcimus has only two-thousand Seleucid soldiers helping him. We can assume he'll abandon the city and flee north for some kind of Syrian support. We can't let him escape. He's gaining support through fear."

Simon glanced over at Judah and could see the shadow of anger on his brother's face. The week before, Alcimus had more than a hundred devout men, women, and children dragged from their synagogues—people whose rabbis openly supported Judah as high priest. All of them had been taken outside the city, executed, and thrown into a mass grave.

"After we take the city," said Judah, "I want you, Jonathan, to remain there with enough men to secure it. Everyone else will come with me to capture that murderer and his men."

Jonathan acknowledged the command with a nod. He was relieved Sarah was not still in Jerusalem, where he couldn't protect her and their unborn child.

"That coward has probably already evacuated the city with his minions," Simon said caustically.

Judah shifted position on his horse, his chest wound dully throbbing. His neck was covered with a large scab surrounded by a dark bruise where the assailant's blade had connected.

He thought about his conversation with Simon the day he had been injured. Though he had said it sarcastically at the time, he truly believed there was more God had for him to accomplish, or he would be dead by now.

I will bring that murdering, power-hungry whore's spawn to justice, he thought darkly. *By the time Demetrius sends his army, I will have gathered mine.* Judah had sent riders to every major city in Judea. He wondered how long Gaddi would take to make it back with their arms. The men would need weapons, because once Alcimus was killed, Demetrius would have his excuse for a war.

§

"What is your business in Narbata?" the old bearded man asked Nabis at the city gates.

"We're just passing through," Nabis answered, "on our way to Dor."

"There's a tax for short-term visitors at Narbata," the old

man wheezed. His words were stressed, as if the mere strain of speaking was pushing him to the point of overexertion.

Nabis was annoyed, but placed two silver coins into the outstretched, furrowed hand. The old man shot Nabis a disdainful look, but let him walk through the gates.

"We'll sell the mule when we get to Dor," Nabis said to Abishag. "Meanwhile, we'll buy some forage for her, and some bread for us." He patted the animal gently on the neck.

Abishag forced a smile, but she felt restless walking through the city. Fear of the unknown had continued to torment her, and now grew greater as they neared the end of their journey. Nabis sensed her apprehension, but said nothing. He didn't know any words that would comfort her. She was headed for a strange world, so unlike her own, where people would look down on her because of her religion and ethnicity. *We can always travel back to Jerusalem when things calm down, if she's too unhappy,* Nabis thought to himself.

After buying fresh bread for the remainder of their journey, the couple continued on toward the city's western gate. The farther they walked, the more poverty-stricken the houses and buildings appeared.

As they stepped into a plaza, Abishag saw a platform with half-naked people on display, their wrists bound. It was a slave auction. She grimaced at the cruelty of the scene and the memories it invoked. Nabis recognized the terror in her eyes.

"Let's go," he whispered, but Abishag did not look away. She saw a young girl handed over to an elderly couple who appeared to be of moderate means. Abishag could almost see the world through the girl's eyes. Her own eyes began clouding with tears. *They're selling people,* she said to herself. *People don't come into the world with chains around their necks. What could be more unnatural and ungodly than selling humans, like animals?*

"Come, Abishag," Nabis said again, but she ignored him. Her gaze was transfixed by a crying Hebrew toddler, with brown ringlets of hair, who now was being brought to the platform.

He looked to be about a year-and-a-half. The auctioneer began shouting out numbers.

A middle-aged woman stepped over to Abishag, seeing her apparent interest. "If you are looking to buy, the choice slaves are auctioned on the other side of the city. It's disgraceful they would sell a lot of such low caliber," the matron hissed in disdain. "That one there—" she pointed at the crying boy. "He's the son of a harlot who was killed on account of some debt owed by her procurer. When he refused to pay, they took their payment out on her—then when they grew weary of the only way she *could* pay them, they cut her throat. Who in their right mind would buy such slaves? It's shameful."

The toddler on the platform began to cry louder, and Abishag's own tears finally spilled down her cheeks. Noticing, the woman gave a sneer and walked away.

Nabis looked down at his wife with concern, and she looked up into his eyes. Her face was filled with pleading and desperation.

Chapter 52

WITH SIMON BESIDE him, Judah strode toward the large tent erected beneath the slope, on top of which Nicantor's army stood, arrayed for battle. The tent was embroidered with the king's standard. No guards were visible—only a single man, dressed in extravagant armor, waiting outside.

Nicantor's army of thirty-thousand waited, formed on the concave slope of the ridge's descending fingers that gripped the valley below. On the rise, the general had positioned his reserve corps, cavalry, and archers. Much of the open ground was covered in brown brush, with a little grass shrouding the hills. Looking over his shoulder, Judah could see how insignificant his small force appeared from where he stood, compared with the massive formations of the Seleucids in front of him.

After regaining control of Jerusalem, Judah and Simon had hastened the army north as planned, trying to apprehend Alcimus, who had fled the city two days prior. A few miles outside of Caphar-Salama, Judah's scouts had ridden into an ambush. Most of the scouts were slain, except for six who were captured and three who escaped. When the three returned, shaken and wounded, Judah had divided his force, ordering his men to take up a defensive position as he waited for some sign of a Syrian advance. Hours passed, but the Syrians never came forward. Finally, nearing sundown, the six captured scouts rode toward them. They had been released, unharmed, with a message of peace. One of the men handed Judah a scroll, which he had hastily read:

To Judah the Maccabee

It is with great reverence that I hope to finally have the honor of meeting you in person. With great sincerity, I must complement you as the most worthy advisory I have ever fought on the field of battle. Fortunately for us both, there is no need to spill our men's blood today. I was dispatched with my force that was stationed in Samaria, after hearing a rumor of possible pending attack from Egypt, and moved south after hearing of the civil war started by Alcimus.

Contrary to what you may have heard, King Demetrius and the Seleucid kingdom in no way support Alcimus, who is spreading false rumors about his Seleucid backing. His men are, according to our intelligence, made up of Seleucid mercenaries—a fact he exploits to support his claim that he has our backing as high priest.

You have my deepest regret about the lives lost by your scouts today. Those that died were slain in self-defense. Your scouts who survived the skirmish, whom we have peaceably returned to you, can attest to this. I am camped only five miles north of your position near Caphar-Salama. Tomorrow I will set up a tent for us to meet—only you, myself, and your brothers if you wish them to be present. My army will be sequestered at a safe distance, so you can meet me without fear for your safety. Together we will put an end to this civil strife, bring Alcimus to justice for his crimes, and end any doubt people may have as to your claim as high priest.

General Nicantor, High Commander of the Seleucid Army

Finishing the letter, Judah had felt shocked that Nicantor could have breached the borders of Samaria without his knowing about it.

Simon read the letter. "It has to be a trap," he said. "It's too good to be true. We should withdraw to Jerusalem and set up defenses."

"But what if it *is* true?" Judah had replied, thinking. "What if their intentions are peaceful and the news about Alcimus having Seleucid support is a lie? The man could just be a power-hungry charlatan."

A long moment hung unbroken in the air.

"I have to meet him," Judah said at last with a sigh. "It might be the only hope we have."

Judah had then spent most of the night praying that his decision was right, that he wasn't acting presumptuously. In the morning, he had felt peace. He rode with his army to the rise opposite the valley where the Seleucid army waited in battle formation. Then he and Simon marched toward Nicantor's tent.

Simon recognized Nicantor's armor as they neared. The general was looking down at something on the ground.

"I wish I could see inside the tent," Simon muttered nervously. They continued walking forward—then Simon stopped and stumbled, as if he had just walked into an invisible wall.

"It's not him!" he blurted out. "Judah, it's not Nicantor!"

Judah drew his sword and signaled to his left. Suddenly, thirty-five Hebrew men who Judah had ordered up the nearby wash, emerged over the embankment, spears flashing. Only yards away, they darted toward the tent, charging past Judah and Simon.

The man dressed as Nicantor disappeared into the tent just in time for one of the Israelites to kick out the stakes, collapsing a part of the tent over him and the eighteen Seleucid soldiers concealed within. Judah's men quickly surrounded the tent as the soldiers within fought to break free.

§

From the slope of the ridge, Nicantor watched the tent fall as the Hebrews butchered his trained kidnapers. *My little ploy failed,* he thought to himself, disappointed. Unfortunately, he would just have to take Judah back to Antioch dead, and risk the king's displeasure.

"Launch the attack," he ordered a commander. A signal officer lifted a banner, and trumpets sounded. The pulsation of synchronized marching shook the ground.

The phalanxes marched forward toward Judah's meager few-thousand men. Judah, Simon, and those who overran the tent, dashed across the open ground to rejoin their formations, falling back into the forward ranks. They watched as the Syrian phalanxes pushed toward the mouth of the valley, closing in fast.

"They're going to try and get behind us," Judah said to Simon as he observed their cavalry trotting slowly along both ends of the ridgeline.

"Begin falling back!" Judah commanded, knowing if his force advanced in an attempt to trap the Syrians, Nicantor's cavalry would maneuver behind them, descending behind both of their flanks. *In fact, advancing is what Nicantor hopes I will do,* thought Judah, with a smirk.

The mass of Judah's men back-stepped, their spears poised toward the enemy. The cavalry continued down the ridge coming straight for them. *Nicantor must be pleased,* Judah thought, seeing the archers move forward between the phalanxes. *He has the high ground, he has two-thirds more men than I. He has archers, and heavy cavalry, and must believe he has every advantage. Only he doesn't know he's already lost.*

Judah gestured toward one of his men, who raised the shofar to his lips, blowing a deafening scream. Like something out of a vision, far above the Seleucid cavalry and reserve corps, five-thousand mounted Hebrews appeared stretching along the hill's ridgeline.

"Now!" Judah shouted. He led his force sallying toward the opposite slope, where half the Seleucid cavalry was advancing. Three hundred Israelites charged the hill to where the slope narrowed, creating a wall of twenty-foot sarissas, waiting for the impending cavalry charge.

The remaining Syrian cavalry near the eastern slope started to panic upon seeing the Hebrew mounted riders descending quickly atop them. Some Seleucid horses tripped and stumbled, trying to turn up the steep rise. Judah's infantry troops cut in just around the inside of the westward slope, redirecting their position toward the Seleucid flanks, now directly opposite the Israelite cavalry.

The previous night, suspicious that Nicantor's offer was a trap, Judah had sent his five-thousand cavalry to scale the ridge behind the Seleucid army.

Now there was mass confusion among the Syrian phalanxes, which tried in vain to redirect their formations toward Judah's attack.

§

From his position on the mountainside, King Mithridates of Parthia stared out at the endless horizon. The land stretched west toward hazy mountains far in the distance. Mithridates glanced down at his young son.

"Do you see all this, Phraates?" he asked. "All of it is yours for the taking. You just have to be strong enough to grab it."

Strong—and ruthless enough to hold onto it, Mithridates thought. "And be in the favor of our God, Ahura Mazda," the king added. There would be a day to teach the boy about ruthlessness when he was older. And who was to say who Mazda would side with in the future? If the Seleucid king hadn't been busy fighting Hebrews to the west, perhaps Mithradates could not have beaten him back this far. If Antiochus hadn't died when he did, maybe the Parthians would have been defeated.

He thought of all of the elders of the old tribes he had murdered to create a united Parthian kingdom, with only himself as ruler. He'd hired the servants of tribal leaders to keep him informed. He'd had men poisoned. He'd had men stabbed to death along with their children to ensure there would be no retaliation years into the future, and embraced the rumors when people spoke of the cruelty associated with his name.

"When will I get to fight the Greeks?" Phraates asked, looking up at his father.

"Soon," Mithridates answered with a smile, "and if you're worthy, you'll inherit this kingdom I've made for our people. But when I give it to you, I must first know you won't let anyone take it from you." *Because they will try,* he thought. *They will try and take everything from you, my son, and now I've placed you in a position where if you don't choose to take the power I shall one day leave behind, they'll kill you just because you are my son, because you will always be a threat to them.* Mithridates pondered all of these things, unable and unwilling to explain them to a boy of ten.

§

Nicantor sneaked into a narrow alleyway, near the Jerusalem square. Two- and three-story houses seemed to rise higher and higher toward the center of Mount Zion. Startled by the shrill sound of a Jewish woman's voice, he glanced back to make sure he wasn't followed. The sweat from his brow streamed down the side of his flushed face.

I should remove my armor, he thought. *How is this happening? This shouldn't be happening.*

He remembered the clash of arms, and the way Judah had shifted the whole battlefield, using the terrain against him. Nicantor had had the advantage. He had the men. His men had advanced forward, every phalanx perfectly placed, and then it had all collapsed.

How in the name of all the gods did he get his cavalry behind me?
Nicantor seethed. *How did you not notice the absence of Judah's
mounted troops? Stupid!*

Nicantor recollected the suddenness of the cavalry element
appearing on the high ground at his rear, their violent downhill
charge sending his own cavalry and rear phalanxes into disarray.

Then Judah had advanced, not up the center, but holding
the slope, preventing Nicantor's cavalry from flanking his left,
turning his men attacking at an angle before Nicantor could
react. Judah had created a very inviting opening—tempting the
Syrians, who outnumbered him three to one, to break and flee.
And so they did. *Cowards,* thought Nicantor, livid.

When he saw his soldiers scatter, Nicantor realized he had
to break and ride for the opening while he still could himself,
before the opportunity disappeared. He rode south, the only
direction possible, following his fleeing cavalry. Looking back,
he saw his infantry retreating up the southwestern heights, under
the cover of archers who protected their retreat. Nicantor also
saw, to his surprise, an element of Judah's cavalry pursuing him.
He rode harder, but they continued bearing down. His own
cavalry scattered until he was all alone, and for over ten miles,
every time he'd glance behind him, he still was being perused.

By the time his horse was on the verge of death, Nicantor
had reached the gates of Jerusalem. He realized his only chance
was to discard his steed and try to lose himself in the city's
crowded streets. Now, weaving in and out of alleyways, he tried
to avoid being seen. He noticed a frail, blind beggar sitting by
a wall. Nicantor looked at him a moment, ignoring his pleas
for alms, and savagely gripped the confused man's ragged cloak,
tearing it from his body. He knocked the beggar face-first to
the ground. The old man tried to stand, letting out a howl
that grew higher-pitched the longer he lamented. Nicantor
could not afford that attention. He swung his fist, his knuckles
slamming into the beggar's jaw, causing him to collapse with

a whimper. Then Nicantor threw the foul-smelling garment over his head and wrapped it over his armor. As long as no one noticed his clean-shaven face, he assumed he would be fine.

Nicantor scurried onto a busy street and mingled among the people. Glancing to one side, he noticed armed riders galloping into the square. They stopped and scanned the crowd. Nicantor looked away, pulling the hood of the cloak low over his face.

As the crowd began to thin, Nicantor realized he was standing in the square south of the temple. The stairs that led up the temple mount were just ahead of him. *I should be standing in this place with my army, preparing to burn the temple to the ground*, he thought, chagrined. Now here he stood in a beggar's garment.

"Sir," a stranger said, stopping him. Nicantor started to draw his blade, then recognized the man as a Seleucid scout.

"Thank the gods," Nicantor gasped in relief.

"Sir, when our riders saw you evade the rebels into the city, we sent men to find you. Almost half the army is gathering south of the city. Most of our cavalry has been accounted for and is along the southern gates. We have people securing the citadel as we speak."

Nicantor could not believe what he was hearing. He discarded the stolen cloak.

"We only lost five-hundred men in the fight, sir. Nine hundred were wounded, and about a thousand are still missing."

"That's it?" Nicantor asked, hope building within him. They still outnumbered Judah's army almost two to one.

"Take me to the men at once," he ordered. "We can still win this! Where's Maccabee's army?"

"The Jewish force is twelve miles north of here."

Nicantor knew with his diminished force he could not occupy the unsecured city and fight Judah at the same time, but he could hunt down the rebel force and then return to carry out his wrath upon the citizens here.

"Wait," he said. He glanced up at the temple and remembered how it had looked when it was under siege a year before. He remembered how Simon had looked descending these very steps, and the bitterness he had felt, being forced to swallow his pride and offer terms of peace to a defeated, broken people. He fixed his eyes upon the steps he and his men could not seize in time, and the temple he'd failed to capture. Even from where he stood, he could see priests scurrying about outside the temple courtyard. *They think they are so secure up there.* They, like the whole city, the whole Jewsih race, believed this temporary fluke of victory was somehow God's judgment upon the Seleuid Empire and a blessing upon the Jews. But it wasn't. It was merely the prelude to their annihilation. He would show them that.

"Order some men to secure the eastern wall," Nicantor barked, "and create a perimeter around this courtyard. Do it quickly." He would show these arrogant priests how vulnerable they truly were. He would teach them how to fear.

Nicantor hated them. He hated the entire Hebrew race. He hated them for not bending a knee even after being beaten. He hated them for the pride they felt, for believing they were somehow chosen by God, for their rituals and the bizarre way they conducted themselves. He hated them for the strife and instability they caused and for their fervent emotions. He hated them for the way they believed their convictions alone were true, and looked down on anyone not of their race. He hated them for the way they talked, the way they looked and acted, the way they hoarded wealth, and the way they judged others but didn't follow their own laws. He hated them for all they were, and he hated their god.

It didn't take long before hundreds of Seleucid spearmen and riders stormed into the courtyard, securing every avenue of approach, keeping the crowd of hostile onlookers at a distance. Now, Nicantor gazed up in the direction of the temple of the people he despised, and ascended the stairs.

Finding himself in the outer temple courtyard, he

meandered forward. His every movement was strained. His mind was weary with fatigue from the lost battle.

Inside, three priests stared wide-eyed at Nicantor's uniform. Two more priests proceeded out of the sanctuary.

"May God bless you, and may you live forever," one of the elderly priests murmured, fear pervading his voice, "but please, do not harm the house of the Lord!"

Two younger men scurried toward them. One held a lamb that was bleating helplessly. "We are not Judah's men," one of the older priests told Nicantor. "We were instated by Alcimus. We're Hellenistic Jews. See?" He pointed at the lamb. "We've ordered a sacrifice to be made here, and burned on the altar, to your king, Demetrius." The lamb let out a high-pitched scream as a knife was pulled across its neck.

Nicantor looked incredulous. "You despicable rodents!" he sneered. "You miserable plague on our kingdom! Hellenistic, Mosaic, Sadducee, Hasidean—you're all the same to me. *Vermin!* You are diseased creatures, low and despised, devoid of any use at all." Nicantor's voice was shaking with rage, the pent-up frustration of his failures overtaking him. "The only reasonable thing for any civilized culture to do is to slay every one of you, like the wretched creatures you are!"

He swung his hand, striking hard across the face of one priest, who at once fell to his knees.

"Please, my lord!" the priest cried, but Nicantor spit in his face. "Please!"

"Your god isn't real, you fool! Any deity that would select a race like yours as *chosen* must be the myth of all myths! You say, don't destroy the house of your god? I will burn it to the ground! I will turn it into the shit heap it always was meant to be! Your remnant will call Antiochus kind in comparison to me! If your people don't bring me Judah Ben Mattathias," he growled, grabbing the priest's throat, "I will kill every one of you. You know how to reach him. Bring him, or I will lay waste to this city and kill every Hebrew inside!"

Nicantor released the man's neck. The priest reeled back, gasping for air, his eyes filling with tears. Nicantor contemplated killing him right there, the man's pathetic pandering only angering him further, but instead he shot him a pitiless look and headed for the gate of the inner courtyard toward the steps he had ascended.

Chapter 53

ARON EASED BACK the reins, slowing his horse to a trot as he entered camp. He and three other scouts of the patriot army had reconnoitered the movements of the Seleucid bivouac. For almost a week, they had lived off of dried salted lamb's meat and the scant amount of water they had in their skins. The scouts had discovered that, in the wake of the recent battle, the Syrians had set up a rally point south of Jerusalem. Once they had gathered the majority of their missing soldiers, they had begun moving northeast, advancing behind Maccabee's position.

"They're camped outside of Beth-Horon," Aaron said to Joseph, his commander, who approached him.

"Get off your horse, get him watered, and get yourself something to eat," Joseph replied. "Where are the others?"

"About three miles behind me. One of the horses died, so I rode on ahead."

"You will likely have to give your report to Maccabee himself."

Aaron nodded.

Walking to the stream, Aaron let his horse drink and filled his water skins. Afterwards, he walked toward the fire, inhaling the smoky scent of oxen meat sizzling on the skewer.

Aaron was twenty-six-years-old and had joined the army of Judah the Maccabee just five years earlier, shortly before the battle of Emmaus. His family was proud of him for fighting for their people, their freedom, and the right to worship the Lord God. Shortly after that first engagement, his commander discovered that Aaron's father raised horses, and selected him for the new cavalry Judah was forming. After Lysias pulled the Seleucid army out of Judea, Aaron had returned home with hopes of marrying a certain girl from his town for whom his father had paid a dowry. Upon his return, Aaron learned the engagement had been broken off. The girl had given herself to another—a young slave who lived in her father's household. The slave had been stoned to death, and the daughter had been taken to a relative's house in Samaria, where she gave birth to her bastard.

At length, Aaron's family finally found a suitable bride for their son. The two were about to be wed when a rider came into town reporting that the Syrians were attempting to start a civil war, had tried to assassinate Judah, appointed a Hellenist as high priest, and massacred many influential Hasideans and religious men in Jerusalem. Once again, the armies were gathering to protect Israel from the pagan enemies of God, and Aaron would answer the call. Aaron knew that God protected Maccabee and his army. How else would he have done so much, vanquishing every hostile nation surrounding them?

"Aaron," his commander called now, waving him over. Aaron rose from the log before the fire and followed the other man through the maze of tents. "Judah will speak with you at once."

Aaron felt a surge of nervousness at the prospect of talking to Maccabee—the general of the army, the ruler of his nation, and liberator of his people. He'd seen him many times at a distance, but never thought he would get to meet him. *God,* he prayed, *help me to be accurate in my report, and leave nothing out that could help Judah, or say something that makes me look foolish.* Aaron felt another wave of nervousness cut through him as he approached the large tent.

Joseph stopped at the entrance. "He wants to see you alone."

Aaron entered, and standing before him was Judah himself. "Maccabee," Aaron said reverently.

"Aaron, correct?" Judah replied.

Aaron nodded.

"Your commander said you and your men scouted out the Syrian camp."

"Yes, Maccabee."

"And your report?"

"Yes, sir. They are holding the high ground at Beth-Horon."

"Can you estimate how many men they have?"

"We estimated between twenty-five and thirty thousand."

Judah's eyes widened. He had hoped they had done much more damage than that at Caphar-Salama.

"Their cavalry?" Judah asked.

"It appeared to be weaker than when we came against them at Caphar-Salama. I think they lost many of their horses in the attack."

Aaron watched as Judah fell deep into thought. Finally he spoke.

"Did it look like they were preparing a defensive position?"

"No, it looked like they would be on the march soon."

"Do you believe with the state and size of our current force, we can win?"

Aaron wondered if Maccabee actually doubted himself. "Yes," he replied with conviction.

"Why?" Judah asked, trying to measure the morale and courage of his own men.

"Because of *you*, Maccabee. You have always been able to turn battles against larger armies. You have always been able to snare the enemy with only a few. You *have* to be anointed by God and favored in his eyes. How else would you be able destroy the Seleucid forces that have always outnumbered us, and have dominion of half the world?"

Pleased, Judah noticed there was no doubt at all in the young man's voice.

"Some of my officers have pointed out to me that you are one of the best riders in the army."

Aaron looked surprised. "I can't claim any such rumors are true," he said, nervous once again.

Judah smiled. "Well, I will take the advice of my officers. I need the best rider we have to lead a major part of the battle that is before us. I'm also told you are an excellent archer and can even shoot while riding, so I'm appointing you my personal scout and making you a commander over one-hundred men."

Aaron looked stunned.

Jonathan walked into the tent, biting off a strip of oxen meat he had grabbed from one of skewers outside.

Before Aaron could protest the honor he had been given, Judah turned to his brother. "Prepare the men for the march. Nicantor's army is at Beth-Horon, and they're readying to move against us."

Aaron gazed at Jonathan. How boyish and young Jonathan had appeared when Aaron first joined the army five years ago! Now, one could barely tell the two brothers apart.

"Good," Jonathan said. "We'll loudly inform the Seleucid king that as long as he keeps sending armies against us, we'll happily continue to destroy them."

Judah wondered if Gaddi would return in time with the weapons and supplies from the Nabateans. It had been far too long. He should have been able to make the journey twice by now, and back. But Judah couldn't wait for his brother or the weapons, though he needed them badly. It was time to march.

§

What an absurd price for passage, Nabis thought, listening to the ship owner prattle. Abishag was bouncing the toddler in her arms, singing to him in Hebrew. She had implored Nabis, her empathy for the child eclipsing all else. It was as though if she could save just that one child from a life of slavery, it would mend all the tragedies of the world, all the pain she had ever felt.

Nabis looked at her tenderly. She smiled back at him.

"It will be sixty-five tetradrachm for three people," the sailor said, pulling Nabis's attention away from Abishag and the little one.

"Come on. That's robbery."

"Ephesus isn't close, in case you haven't noticed, and three people consume a great deal of food which needs to be bought *before* the journey."

"That child could hardly be considered a third person. He's barely weaned."

"If you think you're not getting a fair price, find a different captain and ship. My price for three people is sixty-five."

Annoyed, Nabis pulled the leather moneybag from his belt, opened it, and peered inside.

"Sixty," he said firmly.

"All right, sixty, but I need at least half upfront, and half tomorrow before setting sail."

Nabis nodded, handing over the coins.

"Be here tomorrow at dawn," said the captain. "It will be good to get away from Judea for a while. This whole place is about to be set afire. The king's general is still maneuvering, ready to strike at Maccabee. They're playing cat and mouse all over Judea."

"Who do you think will win?" Nabis asked.

"Nicantor has every advantage and the odds are all in his favor, but who's to say. Judah has already accomplished the impossible."

Nabis looked around at the harbor of Dor. He walked over to Abishag, who was making the toddler giggle with the faces she made at him.

"Look, husband," she said, smiling. "Doesn't baby Asher look like us?"

"No," Nabis answered crossly. She made a pouting face at him, in mock dejection. She smiled again after a moment.

"I love you," she said, wanting to hear the same words directed at her.

"I love you," he replied, taking a moment to absorb her beauty and forget his frustration.

He wondered how he was going to explain to his mother—or his father, if he was alive—why he had returned with a wife not only of the people they'd been warring with for years, but a Hebrew bastard child, begot by a murdered harlot. *Maybe I should leave that part out,* he thought, imagining what his mother's reaction would be.

"I've only been on a fishing boat before," Abishag said.

"It can get tedious." Nabis replied.

"God will get us through," she said smiling, looking down at the infant again. "Hello, Asher," she said, changing her voice to a playful tone.

"We should give him a Greek name," Nabis said. "It would make his life easier, and he'll thank you for it when he's older."

"No," she said defensively. "Our baby is Jewish. He'll have a Jewish name."

She looked at the child again, touching her nose to his, making him smile. *She's already calling him our child,* Nabis thought ambivalently.

"And I'm going to teach him to speak Hebrew and recite the Torah. He'll have it memorized by the time he's six, just like all good Jewish children."

§

"Our informants tell me that Maccabee was last seen outside Adasa," Agrippas, a chief intelligence officer, reported to Nicantor, riding abreast of him.

Nicantor looked out over the two columns of thirty-five-thousand men marching along the dirt road down the hill from Beth-Horon. His cavalry was out front with the exception of the detachment guarding the heavy supply carts. He wondered if Judah's scouts had learned that they had received over eight-thousand reinforcements.

"What do you think their next move will be?" Nicantor asked.

"By the time we reach Adasa, I think Maccabee will withdraw to higher ground, in hopes that we'll chase him. He'd like to draw us into an ambush, which he is so renowned for. It seems to be the only way the coward can win. He won't just stand and fight because he knows he'll lose. Cowards. All Hebrews are cowards. My guess is he'll try to bleed our energy and resources making us hunt for him."

"We'll march for Adasa," answered Nicantor. "Maybe our scouts can pick up which direction he went. When we find him, we'll deploy the men in a three-pronged front, angled to protect our flanks, and place a reserve element at our rear if he tries to get behind us again."

"There are also reports that Judah made a treaty with the Nabateans," said Agrippas. "It's possible that if they do withdraw, they will escape east, across the Jordan."

"Then we'll follow them and kill whoever harbors them."

"Also, there's a rumor that many of Judah's men are departing his army."

"Indeed? For what reason?"

"Perhaps because it's harder to build an army when there has yet been no assault on their freedoms. Perhaps because of our sheer numbers; the odds are hard to ignore. They don't think he can win. And some say," Agrippas added, amused, "that Judah dismisses all men who were just married, or built a house. Then asks which of them are afraid, and dismisses them too."

"Ridiculous," Nicantor scoffed. "No commander would do that."

Agrippas chuckled.

"Again, this all goes back to their religious practices. Because there are stories of their prophets doing such things a thousand years ago, some Jewish sects think they should emulate them."

"Absurd! Maccabee is no fool. I believe the report to be nothing but another romanticized story about the man."

"For recruitment, stories like this could be useful," said Agrippas. "Why not join an army that allows you to leave and go back home anytime you're frightened?"

Nicantor replied with a scornful grunt.

Chapter 54

THE DEEP, MELODIOUS cry of the shofar floated over the heavy sound of marching men. First one shofar, then another, and another—the pitches of the horns varying from low to shrill. While the notes were still ringing, a multitude of Hebrew soldiers rushed over the berm, downhill toward one side of the marching Seleucid column. The experienced Syrian soldiers tried to react upon hearing the sound of the rams' horns, but had no time to ready themselves before the Hebrews drove hard into their flank.

Judah watched as his men, led by Jonathan, attacked in an enfilading charge just before a sharp bend in the road, where the trail descended steeply downhill. Judah knew the majority of Nicantor's cavalrymen would now have to fight uphill, and the infantry would be divided in two.

Judah gestured to his signalman, who let out three blasts from his shofar. Then Aaron galloped forward, leading two-thousand riders, heading right for the bend in the road. The screams and thunderous discord of clashing steel was deafening. The cries of terror, so different from those of pain, rose high above the sound of metal colliding with wood, bronze, and flesh, amid a chorus of unbroken dissident clangs.

Jewish riders formed upon the sloping ridge, looking down at the isolated Syrian infantry and cavalry that tried in vain to wheel around and assault the high ground. Hebrew spearmen moved in between the riders with twenty-foot sarisias poised at the divided vanguard. Every one of the Hebrew riders pulled from their back a short bow, and began nocking arrows into the bowstrings. Upon Aaron's command, they drew, took aim, and loosed into the charging onslaught of men and horses.

Meanwhile, Jonathan's formation swept across the road, pushing the Seleucid soldiers off the edge of the steep cliff, or slaughtering them where they stood. Scores of Syrian men slid off the edge of the road and tumbled to their death.

Judah yelled to his signalman, who let forth two long notes. Jonathan's men immediately reformed along the road, facing Nicantor's advancing infantry. Aaron's riders fought downhill, toward the southeastern slope, and Jonathan's formations faced the west, the two creating outward-facing perpendicular fronts between their divided foes, along the apex of the curving road.

They're forming up for a counter-assault, Judah thought, seeing Nicantor atop his horse, rallying the infantry to form a modified phalanx upon the road. It appeared that Nicantor hoped to push through Judah's ranks, past the bending slope, toward his surrounded men. Judah noticed the Syrian's reserve cavalry, that had been guarding the supply carts, was now pressing toward them.

Judah gave yet another signal, and from behind the berm, his reserve forces and a small cavalry attachment, led by Simon, drew forth. Judah gave the signal to attack, then galloped toward the man wearing the general's armor, who he knew could only be Nicantor.

"Judah, wait!" Simon called, seeing his brother far ahead of the trailing cavalry and his men, who charged behind him on foot, unable to protect their leader.

Judah lunged his javelin into the chest of the first Syrian infantryman who darted at him brandishing a spear and a silver shield. The blow gouged a wide gash into his attacker's neck, sending him whirling. Judah reared his horse, preparing for his next assailant. A spearman charged Judah, thrusting his javelin and narrowly missing. Judah heard his horse whinny in pain, and felt its legs buckle underneath him. Despite its injury, the resolute animal remained standing, remained in the fight.

Judah drove his spear into the abdomen of another attacker and felt the haft snap at the connecting iron tip. Two more men on foot were advancing, closing in. He jammed the broken haft of his spear into the face of one and drew his sword from its scabbard. He could see Nicantor not far away, behind the first ranks. Judah fixed his gaze on him. He saw the recognition in Nicantor's face and the rage in his eyes.

Having already drawn his sword, Nicantor spurred his steed, flailing at Judah. At that very moment, the onslaught of Simon's force crashed headlong into the Syrian ranks.

§

Abishag stared off the stern of the galley and watched, with tears in her eyes, as the land faded into the distant horizon. The sea was calm, but her stomach felt uneasy at the constant rocking back and forth. She looked behind her and saw Nabis walking on the deck, holding Asher on his shoulder. She looked back at the foggy land, wondering if she would ever see it again—the land of her people, the land promised by God to the descendants of Abraham, Isaac, and Jacob.

The Greeks could not win, she was sure. They never had a chance of winning. There would always be someone like Maccabee, someone who would pick up the sword and defend the Jews, standing up for their freedom. Because the land was given by God, and the word of God couldn't be broken any more than light could cease to be, her people would never perish from the earth.

She thought of her parents when they were alive, and the stories that her father used to tell her of great men who would stand up to kingdoms that wished to enslave the sons of Jacob—men like Joshua, Gideon, Sampson, and David. Vile men would keep sending their armies to her land, but she knew they would break themselves against the will of the Hebrews, like the waves always break against the shore.

This place will always be part of me, she told herself as her home disappeared below the horizon.

Nabis walked up, still holding Asher in his arms. "It will be all right," he said, seeing her distressed expression.

She nodded, the lump in her throat making her unable to speak.

§

Flies swarmed about the dead Syrian bodies that littered the winding road. The carnage spanned two miles, clear to the village of Adasa, where the battle had ended.

Both astride their horses, Judah and Nicantor had swung at each other, locking blades. Simon, unable to reach Judah through the sea of bodies, had pressed relentless against the colliding skirmish lines. At last he arrived beside his brother, an instant before a Syrian infantryman would have skewered Judah from off his horse. Simon lunged, driving his javelin into the man's chest, penetrating his armor. Judah swung his xiphos, cleaving Nicantor's forearm. Another Syrian hastened forward directing his weapon toward Judah, but Maccabee's steed, startled, reared up and took the impact of the spear. The spirited horse screamed, reared again, and at last fell, throwing Judah to the hard earth.

Meanwhile, Simon had thrust his spear into Nicantor's side, penetrating his chest and hurling him off of his horse. Simon's men had rushed forward, some to protect Judah, and others to engage the Syrian phalanx.

The Hebrew reserve force then pushed past Nicantor, trampling him underfoot, the broken haft of Simon's spear protruding from his side.

The cut-off forward Syrian element quickly dwindled under the deluge of arrows from Aaron's mounted archers. Their counterattack never drew near enough to be a threat. Once the Syrians broke, retreating down the slope, Aaron gave the command, and his riders secured their bows, drew their spears, and charged downhill, slaying them all.

Nicantor had broken through the trampling crowd, gasping in labored breaths, his face was covered with lacerations and blood. He staggered forward behind the Hebrew reserve element, only to come face-to-face with Judah, who had just been helped to his feet by his men. Judah reached for his blade, but it was gone. He could tell Nicantor was also trying to reach for a dagger, but the general instead dropped to his knees, choking, as blood dripped from his mouth.

Before anyone else could react, one of Judah's men swung his sword into the side of Nicantor's head, toppling him over. The chest wound hemorrhaged, as his blood pooled, darkening the earth. Disoriented, Judah reached down and found his sword. He wasn't sure if Nicantor was still alive when he cut off his head, but once he held it up for all to see, the Syrian army broke in retreat.

"Jonathan," Judah had shouted, "take your men and support Simon. Run them down!" After a mile in pursuit of the Syrian phalanx, Simon's soldiers had neared the village, the whole time attacking from behind. Seeing the enemy running toward their town, the villagers had come forth from their homes, attacking the Syrians from the front and cutting off their only escape route. The Hebrew army gave chase, continuing to sound the shofar, prompting more and more villagers to join in the slaughter.

Almost the entire male populace of the town flooded from their homes, armed with a myriad of weapons ranging from swords and spears, to clubs, axes, and farming tools. When they saw the fleeing Syrian force, they joined battle, feeling ecstasy at the sight of their own people vanquishing their enemy. Astoundingly, when it ended, the villagers had killed as many Syrians as the actual Israelite soldiers had.

"Do you think the Seleucid king will get the message now?" Simon asked as he and Judah stared across the destruction.

"Unless God hardens his heart, to the ends of Demetrius's own reckoning," Judah answered, "to bleed dry every resource, coin, and soldier until they're nothing but the ruins of a once-great empire. And if that is God's will, then *Ratzon ha'El*."

Simon smiled. "I don't think one of them escaped alive."

Staring down the slope at the strewn bodies, Judah recalled what he had said to his men that morning: "Today we will face an enemy who has not only denied our right to exist, but blasphemed the name of the Lord God! We go against an enemy who stood on Mount Zion before the temple of God and spit in the face of his priests, vowing to burn the temple to the ground.

When David faced the giant, did he fear? No, for when Goliath slandered the name of God, David knew that victory was his. Did Gideon not destroy the Midianite army with a paltry three-hundred men? God has laid waste nations that threaten his anointed children with destruction. This battle is already won, because victory belongs to the Lord. Have faith, men, for today you will see God's enemies destroyed before you. They will fall by the sword, in judgment. My people, *you* are the hammer of God, His Maccabee, His instrument of judgment. Today we will crush his enemies and purify our land of the idolaters." Now, staring over the dead, Judah realized that victory had truly been the Lord's, for not a single enemy soldier had survived.

"Maccabee," said an elderly villager wielding a handled plowshare, lowering his head in reverence.

Judah nodded in acknowledgment.

"We heard from Jerusalem today that they're shouting in the streets that you are the undisputed high priest, and the chosen of the Lord. The Syrian puppet, Alcimus, has suffered a stroke."

"The lord has stricken him dumb and helpless as punishment for his sins against Israel," another villager put in. "He can't eat. They are saying he will die within the month."

Judah was astonished. The villagers and his own men gathered near. Quiet descended upon them as Judah raised his hand, preparing to speak. "From this day forth," he began, "we will celebrate this battle, and the victory the Lord has given us. We'll remember the fall of our enemies, and the liberty they can never take from our hands!"

Before he could continue, deep baritone cries of victory began echoing from the hills and canyons below, as the crowd once again chanted the name they had now come to know him by: Maccabee.

רֶפֶס הרשע

Book X
Maccabee

160 BC

"The Lord is my light and my salvation. Whom shall I fear? The Lord is the strength of my life. Of whom shall I be afraid? When the wicked came against me to eat up my flesh—my enemies and foes, they stumbled and fell. Though an army may encamp against me, my heart shall not fear. Though war may rise against me, in this I will be confident."

~ King David

βιβλίο δέκα

Chapter 55

"CAN SOMEONE GET something for her?" Demetrius asked one of the physicians, annoyed at his mother, who was groaning miserably. Laodice held her stomach and forehead, lying on the sofa curled on her side. "She's been going on like this all morning."

He turned back to the architect. "Is there any way to make the statue taller?"

"We can place it on a column," the man answered with a grin, "but according to the plans, it's already going to be the largest likeness of any king who ever sat on the Seleucid throne."

Demetrius responded with a smile that barely disguised his dislike for the man. "I've seen larger statues in Rome."

"With all due respect, Your Majesty, given the space we have, and the kind of stone we use, it might not be practical. After all, you don't want the Colossus of Rhodes ready to fall upon your city."

The door opened, and Demetrius looked up to see Pedocles, his advisor, walk in. "Your Majesty," he began.

Demetrius turned toward the architect. "We'll discuss this later. Would you excuse us?"

The man bowed and departed.

"We've received word from Judea," said Pedocles. Something in the advisor's tone disturbed the king immediately.

"Your Majesty, General Nicantor was slain in battle, and his army was defeated by Judah the Maccabee in an ambush at Adasa."

"He's dead?" Demetrius asked, unable to believe it.

"He was beheaded by Judah."

"By the gods!" Demetrius cried. "Where is the army now? What is their strength? We need to send Bacchides with reinforcements to take command."

"Your Highness," Pedocles said, his voice becoming a whisper, "they are *all* dead. Not one of our soldiers survived." He could see that Demetrius was becoming irate.

"How is that even possible?" the king screamed. "They had over thirty-thousand trained soldiers against a pack of wild dogs!"

Demetrius heard another whimper from his mother, who remained attentive only to her own agony. The sound, an irritation to Demetrius before, now vexed him to the point of outrage.

"Somebody get that old whore out of here!" he yelled.

Two servants scurried to the sofa and helped Laodice to her feet. She struggled to stand, then staggered to her son and smacked him across the face. Demetrius glared at his mother with burning eyes, wanting to strike back, but he wouldn't let her rob him of further dignity in front of his advisor and servants. Too ill to speak, Laodice shuffled out of the room with the aid of the servants.

Breaking the tension, Pedocles murmured, "I'm afraid there is more, sir."

Demetrius snapped, "Well, out with it then!"

"Apparently the people of Adasa came forward to help during the fight, slaughtering our men on their retreat."

Demetrius thought for a moment, trying to calm himself.

"Order conscripts for another levy," he said finally. "Call up every retired soldier who still can march. I want as many experienced men as we can manage—men who won't get rattled and run when they see a little blood. We are *not* giving up on our southern border, and we *shall* make those bastards pay dearly for what they have done. Our men will not have died in vain. Not while *I* wear this crown!"

"Your Majesty, levies cost money, armies cost money, and the treasury is already—"

"Raise the taxes on all non-Greek lands outside of Antioch," Demetrius snapped.

"Sir?"

"Placate the nobles, but tax the peasants and landowners. The foreign middle class is where we'll pull the wealth from for this war. Now bring me Bacchides. Our response must be as swift as it is harsh."

"I'm sorry to say there is still more bad news," the advisor continued. "Alcimus has suffered an ailment that has deprived him of speech. The physicans believe he will die, so Judah now has no dispute to his claim as high priest."

Demetrius blanched. *Can anything else go wrong?* he wondered.

"But Alcimus is alive?"

"For now."

"As long as he lives, he is the only high priest of the Hebrews, recognized by the empire!"

§

"The Hellenistic Jews have all fled the city," Jonathan told Judah over the noise of the crowd. The entire street was lined, packed with cheering masses wanting a glimpse of the man on the magnificent horse who was now their undisputed leader—the man who had saved Israel, restored their liberty, and returned their freedom to worship their God. Judah raised his hand in benediction.

The helpless Alcimus had been taken north for protection. *What a fitting punishment,* thought Jonathan, *being trapped in the shadow world between life and death.*

"Still no word from Gaddi?" Judah asked.

"No word at all," Jonathan answered. The worry that something had gone horribly wrong was increasing with each passing day.

"Send Aaron out with some of his scouts to the Nabatean chieftains. See if they can find out what happened."

"If he had been harmed, his men would have sent word," Jonathan answered. "We'll find him, Judah."

"We need to finish rebuilding the city walls," Judah said, shifting his mind from the troublesome subject. "If Demetrius tries to invade, we can't have Jerusalem unfortified."

How he wished he could return to Modein! He longed to rest, to lie down in his own bed—not on the stony dirt beneath his tent.

And he missed Martha. He remembered the touch of her lips when they had kissed. He wanted to have that feeling again, to look into her eyes again.

You should remarry, he told himself. *Adi was the love of your life, but you didn't die with her. There's no reason to put yourself through hell until the end of your days.*

Judah knew if he married Martha, he should relinquish the office of high priest. It was unlawful for the high priest to take a widow as wife. Yet he needed children, to secure a lineage and pass down this order he had created. An order of high priests ... Marrying Martha meant giving up that office. The prophets said a son of David would return to rule the throne and be lord over Judea one day—a messiah—but until that time, Judah and his lineage should rule Israel. He would name his first-born *Hasmonai* after his own grandfather ... a Hasmonean dynasty.

I will rule Judea today, and soon I will take Samaria and Galilee, restoring our true borders. I will pass the rule of Israel on to my lineage, and they will reign as long as the Lord is pleased with my descendants. I will destroy anyone who tries to take this from me.

Judah was suddenly startled to hear his own thoughts. *How long have you been so infatuated with power?* he asked himself.

Power like this—could you give it up? He glanced over the raucous crowd still cheering his name.

Yes, he answered himself, he could. But if he did, he would always be a threat to the next man to take power. The people would always rally to him anytime something politically unsavory happened, and therefore, if ever he did relinquish power, he always would be a target, as would his family.

He almost wished he could give it all up and disappear from the sight of the people, with Martha. He thought of her often throughout the day. At times he imagined her watching him. He hoped she thought of him, too. At other times, he imagined her in his bed chamber, coming to him at night, slipping the sleeves of her dress down, looking at him with her tantalizing gaze, and letting herself be taken by him.

Then he would force the thoughts from his head, purging them from his mind, not wanting to lessen her or degrade her purity in his heart. Maybe if he sent for her, she would come to Jerusalem. Then he could decide whether to ask for her hand. He knew she would make a good and suitable wife.

But there was the statute—right in the books of Moses—decreeing that the high priest could not marry a widow, but must marry a virgin. Part of him was tempted to ignore the statue. After all, Martha was a resident of a faraway border city and had no family, so few people would even know she had been married before. Even if he didn't conceal the fact, many people would not care.

Then Judah's conscience screamed within him, as if he were hearing the echo of his own father's voice. *Fear the Lord your God, and never disregard his statutes,* he admonished himself. *Never place yourself on the wrong side of righteousness, lest you force the hand of God to judgment—not after all the blessings He has bestowed upon you and your people.* At once Judah decided he would give up the high priesthood if he chose to marry Martha.

But that would not require relinquishing his power. He

could pass on the office to Simon or to Jonathan, and still hold sovereignty. Simon, Judah contemplated, could lead men both spiritually and militarily, but he was also idealistic and would prove difficult to compel on issues that Judah felt strongly about. On the other hand, Jonathan would doubtless heed his every word, and the young man was far wiser than his years. In any case, Judah would retain full control over the army in accord with their father's wishes. With that, he would have control of the political dominion of Judea.

I could create a dual system of power, he thought to himself, *like Moses shared with Aaron.* Moses had led the people, and Aaron had administered the office of high priest. Why could Judah and Jonathan not do the same?

§

"It's good to have you back in Rome," the magistrate Ovidius Tiburtius, said to Diomedes.

"I'm pleased to have returned. It's been years since I was last here."

"Were you able to visit your family?"

"I'm hoping to do so as soon as we're finished with our business."

"How long have you been stationed in Judea?" Tiburtius asked.

"We call it 'placed'," Diomedes answered, realizing the man had no military experience. "There's no actual base of operations in Judea to be stationed at, so ..."

"Of course," the magistrate smiled. "But that is one of the things we are hoping to change, you see."

Diomedes eyed him suspiciously. He had come to feel much more akin to his mother's people, the Jews, than to his father's, the Romans.

As if the man could read his thoughts, Tiburtius answered, "We feel it would be mutually beneficial for both Judea and

Rome if we could place a small garrison in Judea, for the dual purpose of protecting the Jews from the Seleucid threat to the north, as well as protecting Rome from eastern threats that lie across the great sea."

Diomedes tried to keep his face from revealing the contempt he felt for the man in front of him, whose hypocrisy was so evident. "In fact," Tiburtius continued, "word is spreading all over Rome about this treaty. Judea has become a household word. Before, the average Roman had never heard of the place unless they happened to have a Jewish neighbor. Even then, most educated men would never have been able to find it on a map."

"Will the garrison be prepared to help the Hebrews fight?" Diomedes asked, already knowing the answer.

"We will send grain, Roman weapons, and armor to aid them in winning their war. You shall have a small detachment from the fourth legion, but they are solely for training purposes and your protection. At the moment, Rome is not prepared to send soldiers to fight. The senate wants to wait until things are a little less . . . precarious."

How predictable, Diomedes thought. *Rome wants to reap all the benefits without offering any labor. That's because they are acting solely for their own benefit, not Judea's.* Not that this was surprising. Rome had always sought nothing but its own gain, whatever that happened to be at the moment. Judea must take care of itself now, with the help of God.

"The good news," said the magistrate, "is that in an eternal war, everyone has a chance for revenge as well as for gain. You will be given charge of three ships with arms, supplies, and soldiers, and you will sail them back to Judea. We want you to deliver the arms and supplies to Maccabee. Then you will simply resume your position there, collecting intelligence. Your second in command will return to Rome for a second shipment, which we hope to deliver six months later. The agent you met, Crassus, would have been our first choice to accompany you, but the fool has disappeared."

"Disappeared?" Diomedes wondered if the magistrate was suggesting some kind of sabotage or assassination.

"Oh, the fool ran off, probably to the north," Tiburtius said, with a dismissive wave of the hand. "As I'm sure you know from personal experience, at times our men go through stress, which sometimes manifests in their personal lives as well as in their careers." He turned and walked toward the door.

"But I'm taking up far too much of your time, and keeping you from your family. The ships will be ready to sail in three days. Report back here at dawn three days hence, and you will be given command of your fleet."

"Understood," Diomedes replied as the magistrate opened the door for him. After his agent stepped out into the street, Tiburtius walked to his desk and looked at the crooked, hand-drawn map of the Mediterranean. *Judea is the key,* he thought. *We'll establish our foothold there today. In a generation, it will be ours. Then all of the Seleucid kingdom, then Parthia to the east, and then the world!*

He guffawed out loud. *Of course that's all a dream,* he told himself. Though there were those in senate seats who believed power, expansion, and creating an empire of provinces should be their focus, Rome was, in fact, a republic. Republics were supposed to have no such ambitions, but only value freedom. The wars of republics were only fought to protect their freedom, or that of their allies. Tiburtius tried to imagine the whole world under the realm of one united empire—every foreign land, a province under the might of Rome. *Is it really that hard to imagine?* he asked himself. *No, it isn't,* he decided with a smile.

Chapter 56

"I SENT RIDERS TO Modein with Jonathan," Simon announced, sitting down on the luxurious sofa inside the governor's palace. "He insisted on bringing his wife back himself."

Judah poured wine from a golden chalice into two Syrian cups made of refined silver. He handed Simon one of the cups.

"He knows to contact Martha and that you wish her to come to you here." Simon's voice was tired. Jonathan also knew not to contact Simon's wife, whom he had no desire to see.

"Is there any word from Aaron and the riders we sent east?"

"No." Simon cleared his throat. "They've been gone far too long now too. If we don't hear something within the next few days, we'll have to conclude that they have met with foul play."

Judah's mind was spinning with dire possibilities, none of which were probable. He thought out loud, "Do you think there's a chance the Nabateans could have betrayed us, or joined sides with the Seleucids?"

"I doubt it. We've given them no reason to betray us. They've seen what you did to the Ammorites, Idumeans, and Philistines—all at once—for making war on us. We've beaten back the army of one of the most powerful principalities on earth. Why would they want a war with us?

"Maybe because they think they can win."

"Maybe the Nabateans aren't the problem," Simon retorted. "There are Ammorites and Idumeans all around that area, and gangs of thieves with no allegiance to any side. They could have attacked our men. Or maybe Gaddi fell ill, and the others thought it best not to leave him."

"There is another possibility," Judah said, after a long pause. "I have trouble even speaking of it."

"Oh?"

"What if Gaddi didn't return to Judea with the weapons and gold because he didn't want to?"

Simon looked confused. "Why would he not want to return with our weapons and money, especially when we needed them so badly?"

"What if he was counting on us being defeated by Nicantor? Counting on us—on *me*—being killed?

Simon's face flushed. Judah could tell he was angry.

"And why would Gaddi do that?"

"You've seen it. I know you've seen the way Gaddi eyes the seat of power. If I die in a defeat, it gives him claim to the office of high priest and commander of the army. He'd have the money to supply and pay for an army, and the weapons to arm them. He could inflame the patriotic sentiment of the people by using me as a martyr."

"That's outrageous!" Simon said, further angered. "Gaddi would never do that! He is an upright man, who cares about his standing before God. And he'd never disrespect Father's wishes. I know him better than you do. I don't believe for a moment he has it in him to be a traitor."

"I'm not accusing him," Judah shot back. "I'm just saying, he is the eldest, who didn't inherit the position of power, and in examining all scenarios, we should address it as a possibility."

"You go too far with your words, Judah. It's not a possibility."

"Probably not, but we should consider it anyway."

"Rather, we should beware of unreasonable suspicion that can rip our family apart, and our country with it. Suspicion breeds evil."

Judah decided to drop the subject until Simon was less

angry. He walked across the room and gazed out the window at the courtyard.

"Demetrius plans to attack us again," he said finally. "He's summoned all his reserve and retired soldiers and has levied new conscripts."

"The arrogant fool!" Simon blurted. "This will never end. They can't just let us live in peace."

"No," Judah replied. "It will end. This will likely be that last major battle we need to crush them. Their kingdom is crumbling. They have far too few soldiers to maintain their empire. The Parthians are taking more land to the east. Demetrius has had to raise taxes on all foreign-held lands to finance a new army. If we shatter their army just once more, it will be over. If we have just *one* more victory like we had at Asada, the Syrians won't be able to launch another full-scale campaign for the next decade. We'll have completely broken them and secured our freedom for years."

"*Ratzon ha'El*," Simon replied.

"Even at this rate, it will take them a year to launch a campaign with any kind of formidable force. That is at least a whole year we have to prepare."

§

"A month! We'll be able to launch our forces in *less than* a month!" Bacchides said excitedly to Demetrius. "The foreign middleclass landowners in the cities outside of Antioch have decided they'd rather part with one of their sons, and take advantage of the exemption on all new taxes for those with an enlisted family member. And the recall of retired soldiers has been most successful. Thirty percent of our conscripts are veterans. Many of them were overwhelmed with joy, because previously they'd been barred from re-enlistment due to their age."

"So we will catch Judah with his guard down, unprepared,"

Demetrius said gleefully, the strategy growing clearer in his mind.

"According to our reports, Judah had about nine-thousand men with him. We already have seventeen, and in a month's time we'll have over twenty-five thousand."

"My worry," mused the king, trying to find the best way to word what he wanted say, "is that Judah has always had fewer men. Nicantor had over thirty-five thousand, and every one of them was butchered by Judah and his animals."

"But he isn't expecting us, not this quickly and not after such a great loss. Our spies tell me he has sent most of his army home for the winter months," Bacchides said. "So we'll strike quickly and hard, before he has time to rally his forces. Before they even know what happened, Judah will be defeated, and Jerusalem and the citadel will be in our hands. If we have *that*, we can control the whole land."

"Don't you think it's risky, marching an army in the winter?"

"It can be. It's seldom done, but the farther south we move, the safer it is, and when we cross into Judea, they'll be completely caught off-guard."

The excitement in Bacchides' voice was unmistakable. *He's not just telling me what I want to hear,* thought the king. *He really believes he can win.* "I will authorize your winter campaign, but I want complete and total victory."

"You will have it, my lord. I promise you."

§

"You know if they find out about this meeting, we will all be executed for treason," Exudoxi, the Seleucid nobleman, said to Hilarion and Solon—two nobles who controlled more influence within the kingdom than anyone except for the king himself.

"We're just three men having a social visit to discuss business," Solon replied.

"Yes, and the business of today is?" Hilarion asked with a smile. "Oh, I remember. Supplanting Demetrius from the throne, I think."

Solon laughed. Exudoxi stood and checked to make sure the door was tightly closed.

"You shouldn't say that out loud," he said in a hushed voice.

"Why not?" Hilarion replied, his tone cavalier. "That *is* what we're trying to do. He's raising taxes at an absurd rate— to where landowners are harvesting fewer crops—food sorely needed outside the capital. He's acting more Roman politically. He's thrown our military away against the Hebrews, who have bested him, and the Parthians are conquering the heart of our empire—taking control of the trade routes to the east. They're on the outskirts of Babylon, in the name of all the gods … *Babylon!* And the fool has done absolutely nothing."

"I agree," Solon interjected. "He is a Seleucid, but he's been raised Roman his entire life. His very presence in the palace is a disgrace. The way he took power and murdered his half-brother openly like that!"

"Demetrius has more promise than Antiochus ever did, that madman!" Exudoxi scoffed.

"He can't stay on that throne," Solon answered. "He's making too many enemies, he's a naive idealist, and completely unrelenting in his folly."

"I am no supporter of the king," Exudoxi said defensively. "He's costing me more money than either of you, but even if we could replace him, who would we replace him with? The king has to be from the royal line, and there are no viable candidates."

"That is because Demetrius killed them all," Solon remarked dryly.

"That's why I called this meeting," said Hilarion. "There is a man who could be placed on the throne of Seleucus, who I think would solve all of our problems."

Hilarion waited to see the curiosity build in the eyes of the others before he continued. "Antiochus IV, years before he died—shortly after he himself was traded for Demetrius—had a bastard son named Alexander."

"You would hand the crown to an illegitimate ... a bastard?" Exudoxi asked, incredulous. "This is your plan?"

"*Yes*, I would. The young man is not the son of a slave or harlot, but of a noblewoman. Also, he is now betrothed," Hilarion paused for effect, "to Cleopatra Thea."

"The daughter of Ptolemy," Solon said, impressed.

"And a marriage to a Seleucid king, by the daughter of the king of Egypt, would strengthen us by pacifying our greatest threat to the south," said Hilarion. "Not to mention it also removes the need to hold onto Judea. Maybe we can, by way of treaty, restore all lands conquered by the mad Antiochus's father, returning Judea to the Ptolemaic realm and removing that problem from our hands. Or we can just let Judea go entirely."

The other two noblemen contemplated the notion.

"And Alexander?" Exudoxi questioned. "What are his ambitions in all this? Does he have the inclination to take his father's kingdom? Does he even know about us?"

"He is very—shall I say, *anxious*—to take up his father's kingdom, and Ptolemy looks forward to the day as well. He has been educating the young man in political matters. Politics that, I should add, are in line with our own."

Chapter 57

THE WOODEN PRACTICE swords rattled and clapped as John Ben Simon swung at Saul in the courtyard of the governor's palace. Saul, a young officer over fifty men and an expert at arms, had been asked by Simon to personally train his son.

John held his heavy weapon the way his father had shown him. Even for the mere adolescent that he was, his stance and movements were correct. In his imagination, he was fighting a Syrian soldier in the north.

Saul lifted his weapon to block the boy's vertical blow, as John brought his sword down again. Saul blocked it, redirecting his swing toward John's shoulder. John side-stepped but stumbled, trying to keep his balance. Saul swung again, and his practice sword lightly connected with John's back.

"I killed you," he murmured.

"You didn't," John shouted back, wanting to fight again.

"Alas, I'm afraid you are dead," said Saul, with a benevolent smile.

"No, I was only wounded!"

John swung again at his trainer, who in turn blocked another series of blows. Saul counterattacked, and one of his strikes came down upon John's fingers that were wrapped around his practice sword.

"Ow!" John groaned, dropping his weapon to the ground and cradling his hand. He looked up and saw his father walking by, toward the palace. Simon looked right at him. John didn't want to show pain in front of his father. He picked up his sword and swung hard at Saul, who barely managed to block the blow.

Watching the little drama out of the corner of his eye, Simon smiled, then entered the palace, as Saul delivered a quick series of retaliatory strikes. At last jabbing his sword into John's shoulder, he jolted him backwards. John stopped to rub the spot where the wood had struck, knowing it would leave a bruise.

"You mustn't stop," said Saul, firmly. "When you are wounded in battle, your enemy will not stop and wait for you to recover, but will keep coming at you until one of you is dead. Now defend yourself."

Saul quickly attacked again. John barely had a chance to parry the assault.

When the session was over, the boy wandered out of the courtyard, looking for a place to sit down. The swordplay challenged him, but he could feel his skill and strength growing with each day. He could hardly wait until he was old enough to fight in a real battle at the side of his father and uncles. Simon had promised he could join the army in two more years, if that was still his wish. *I'll lead an army,* he thought, *and fight the Gentiles and be a great warrior.* He imagined himself turning the course of a battle and saving his father or Judah's life, fighting off a host of Syrians.

§

Martha's deep-brown eyes shone in the sunlight, accentuated by the contrast with her fair brown skin. A red shawl draped over her shoulders and long black hair. Her features, still youthful, bore a trace of the sadness she had long carried, like a scar. *We have all lost much,* Judah reminded himself.

"It seems they're speaking your name all across the earth," Martha said, smiling. "Last week, in Modein, I heard travelers passing through from Corinth, talking about your victories."

Judah's own smile broadened. He had tried not to be obvious about how mesmerized he was by her beauty, but he cared less and less about concealing it.

Martha had accompanied Jonathan with his family from Modein to Jerusalem. When she arrived, she had been amazed at the foreign extravagance of the governor's palace, in which Judah and his brothers now resided.

Now, she stood on the parapet of the palace, watching the sun set behind Jerusalem's city walls. From a distance came sounds of children playing. "And now you have brought peace to the land—peace and freedom, and faith in God," she said admiringly.

"Not yet," Judah said, his voice low. "Not peace. It's not over yet. Next year, after the winter ends, Demetrius will mount another invasion of Israel, for one last attempt to regain control of our people."

Martha recoiled at the statement. "Will it never end?" she asked, a hint of fear entering her voice.

"It will," Judah replied. "This will be the last campaign the Seleucid kingdom can afford to launch against us. They don't have the strength to keep going."

She gazed at him, rays of light illuminating her profile.

"If I beat them back once more, it will end this war, or at least stop hostilities for the next decade. By *then,* the Seleucids will have other problems to focus on."

"I just worry for your safety." She hesitated, hoping not to appear too forward or assuming. "I ... care for you."

Judah enjoyed the way she was looking at him.

"I'll be fine," he said emphatically. "The Lord has kept me alive through all of this for a reason. I don't think He'll send me to sleep with my ancestors until I've finished serving His purpose in this life."

She forced a cheerful smile, her worry somewhat lessened. Everything about this man impressed her—he was august, venerable, self-assured, confident in his cause and in the Lord

God. There were so few men who had done what he had done. So few pillars of power who weren't handed their authority as an inheritance, but who had the prowess to create a principality from nothing— and who had such love from the people that they were able to keep it. There were even fewer men who didn't let power corrupt them.

She thought of the stories her father had told her as she was growing up, about King Solomon, the son of David, who inherited David's throne. Though unparalleled in wisdom, Solomon let himself be corrupted, taking for himself over one-thousand wives and concubines, who directed his attention away from their God to the worship of foreign idols.

Judah and Martha stared at each other. They had kissed only once, and since then, with all that had happened, they both had wondered if it had been just a fleeting moment, or if it meant something more.

"I care for you, too," said Judah. The sweetness in her eyes made it easy for him to continue. She smiled and took his hand in hers. She placed her head on his shoulder.

He felt her warmth against him. It all seemed so clear to him now. To give up the high priesthood would be easy if Martha were beside him. Having her as his wife would make it worth it.

He turned her toward him so he could look directly into her face.

"Martha. You mean more to me than . . ." he felt lost for words. He tried again. "It's thoughts of you that give me hope, that give me a reason to return from every campaign. If you would have me, I want you to be my wife. I'd no longer be able to hold the position of high priest, but—"

"Yes," said Martha, stopping him mid-sentence. She had tears in her eyes.

A cool wind rose from below the parapet, brushing across their garments. The setting sun, now almost hidden behind the city's western wall, cast a shadow upon all of Jerusalem.

"Stop," she whispered. "It is you I wish to marry, my love, not some position. I adore you."

§

"It's been following us since we left Crete," the captain said to Nabis, who was watching from the stern of the ship. The vessel that had been shadowing their movements was following about a mile behind. "It's a lembus—an Illyrian galley. Those are light, maneuverable, and fast."

Nabis squinted to see the ship better against the clouds on the horizon.

"It's rare to see them this far east. Usually they're busy harassing the Romans and Athenians."

"Illyrians?" Nabis asked.

"Pirates," the captain said.

"How long until they catch us?" Nabis was suddenly worried for Abishag and the silver coins he had hidden below.

The captain snickered. "They could have caught us any time they wanted. Right now they're just checking us out, trying to gauge if we're worth the trouble. Unfortunately, this is a nice ship, and they might assume it has plenty of goods they can steal. On the other hand, any competent captain would see that our galley isn't that low in the water and probably has a light cargo. Where they really make their money is from kidnapping dignitaries, or estate holders, and ransoming them to their families. So not sitting low in the water is no assurance we won't be boarded."

"Can any of the oarsmen fight?" Nabis asked.

"Not well. The Illyrians are pure savages, barbarians. But pirates have plagued these waters ever since man learned to carve a piece of wood. The Egyptians used to welcome them, as long as they didn't rob their exports. Ramses, I'm told, used them to attack Hittite ships a thousand years ago. The Romans have a solution for them, though. They built the corvus—a long, adjustable plank with sharp blades on the end, that is tied upright against the mast of their ships. When pirates try to get close enough to ram or to set fire, the Romans cut the ropes, and the corvus blades slam down on the enemy deck, locking it in place. Then Roman marines board the pirate ship across the plank."

"Well, we have no corvus that I can see," said Nabis, "nor Roman marines."

"Very true," the captain said with a smirk, unfastening the lacing and pulling away a large sackcloth sheet. This revealed a small torsion catapult on the deck, aimed over the stern. "Fear not!" he said with a grin and a flourish. "I have fifteen jugs of Greek fire down below, gotten— illegally, of course—from a Macedonian naval commander. They keep the concoction a secret, but sulfur, niter, and quicklime are among other ingredients. Only a handful of alchemists know how to make it."

Nabis had heard rumors on the Egyptian campaign that Ptolemy's army had fortified the walls of Memphis with archers and catapults armed with Greek fire. Despite the name, it was the Assyrians who, centuries before, had developed the stuff. At the battle of Delium, the Boeotians used Greek fire to burn down the walls of the temple of Delium in Athens. They applied it through a pressurized pipe that shot fire. After burning the temple, they used the device to chase the Athenians from the battlefield.

"Do you think they'll make a move on us?" Nabis asked, feeling only slightly more secure.

"It's hard to know. Right now they're stalking us, but keeping their distance."

"Will we keep sailing forward?"

"I haven't decided. I may turn back for Crete and force them to either engage or to cast off—sooner rather than later when we're far out and secluded in the middle of the sea."

The captain had once seen a warring ship slam into a galley, the water pouring into the hull, crippling the attacked vessel before the bow sunk into the depths. *Better to have done with it, he thought, before we're too far out at sea, where there's no chance of surviving a direct hit from the ram of a lembus.*

§

Going south to war once again,

to fight the rebels who would tear apart our lands,

and if the cause would trade my life for the corps,

then I'll follow where our empire's fathers and brothers have fallen before.

Bacchides hummed the tune in his head. It was a song the soldiers had sung around the fire that morning. The lyrics promoted the virtue of defending the homeland, defending the king. It made reference to Seleucus, the right-hand man of Alexander the Great. The song provoked an emotional response of overwhelming national pride.

"What's our current strength?" Bacchides asked his logistics officer, scanning the roster listing supplies, weapons, and food. The camp was busy, with slaves folding up the last of the tents, and carts moving into place. The infantry and cavalry stood in their respective formations, awaiting orders.

"As of this moment, twenty-seven-thousand-nine hundred-and-forty-three men who are combat-ready, sir," the officer announced.

Bacchides rolled up the parchment and placed it in his horse's saddlebag. Patiently, he took hold of the reins and mounted. He looked toward a subordinate officer, sitting astride his own steed. "We have the king's wish, son. Now, give the order," Bacchides said.

The young man galloped across the parade field, while the

last of the supplies were still being placed into carts. He moved to the front ranks and wheeled his horse around.

"Forward!" he yelled, waiting for the command to be echoed by each phalanx commander.

"Forward!" he heard back in a chorus of shouts.

"March!"

The drumbeat sounded, and the leading formation of cavalrymen moved out at a trot. The leading infantry formation followed, marching in unison from the field toward the road south.

The words of the song kept repeating in Bacchides' head, *"Going south to war once again . . ." This is it—* he told himself, *my chance to redeem my name, regain the glory of the Seleucid kingdom, and destroy this insurrection once and for all.* He knew he had far fewer men than Nicantor had when he was defeated, but Bacchides had the surprise and speed of the attack on his side. He would consume Judea like a flame. In the end, all that would be left is the world he would make.

Chapter 58

AARON AND HIS three companions drove their horses over the dry desert floor. He had started out with twelve scouts to find what happened to Maccabee's brother. Now only three were alive.

The journey had been fraught with disasters. First was the viper nest one of the riders had disturbed while crossing through brush. No one had been bitten, but the hissing serpents startled the horses, and one of the riders was thrown. The man broke his back on the ridged stones. He survived for three days, awakening periodically, then his body gave out in the night, and he died.

Then they had been attacked by more than twenty Idumeans not long after they crossed the Jordan River. Close to being overwhelmed after losing two of their men, they tried to escape to the north.

The Idumeans had been relentless in their pursuit, killing five more men on the long chase. More than once, they were pushed toward the low ground, forced to slow down. Arrows were fired, causing more casualties and forcing them to dig in under fire.

They finally broke and escaped at nightfall with six men on four horses. Three of the scouts were wounded, one with a gash in his side and two with arrows. By morning, two of them had died.

From there, Aaron rode toward the Nabatean city. He was greeted respectfully and immediately given an audience with the city elder, who told him Gaddi had indeed come and taken the weapons and gold that Judah had stored with them. He said he thought it odd that Gaddi did not immediately travel back across the Jordan, but headed north and set up camp with his men.

When that happened, explained the Nabataean elder, he had contemplated sending riders to Judah himself to confirm that Judah's intention was to have his brother collect all the arms and money they had stored on his behalf.

Before he could do that, though, Gaddi had traveled west toward the Jordan. Then word came that Gaddi had been attacked by a tribe of bandits called the Medeba, descendants of the Moabites, who had plundered all of their gold and arms. According to the report, most of the men were killed, but Gaddi was not among the dead, so it was believed he had been taken hostage.

Rumor had it that Gaddi had been taken north into the camps of the Medeba, where they were holding him. The elder said he had sent riders to warn Maccabee, but they never returned, so they must have been killed by Nicantor's Seleucid soldiers. Other men of Judah's had come searching for Gaddi months before, and when they were told what had happened, they headed north toward the Medeba city, but never came back.

After talking to the elder, Aaron decided to divide what was left of their scouting party, sending two scouts back to Judah to inform him of all that had happened, while Aaron and the other scout would go north to the Medeba villages to learn if Gaddi was dead or alive.

Aaron wondered what Maccabee would do when he learned the Medeba had his brother, that his scouts had been attacked by Idumeans. If there must be a war with the Medeba or the Idumeans again, better now, while the Syrians were crippled, than later. *Arrogant fools,* he thought, *kidnapping the brother of Maccabee!* Did they actually think they would live to collect a ransom? He wondered if they even knew who they had.

§

"It feels strange to sleep in a bed now," Jonathan said, sitting at the table with Judah and Simon. "And having all of this—" he gestured toward the ceiling of the governor's palace. On their plates was meat of a fattened calf and unleavened bread, set next to silver chalices filled with wine.

"It's almost hard to live like this," Jonathan went on. "It feels so different."

"I don't have any problem with it," Simon replied with a grunt. "It doesn't feel strange, it feels *nice*. You've just forgotten what *nice* feels like because we've been living on the plains like animals for the last five years."

"Maybe, but it's so different even from life in Modein. We were simple townspeople then. Now we're aristocracy. Doesn't that ever bother you?"

Simon just shook his head. He glanced at Judah, who had not spoken and seemed absorbed in thought.

"So, brother," Simon said, cutting into his food. "Why are we having this meal by ourselves? Jonathan misses his wife," he joked. "What's going on?"

"One of the scouts returned today from the Nabataeans."

"And?" Simon asked, putting down his knife.

"Gaddi tarried in the east longer than he needed—for what reason, we don't know—but the report is: the Medeba attacked him. The weapons and gold were stolen. Gaddi was taken for ransom."

"Ransom!" Simon repeated, in shock.

"Is all of this from Aaron?" Jonathan asked.

"From two of his men he sent back. He's still in the east trying to learn if Gaddi is alive. Most of Aaron's men are dead. They were attacked, by Idumeans."

"Those swine-raping sons of whores!" Simon raged.

"So when do we march?" Jonathan asked, staring at his plate of food.

"At once!" yelled Simon. "They kidnap our brother and think they can get away with it?"

"No," Judah said, raising his hand. "There's more. It could be rumors, and I pray that's all it is. Reports have it that Bacchides, Nicantor's replacement, has already departed Antioch with a host of thirty thousand for an invasion of Israel."

Simon and Jonathan looked stunned.

"But that's impossible!" exclaimed Simon. "They just lost their whole army. We knew they'd probably recruit conscripts for one last attempt, but it's far too soon."

"It could be disinformation to get us to call up our forces repeatedly until people stop reacting to our call to arms," Jonathan said, thinking out loud.

"Whether it's true or not makes no difference," sighed Judah. "We'll have to respond as if it were true. We'll need every man in Israel who can bear arms."

"And Gaddi?" asked Jonathan. "We just leave him to rot, a prisoner of the Medeba?"

"Right now we have no choice. First we'll stop the Seleucid invasion. Then I'll find Gaddi, destroy the Medeba, and lay waste to their cities. After that, I'll send soldiers south to teach the Idumeans the cost of attacking our scouts."

Once again, Jonathan thought, *we're at war with the whole world.* And there sat Judah, shouldering the burdens of all of their people, making every decision and living alone with the consequences. Some people were just born with that ability, it seemed—the ability to always know what to do, without help or advice. They just knew. Jonathan despaired of ever being like him. The man was larger than life.

"Tomorrow," Judah continued, "I want riders dispatched to every major city. They will begin gathering the men in case the threats are legitimate. We need to put someone in charge of stockpiling weapons and food. I would have Gaddi do it, but until we get him back, someone else has to. Now, more than ever, we could have used what we stored with the Nabateans."

"I'll have someone take care of it," Jonathan murmured.

He could tell that Simon was still seething, wanting to act.

"What if I just take a few-score men and try to rescue Gaddi?" Simon asked. "If it's true about the Syrians, we might have time to get our weapons and gold back before they arrive."

"No," Judah said firmly. "I need everyone here. Besides, you will need more than a few-score men to accomplish the wrath I have in mind to bring down on the Medeba."

§

Demetrius could hear, through the walls, the dratted noise his mother was making. It had been every night that week. She just hung on, groaning in pain. They had bled her to balance her humors, and increased the dosage of mercury, but it failed to give her relief.

Mostly when she spoke, it was to complain. "My head hurts," she kept saying. The only other time she spoke was when she talked about her darling son, Antiochus, who she thought was still on a military campaign in Judea. She went on and on about missing him, asking again and again when he would be home. *She's lost it,* Demetrius thought to himself. *She can't cope with all that's happened, that I am king and that her son is dead.*

They'd had all the physicians and priests in the kingdom try every kind of remedy they could conjure. Still, Laodice slowly grew worse. And now she looked like someone he could barely recognize. In all this time, since he was taken away to Rome until he returned, a man, his mother had looked almost exactly the same. Now, her hair was gray, her skin sagged around the eyes and mouth, and her brow was furrowed and shriveled. *She's transformed from a seductive, beautiful woman into a repulsive old gorgon, almost overnight,* he thought in disgust.

If she wanted to believe her whelp of a son was still alive, he would let her. It seemed to bring her some comfort. Another long cry of pain reverberated along the stone walls, and Demetrius sat up in bed. The sound sent chills down his spine and made his heart race. It was a sensation he could not identify, running through him like a sword, making him feel hollow.

Shut up! he longed to shout, annoyed at the woman's every sound. Amidst the din, sleep was impossible. Drawing himself up from the bed, Demetrius shuffled down the cold stone floor into the hallway, then down the hall toward his mother's room. He stopped outside the door, hearing another groan of pain. *Maybe if you wake her, you won't have to listen to her go on like that,* he thought. He wondered where her physicians were. He opened the door. Next to the bed, sleeping in a cushioned chair, was one of the queen's slaves.

Demetrius walked over to the sleeping Laodice. Her face looked like it had melted away with age. Beads of sweat rolled down the side of her brow. The smell in the room reminded him of a sepulcher.

He was about to shake her awake, when a thought occurred to him. He stood motionless for a moment, then reached for the extra pillow. Taking hold of each end with a firm grip, he aligned the pillow carefully before shoving it down over his mother's face.

He felt the queen jerk awake, but pressed down tightly, pushing his weight forward, savagely, clenching his knuckles against the bed. He could hear her cries muffled beneath the pillow. Looking up, he saw the slave girl was on her feet, shaking in terror, her hands covering her mouth against the scream that would not come. All he could do was smile at her, as he struggled to keep the pillow over Laodice's face.

She kicked her feet, trying to push up, using the bed for leverage. She tried to turn her head. *I hope she doesn't realize it's me,* Demetrius thought, pushing down even harder. He felt his mother's clammy fingers slide over his, clawing and digging her nails into his hands. Then after a long, suspended moment, he felt her body go limp and her chest spasm, as her hands slid off his own.

He felt the sting of the cuts from her nails, but kept the pressure of the pillow tight over her face for a few more moments. He looked up again, smiling awkwardly at the slave girl, who stood frozen in horror. His brow was dripping with sweat.

At last he let go of the pillow, his hands numb from exertion. He nodded at the slave girl, then strode from the room, leaving the pillow over his mother's face. He didn't want to look at her.

Maybe now I can get some sleep, he thought. *I did her a favor, putting her out of her misery,* he told himself when the odd, hollow feeling shot through him again. After all, he was king. His subjects lived and died at his discretion. The odd feeling closely resembled guilt, but since Demetrius had never felt guilt in his life, he didn't recognize it.

Reaching his quarters, he entered the door, and the high, shrill screech of the slave girl pierced the air. Footsteps and cries erupted from every direction. Would there never be a moment's peace?

Chapter 59

JUDAH AWOKE WITH his heart racing. He sat up and reached for his sword, but it wasn't there. Confused from the dream, he lurched out of bed, believing he was in camp, knowing something was wrong. On his feet, he fully awakened: he was in the governor's palace, after all. Calming himself, he sat back down on the bed.

He couldn't remember the dream, only the feeling of danger and foreboding it gave him. The feeling lingered—like a disturbing face he couldn't remember, that he *had to* remember. If only he could recall what he had been dreaming . . .

Glancing around the dark room, Judah saw his sword leaning against a chair several yards away. *Stupid. You should never sleep that far from your weapon,* he admonished himself. He was getting too comfortable. Even in Jerusalem, the Seleucids could try to kill him as easily as anywhere else. The attack in Modein had been a very close call. The scar on his neck would fade over time, but the one across his chest he would carry the rest of his life.

Judah walked to the balcony and looked out over the ledge at the crest of the rising sun. The riders he had sent to call the sons of Israel to arms should be well on their way, gathering men for war.

He had defeated Nicantor with nine-thousand men. Nothing begat confidence like victory. Hopefully, the people would respond to the new threat. If it turned out to be a lie, and the Syrians had no intention of invading until spring or summer, then he would use the army to attack the Medeba, and rescue Gaddi. *I hope he's okay,* Judah thought, imagining Gaddi tied up, under guard, surrounded by Medeba idolaters.

Someone knocked at his door, and Judah called, "Come in!"—his voice still raspy from sleep.

Simon entered the room, sweat on his brow. Judah could tell by his unsettled manner that what he was about to say was not good.

"Judah," said Simon, his voice shaky, "the Syrians just crossed the border of Samaria with more than twenty-five-thousand soldiers."

Judah felt breathless. After a moment, he shook his head. "The riders?" he asked.

"They left an hour ago. But even if they move fast, only the ones going to nearby cities will be able to make it back in time, and who knows what their numbers will be."

"Gather every man in the city who is willing to fight. We can't let them take Jerusalem. If they capture this city, they will seize the citadel. They'll control it all and mount unlimited assaults against us. We'll never be able to force them from our country."

"We don't have the food or the arms to hold out in a long siege," protested Simon.

"Our strategy hasn't altered. We must hit them before they make it here. We'll have to hit them so hard they'll not only stop moving forward, but won't be able to regroup without reinforcments before launching another attack. It ends here! We *will* drive these heathens from our land. With thirty thousand or three hundred, I will end any illusion that dog in Antioch has of taking our people again for his slaves and our land for his plunder."

Simon forcibly straightened himself and cast his eyes toward the balcony and the rising light in the east.

"Let's do it," he said. "Let's finish this."

§

Nabis stepped from the beached galley onto the dense wet sand. He breathed in the air of his homeland for the first time in more than ten years. Turning back, he helped Abishag down from the gangway plank, bearing Asher in her arms. She looked at Nabis and smiled, seeing his happiness.

Abishag had been terrified when they had been caught in a small storm, and more so when Nabis had told her of the Illyrians, who had been stalking them. The captain had decided to continue on their course, with the Illyrian ship following them for two days, at times gaining on them, and then giving way. No one knew whether the Illyrians finally decided they weren't worth the effort, or if the captain, as he boasted afterwards, actually lost the ship in the storm. They had stopped in Xanthus, resupplied, and then moved around the land formation northwest toward Ephesus.

"Do you feel like you're home?" asked Abishag.

"Wherever *you* are, I'll be home," he said, kissing her forehead.

"Will it take you long to find your family?"

"Maybe a few days. Let's move away from these harbor shops before we buy anything. Everything near the ports is overpriced."

He looked around the port. It hadn't changed that much in the ten years he had been away. He remembered, as a child, coming to the sea with his mother and playing along the harbor. There were a few new shops, but mostly the port remained unaltered. He knew he would probably find many of his childhood friends working inside those shops, practicing their father's trade, never having traveled more than twenty miles from home in all their life, with little more knowledge than they had a decade earlier. They wouldn't be able to comprehend what it was like to march to Egypt, or to be stationed in a foreign land for years in the midst of an endless war. Nabis found himself indifferent at the thought of seeing the friends from his youth.

Abishag picked Asher up and carried him as they hastened inland on foot, approaching the city. Two barking dogs ran past toward the water. Abishag stood amazed at the size of the buildings in the distance, which looked huge even from where she stood. She saw wide colonnades encircling strange marble structures, unlike anything she had ever seen.

Nabis walked with the heavy satchel containing the silver coins, over his shoulder. His xiphos was concealed beneath his cloak. Passing by a man who eyed him warily, Nabis realized that his dress, demeanor, facial hair, and especially the woman and child by his side, were all Hebrew. Despite his light coloring, all would assume he was a foreigner.

"Why are people looking at me that way?" Abishag asked, after noticing a scowling glance from a fat Greek woman who walked past in the opposite direction.

"We look like foreigners," Nabis answered, smiling. "Here, *we're* the Gentiles." He could see the uneasiness on his wife's face, but she kept silent. Some priests of Apollo walked by, and Abishag looked appalled.

They continued into the city. To Abishag, the air smelled distinctly different. She picked up a strange scent. It was burning meat, rich and smoky, the aroma excellent. Walking toward the smoke, where meat roasted over a fire pit, she felt her stomach ache in hunger. She wondered if Nabis would want to stop or hurry forward to find his family. Then she realized that the wonderful scent she had never encountered was actually roasting pork, and suddenly, she felt ill. Her body felt numb from the journey, and her arms were tired from carrying Asher.

Noticing her weariness, Nabis took the boy from her arms. "It isn't much farther," he told her. "Shall we rest? Are you hungry?"

"I don't know if there's any food we can eat."

Nabis glanced at the burning meat that Abishag was staring at ruefully. "Don't worry. Pork isn't the only thing people eat here," he said, cheerfully.

Passing a semicircular amphitheater, Abishag saw on a distant hill a structure so large that she stopped and gaped in amazement.

"It's the Temple of Artemis," said Nabis proudly, "one of the oldest temples in the land. It was built by the Amazons."

"Amazons?"

"A tribe of warrior women who emerged out of Scythia. They founded not only this city, but Paphos and Smyrna as well. They were called *Oiorpata* by theScythians, which in their language meant 'killers of men.' They were as fierce in battle as any man, and their warriors as renowned as the Spartans. The historians say no man was ever permitted to touch them."

Nabis stopped, stepped behind Abishag, and teasingly kissed the side of her neck. "Except once a year, when they would allow the men of a neighboring tribe to visit them, and sire them children." He kissed her neck again, but she remained unresponsive, still staring up at the pagan temple.

"In the war against the Trojans, they sided with the Greeks. They conquered vast amounts of land and territory across Asia."

"What happened to them?" she asked, absently.

"They've all but disappeared. They were taken as wives by the Scythians, perhaps by choice, perhaps by force—no one knows. They say a remnant still remains on Leuce Island."

Abishag could see, even at this distance, that one of the statues near the temple's marble steps was that of a huge, multi-breasted woman. Her whole body was covered in mammaries. In her hands was an Ouroboros ring, a carved serpent eating its own tail.

They're the same, she thought, in revelation. *The same images I saw from travelers from Egypt, the same as the worshipers of Moloch, the same as the Ammorites, and the Assyrians, and the groves where the idolaters of Israel's past would conduct their orgies after offering human sacrifice!*

She felt sick again. All of it sickened her—the pagan temple, the priests, the graven images, and the stench of burning swine she could not expel from her nostrils. She felt dizzy. It was all unhallowed adulation to Beelzebub. In that moment, she wished she could return to the ship and set sail back to Judea.

Then Asher lifted a tiny hand and placed it on her cheek. She looked into his eyes and saw his playful smile. "Horsey," he said, pointing to a mule passing by.

Abishag looked at Nabis—his eyes showed so much ... eagerness, pride in his homeland, fear that his wife might never find happiness in this place.

Abishag straightened her shoulders. "Let's keep going, Nabis," she said, placing a kiss on his cheek. "I'm eager to meet your family."

§

"How many of the landholders have you convinced?" Solon asked Hilarion as they strode down the promenade outside the imperial palace of Antioch. There was ice along the river bank. Every time a gust of wind blew in from the water, it added chill to the air.

"Almost half the men with allegiance to me have already secretly pledged their loyalty to Antiochus's royal bastard, " Hilarion replied. "I've convinced them that the royal lineage of Demetrius's father died with him and that the power fell to Antiochus and *his* children."

Solon smiled sardonically. "And were there any of your people who refused loyalty and sided against us?"

"There were three," Hilarion said, thinking back to his final warning to one of his noble landholders, and the man's heated refusal to side with them. Hilarion had walked out of his home, giving a fateful nod to the armed men waiting outside. They entered and strangled the aristocrat to death, while Hilarion waited, listening to the struggle.

"*Were?*" Solon asked confirming.

"Were," Hilarion repeated coldly, remembering the

murders he had ordered of the other two nobles who had also refused to comply. He wished politics didn't require such sordid measures, but then, that was life.

"We can't be too cautious," Solon said softly, looking across the water at the palace. "You almost have to admire the royal shit. He managed to take the kingdom by surprise, only spilling the blood of those in power. If only we could be so fortunate! If we can't accomplish the same feat, the country will succumb to civil war."

" And that would be the end of the empire. In a civil war, nobody wins."

"If the Hebrews defeat Bacchides, and have one more of their devastating victories, it will be over. They'll have won their freedom, and the borders of our empire will slowly dissolve away. One last fight remains, and that will determine the fate of the world."

Hilarion shrugged. "Maybe it's better if they win. After all, that land was never part of the empire to begin with. It was Ptolemy's. That whole conflict has become a very unpopular war. Most people have no idea anymore why we're even fighting Judea. Probably best to just let it go."

"If the Hebrews defeat this army, or even prevent them from taking Jerusalem, we'll have no choice *but* to let it go."

"It's disgraceful what our empire has been reduced to."

Chapter 60

"WE HAVE THREE-THOUSAND men," exclaimed Simon to his brother, who eyed the army from atop his horse. "We were able to draw in seventeen hundred from Jerusalem. Most the others are from Mispha, some from Modein. The riders haven't returned with the men from the northern cities yet."

"It's hard to believe they number even three thousand," Judah said grimly, looking at the paltry company at arms. "We can't delay any longer."

The Syrian army had passed Galilee four days ago. They were moving fast, and Judah knew they would soon reach Jerusalem, if he didn't stop them."

"I don't know how we'll stop thirty-thousand soldiers with three-thou—"

"We don't have a choice," Judah interrupted fiercely. "We either fight them and win, or all that we have fought and suffered for is lost."

Simon tried to keep the dismay from his face.

"We don't have to obliterate them," Judah continued. "We just have to hinder them enough so they can't take Jerusalem before we gather our full strength from the northern cities. If we halt them and cripple them, they'll have to remain exposed, waiting for reinforcements that won't come. Because we'll destroy the force before Demetrius has time to send reinforcements."

"They may try to take a smaller, less fortified city for protection," Simon said, thinking.

"In which case, we can besiege them once we have the men."

"Jonathan's not exactly happy that you wanted him to remain here," Simon pointed out, seeing their brother draw near.

"His wife is expecting his firstborn," Judah replied. "As much as he wants to be in the battle, he'd be distracted and hesitant, and he needs to be here to take care of her. Besides, I want someone in Jerusalem I can trust while we're away."

Judah remembered their bitter disagreement, Jonathan's protests of his decision to leave him in the city.

"Until I return, you are high priest in my stead," Judah had told him.

He then had elaborated on the need for someone to protect his office and to protect against political opportunists and Seleucid agents, like Alcimus.

Disappointed, Jonathan had finally capitulated.

"Someone has to stay with the women," Simon now declared caustically, loud enough for Jonathan to hear as he approached them.

Jonathan glared at Simon, who towered above him on horseback. Then he turned toward Judah.

"No word from Aaron?" he asked.

"No," Judah replied. Now more than ever, he wished he had Gaddi at his side with the arms and gold he had stored with the Nabataeans. He wished he had ten times the men he had present. He wished he had cavalry. He wished the Romans would show up with support before the battle, but the meager band of men who stood before him, spears in hand, were all he had. *God,* he prayed mentally, *give us strength. Gird our hearts. You used Gidion, with only three-hundred men, to defeat the whole Midianite army. Be with us, and let us be content and fearless with three thousand.*

"If Gaddi were here," Jonathan interjected, "he would be advising you, with everything in him, not to commit to a fight with so few men."

"We both know, if Gaddi were here, Judah wouldn't listen to him anyway," Simon said.

"If we had just a few hundred more, it would inspire men to join the ranks. They are afraid, Judah."

Judah looked down at his youngest brother. "Then let them stay here in the city and fear," he said. "I'd rather have a few hundred fearless men, with faith in God, than fifty-thousand cowards, without faith, who are poised to flee."

"Let me come with you," Jonathan pleaded once more, fervently. "It may inspire more men to join, and will show you have unyielding faith in your resolve to win, and no need of your brother to remain and secure the city—"

"I *do* need you here," Judah replied firmly. "And you should be here with Sarah." Judah remembered Adi's pregnancy, being absent when she gave birth when she needed him the most, and how horribly her health had turned.

"If Aaron does return with news of Gaddi, send a rider to bring us word," Judah told Jonathan, who nodded despondently.

"We have no more time to waste," Judah said.

He spurred his horse, and Simon followed. As they trotted down the road toward Jerusalem's northern gate, their men fell in, marching behind them. Jonathan noticed there were almost as many onlookers who watched with guilt-stricken eyes as the men who marched from the city. *Cowards!* he thought, angrily.

"For God and for Israel!" one of the soldiers shouted in Hebrew. Others in the ranks repeated the ancient Israelite battle cry. *The recruits seem fearless,* Jonathan thought, as he watched his fellow countrymen disappear beyond the city gates. *May God go with them.*

§

Laria, the family household slave, stepped into the doorway, shielding her eyes against the glaring midday sun. *No.*

It's impossible, she thought. *Nabis died in the Jewish revolt. The messenger told us so.*

But, indeed, it was Nabis—ten years older, dressed like a Hebrew, a woman and child in tow, but the beloved son of her master, all the same.

"Oh, by the gods!" she cried, running to meet him. Nabis's face broke into a huge grin. He handed Asher to Abishag and grabbed the diminutive slave woman in his big arms, lifting her off the ground and spinning her round in a circle.

"You're alive! You're alive!" she kept shouting. Neighbors came out of their houses to see what the commotion was about, smiled, and went back inside.

But no one came out of Nabis's parents' house. He felt gripped by dread. "Laria, where is my mother?"

Tears filled the slave woman's eyes. "Oh Nabis, so much has happened since you left. Your mother . . . died last year. We were told *you* were dead!"

Nabis felt a pain in his chest and his own eyes well up, which he tried to control by looking away for a moment.

"She was never the same after they told us you . . ."

Nabis swallowed hard, his throat burning. Abishag stepped closer and took his hand.

"Even with your father, things were never the same."

"Father is alive?" Nabis said, surprised, wiping a tear from his cheek.

"After you left, Agis fell sick, but then he got better. He was well for years, but when your mother died, his health worsened. He stopped being able to work, and had to borrow some money. When he couldn't repay it, the lender made threats. He's been coming around saying he'll burn the house down if the loan isn't paid. And he said he'll take me in payment, and turn me into one of his whores."

"Who is the man?" said Nabis, the anger surging within him.

"The local money lender. The whore master. He controls much of the city in one way or another. I knew it meant trouble when your father went to him. He sold all the good furniture just to pay for food, and then when that money ran out, he went and crawled to that scoundrel for help."

"Where is my father now?"

"Taken to bed, these three days past. You know him— never the type to admit he's sick, but now I can't even get him to eat.

"Take me to him, Laria."

Nabis followed her into the house. She led him through the rooms that were once so familiar. He noticed that the table, where he had eaten every day as a boy, was gone. The whole house was bare of its old beautiful furniture, stripped of everything of value. Nabis entered the back room behind Laria, with Abishag and Asher following.

Lying on the bed, his body propped up with pillows, was Agis. Nabis was struck by how thin he appeared. He had become frail and gray.

The old Spartan opened his eyes upon hearing the shuffle of feet and looked at Laria. "Your son is alive and has returned home," she said gently, touching his shoulder.

At first he looked stunned, like he didn't understand. Then he slipped out of his dream-like daze and looked up in disbelief. Unsteadily, he brought himself to his feet. Nabis saw he was fully dressed and that next to his bed lay his sword, the only thing of value still in the house.

Agis looked at Nabis, not believing his own eyes. When he realized what he saw was not a hallucination, he exclaimed, "By the gods! Is it you, Nabis?"

"None other, Father."

The old man put his good arm around Nabis's shoulder. "They told us you were dead!"

"It seems fate has smiled on us."

"Laria, go to the grocer and buy food for a feast!" said Agis, looking deeply into the face of his boy—now grown way past boyhood.

"Master," Laria whispered. "The money is . . ."

"Sell my sword," Agis commanded.

Nabis knew his father had kept his sword since before he was born, and the Spartan blade was his most prized possession. Agis had held it in his hand when he had been knocked to the ground, his forearm severed by the battleaxe. After wrapping his arm with one of the leather straps that laced his armor, Agis had pried the blade from the fingers of his own amputated hand and returned to the fight.

"Father, I have money, more than enough to take care of us for the rest of our lives," Nabis murmured.

"Your mother would have been so happy to see you well." Agis looked past Nabis to the woman and child standing behind him. He looked back at his son, his eyes a question.

"My wife, Abishag," Nabis said, bringing her and Asher forward.

"She is a Hebrew?" his father asked, surprised.

Then, greeting her with a smile, he repeated, "Abishag," trying to pronounce the name correctly.

"And this is your son?"

"My *adopted* son."

"Oh," said Agis, a hint of disappointment in his voice. He had a thousand questions for Nabis, but all he could manage to say was, "I'm happy."

§

"General," the adjutant galloping up to Bacchides called out to him. "Our scouts met with skirmishers of the Maccabean force."

"How far?" Bacchides asked, trying to assess the situation.

"Almost seven miles. Over half the scouting party has been killed."

"Move the heavy cavalry toward the front with the infantry and ensure the men are fully arrayed for battle," Bacchides commanded, hiding his nervousness. He wondered if the Hebrew men he was about to fight had heard about the massacres he and his men had committed in the Galilean cities they passed through. He had burnt the homes to the ground, with the families barricaded inside. It was a strategic move meant to incite their enemy to act.

"The scouts who lived said they could see the Israelites begin to withdraw south," the adjutant explained.

"It could be a trap. They may want us to give chase. Make sure the men are formed up, to protect our ranks against possible ambushes."

What are you planning, Maccabee? Bacchides thought. "Order the overwatch to skirt the roads." he continued. "If Maccabee does hit us, we'll counterattack and surround him."

Chapter 61

"WE CAN'T WIN this fight!" Tamar, a commander of one hundred, said. The mass of insubordinate men behind him let out a murmur of agreement. "They have over twenty-thousand soldiers and five-thousand cavalry. We have no cavalry, and *three*-thousand men. *We cannot win!*"

"We can fight, and we *can* win!" Judah shot back. "We destroyed the enemies of God at Wadi Haramia, at Beth-Horon, at Emmaus, at Beth-Zur, and obliterated Nicantor's army with him at Adasa. Not once did we ever outnumber their forces. Every single time, God granted us victory, and we defeated the Syrian force. And still, you have no faith!"

"Even if we had three-to-one odds, at least then we'd have a chance," Joseph, another commander of one hundred, blurted out. Another murmur rose in support. "You are sending every one of us to our deaths!"

"We know you're anointed as high priest," Tamar argued. "No one doubts you're a genius on the field of battle, and the hand of God is on the people of Israel. But you have an obligation to rule your people. You can't do that buried in a grave."

"We should withdraw, and wait for the gathering army from the north," another recruit interjected.

"In Galilee," said Judah, "they are still putting out the fires of the dead that the Syrians massacred as they passed through. If we don't stop them here—if we withdraw—the Syrians will take Jerusalem, and in two days it will be *our* families who are burned alive. We don't have the men or the provisions to withstand a siege in the Seleucid citadel, let alone Jerusalem. If we run, the only option we'll have is to evacuate the city, gather an army, and spend the next five to *twenty years* trying to root them out of Jerusalem, after they've slain all the inhabitants. *Or* we can fight them here. If they do take the city, they won't stop. They will reestablish their dominance and use the momentum to track us down and execute every one of us. Our army could be completely gathered in a matter of weeks, if not sooner. If we halt them—not defeat them, but just stop them from entering the city—it will give us a chance to gather our forces, and then we can drive them from our land forever."

More complaining murmurs erupted from the men.

"We won't stop them," Tamar interrupted. "They'll crash right through us and still take Jerusalem."

Simon stood by Judah's side silently, deep in contemplation, searching his heart and soul, trying to discern the wise answer, but he could find none.

"The army of God's chosen will not let His holy city be taken without a fight," said Judah. "Far be it from us to flee like cowards from the heathen armies. If our time has come, then let us die bravely for our brothers, and not leave any cause to question our glory." A silence descended upon the men. "But I will not force any man to fight. If a people are unwilling to risk their lives for freedom, they no longer deserve it." Judah took a deep breath, looking to heaven.

When he looked back down he said, "Whosoever has just been engaged, has had a newly born child, built a new home, or harbors fear in his own heart, he may now leave the army."

A hush fell over the men, and the air became still and breathless as the moments waxed. Tamar was the first to step forward. The army at his back remained deathly still as, with a dagger, he cut away the straps that secured his armor. It slid from his body and smote the earth with a crash. Then he laid down his spear before Judah's feet. Judah could see that the fear that had overtaken Tamar now manifested as hate, evident by the glare in his eyes. He turned and walked away along the southern road.

After another still, silent moment, Joseph stepped forward. He kept his armor, but he, too, laid his spear down before Judah, staring at the ground in shame, unable to look his high priest in the eyes.

Another moment passed, and then the whole army began to stir. Scores of men moved forward, dropping their arms. Some kept their weapons and just walked away, following the men before them on the road. As more recruits laid down their arms, those who remained grew further disheartened, provoking more to follow the deserters in fear.

Judah looked at the faces of his men and felt overwhelmed by a sense of betrayal. The onset of the pain struck him deep, in a way he could not have imagined. He looked into the eyes of the men who passed before him, and found he could not speak. He could only pray, silently—asking God why, hoping his demeanor did not betray the distress he felt. He stood incredulous, his heart writhing within him, watching his army melt away.

Men by the hundreds turned their backs and departed. Judah was about to raise his voice to try to say something, anything, that might inspire his men to courage, but before he did, Daniel, one of his captains of fifty, came before him. Amidst the noise and bedlam, he said, "Maccabee, I beg you not to stay, *not now.* It would be suicide! Come with us, and at least wait until enough men have gathered from the northern cities and we have a chance of winning. They *will* come, I'm sure of it, but we have to wait. Trust in the Lord. They will come."

Raising his voice, Judah replied, "And defile my name, and all I've done, by turning my back and retreating? I have more faith in the Lord God than that."

"You are not Gideon, and God has not shown you signs with a woolen fleece!" Daniel pleaded. "God isn't going to lengthen the day for a massive victory for Israel tomorrow. Look at your army. *It is broken*, and they know it. Lead us south. Wait for the men to arrive from the northern city, and then we'll take back Jerusalem."

"If I do *that*, I betray all that I am," Judah said calmly, "I would betray my soul. If I am to die—if my time has come—then let it come, but I'll go to sleep with my ancestors *knowing who I am*. I will not blemish my honor before the Lord by letting the people in Jerusalem be massacred by the heathens, while I run in fear."

As soon as Daniel left, Simon approached Judah and said in a low voice, "They may be right, Judah. A fight now may not accomplish anything but our deaths. Are you sure this is your decision? Are you sure this is the *right* decision?"

"Have I not commanded you? Be strong and courageous. Do not be afraid; do not be discouraged, for the Lord your God will be with you wherever you go." Judah quoted in Hebrew God's command to Joshua before the invasion, as the Israelites were crossing the Jordan River.

"Then I will fight by your side, and put my faith in the Lord, Maccabee," Simon said, bowing his head. He thanked God that it was not he who had to make a decision between life and death, honor and survival, and trading the lives of the men—and probably their own—for the innocent souls in Jerusalem.

He knew at that moment that he wasn't meant to be high priest or the leader of the army, and didn't ever want to be. *We're all going to die here,* he thought, *every one of us. Any who remained will never see another summer or winter.* He wished he could have seen his sons one more time. He thanked God his eldest, Mattathias, was one of those sent to the northern cities to gather the army and that he was not here, a part of this sacrifice. He wished he could have said goodbye to Jude and John. He wished he could live to see what kind of men the boys would one day become. *I should have reconciled with my wife,* he told himself, sorry that he had left things to end so bitterly. *There's not enough time. There's not enough time,* he kept repeating to himself.

Judah looked at the ground before him, littered with strewn weapons and armor. It already looked like a battlefield after a massive clash of arms, only without bodies or the smell of death. A battle *had* taken place here, he thought: a battle in the hearts of God's people, and fear had won.

Along the road, disappearing into the distance, hundreds of men walked away in shame—some hanging their heads, some indifferent, some scoffing with laughter about the simplicity of the decision, trying to numb their consciences. It took Judah a long moment before he could speak again.

Before him, in formation, arrayed for battle and with hardened eyes, stood the eight-hundred men who remained. Eight-hundred men, ready to fight to the death for their God, the freedom of their people, and the salvation of Jerusalem.

Judah looked into their eyes and could see their resolve. Nothing would break the spirits of these men, and Judah suddenly felt comfort at having eight-hundred such stalwart souls at his side.

It's not about whether or not you feel fear, he said to himself. *That feeling always comes. It's about overcoming it, not letting it undo you.*

"Gather the weapons," Judah ordered.

§

Aaron rode hard, heading west toward Jerusalem. The city seemed to expand as he drew near. He had scouted out the lands of the Medeba, riding as fast as he could, then had crossed the Jordan and continued his journey. The only man he had left galloped behind him, his horse slowing from fatigue. They reached the wall of the city and moved through the streets toward the governor's palace.

Aaron's horse snorted and reared up, halted by twelve Hebrew guards.

"I'm here to see Maccabee," the young man announced. "I bring information directly for his ears. Tell him Aaron Ben Malimalck is here."

One of the guards took hold of his horse's reins. "Maccabee has taken all the men he could gather in time, and marched north to meet the Syrians," he declared.

"The *Syrians?* The Syrians are marching on Judea?"

"They're *in* Judea," the guard said, emphatically. "Last reports said they were only miles from the city."

God protect us, Aaron thought.

"Judah could only gather a fraction of his army in time and marched north to face them.

"Who's left in charge here?" asked Aaron.

"Jonathan, Maccabee's brother."

"Take me to him," Aaron demanded.

"I'll see if he will receive you."

It was only moments before the guard returned to escort Aaron into the palace.

"What news have you of my brother?" Jonathan asked when Aaron stepped into his quarters.

Aaron responded by shaking his head. "Sir, I am so sorry. The rumors were true. Your brother, Gaddi, has been murdered." Jonathan averted his eyes, holding back the tears. "Tell me all of it," he murmured at last.

"We spent a week, sir, reconnoitering the Medeba village before we captured one of the guards on patrol. We dragged him to a cave and made him talk. They had captured Gaddi, and brought him to their village, not realizing who they had."

Jonathan wanted to sit, but forced himself to remain standing.

"Once they knew, apparently they argued. Some said they should demand a ransom. Some wanted to release him and give back the weapons and gold. Others said that even if they did that, Maccabee would be enraged and take vengeance upon them for the Hebrews they had slaughtered. And they would lose the respect of their neighboring tribes, becoming objects of ridicule and attack. They decided the only solution was . . . death. If Gaddi disappeared, so would their problem."

Aaron looked at Jonathan, not knowing what else to say.

"How did he die?"

"The guard we captured said . . . he said they they dragged Gaddi from the tent, where had had been listening to them argue the whole time, and then drove a blade into his chest. He died well, and did not suffer long."

"Did they bury him?" Jonathan asked hoarsely, swearing revenge in his heart.

"They took him outside the camp and burned the body."

Jonathan finally collapsed into a chair. Although he had been much closer to Eleazar and Judah—even to Simon—than he was to Gaddi, who seemed a generation older, Gaddi was still his brother, the son of his father and mother. *I will destroy them,* Jonathan thought to himself. *When Judah hears of it, nothing will save them. We'll lay waste the villages of the Medeba until their name becomes forgotten with time, only remembered for the vengeance we will bring upon them.*

"With your permission, sir, I would like to ride north and help Judah with the fight against the Seleucids," said Aaron.

"Yes, and you must bring him this news," Jonathan replied—wishing with everything in him he was with his brothers now.

§

"How much longer will I have to be on this god-cursed boat?" barked Diomedes in Latin to the ship's captain.

"We're almost there. A day and a half, maybe two," the captain answered leisurely.

"You said that two days ago." Diomedes swore under his breath.

"The sea is vast, and these things take time," the captain responded.

This place is a prison, Diomedes thought, *and the water is the bars. I'm shackled to these fools, and the jailer is that fornicating Roman magistrate.* Frustrated and exhausted from the long journey, Diomedes felt less love for Rome every day, and more appreciation of his mother's Jewish blood that ran through his veins.

He stared off the stern of the Roman war galley at the other two ships. On the deck of the one closest to him, he could see Roman soldiers wandering aimlessly. The sun was out, the day clear, and the ocean calm.

That magistrate, Diomedes lamented to himself. *I swear the world is ruled by fool politicians who haven't a clue how their decisions affect the fate of armies and nations.* The senators weren't any better, absorbed in swindling money through exorbitant taxation from the aristocracy and commoners. The consuls were the worst of them all. They encroached upon the role of the senate, all the while professing their loyalty to the republic. *Cincinnatus would fall on his sword if he saw his republic today,* thought Diomedes. It was just a matter of time before one of the consuls got power-hungry enough to declare a national emergency, assume the office of dictator, and declare himself king.

Diomedes looked again at his men. They gave him a detachment of soldiers, and they really expected him not to use them? It was too tempting, too easy. He would simply use his soldiers to support Maccabee and fight the Syrians. If he faced retribution afterwards from Rome, he would simply lie. It wouldn't be hard to convince that fool of a magistrate, or any other Roman official, that he had no choice—that his men, who were just carrying out orders in training the Hebrew rebels, were attacked by Seleucid soldiers and forced to defend themselves.

If there was an incident, and Rome went to war with the Seleucid kingdom, there would be no possibility of Syria holding onto Judea. The Syrians were already fighting two wars. The only thing that would be worse for them was if they started fighting each other.

§

"We should take Antioch by force," Hiliarion insisted. "An open proclamation to the empire—not some vile assassination."

"We should avoid a civil war at all costs," Solon protested calmly.

They walked along the horse trail on Solon's land, four miles outside the capital city. The sky was partly gray from clouds, but the sun broke through overhead. Solon's armed servants traveled at a distance ahead and behind them on the trail, out of earshot.

Hilarion clasped his hands together, intent on making his point. "The more I persuade the nobles under my patronage to side with us, the more it becomes apparent their problem doesn't lie with killing Demetrius. They have a problem *murdering* him, like a band of criminals waiting to usurp the throne. The only way we can keep power, and make and keep Alexander king, is if we have the perception of legitimacy. We can't have that if we murder Demetrius in secret."

"It will be harder to continue ruling if this turns into a long, drawn-out war," answered Solon, "especially if Alexander rises to power. Whoever ends up with the throne will have a completely depleted treasury and a shattered empire. And if Demetrius does succeed in Judea and manages to reconquer the region, he'll have an already strengthened army to the south at his disposal—ready to come to his aid."

"If Demetrius manages to retake Judea, popular opinion will change, and we might as well call the whole thing off," Hilarion muttered, reluctantly. "There will be too many disadvantages—tactically, politically, and financially."

"Alexander is in Cyprus now," Solon said, thinking out loud. "When he leaves, he will sail to Alexandria, where Ptolemy will provide him with vast wealth to support his claim to the throne. He's of a mind to take it in the same way Demetrius ousted Lysias. But if that proves impossible, he'll have no choice but to gather men from Egypt, as well as his supporters here, and declare full-scale war. If Alexander doesn't take the throne immediately, civil war could rage for years. Who knows who people would side with then?"

"So perhaps we should strike soon, in secret, while popular opinion is still against the king," Hiliarion urged. "Still," he added, "it won't look good for our side."

"Yes, soon. After we consolidate our support, and Alexander has his Egyptian soldiers and our Seleucid support from inside the empire. *Then*, we destroy Demetrius."

Chapter 62

PARIS TOOK A drink of ale from his clay cup without glancing away from his ledger. On the second floor, the rooms rented out by the hour were all occupied by the girls who worked for him. He heard the quiet conversation of three of his men outside his office, which opened into what, he felt, was a sad excuse for a tavern.

In his late forties, Paris had been in his trade since he was a boy. He worked first as a collector and later as the middleman, slowly rising up the ranks until he was the boss. Hearing the door open, he glanced up at the man who entered. *He must want to borrow money,* thought Paris. Most clients didn't come by for the girls until later, unless they were rich men, which this one didn't appear to be. At first glance, the stranger looked foreign, but as he moved closer, the light from the window showed he had Greek features. "Hello," Paris said greeting the man respectfully, gesturing to the small seat before his table. "Jason, bring ale for our friend."

"So how can I help you?" he asked, smiling in anticipation like a salesman.

"I'm here to settle an outstanding debt."

"And which debt do you speak of?" said Paris, his excitement disappearing. Settlement of debts was not generally to his liking, as it meant the interest income disappeared.

"Agis, the Spartan," the man answered.

Paris searched his memory, "Ah, Agis. Agis owes thirty-five tetradrachm," he said, exaggerating the number.

"Yes," the man replied.

"And you have *thirty-five* tetradrachm?" Paris asked doubtfully, thinking *the man can't even afford a decent set of clothes.* He smiled sardonically.

"Yes," the man said, pulling the money pouch from his belt, drawing from it thirty-five tetradrachm, and laying them on the table.

Paris looked shocked, but betrayed his surprise for only a moment before his face became stern once more. "He also owes interest," he said. "These debts have gone unpaid for so long now. The added interest is an additional . . . " he mentally computed the largest number the man could possibly pay . . . "fifteen tetradrachm. Unless you can pay that in addition, I'm afraid the debt has not been settled."

The man across from him pulled out an additional fifteen tetradrachm from his bag and set it on the table. Paris's eyes lit up at seeing all the money—more money than a relatively wealthy man would make in a year.

Who was this stranger? How could he, dressed in something a beggar would wear, flaunt money like a king? And why would he want to pay off that decrepit old cripple's debt?

"Might I inquire your name?" Paris asked, curious. There were small beads of perspiration on his upper lip and forehead. The stranger's noble demeanor irritated him.

"Nabis," the man replied coldly.

"Well, I don't know you," Paris answered. "Tell me, why in the names of the gods, would you want to pay the debt of an old, broken-down, one-armed fool?" He felt like making insults, suddenly angered at the man's presence and the arrogance he projected.

"Are we considering all debts paid in full?" Nabis asked.

"No! We are not," Paris shot back.

"That old bastard insulted me. He cursed and insulted me in front of my men. *I* can't afford to look *foolish* in public! I promised that simpleton I'd make him pay more than just money!"

"I will pay five more tetradrachm for the insult." Nabis

kept his voice low, standing up to leave. His gaze was full of ice.

"Who do you think you are, coming into *my* place, throwing your money around? Do you think you can insult me like this? Don't you know who I am? Let me inform you: I control this city, and I'll get what I want. What I want is his slave, that bitch that has taken care of him, keeping him alive the past two years. She will earn money for me as one of my girls. Bring her in, and *that* will settle the debt. If I don't get her, I'll kill him, burn his dilapidated house to the ground, and then fuck his slave, just like I fucked his whore of a wife, when she came begging me to extend the debt deadline, the last time he owed money."

Nabis looked into the moneylender's eyes and knew he wasn't lying.

Paris barely had time to react as Nabis sprang forward, shoving the table aside that separated them. He took hold of the moneylender's wrist, as Paris drew his blade. Nabis grasped his forehead with one hand and, with all his might, brought down his weight, slamming the man's head into the wall, tightening his grip and trying to control Paris's hand that held the knife, now poised at his center. Paris let out a yell, alerting his comrades. Nabis slammed Paris's head once more into the wall, feeling the skull crack, blood smearing the stone and mortar.

From outside the room came a cacophony of shouts and rushing footsteps. Three armed men, two brandishing daggers and one a sword, entered and closed in quickly. Nabis drew the xiphos from under his robe and swung it in a horizontal arc, cleaving through the bridge of the nose and eyes of his first attacker. The man recoiled and fell, uttering shrill, blood-curdling yelps.

The other two, together, began to close in on Nabis. The first struck with a sword blow, which Nabis parried, while the other man lurched forward. Nabis felt a sharp pain pierce his side. He gripped the second man's wrist, keeping him from wresting the dagger free and using it again. Then Nabis lunged his xiphos into the abdomen of the man wielding the sword and twisted, opening up the wound. Going ashen, the man staggered back, lost his balance, and dropped to his knees.

The assailant whose dagger was buried in Nabis's side was trying to pry the blade free, but Nabis held firm his grip on the man's wrist. The knife wrenched back and forth, tearing the wound. The attacker used his free hand to grip Nabis's throat. As Nabis brought the tip of his xiphos up and aligned it with the assailant's throat, he let go of Nabis's neck and gripped the back of his head, digging his thumb into Nabis's eye. Nabis jerked his head back and then drove the point of his sword into his enemy's neck.

Nabis saw the familiar desperation in the man's eyes, as they fogged and glazed over. Convulsing and bleeding, his attacker fell to the floor.

Nabis looked around him. All of his attackers were wounded or dead. Paris lay on the floor, a pool of blood gathering around his head. The man he had slashed across the eyes was still screaming, on his knees. The other was curled in a ball, holding his stomach, mouthing a prayer to the gods.

Nabis looked down at his own wound. The cut was deep, torn almost an inch-and-a-half wide during the struggle. A wave of nausea hit him, and he had to lean against the wall as his knees buckled. He touched his face with bloodstained fingers, and felt numb.

He staggered toward the door, leaving the coins he had paid in the spilled ale under the overturned table. For a moment, he thought he would vomit. He leaned against another table, but it slid under his weight.

Girls came screaming out of rooms on the second floor. Nabis shuffled outside, the cool air helping. *You have to get home,* he thought. *You have to get back to Abishag and your father. It's all right,* he told himself. *You've been here before. You've been through worse. Just get yourself home.*

He breathed hard, and his heart was racing. He moved around the corner through a back alleyway. *Calm down,* he ordered himself, as he applied more pressure to the wound. *Just make it home, and you'll be okay. It's a flesh wound. Nothing to worry about.* He took another deep breath. *Keep moving,* he demanded of himself, afraid he would collapse.

Nabis began praying again to the Hebrew God. *Get me home to Abishag,* he asked, the same way he had years before when he had taken an arrow in his shoulder at Beth-Horn. *Don't let me die in the streets and leave her abandoned in this strange place.* He stopped a moment, his face dripping sweat. He leaned against a wall, removed his hand from the wound, and peered down at it again. That's when he knew he wasn't going to survive.

§

The Greek trumpets pierced the silence. The phalanxes marched forward in unison. The earth shook with the beat of the marching, as the seemingly infinite body of Syrian troops flowed like a tidal wave toward Judah's men.

The earth began to vibrate as the ground shook all around them.

I suppose there are worse ways to die, Simon thought, breathing in the cool air of the dawn morning, seeing the force as thick and dense as a forest, that seemed to stretch miles wide. He wished he could see his family once more, just to say goodbye. At that moment, there was nothing more he'd rather have. *God, take care of them,* he prayed. *Best not to think on it now, Ratzon ha'El,* he told himself, hoping the prayer he had given before the army was enough to comfort the souls of the men, and prepare them for their end.

Across the open ground, flanking the massive force on either end, were the companies of Syrian cavalry. What seemed more impossible to believe than the endless army approaching, was how very few men they numbered themselves. Their company of eight hundred, which didn't stretch even a hundred yards across, seemed to Simon like a single man standing firm against the tempest of an engulfing ocean.

"See the cavalry?" Judah asked, composed. "Look how heavy it is on their right. They are planning on flanking our left."

Flanking our left? thought Simon. *They have more men then sand on the seashore. What strategy do they need? We might as well march off a cliff.* Since the Syrians had spotted them, Judah's little band didn't even have the element of surprise, but were forced to retreat or fight on open ground.

"Their cavalry on their right will be the first to charge and get behind us, just as soon as their phalanxes have moved forward far enough," Judah yelled over the thuds of marching and squeals of Greek trumpets. "Which means General Bacchides will be on their right, behind the brunt of the fighting."

Before Simon could ask how he knew that, Judah said, "Bacchides was a cavalry officer. He'll be there with the men."

"So?" Simon asked, swallowing hard, trying to control his shaking limbs.

"So, we attack their right. We avoid the slow-moving phalanxes entirely. See that berm?" Judah asked, gesturing to his left at a shallow rise in the mostly flat terrain about three-hundred yards in front of them.

"Yes," Simon replied, his voice quavering.

"When I give the order, we'll charge that berm and get there at the same time their cavalry does. We'll use our sarissas to bear down on them while our men behind us fire slings and javelins over our heads."

"It'll never work," Simon murmured.

"If we break their cavalry and kill Bacchides, if we can fold their lines into each other, we can halt them, and that's all we need to do. Then we'll return to Jerusalem and pray our men from the north arrive in time."

Simon nodded, overwhelmed. He could see the cavalry begin to trot forward on the flanks of their formations.

"Give the order to the commanders of one hundred. It won't be long now."

It took Simon no more than a minute to disseminate the order and explain the simple plan to the eight commanders who gathered around him. A few more minutes passed, and the massive army was almost on top of them. Simon could almost make out the faces of the men in the colossal force. He glanced over his shoulder, hoping with everything in him that at his back would appear all the men from the north they had prayed would show up, or the men who had abandoned them, returning to support them now, but there was no one—just the eight hundred who stood tall, holding their long pikes ready for battle, ready to die.

"When this is over, you can marry us," Judah said.

"What?"

"Martha and I."

Incredulous, Simon looked over at his brother. *How can he have such faith?* he asked himself, amazed. *How can he talk like we'll be alive tomorrow?*

Suddenly he was ashamed of how afraid he really was. "I'll be happy to," he replied.

Judah regarded the movement, the placement, and position of every formation expanding across the field. "Get ready," he said to his signalman, who placed the shofar to his lips.

He waited. The seconds seemed suspended. Judah gauged the distance between the leading cavalry on his left, and the distance to the berm.

"*Now!*" he bellowed. The shofar sounded, and the small force broke into a run, heading diagonally toward the berm.

The Syrian infantry, locked in their dense phalanxes, did not seem to react, but the cavalry did, breaking into a gallop, charging toward the berm—three thousand of them. Judah felt his lungs burn with exertion. He and his men took the elevated slope just seconds before they became hemmed in on all sides by the Syrian horsemen.

And then the enemy was on top of them. The slow, armored horses tried to advance up a rise barely wide enough for all eight-hundred Hebrews to occupy. Jewish javelins began to fly spiraling through the air, killing horses and Syrians. Rocks from slings began flying down on the mounted soldiers in every direction. The Hebrew soldiers were shouting, gritting their teeth, negating the daunting terror which gripped them, as they watched the Syrian riders trudging uphill and closing in around them. The Israelites lowered their sarissas, pointing them in every direction, poised at the surrounding riders. Judah heard a Syrian horse whinny as it moved toward their dense circumference atop the berm. Judah aligned his spear and took aim.

Chapter 63

"HOW IS HE?" Agis asked, his voice a whisper. Nabis lay on the bed—his heartrate fast, his breath labored, his wound infected.

"Not much different than when the doctor came," Abishag answered. The physician had been delayed in getting to the house. He said he had been occupied at a tavern, where someone had killed the moneylender and two of his employees, severely injuring a third. The doctor didn't offer much hope for Nabis.

Sitting at the bedside of her husband, Abishag had cried all night. She was terrified of losing Nabis and being left alone in a foreign land. And now it appeared she was with child. She had missed two monthly cycles and had only been waiting for the perfect time to tell Nabis the happy news—news that now had turned to a yet another worry, another fear. What if Nabis and his father both died, and she was left in this country with two children? There was enough money now, but how could she survive alone in a place so strange it seemed like another world? A world without her people, without her God. She prayed to Him now. All her hope hung on Him.

Abishag looked up at her father-in-law. The distress she saw in his face made her feel ashamed for her self-pitying thoughts. *How terrible,* she told herself, *to be deprived of your son for a decade and then to be given him back, only to lose him once more.* Weak as Agis was when she and Nabis arrived, Abishag believed the old man could not withstand the heartbreak of losing his son again now. She was almost certain he would follow his son into the grave.

The day before, Nabis had given his father and Laria an abundance of money, to refurnish the house and stock up on food. It was enough money to buy a new house, if Agis so wanted. Later that day, Nabis had staggered home from the moneylender and collapsed on the walkway that led to the front door. Laria found him, and Abishag had rushed out in a panic to help when she heard Laria's screams.

Nabis had barely been conscious. A dark-red patch of blood had spread from inside his garment, down his side and leg. Abishag had torn away his robe and found the wound. It didn't look to her like vital organs were injured, but the massive loss of blood caused immediate alarm.

That night, Nabis had broken out in a fever which they all knew would be his biggest risk, if he did not die immediately. The infected wound was worsening rapidly. His ashen body was shaking, his hands were cold and clammy, but his temperature was scalding.

Agis had Laria purchase strong drink, telling her to soak a cloth in it and apply it to the stitched wound and the surrounding areas. "Sometimes," he said, "it keeps the wound from festering, and helps prevent infection of the blood, which sends the humors off-balance."

Abishag had never seen Nabis in such a dismal state. She tried to be strong, tried to show faith in God, especially in front of his father, but she couldn't help what she felt. She imagined Nabis dying, superstitiously thinking that if she could imagine something as horrifying in grim detail, that would somehow prevent its actual occurrence.

Agis took a seat beside his daughter-in-law. "When he left for the army," Agis began, "I didn't want him to go. He was like me when I was young, wanting to see the world and find some kind of meaning in it all, put some sort of perspective on life, following that ineffable yearning all young men seem to have to face the worst." Abishag watched the old man's face as he spoke. In spite of the lines and the suffering there, she found it noble and beautiful.

"I knew then I might never see him again," he went on. "When you're young, you have no concept of mortality. You think nothing can hurt you. Not until you're there, before the battle starts, do you have any realization. You see all the other boys standing next to you begin dying, boys who will never see home again. Some of them, you can tell, were never meant to see old age. They just had . . . ," he paused, "they had something about them, like you could almost see their fate. Not that they weren't good soldiers, or strong people. Some of the men I thought wouldn't get a scratch, didn't come home. Some I thought would die in their first battle lived, but some— you just knew their fate was sealed. I didn't think Nabis was one of those, but a father can't be sure. It's hard to read the fates where your own child is concerned. That's why I never wanted him to go." Abishag's lips were quivering as she stared deep into Nabis's face. He looked calmer now, and his breathing grew heavy and slow.

§

"They're breaking!" Judah shouted in ecstasy, peering across the battlefield.

"I don't believe it!" Simon said, seeing the Syrian cavalry in retreat, inadvertently crashing into the right side of their own formations of archers, causing the ranks of the first phalanx to falter and break.

After Judah's men held the berm for almost two hours, fighting off the repeated waves of charging cavalrymen, the Syrian archers, believing the Israelites to be pinned down, had moved forward, ahead of the infantry, to bombard them. They had to wait for their enveloping cavalry, to move from behind the berm which the Hebrews held, but when they had, Judah and his men charged. The unorganized attackers panicked and wheeled right into their own phalanx that was hastening toward the Hebrew right flank.

"I don't believe it!" Simon said again, this time more loudly.

"Charge them!" Judah ordered, pressing his men forward in pursuit. The Israelites rushed at the fleeing Syrians. A cavalry officer turned in panic, trapped between the deluge of Hebrews and the barricade of fleeing Syrians. Judah lunged with his sarissa, impaling the rider through the chest. Judah had lost nearly fifty men, most of whom had fallen holding back the cavalry that had attacked the rear of the berm.

"We've done it!" Judah shouted to his brother, in triumph amidst the foray. He could see the ominous, chaotic flight of the first two phalanxes. No matter what, now they wouldn't be able to take Jerusalem without regrouping. If the Jews now could shatter their cavalry, and kill Bacchides—assuming he wasn't already dead—they would completely paralyze the Syrian force.

The Israelites charged down the shallow embankment on foot, engaging the Syrian cavalrymen trapped in the consternation of retreat. The left flank of the Syrian infantry, Judah realized, would attempt to maneuver and envelop them, but they were far too slow. Judah contemplated for a moment if they should fall back to the berm, and again hold their defensive position, but this was the only chance they had to use their momentum and break them. He knew if he could, they'd never recover. He drove his spear into the hind leg of a fleeing horse, causing it to stagger and throw its rider. The rider, fully armored, tried to bring himself to his feet, but was skewered by three spear tips before he could rise to his knees.

Suddenly almost thirty cavalrymen, seeing they could not flee quickly enough through the barrier of men, turned and charged their position. Judah raised his sarissa and pierced the abdomen of one of the bounding riders. He felt his spear snap in the center. He threw down his broken pike and drew his sword. Another Syrian on horseback, with a spear cradled in his arm, rushed at him. Judah sidestepped to his left and slashed through the side of the man's armor. The rider hunched forward, dropping his spear, and slid from his saddle, tumbling to the dirt.

"Keep pushing forward!" Judah cried, seeing the panicked desperation in the Syrian cavalry as they began to collapse. Judah glanced at Simon, and terror suddenly gripped him, seeing the blood rushing down his brother's face, down the sleeve of his priest's raiment, and over the side of his armor. Then Judah realized it was only a cut that had grazed Simon's forehead along his hair line. Though it bled profusely, it didn't seem to hinder Simon amidst the heat of battle, and he continued fighting viciously, grabbing hold of one of the riders and hurling him off his steed, then hewing him down with his kopis. All of Judah's men were attacking just as rapaciously.

Fewer men on horseback attempted now to advance them or hold their ground, but instead began riding around their own formations like pincers, past the massive phalanx that blockaded their front.

Though trapped in the fulcrum of battle, Judah felt an ineffable serenity come over him, and he silently began to praise God in those passing, savage moments. *Thank you, my Lord my God, for giving us this day, for giving our enemies into our hand.*

As the chaos ensued among the disjointed Syrian ranks, he knew there would be no way for the Seleucids to advance further. All around him was crashing metal and shouts. The sun was overhead, beating down on them, warming the day. Judah looked down at his sword, the same sword he had taken from Apollonius all those years before, when he had won his first major victory at the Wadi Haramia Pass. He sheathed the blade and picked up a Greek spear which he found discarded on the ground. He looked up at the army retreating before his men, and ordered his men forward once more.

§

Diomedes stood on deck, watching his ships glide through the rising waves toward shore. Men tossed rope ladders and leapt from the side of the galley. Those on the bow tossed lines of thick rope to them, to tie down the Roman warship. The evening was warm, and the waves looked green except where they broke against the shore and frothed glistening in the sunlight. On deck, Roman centurions were shouting instructions, treating the landing like an amphibious combat assault.

More rope ladders poured over the sides of the three ships, and more soldiers climbed down into the waist-high surf. The galleys rocked up and down as the surf moved in and out, the waves slapping against the hulls. The first teams of five crept forward, javelins ready, moving inland onto dry sand, as archers provided over-watch from the deck. Diomedes saw one of the soldiers trip as a wave knocked his feet out from under him, rolling him in the break. He was quickly helped to his feet by the man next to him.

The first groups on the beach began setting up defensive positions in short modified cohort formation. Once enough men had fallen into their respected ranks, the units began moving inland toward the beachhead. The small attachments of archers formed up behind the infantry lines and began moving forward. They had all rehearsed the landing routine countless times before, but always expected it to be under barrages of arrows, facing an adversary attempting to push them back into the sea. This was different. There were no opposing forces and no major city in sight. Diomedes had ordered the captain to make their landing on an isolated beach, far from any major port.

Once the defensive positions were established and every major avenue of approach secure, Diomedes ordered the ranking centurion to have the men fall in. Once they did, he gave the order to begin the march east toward Jerusalem.

§

Simon's heart raced as a Syrian rider galloped past the left wing of the Hebrew mass, hurling a javelin in his direction. It soared just over his shoulder, lodging deep into the chest of the man behind him. Simon thrust his sarissa at the rider, narrowly missing him as he galloped past, kicking up cyclones of dust. Sweat and blood ran into Simon's eyes from the cut on his brow. His mouth was parched, and he could barely move his arms.

"We have to make it back to the berm," Judah bellowed. "We're getting massacred here!"

It was nearly dusk. Judah's men had fought all day, losing one-third of their force. They had successfully halted the Seleucid advance and routed the massive infantry phalanxes, sending them crashing into one another. The confusion caused other formations to assume Judah had once again formulated some artifice that they could not perceive. This sent them into flight. Soon the largest portion of the army was in a full retreat.

Judah had kept pushing his men forward, knowing if he could get to Bacchides and kill their general, the Syrian's would completely lose command and control of their army. Then amidst the rout, two-thousand Syrian cavalrymen on their right had managed to get behind them, surrounding them. Judah amassed his survivors within a defensive perimeter, their twenty-foot pikes poised in all directions, as the riders galloped past, hurling javelins, trying to crash and break their lines.

Another javelin slammed into Simon's shield, jutting it into his face, momentarily stunning him. More riders approached, and Simon saw the man next to him drop to his knees, a spear haft protruding from his stomach. One by one, they all were being killed.

Judah caught one of the riders with his sarissa, stabbing him in the head, knocking him from his steed. Simon braced himself for another rider coming in from the opposite direction, every volatile breath ushering in the coming end.

Then he saw the rider loose an arrow into the center of a charging Seleucids, and Simon realized the rider wasn't Syrian, but Hebrew. It was Aaron. Aaron had somehow broken through the enemy cavalry where they had been the thinnest. In the disorientation of battle, he had fought his way to the Jewish perimeter. Simon wondered if he had found Gaddi, but there was no time to ask, focused on the need of the moment to survive.

Aaron dismounted his horse and slapped its hind leg, sending it galloping away, before he sank into the swarm of fighting Israelites. He fired another arrow into the neck of a Syrian rider and emptied what was left of his quiver before gripping the bloodied haft of a fallen man's sarissa.

"Simon!" Judah cried. "there are few riders behind us. On my command, break for the berm!"

Simon nodded, sending the order down the line. They waited for the next wave of riders to pass, and Judah shouted, "Now!"

All at once, the Hebrew force darted two-hundred yards south for the berm they had held that morning. Pursuing riders hewed down scores of fleeing Israelites, but soon they reached the incline of the slope, slowing the exausted enemy steeds, then halting them. Some of the Syrian cavalrymen dismounted and tried to advance on foot.

Simon peered around at their men. More than half had been killed. Judah was scanning the scene behind them. No enemies had yet made it up the berm, and there were no enemies at their back. "Now's our chance," Judah said. "We'll fall back in staggered lines. Even numbers will hold the line, while odd numbers fall back. Then the even numbers will fall back while odd numbers hold the line."

The dismounted Syrian cavalrymen were nearly up the rise.

"Now!" Judah shouted. In sequence, half the Hebrew force held their lines, facing the enemy, while every other man fell back one-hundred yards. Then the first element fell back, while the second held their ground. The sun was nearly set, with the shadows of distant mountains expanding as it made its final retreat. "We can lose them in the dark!" Judah cried, continuing his organized retrograde south, back to safety, back to Jerusalem.

Without warning, a small Syrian phalanx of light infantry appeared from a subtle incline just to the east. It bore down on them. Instantly, two-score riders who had managed to circumvent the rugged terrain around the berm, charged in from the north.

"They're going to try to surround us again," Judah shouted. "Keep falling back! Don't let them get behind us!"

Judah's men continued moving back until the riders crashed into their left. The infantry slammed into their right. The lines intermingled. Simon thrust his sarissa into the throat of a Seleucid rider, bringing him down. He glanced to his right and saw Judah plunge his sarissa deep into the abdomen of an enemy infantryman. The haft of his spear cracked, and the spearhead remained lodged in the dying man's corselet. Judah flung aside the broken sarissa and drew his sword. Another Seleucid came at Judah, but he darted from beneath the attacker's spear before cleaving his neck, nearly taking his head off. Then three Syrians charged Judah all at once, each wielding a javelin. Judah parried the spear tip of the first. Then the second attacker plunged his javelin into Judah's right side. The third attacker drove his spear into the left side of Judah's chest.

"Judah!" Simon bellowed.

Judah staggered and fell backwards. Simon sprang for his brother.

Seeing Judah fall sent a tumultuous roar through the remaining Hebrew force who, with a shout, charged their leader's position, pushing the Syrian line back. Simon crouched over his brother, gazing into his face. The blood was everywhere, pouring out of his chest and his side.

"Judah, stay with me. We'll get you help." He put his hand over the chest wound, trying to somehow stop the bleeding.

Judah's face tightened, his eyes were shot with pain, and blood pooled in the corner of his mouth. He groaned, trying in vain to rise. His blood-soaked and shivering hand inched toward Simon's. Simon grasped it. Judah didn't speak, he could not, but his eyes beckoned Simon, as if telling him, "Take care of our people. Take care of our nation. Take care of Jonathan." Then, in a moment, he was gone. There was no more fear in his face nor pain, just a fierce expression and empty eyes. His warm hand stopped fluttering, but Simon could not look away. He could not believe what had happened.

"We have to get out of here!"

It was Aaron. He was standing over them. "They can't hold the lines any longer. Syrian reinforcements are coming! We're about to be overrun!"

Simon glanced up, frozen. Aaron looked at Judah, knowing he was dead, and hoisted his body unto his shoulders. "Sir, we have to move!"

Simon felt removed from himself. He clutched his brother's sword that had fallen next to his body, and felt himself being helped to his feet, as the remaining survivors of the Hebrew force retreated south, before being completely cut off.

Chapter 64

A BLEAK GRAY DAWN was rising in the east as Jonathan strode toward the well outside the steps of the governor's palace. He had been awakened by one of his servants, who informed him that the army had returned.

The previous day Jonathan fought every temptation to mount a horse and ride out to help the army himself, after hearing the disquieting news that two-thousand men had abandoned his brother on the eve of the battle. In a panic, he had strapped on his armor and sword. It was his wife, Sarah, who convinced him not to foolishly ride alone toward danger.

"Judah ordered you to remain here, where he needs you," she had said. "Don't abandon your post and leave Jerusalem leaderless. "The Lord will take care of your brother," she told him, placing a comforting hand on his shoulder.

Now, having been informed of the army's return, he rushed from his bedchamber. He hastened toward Simon, who was pouring water from a well bucket into a basin. He was about to ask if they had fought or evaded, but the dried blood on Simon's face and the bloodstains on his robe were evidence enough.

"We stopped them," Simon said hoarsely, splashing the cool water on his head, causing the dried blood and dirt to streak down his face.

"What happened?" Jonathan asked anxiously.

"We didn't defeat them, but we halted their advance at Elasa," Simon said, turning to look at the younger man. Jonathan looked into Simon's eyes and saw utter despair.

"Judah is dead," Simon said, his eyes tearing up.

Jonathan seemed unable to comprehend it. *It's impossible*, he thought. As the realization slowly set in, his stomach twisted inside of him. It seemed as if the world came apart with the muttering of those words, and for the first time, he felt completely alone. Neither man spoke for a long moment.

"In the beginning, we were spotted by the Seleucid scouts. So we lost any possibility of ambushing them or setting a trap. Judah refused to fall back and let Jerusalem be captured. Once the battle began, we took up a defensive position on a berm surrounded by a deep wash, and held off their cavalry for over an hour as they advanced in all directions." Simon continued, telling his brother how they had routed the cavalry and sent their whole army into disarray, before finally the enemy riders had managed to get behind them. He told him of their break for the berm, their retreat, and then of the final attack by the Seleucid light infantry.

"How did he die?" asked Jonathan, tears streaming down his cheeks.

For a moment Simon relived those last painful seconds with Judah, as he clutched his hand.

After a long moment he replied in a shaking voice, "He was lanced in the chest, Jonathan."

"Did he suffer?" Jonathan asked in a whisper.

Simon sighed heavily, fighting back his emotion. "No," he lied, unable to get the image out of his mind.

"How many people made it?" Jonathan asked, wiping his eyes.

"Only about two hundred and eighty of us. We escaped just before the Syrians cut off our retreat. We were able to lose them in the night. Judah had his strategy. Even against the outrageous odds, he knew we could succeed. And we did. Because of him."

Jonathan nodded. He didn't remember if he'd ever seen Simon weep before in his life until now.

"It's been confirmed. Gaddi too has been killed," Jonathan murmured.

"I know," Simon replied. "Aaron arrived almost an hour after the battle started. He was one of the few who survived. He told me what happened on the retreat this morning."

Jonathan walked wearily to the steps leading to the back of the governor's palace and sat down. Simon followed him, but Jonathan just wanted to be left alone.

He heard distant shouting, coming from the streets outside the palace walls. "How has the mighty man fallen, that saved the people of Israel!"

He wanted to burry his face in his hands and scream, but all he could do was repeat, "How has the mighty man fallen, that saved the people of Israel? *Ratzon Ha'el.*"

"Where's Judah's body?" he finally asked, mournfully.

"I ordered ten men to take him to Modein in a cart. They will prepare the body with myrrh for burial at father's tomb. I told them we'd be there after the Sabbath for the burial ceremony."

Minutes passed while both brothers remained silent. The question lingered in Jonathan's mind: *What are we to do now?* All their hopes and all their strength had rested in Judah. Jonathan could see, by the look in Simon's eyes, that he was still lost in the events of the previous day.

Jonathan glanced up and saw a servant walking toward him, leading a man in foreign dress who appeared to be a dignitary of some sort. Behind them, surrounded by Hebrew guards, were thirty other men clothed in strange armor with crimson colors. One of the soldiers carried a standard with the letters SPQR.

It took a moment before Jonathan recognized the dignitary. He was one of the Romans who had facilitated the treaty between Judah and Rome. Simon recognized the man also, and remembered his involvement in the incident of the escaped, so-called "Greek spy."

Diomedes gestured for his men to wait as he approached

the white stone steps of the governor's palace. Jonathan and Simon descended the stairs to meet him.

"Greetings from Rome. I am here to see Judah the Maccabee. I have arms, supplies, and soldiers for his efforts against the Seleucid kingdom. Do you remember me, sons of Mattathais?"

Simon nodded.

"Where's Judah?" Diomedes asked more informally. "I'm sure he and your army have need of the help that I bring."

After long pause, Simon answered. "Judah was slain yesterday in battle."

Diomedes looked like he couldn't believe his ears.

"We halted the Seleucid invasion," Simon explained. "Judah died in the fight."

Diomedes looked undone at the news. He brought his hand to his forehead in frustration. "It couldn't have come at a worse time," he murmured.

"So who do I report to and give these weapons and supplies to? I have two-hundred-and-eighty more men with carts of cargo right outside the city, and three-hundred-twenty-three soldiers at your leader's disposal." He looked back and forth, from one brother to the other. "Who will lead the army now?" he asked.

"Jonathan was placed in the office of high priest by Judah before he died," said Simon. "*He* will lead the army." Simon knew he could not bear the yoke of high priest. "In the meantime, Jonathan will make sure that the weapons are distributed, and that your men are fed after their long journey."

Jonathan looked at Simon in shock, overwhelmed at his brother's words. He wanted to protest and tell him Judah only left him as temporary high priest because he was the only one Judah could afford to leave behind, and if anyone should be made high priest now, it should be Simon. But Jonathan remained quiet, knowing he shouldn't say anything in front of the Romans.

Suddenly the weight of the office bore down on him. *I can't handle something like this,* he thought. *"I can't do it without Judah. I wouldn't even know where to begin."* He knew how to lead a thousand men on the field of battle when Judah directed him, but was lost with him gone. And Gaddi gone, too! Jonathan felt benumbed. But the Roman diplomat was looking at him, courteously awaiting instructions.

He made the only decision that came to him, the one he thought his brother would have made. "Bring the supplies into the city and store them in the palace armory," he ordered a servant. "Bring the Roman soldiers in, and set up a banquet for them, with the finest food and wine."

"Yes, Maccabee," the servant replied.

"*What?* What did you call me?" Jonathan asked in shock.

"You are the high priest, correct?" asked the servant.

Jonathan stood there, his mouth agape. He never had thought of the title as anything other than another name for Judah.

"Gather the men of the city who can fight!" Simon commanded. "We still must push these Seleucid dogs out of our country, and we'll need more men for that. Tell them that Judah Ben Mattathias gave his life so they can be freed from tyranny and so they can worship the Lord their God. Tell them that the nation of Israel needs them now as never before!"

The servant bowed his head in acknowledgment of all this, and walked past the Romans, along the perimeter of the palace.

§

Abishag gazed over the green hills toward the cliffs that dropped into the vast sea. From the stone terrace behind Agis's home, she could make out the pale blue of the water, reflecting luminous against the radiant sunrise. She took in every inch and breathed a sigh. Nabis approached from behind her, his shoulders wrapped in a cloak. He pressed his body against her back, feeling her warmth. She smiled, relieved, knowing that he would be all right.

That morning he had finally awakened. The fever had completely subsided, and though he was still weak, with pale skin and dry lips, it was clear he was recovering and would live. That morning, privately, Abishag had released her pent-up tears, relief pouring over her, washing away all of the fear and worry and pain.

She smelled her husband's hair and skin now, and felt comforted. He placed his arms around her. "You shouldn't be walking around yet," she said gently, turning toward him and looking into his eyes.

He smiled at her, his eyes absorbing her beauty. He leaned forward and kissed her.

She wanted to ask what had happened with the moneylender, and if they would have to flee. She had heard he was a powerful man, with powerful friends, and wondered if they, along with Agis and his bond slave, should prepare to leave the city once Nabis was able to move about. Yesterday he was on the verge of death, but now that he was lucid and healing, she feared people might come after them. *There will be time to talk of that later,* she thought, looking at Nabis, loving him.

She turned again to look at the horizon, while Nabis held her close, draping his arm across her breasts. *We've been through so much,* she thought, *but now it's a new day, and the sun is shining.* She silently prayed, thanking God for Nabis and his recovery, for all they had overcome, and for all the love He had given them. She thought of her people. Then she turned her head in the direction of the carrying breeze, in the direction of Israel. She stared out across the vastness into the sunrise, and wondered.

Chapter 65

JONATHAN STOOD ON the small green mound facing his father's tomb. It had not been opened since Mattathias's death. Eleazar's body was never recovered, and it was unlikely they would ever find anything of Gaddi's remains.

His back to the tomb, Simon stood at the top of the mound. He was giving the eulogy in Hebrew. His words were powerful, riveting, but Jonathan was tuning them out. *It all falls on me,* he thought to himself. *There is still a Seleucid army of seventeen-thousand men camped just north of the city, unwilling to retreat, and unable to move forward to take Jerusalem.* Jonathan fought the urge to turn his head and look back at the seven-thousand men and their families who had gathered for his brother's funeral. There were nearly four-thousand more men in Jerusalem, having finally been gathered from the northern cities, and more were arriving every day as word of Judah's death spread, enraging the people who heard the news. *He has become a call to arms,* Jonathan thought grimly.

Simon's words carried over the massive crowd, who listened in silence. Jonathan noticed that many of the men were already armed, and the general sentiment of loss and outrage was very much like when Antiochus had desecrated the temple, all those years before.

Despite the nation's mourning for the loss of Judah, there had been celebration in the streets two days after, when word that Alcimus, the fraudulent high priest, had finally died from the stroke that paralyzed him months before. Jonathan was now the only acknowledged high priest of Israel—at least until some heretic bribed Demetrius with enough money to arbitrarily appoint him to the office in hopes of regaining control of the Jews. But Demetrius would not be able to send another army if Jonathan annihilated the seventeen-thousand men who remained with Bacchides, camped north of the city. *I will destroy him*, Jonathan promised himself. *I will utterly remove the Seleucid hold over us forever. And the men will fight. They will fight for God, they will fight for me, and they will fight in the name of Judah, the Maccabee. Then I will lay waste the tribe of Medeba, for killing Gaddi, and I will fulfill Judah's wish of establishing a priestly dynasty of our blood, of our father, Mattathias, and his father, Hashmona'i, and we will rule Israel like the judges of old, until there comes a son of David.*

Looking to one side, Jonathan saw Martha crying bitterly as they placed Judah's body, wrapped in a shroud, into the tomb beside his father. There was so much Judah had left undone, so much more he still had left to do.

Jonathan remembered giving Martha the news that Judah was dead. She began to cry, first in a whimper, and then uncontrollably, collapsing to the ground. Now, as then, Jonathan wished there was some way he could comfort her, something he could say or do to help, but he knew there was nothing. He thought of how Simon had told him, before he died, that Judah had asked if he would marry him to Martha. Jonathan didn't know whether or not to tell her this, thinking it might only cause her further grief, but he knew it was only right that he do so. Jonathan felt Sarah's hand tenderly take hold of his own. *So much loss,* Jonathan reflected … his father, Eleazar, Gaddi, Judah, and all the countless men who had served under him who had left this world. *Ratzon ha'El.*

Jonathan's mind turned to a memory from his boyhood. His father had taken him to the synagogue where he taught. An infantry patrol of Syrians had marched by outside, and a look of sadness had crossed his father's face Jonathan had been terrified, not only by the tramp of marching soldiers but by his father's pained reaction. Then Mattathias had whispered to him,

"One day soon, we will be strong again. We will not always be trodden down by the pagans. There will come a day when God will remember his chosen and anoint us with a leader who will throw off the yoke of the idolaters, and Israel will once again be free." Just before the soldiers pounded on the doors, demanding to search their place of worship, Jonathan had asked his father if kings would ever rule again in Jerusalem. His father had answered, "Yes. One day, I promise you— one day, they will." Then the solders had kicked the doors in.

I'll never forget that, thought Jonathan. *I'll never forget the look on his face when he said that, because it was a look of hope.*

As they moved the flat stone into place that would cover the tomb, Jonathan prayed, asking God for help and the strength to live up to his father's and his brothers' memories and the people's expectation of him.

There was another matter that weighed heavily on him. He had to reply to the message, sent in secret, from Alexander, the illegitimate son of Antiochus, stating he wished for them to meet. The only reason Demetrius had not had Alexander killed was because he had been in hiding, protected by Egypt. *There is only one reason he could have for contacting me,* Jonathan thought. *He wants help in trying to take the Seleucid throne, and would offer Judea its freedom in exchange for our support.*

Jonathan contemplated it, weighing the potential dangers of bartering a deal with the son of a madman who thought himself a god, the very man who had started this war when he desecrated the temple and erected an idol to Zeus in the Holy of Holies. The same idol Judah smashed, just as he smashed the Syrian armies over and over again. Jonathan considered the idea for a moment. Autonomy was the key, he decided. Judah would not have compromised for less, and neither would he.

The round stone slab finished rolling into place, and then a breathless silence fell over the multitude. Jonathan realized that everyone was looking at him. He turned around and saw the faces of his people, staring. He saw Aaron in the crowd, as well as others he knew. His mouth grew dry, and his heart started to pound. The crowd was waiting for him to speak, to answer the question—the question of questions—what would they do now?

Jonathan finally said over the silence, "Shall we find another man such as *this*?" he gestured back toward his brother's tomb. "For how the mighty *have* fallen!" he said raising his voice. "The battle is before us. The armies of the enemies of God, the enemies of Israel, are to the north of the City of David. They have the Jordan to their left, and have invaded our Promised Land. They have spent the last decade turning the land of milk and honey red with the blood of the children of Jacob, and wish to lay low the chosen people, to destroy our homes and make us their slaves forever!" There was a murmur from the crowd.

Jonathan's voice grew quieter. "But we are *not* slaves. God, the one God, who gave us life, gave us freedom. A thousand years from now, when the kingdom of Seleucus is forgotten and nothing more than scattered ashes, they will look back on *us* and *our names* and remember what we did here, and know that we lived our lives as free men. They will know that there is a God, and the name of his chosen people is *Israel*! They will know that in us lie the blessings and the curse of all nations!

"Cry out to Heaven, that you may be delivered from the hands of our enemies, *for the battle is before us*, and you, that are here now, are the chosen, who will be remembered for what we will now do to the enemies of God!"

The crowd erupted in a riveting uproar of shouts and cheers. Jonathan wanted to say more, but through the roar he heard a subtle chant, which grew louder. Soon it was the only thing that could be heard. It was the familiar chant Jonathan had heard many times after his brother's numerous victories. They were chanting the name, *"Maccabee, Maccabee, Maccabee!"* but this time they weren't chanting his brother's name, they were chanting his.

He looked over, surprised, as Simon stood there with

outstretched hands, offering him Judah's sheathed sword. Jonathan slowly drew the blade from its scabbard and held it firm in his grip, for all to see. The crowd's roar of elation grew stronger. The chant grew louder and louder. Jonathan lifted his brother's blade aloft and shouted over the roar, the ancient Hebrew war cry, *"For God … and for Israel!"*

And now I free you and exempt all the Jews from payment of tribute and salt tax and crown levies, and instead of collecting the third of the grain and the half of the fruit of the trees that I should receive, I release them from this day and henceforth. I will not collect them from the land of Judea or from the three districts added to it from Samaria and Galilee, from this day and for all time. And let Jerusalem and her environs, her tithes and her revenues, be holy and free from tax. I release also my control of the citadel in Jerusalem and give it to the high priest, that he may station in it men of his own choice to guard it. And every one of the Jews taken as a captive from the land of Judea into any part of my kingdom, I set free without payment; and let all officials cancel also the taxes on their cattle. And all the feasts and Sabbaths and new moons and appointed days, and the three days before a feast and the three after a feast— let them all be days of immunity and release for all the Jews who are in my kingdom. No one shall have authority to exact anything from them or annoy any of them about any matter. Let Jews be enrolled in the king's forces to the number of thirty-thousand men, and let the maintenance be given them that is due to all the forces of the king. Let some of them be stationed in the great strongholds of the king, and let some of them be put in positions of trust in the kingdom. Let their officers and leaders be of their own number, and let them live by their own laws, just as the king has commanded in the land of Judea. As for the three districts that have been added to Judea from the country of Samaria, let them be so annexed to Judea that they are considered to be under one ruler and obey no other authority but the high priest.

~ Letter of Demetrius Sotor,
King of the Seleucid Empire
1 Maccabees 10

When Jonathan and the people heard these words,
they did not believe or accept them, because they remembered
the great wrongs which Demetrius had done in Israel and
how he had greatly oppressed them.

~ 1 Maccabees 10:46

Glossary of Characters

Abishag–Sexually abused, her whole family butchered in the massacre, she is sold as a slave to Nabis. Devoted to God and to her people, she hates all things Greek, including her new master. Over time, she recognizes his humanity and becomes infatuated with him.

Adi–Judah's loving but barren wife, to whom Judah is powerfully devoted.

Agis–A former Spartan solder who lost his hand in combat. Father of Nabis.

Alcimus–The Hellenistic and fraudulent Jewish high priest who is a puppet of the Seleucid Empire.

Alexander–The illegitimate son of Antiochus IV, whom the Seleucid nobility hope to supplant Demetrius with toward the end of the story.

Antiochus (Antiochus IV Epiphanes, "King Antiochus")–The maniacal king of the Seleucid Empire, who reigns through the first half of the story. Sadistic, plagued with bouts of delirium, he believes himself to be a demigod who can bend the world to his whim. Holding no regard for human life, he seeks only to further his power and re-create the empire of Alexander the Great.

Antiochus the first child–Nephew of King Antiochus and second son of Laodice (from her brother/former husband, Seleucus). Although just a boy, Antiochus is heir apparent and rightful king when the story opens. King Antiochus, to solidify his control of the empire, has the child poisoned.

Antiochus the second child (Antiochus V)–The son begotten of the rape of Laodice by King Antiochus. The king committed rape to solidify his position on the throne by providing an heir, after murdering the other child Antiochus.

Apelles–The flippant and cynical Seleucid cavalry officer who works with Onias to subject the local Jewish population.

Apollonius–The Seleucid governor of Judea, later demoted to serve under Governor Seron.

Bacchides–Rescuer of Demetrius, and former general under Demetrius's father, Seleucus.

Crassus–An outspoken, cynical, yet spirited Roman agent and companion of Fabius, sent with him to oversee the signing of the Roman/Jewish Treaty.

Demetrius–Son of Seleucus and Laodice and eldest child of Laodice. Demetrius has been presumed dead since taken to Rome as a hostage and traded by Antiochus III in exchange for the release of his son, Antiochus IV.

Diomedes–Son of a Roman ambassador and Jewish mother, he is Rome's agent in Judea. Being a prior Roman soldier and multilingual, he is influential behind the scenes, working to establish the Roman/Jewish Treaty.

Eleazar–Judah's younger brother. He is kind, good-natured, but innocently naïve in the beginning of the story. After his father's death, he matures.

Eugenio–A Seleucid soldier who trains under Nabis as an Argyraspides (Silver Shield).

Exudoxi–One of three leading Seleucid nobles who plot to overthrow Demetrius.

Fabius–A disciplined Roman agent, driven by a sense of duty. One of two men sent to oversee the signing of the Roman/Jewish Treaty.

Gaddi–The eldest brother of Judah, he is bureaucratic by nature and feels passed over by his father.

Gorgias–A Seleucid general, known for being boisterous.

Hilarion–One of three leading Seleucid nobles who plot to overthrow Demetrius.

Isokrates–Head of the Seleucid espionage network that operates inside Jerusalem, routing out loyal and religious Jews. More Jewish than Greek in appearance, he is distinguished by a wide scar that runs across his chin. His name is not revealed until later in the story.

Jesse–A Hebrew soldier, who joins the revolt out of a sense of patriotism.

John–the youngest of Simon's children. Though merely an adolescent, he is sharp, strong, and morally grounded.

Jonathan–The youngest of Judah's brothers. Though just an unsure adolescent when the story begins, he grows up to be close in nature to Judah. During the early part of the revolt, he falls in love with Sarah, the daughter of one of Judah's captains.

Joel–A captain in Judah's rebel army, and a daring soldier.

Judah (Maccabee)–The third son of Mattathias. Trained as a priest, he makes his living apprehending brigands prior to the Jerusalem Massacre. He is possessed by a haunting love for his wife, Adi, even after her death. Known for his uncompromising patriotism and love for God, he is tough, intelligent, strong, and an ingenious tactician, who will stop at nothing to free his people.

Jude–the second son of Simon.

Kalisto–A flawless sailor, and admiral of the Seleucid navy. Driven by wealth, he soon finds himself in the service of his former enemies, the Romans. His arms are scarred from being burned in a fire on board his first ship. He is haunted by the news he receives while away, that his family perished in a plague that swept through their village.

Laenas (Gaius Popillius Laenas)–Former consul of Rome, and ambassador. Protecting the interests of Rome, he is sent to halt the Seleucid invasion of Egypt.

Levi–A captain in Judah's rebel army and father of Sarah, Jonathan's sweetheart.

Laodice–The wife/sister of King Antiochus, and mother of Demetrius. She is manipulative, beautiful, and driven by a lust for power.

Lysias–Cousin to King Antiochus; placed in charge as viceroy while the king is away campaigning in Parthia.

Martha–A widow from an eastern Hebrew city across the Jordan. She is rescued, with the other survivors at Dratma, by Judah and his army. She and Judah come to love each other years after the death of Judah's wife Adi, but his continuing devotion to Adi impairs his relationship with Martha.

Marcus Cornelius–A Roman ambassador who negotiates with Gaddi

Mattathias–A priest and widower, he is father to his five sons Gaddi, Simon, Judah, Eleazar, and Jonathan. It is the unwillingness of Mattathias to be ruled over, and his uncompromising faith in God, which spark the beginning of the insurrection.

Mattathias (Mattathias Ben Simon)–Eldest son of Simon, named for his grandfather. He is rash, bold, and yearns for glory.

Mithridates–King of Parthia, who has united all the old tribes in hopes of carving out the eastern portion of the Seleucid Empire for himself.

Nabis–Member of an elite Seleucid infantry unit, The Argyraspides (or Silver Shields). He tries to live up to the expectations of his father, a former Spartan soldier. An excellent soldier himself,

Nabis is disillusioned during the Egyptian campaign, and more so after the massacre. He becomes sympathetic to the Israelites when he falls in love with Abishag, his Hebrew slave.

Naomi–A resident of Hebron and wife of the Hebrew soldier, Jesse.

Nathan–A priest and friend of Mattathias. Though a good man with a similar vision, he is uncompromising in his interpretation of the letter of the law, causing a rift between Mattathias and himself.

Nicantor–The best military tactician and general in the Seleucid Empire, and the only man whose prowess can match Judah on the battlefield.

Nina–A priestess of Apollo and a lover of Laodice.

Onias–A Jewish traitor and informant, helping the Seleucids enforce their mandatory worship of Greek gods among the Jewish population.

Orestes–A patriotic Selecuid soldier who trains under Nabis as an Argyraspides (Silver Shield). He is one of two men who ends up saving Nabis's life at the battle of Beth-Horn.

Paris–A greedy and prideful moneylender, who runs prostitution and gambling within parts of Ephesus.

Philip–The lover of King Antiochus who was arbitrarily made general and later viceroy.

Sarah–Beloved of Jonathan and daughter of Levi, one of Judah's captains.

Seleucus–former general of Alexander the Great (Alexander of Macedon) and founder of the Seleucid Dynasty.

Seleucus IV–The deceased older brother of Antiochus IV. Former husband of Laodice and father of Demetrius.

Simon–Judah's older brother, a priest, who leads the rebellion in spiritual matters. Quick-tempered and cynical by nature, he is a loyal supporter of Judah and courageous warrior on the battlefield.

Solon–One of three leading Seleucid nobles who plot to overthrow Demetrius.

Seron–Seleucid governor of Judea after Apollonius's demotion. He is an inferior military strategist and out of his depths as governor.

Theophilus–Head cook of the king's royal kitchen and lover of Queen Laodice, who uses and manipulates him for the purpose of having her husband, King Antiochus, killed.

Tiburtius–A Roman magistrate. Gives orders to Fabius and Crassus.

Timothy–General of the Ammorite and Idumean coalition against Judea. He has an undying hatred for the Jews.

Urion–The king's former slave and loyal advisor to King Antiochus.

Acknowledgements

I WOULD LIKE TO thank God for the countless gifts He has bestowed upon me . . . my wife, Cori, the most genuinely kind person I have ever met, for her undying love and dedication over the years... my parents, Steve Teskey and Susan Teskey . . . my grandparents, Robert and Barbara Teskey, for everything, especially the trip to Israel without which I don't think I could have written this novel. . .Virginia Mort, my grandmother, who painstakingly read through, and helped me correct, the first draft of this manuscript ... Kay Frenzer-Zeeh and Nick Frenzer, for believing in my book and assisting with the early editorial process . . .Jessi Rita Hoffman, for her vigilant work as she skillfully edited this book . . . and, not least of all, the soldiers I've had the privilege of serving with. My heartfelt gratitude.

About the Author

Brandon Teskey spent three years as an enlisted infantry soldier and commissioned as an infantry officer in 2012 from Officer Candidate School. During his service, he developed a keen interest in history, particularly ancient warfare. Brandon currently serves as a 1st Lieutenant in the U.S. Army NG (National Guard).

Brandon holds a bachelor's degree in philosophy from Arizona State University and is an avid researcher, writer, and musician. With his wife Cori, he owns and operates a medical staffing business. The couple lives in Arizona with their infant son, Troy. *Insurrection*—volume one of a trilogy—is Brandon's first novel. He is working on volume two.

Made in the USA
Middletown, DE
17 January 2021

31779910R00333